THE DOMINO TATTOO

He touched her as she herself had touched Lucy the maid, running his hands lightly over her bottom, examining its curves and crevices, palpating its flesh.

Then he came round to the front of the chair, where she could see him. Plucking the knees of his trousers, he squatted easily before her. He reached out his hand and caressed the back of her head; she felt herself shudder with anticipation.

'Would you like a gag?' he asked her. 'Or would you prefer to scream?'

A NEXUS CLASSIC

THE DOMINO
TATTOO

Cyrian Amberlake

This book is a work of fiction.
In real life, make sure you practice safe, sane and
consensual sex.

This Nexus Classic edition published in 2006

First published in 1991 by
Nexus
Thames Wharf Studios
Rainville Road
London
W6 9HA

www.nexus-books.co.uk

A catalogue record for this book is available from the British
Library.

ISBN 0 352 34037 1
ISBN 9 780352 340375

The paper used in this book is a natural, recyclable product made
from wood grown. in sustainable forests. The manufacturing
process conforms to the regulations of the country of origin.

Typeset by TW Typesetting, Plymouth, Devon
Printed and bound in Great Britain by
Clays Ltd, St Ives PLC

For Ellen, who let me know

Prologue

Josephine's watch chimed softly. It was six. Over the cold city, the daylight was beginning to fade.

She pressed two buttons on her desk. One lowered the blinds over the windows of her office; the other rang her chauffeur.

'Yes, ma'am?'

'We'll be leaving in ten minutes, Francis. Have you got an overnight bag?'

'Of course, ma'am.'

'Ten minutes, then.'

Josephine rose from her desk and took a black leather attaché case from a cupboard. She laid it on a table, pressed the catches and lifted the lid an inch or two to glance inside. Then she closed it again, looked at her watch, and went out of her office along the corridor to the lift.

On the way down she looked at herself in the mirror.

Her suit was French, white linen, a little lightweight for the time of year, but Josephine rarely had to set foot out of doors. Her shoes were Italian, her neckscarf too. Her hair, blonde already, had been bleached and cut in a perfectly balanced shag style at a Zurich salon. Her eyes were pale, with a very discreet blue eyeliner; her lips were bold, sharp, raspberry pink.

'Where to, ma'am?' asked Francis.

'Estwych,' said Josephine.

It had been a while since she had had him drive her down to Estwych. If Francis was curious, he didn't show it.

In the gathering dusk they left the city and entered a landscape of rolling hills and winding lanes overlooked by dark woods. The head-lights of the Mercedes raked the stone walls of cottages, stableyards, orchards. Josephine lay back, relaxing. She did not speak. She looked at her reflection in the darkened windows, and, beyond it, the shrouded scenery of other people's lives. She had not felt this way for a while.

The sign for Estwych stood half hidden in bushes at the side of the road. Francis drove into a small village, and out the other side. A mile or two further on he turned down a steep lane that led at last to an old half-timbered house standing alone by a swift, silent river, a house that might have once been a fishing lodge. A light was burning in the porch.

Francis opened the door and Josephine stepped out. Francis ducked in to retrieve her attaché case from the back seat and handed it to her.

'What time tomorrow, ma'am?'

'Shall we say nine?'

'Nine it is. Goodnight, ma'am.'

'Goodnight, Francis.'

As the car drove away, Josephine turned and went into the house, stooping at the low door. Inside it was warm. The carpet was thick, deep red, the lamplight gentle, the hall furniture old wood with a comforting patina of age. Nothing had changed.

One of the maids was crossing the hall, a young girl in a long black dress, white apron and mobcap. She saw Josephine and came towards her.

'Good evening, madam.'

'Good evening,' said Josephine. She did not recognise the girl. She put her case down beside the table with the open ledger and unbuttoned her jacket. She took off her neckscarf, and began to unbutton her blouse. The maid watched her, saying nothing.

Josephine unfastened three buttons of her blouse and drew it open, releasing a breath of Chanel Surtout into the warm air.

Beneath the blouse, a bra of dove-grey silk contained her ample breasts. Between them she displayed a small, discreet tattoo of a carnival mask, a black domino. The elegant design suggested gaiety, harlequins, Venice, the *bal masqué*. Yet there was something just a little sinister about it, a hint of secrecy, of nameless crimes and assignations in the shadows of night.

If the maid thought any of this, her innocent young face showed none of it. 'Thank you, madam,' she said. 'If you'll please wait here a moment, I'll fetch the housekeeper.'

Josephine waited, buttoning up her blouse. She looked at the picture on the wall above the little table, an old hunting print in a walnut frame. Nothing had changed here at Estwych.

The maid came back into the hall with the housekeeper bustling along behind her. She was a small woman, slightly stout, but dapper as always in a smart mauve dress with a diamond brooch. When she recognised Josephine, she gave a beaming smile and clasped her hands together with pleasure and satisfaction.

'How lovely to see you, Ms Morrow,' she said. 'You've been neglecting us. Why, it's months since you last came down,' she said, chidingly.

'Yes, Annabel, I'm afraid I have,' admitted Josephine. 'I'm so busy these days. But I'll make up for it tonight.'

'I'm sure you will,' said Annabel, precisely. She turned to the table and consulted the ledger. 'Let's see, now. Room 3 is ready for you. That was always a favourite of yours, wasn't it?'

'It was my first room,' said Josephine. 'The first time I came to Estwych, not knowing anything or anyone.'

'Ah,' said Annabel, 'we've got a couple arriving later tonight. One of them has never been here before.'

Josephine smiled. 'Would you like me to look after them?'

'That would be splendid. If you won't be too tired.'

'That depends,' said Josephine.

'We'll see how you feel later,' said Annabel. 'Have you eaten? Shall I have something sent up?'

Josephine stretched and rubbed the back of her neck. 'No, Annabel,' she said. 'I want to get started straight away.'

'Of course,' said Annabel.

She picked up a slender black pencil and made a swift mark in the ledger. She didn't ask Josephine to sign. Then she opened a drawer in the table and took out a key attached to a black disc. She signalled to the maid.

Josephine took the key, its tag clinking softly against her signet ring. On the tag was engraved an emblem of a domino mask, the same as that tattooed between her breasts.

The maid picked up her attaché case. 'Would you like to follow me, madam?' she said.

Together they went upstairs. Brown pictures glowed dimly on the landing. There were several doors, all closed. Dull brass numbers identified the rooms.

There was not a sound in the house. Josephine unlocked the door of Room 3 and went in. The maid followed, bringing the case.

But for the shaft of dim light from the corridor, Room 3 was in darkness. The maid reached for the light switch.

'Don't,' said Josephine.

The maid withdrew her hand.

Josephine stood in the shadow.

'Put the case on the bed,' she said.

The maid obeyed.

'Open it,' said Josephine.

She thumbed the catches and lifted the lid. The light from the corridor came in and showed her what was inside. The maid displayed no more reaction than when Josephine had shown her the domino tattoo between her breasts.

'Come here,' said Josephine.

The girl came towards her.

'Closer.'

The girl obeyed. She stood a foot away from Josephine, looking up at her in the darkness.

'What's your name?' asked Josephine.

'Lucy, madam.'

'Lucy,' said Josephine.

She reached out and put her hand behind the girl's head, clasping the back of her neck.

'Have you been trained, Lucy?' she asked casually.

The girl did not flinch. 'I hope I can give satisfaction, madam,' she said calmly.

Josephine looked her over. 'I hope you can,' she said.

She released the girl and stepped back, folding her arms.

'Lift your skirt,' she said.

Unhesitatingly the maid reached beneath her apron and gathered her long black skirt in both hands, revealing layers of petticoats.

'And your petticoats,' said Josephine.

The maid scooped up her petticoats, baring her legs. They were short and chubby. In the dark room pale bands of bare thigh gleamed between white knickers and the tops of black stockings, held up by plain elastic garters. The garters were quite tight, and cut into her flesh. Unquestioningly the girl stood, showing herself to Josephine.

'Turn round,' said Josephine.

The girl turned. Without further instruction, she lifted her dress at the back, gathering it up to her waist.

Her knickers were old-fashioned, cut loose with buttons at the side.

'Bare your bottom,' Josephine said.

The maid reached down and unbuttoned herself. The flap in the seat of her knickers fell open.

The pale mounds of her bottom shone dimly in the darkness.

Josephine stepped up behind her. She put her left hand on Lucy's left shoulder, and laid the palm of her right hand gently on the girl's right buttock. Her flesh was warm and soft.

'You have been trained well, Lucy,' said Josephine quietly.

The girl inclined her head slightly, turning to look at the woman behind her with a tiny smile, gratified.

Josephine lifted her left hand and ran the knuckle of her middle finger down the girl's cheek, stroking the invisible down.

Then, all at once, she let her go.

'Dress yourself,' she said.

'Will that be all, madam?' asked the maid. She glanced involuntarily at the bed, at the open attaché case.

'Yes, thank you, Lucy,' said Josephine.

She stood and watched as the girl buttoned her knickers and twitched her petticoats and her skirt back into place, and smoothed her apron. The girl patted her head to make sure her cap was straight, then bobbed a curtsey and scurried from the room. She seemed to be in a hurry, as if expecting Josephine to change her mind and call her back.

Josephine smiled.

She went and closed the door, switched on the light and looked around.

It was not the first time they had given her Room 3. It was just as she remembered: spacious, low-ceilinged, with a double bed, night table, a wardrobe and a low armchair. Anything else a guest might need could be provided. A bell rope hung by the fireplace. Unlit candles stood on the table, on the mantelpiece and the deep windowsill. The curtains were closed. On the far side of the room a second door led to the bathroom, a modern addition.

Josephine snapped the locks of the attaché case shut, and left it on the bed where it lay. She took off all her clothes and went straight into the bathroom.

Critically, she examined herself in the mirror.

She saw a blonde woman of medium height, young, slim, her skin still bearing a trace of a golden week spent lazing nude on a private beach on Evvoia. Her shoulders were narrow, her chest seeming almost too small to bear the weight of the high-peaked breasts that swelled proudly before her. Josephine cupped them in her hands, running the tips of her thumbs lightly across her nipples with a small shiver of pleasure. She ran her hands down her sides, pinching the skin of her hips critically with thumb and forefinger, stroking her flanks, swivelling in front of the mirror to examine her high round bottom and the taut curves of her thighs. Her skin was clear, unblemished, unmarked. These days she enjoyed the best health and beauty preparations money could buy, and spent three hours a week in the company's executive gym. She made a point of taking suitable clients there. A deal that was proving tricky in the boardroom could often be sealed in a leotard damp with sweat.

Josephine took a long, hot shower. When she was finished, she dried herself, wrapped the capacious bath towel around her, and stepped back into the bedroom.

The room was in darkness again. Someone had turned out the light.

Josephine could barely make out the shapes of the furniture. She remembered there was a second light switch, a cord over the head of the bed. She stepped towards it.

He came up behind her and put his hands on her shoulders.

She stopped, turning despite herself.

'Don't turn round,' he said. His voice was warm and pleasant.

Josephine stood still, breathing quickly, facing the darkened wall.

He put something into her hand: something small, hard and rectangular. Josephine knew what it was. She grasped it firmly between finger and thumb.

Her visitor's hands moved to her throat, stroking her, and then to her face, exploring her gently, as if he were a blind man seeking to identify her.

She felt him take hold of her towel. She relinquished it. He drew it from her body and threw it aside. She heard the soft sound it made as it fell to the floor.

His hands moved to cup and squeeze her breasts, stroked down her stomach. He moved closer to her. His left hand probed between her thighs, cupping her groin, rubbing her there, while his right hand fondled her right buttocks. Josephine gave a little gasp. She bent forward from the hips, submitting to his exploration.

Then abruptly he let go of her.

She stood, irresolute, wanting to turn, knowing he would forbid her to.

She stood there for what seemed a long while. She found herself straining to hear the sound of his breathing. She heard nothing.

She wondered who he was. She knew it did not matter, never mattered, yet she could not help wondering.

Just then he said: 'Light the candles.'

Josephine went to the mantelpiece. She glanced at what she was holding in her hand, the thing he had put there.

It was a playing piece, a stone from a game of dominoes.

She put it on the mantelpiece, picked up the box of matches that was lying there and moved around the room lighting the candles. He had moved when she moved, keeping himself behind her. She passed the damp towel, discarded on the floor, but she did not pause to pick it up. She did not look at it, or at anything else but only at each candle as she lit it.

She felt she was leaving a trail of light behind her, that each candle she lit exposed her more, and that his eyes were on her. Did he admire her? Was he aroused by the sight of her, naked, walking calmly about the room like a servant at her work? Or did he despise her? Did he know her of old, and feel contempt for her for coming back here again, for seeking him out, whoever he was?

None of these things mattered either. Josephine realised she was nervous. It had been a long time. She had grown out of touch, too used to the ways of the world of business, the consultations and negotiations, seeking ascendance over colleagues and competitors, looking for leverage and advantage. Here at Estwych, there was no need for opinions and decisions. As she recalled that, she relaxed. A familiar deep calm came over her. She lit the last candle.

'Turn around,' he said. 'Let me look at you.'

She turned.

She saw he was lounging on the bed. He was a dark young man in a dark suit, a good suit, black or perhaps dark grey. He was not any of the men who had previously dealt with her here at Estwych. His good looks were vaguely East European, she thought. His jacket was open, his hands folded carelessly on his stomach, a gold signet ring on his finger catching the candlelight. They were slim hands. Josephine could still feel the places where they had touched her body. His eyes were on those places now, assessing her. She felt them linger on her breasts, on the tattoo between them.

She saw that her case lay at his feet, open, the contents jumbled. He had been rummaging through them. They were not the sort of contents one might expect to find in the attaché case of a wealthy businesswoman.

'Get dressed now,' he said.

Josephine was surprised. 'Dressed?'

He raised his eyebrows. 'Are you questioning me?'

'No,' said Josephine quickly. 'No. Of course not.'

He indicated the case. 'Stockings,' he said, 'would be suitable. And your shoes.'

'Of course,' said Josephine.

'There's no need to speak,' he told her.

'Sorry,' she said automatically.

'Nor to apologise,' he said. 'Your penitence is assured. You may approach the bed.'

Josephine dropped her eyes and went to the bed. Looking nowhere but in the case, she found the suspender belt she'd brought, a black one with the most minute lace trim, and fastened it around her hips. She found her stockings, black too, a fresh pack. She broke open the cellophane. She stretched each stocking carefully into shape and rolled it before drawing it on, setting her foot up on the bed and smoothing the stocking up her leg, straightening the seam, turning over the top and fastening the suspender. She knew he was watching her. She did not look at him.

Her shoes were glossy black, with heels higher than anything she would wear on any other occasion. She put them on and stood before him, her eyes still cast down.

'One more item,' he said.

She reached into the case again and found it.

'Bring it here,' he instructed.

She held it out to him in both hands, not looking at his face.

It was a collar of soft black leather.

He took it from her.

'Kneel,' he said, and when she did, bowing her head, he fastened it around her throat.

He left her there like that a moment, to savour the completeness of her subjection. Some of them would caress her head while she knelt before them. He did not. He did not touch her.

'Get up now,' he said.

She got to her feet.

'Go and stand in the corner,' he said. 'Face the wall.'

Josephine walked over to the corner by the wardrobe, feeling her height in the unaccustomed shoes. She stood and faced the wall, linking her fingers and putting her hands on her head.

She heard him follow her, speak to her quietly from just behind her. 'Clasp your hands behind your back.'

She did so, and felt the touch of cold metal as he fastened her handcuffs about her left wrist, and then her right.

He caressed the bare cheek of her bottom once more.

Then he left her. She heard him return to the bed, heard the whispering jangle of the bedsprings as he lay down.

'I can see it's been quite a while for you,' he said.

Josephine did not reply.

'Why are you here?' he asked.

Josephine's lips were dry. She licked them, surreptitiously.

'You may answer,' he said distantly.

'I am here to obey,' said Josephine. Her throat felt tight.

'Obedience!' he said. 'At Estwych, obedience is the law. Had you forgotten?'

'I – ' said Josephine. 'I have been obedient to no one's will but my own,' she said.

'Indeed,' he said. 'What am I to do with you?'

He spoke speculatively, almost whimsically. He spoke with a slight accent when he was amused.

Josephine took a deep breath.

'I need correction,' she said.

'Corrective treatment,' he said. 'Would you have me take care of it?'

Josephine realised she was staring blindly at the wall. She closed her eyes. 'Yes, sir,' she said. 'Yes, master.'

'You may ask me,' he said.

Josephine felt as though the floor had given way beneath her. She wanted to crumple at the knees. She knew she could not.

'Master,' she said. 'I have been wilful and disobedient and I beg you to discipline me.'

As soon the words were out she felt better, stronger. She opened her eyes. She was standing firm, facing the wall, her hands behind her back.

'What degree of discipline would be appropriate?' he asked her.

She closed her eyes again. 'Severe,' she replied. Her voice was no more than a whisper.

'Severe discipline,' he repeated, equably. 'Well, we have all night.'

Josephine said nothing. The room was warm. She did not shiver. She waited. There wasn't a sound from anywhere. The house might have been deserted.

In a while, she heard him move. Involuntarily she tensed; but he did not come over to her. She heard the squeak of castors. He was moving a piece of furniture.

'Turn round now,' he told her.

She turned. He had moved the armchair into the space between the bed and the fireplace.

'Come here,' he said.

He led her out of her corner to stand behind the armchair.

'Bend over the chair,' he instructed her.

As gracefully as she could with her arms handcuffed behind her back, Josephine bent over the back of the chair.

She overbalanced, her head on the seat cushion, her bottom in the air. Her arms were awkwardly twisted behind her. She turned her head on one side so that her cheek was against the fabric. It was rough, and smelt of dust and age. With one eye she could just see the foot of the bed, a corner of her case, and the bedroom door beyond.

He seemed to have moved from his place beside her. She did not know where he had gone to. She waited to feel his hand. Then she heard him, by the fireplace. Faintly, she heard the creak of the bell rope.

A minute or two passed.

There came a knock at the door.

'Come,' he said, clearly.

The door opened, and a maid came in. It was Lucy, Lucy who had bared her bottom for Josephine here in this room, not an hour ago. Lucy glanced at Josephine now, bent half-naked over the back of the chair. Her face revealed no particular expression. She looked past her.

'Yes, sir?' she said.

'Bring me a cognac, would you, Lucy?'

'Yes, sir,' said Lucy. 'And for madam?'

There was a pause. Out of the corner of her eye Josephine glimpsed him at the bed, looking through the contents of her case. She heard the chink of metal, and fainter still, the slither of leather.

'Nothing for madam,' he said.

'Thank you, sir,' said Lucy.

She went out.

He stayed for a moment by the bed, then came around behind her. He touched her as she herself had touched Lucy the maid, running his hands lightly over her bottom, examining its curves and crevices, palpating its flesh, feeling the weight of her buttocks, the tautness of her flanks. He traced the crease of her underhang, dipped his fingers into her cleft, let them linger a moment on the backs of her thighs.

Then he came round to the front of the chair, where she could see him. Plucking the knees of his trousers, he squatted easily before her. He reached out his hand and caressed the back of her head; she felt herself shudder with anticipation.

'Would you like a gag?' he asked her. 'Or would you prefer to scream?'

|1|

Josephine had been working for the department since her divorce. It was a responsible job, lower-middle management, but a bit boring. The prospects weren't that great, not least because she couldn't really get motivated enough to push her way on up the ladder. The pay was okay, nothing special.

There was nothing very much in Josephine's life that was special any more.

She wouldn't have said she had a Problem. She was shrewd enough to know that once you admitted that, it became one, whether it had been before or not. Her marriage to Larry had taught her that. Larry had decided they had a Problem, and so they did. She had mothered him through the crisis as long as she could stand it, then she'd gotten out and never looked back. She'd found, at first with a kind of guilty pride and then just with pride, that she preferred living on her own. She put everything she'd got into finding a job, and then she put everything into the job.

It was just that lately she seemed to be living on a different planet from everyone else. She'd lose her temper over the least little thing, then sit staring out of the window all afternoon when there was something sitting on her desk that was supposed to be finished yesterday.

She was all over the place. She would wake up and find herself having the most incredible fantasies, fantasies she'd been having for days and thinking they were true. She had been convinced one of the accountants was the bank robber whose photo-fit she'd seen on the front of the *Evening Standard*. She had only snapped out of that when she'd caught herself following him after work and trying to think of ways of waylaying him and leading him into the police station without him realising what she was up to. Several times she had come home and been sure someone had been in the flat while she was out, some-

1

one very clever who hadn't left a single trace that they'd been there.

She had started masturbating again.

That was something else she had stopped feeling guilty about. She'd always assumed it was something you grew out of, like spots. You only did it until you started having regular sex, and then you handed responsibility for your orgasms over to your partner. But after Larry, for a long time she really hadn't felt like having a partner, and rather to her astonishment, she had started bringing herself off again, again and again, just as if she'd never been away. And once she had learned to relax and enjoy it, she discovered it was better than anything she'd ever had with Larry.

She did it in the shower, in the sitting room, in the kitchen, pressing herself up against the sink. She started sometimes almost without knowing it, waking up in the middle of the night from a wild confusing dream, gasping as if she was running for her life. In the dark and silence of the bedroom she felt suddenly very empty and alone. Seeking comfort she slipped a hand down between her legs and discovered to her surprise that she was hot and wet, her lips swollen and yielding, as if a phantom lover had just slipped out from between the sheets. With two moist fingers she would coax the trembling knot of her clitoris into full arousal, panting and gasping, arching her back until she stood up from the bed on her heels and the back of her head, thighs taut as a bow, sweat running from her breasts and belly. Sometimes she would come with a great shout, a cry more of despair than triumph.

There was nothing on her mind while she worked her body to a climax of frenzy, no imaginary men, no gratifying fantasies of throbbing cocks and tight-muscled buttocks — just Josephine and her fingers, working, working.

She was over the reaction, the never wanting to look at another man. Still, there was nobody she felt particularly excited about: not in the office, not even on the tube or on the street. Men fancied her, they always had. She had a desirable figure, she knew that: good breasts and a firm, round bottom. She never ate enough to put on an ounce around the middle. The men came after her, paying her attention, seeking her attention in return. But somehow she just couldn't be bothered. She seemed to have no patience with them, though she had patience. She could be very patient indeed, when she was after something she wanted.

She knew she wanted something now. But she didn't have any idea what it was.

What did other women want, apart from affairs and promotions? Babies? Josephine winced at the thought. To have something small and wet and helpless growing inside you, something that would demand all your attention and ruin your independence: no, thank you. Something simple, then. A holiday. Two weeks in Spain, or getting away from it all in the wilds of Scotland. That didn't sound any more alluring. She didn't want to relax, but she didn't want to take up anything new. There wasn't anyone whose company she wanted, but she couldn't stand the idea of going off somewhere on her own. Who could she go and see? Nobody.

She read the women's magazines, looking for a clue, but none of them held her attention. Royalty, anorexia, how to make paté, the trials of staying married to an alcoholic soap star: what did any of it have to do with her? She didn't even recognise herself in the fashion and self-management articles. These modern women were all concerned with projecting a smart and capable image. It was reality Josephine was losing track of. She read about somebody's midlife crisis, but it was hardly that, she was only just thirty. Maybe what she needed was a challenge. Sky-diving. Big game hunting. Famine relief in Ethiopia. She sighed and looked out of the window. It was July in Marylebone, and pouring with rain. People with umbrellas were scurrying out to lunch. Josephine looked at the time. The morning was gone, and she hadn't even finished the memo she was supposed to be writing. She'd have to have sandwiches brought in again.

Calling Dr Shepard was not a last resort, exactly, though it was certainly a cry for help. She'd been to her two or three times over the years, usually on some kind of gynaecological matter she didn't want to take to her GP, stuffy old man with an incomprehensible accent. Dr Shepard was a friend of her mother's who'd phoned her one day out of the blue, shortly after her wedding.

'Let me know if there's anything I can do,' she'd said. 'I'm not far away.' Josephine knew, though it hadn't ever been said in so many words, that her mother had asked Dr Shepard to keep an eye on her. In fact. she and her mother had never really spoken about Dr Shepard. She wasn't even sure how they knew each other. Some wartime friend, Joephine supposed, or one from schooldays.

Dr Shepard had been in private practice. When Josephine phoned, she found she'd retired since she'd last been to see her, 'but don't

<hr />
3
<hr />

worry about that,' Dr Shepard told her. 'You must come and visit me at home. Come to dinner.' She wouldn't let Josephine go without making a definite date.

Dr Shepard was an energetic, kindly woman, who could have been any age from fifty to seventy. She lived in a large, secluded house in Hampstead, surrounded by cherry trees. The door was opened by another woman, a short, slightly stout woman a few years younger who didn't offer to introduce herself: a housekeeper, Josephine supposed. Otherwise Dr Shepard obviously lived on her own, widowed or never married: never married, thought Josephine to herself. Dr Shepard was sensible enough to have managed that one.

It was a lovely house, thirties mock-Tudor, but done with enough money and taste to make it very comfortable. Nothing had been modernised, but everything was in perfect condition. Goodness knows what it cost to maintain. The housekeeper served a delicious dinner, veal with apricots and a perfect Queen of Puddings. She didn't eat with them. 'I wanted to be nosy,' said Dr Shepard. 'Find out how you're getting on. What it's like out there for a working girl these days.'

'How much of this will get back to Mummy?' Josephine asked her with a little smile.

Dr Shepard tut-tutted and held up a hand as if she was swearing her Hippocratic Oath. 'Strictest confidence,' she promised, chewing. 'I may be a nosy parker, but I'm not a gossip.'

So Josephine found herself telling her even more than she'd intended to, this woman she hardly knew: telling her how, in one sense everything was going so well and how, in another, it all seemed to be coming to pieces.

'I feel I've got stuck somehow,' she said, over coffee and Cointreau. 'Stuck in a corner. It isn't that I don't like my life, or my job or anything. It's just that something's missing, and I don't know what it is.'

'What about sex?' said Dr Shepard.

The very frankness with which she asked made Josephine want to be equally frank with her. She shook her head, and looked into her liqueur glass.

'Not for a long time,' she said. 'Not since the divorce.'

'But you must have had offers,' said Dr Shepard, just as bluntly. 'A juicy young woman like you.'

Josephine shrugged. She looked Dr Shepard in the eye. 'Would it make any sense,' she said, 'if I told you I've had offers, but right now

4

I can't even remember who from?'

Dr Shepard grunted. 'Gone off men, have you?'

'I did,' she said. 'For a while, I did.'

'Only natural,' Dr Shepard murmured conversationally.

'I don't know,' Josephine went on. 'I think I'd quite like a man now, but there doesn't seem to be one my size. Oops,' she said, with an embarrassed laugh.

Dr Shepard ignored the slip.

'What I mean to say is,' said Josephine, pulling herself together, 'I haven't found one; I can't be bothered to look for one; and if the right one threw himself at my feet, I can't even be sure I'd notice. I always seem to be thinking of something else,' she said.

'Oh, well, it might just be blood pressure, iron deficiency, something like that, you know,' said Dr Shepard. 'Are you eating properly?'

Josephine shrugged non-committally. Last night she'd been reduced to a Chinese takeaway. She'd meant to cook, but going into the kitchen she'd brushed her pubis against the door of the fridge and that had set her off. Instead of cooking, she'd stood there in the darkened room, her skirt up to her waist and her knickers down around her thighs, her bare bottom thumping softly against the fridge as she gasped and thrust, slicking herself to a long and complicated string of climaxes.

Should she tell Dr Shepard about that?

Better not.

Dr Shepard was still talking to her. 'Have you had a check-up lately? No? Would you like me to take a look at you?'

'Please. If it's not too much trouble.'

Dr Shepard drained her cup and got out of her chair. 'You are staying the night, aren't you,' she said, as if it had all been arranged.

'Oh,' said Josephine, 'I don't think I ...'

Dr Shepard interrupted, overriding her. 'There's a bed made up, and you can get in quite quickly from here in the morning. I'm sure we can find you a nightie, though I don't usually bother in the summer, do you?' Without waiting for a reply, she went on. 'You don't want to have to leave now and look for a taxi at this time of night.'

'All right,' said Josephine. 'I will. Thank you.'

'Come up and I'll show you where everything is.'

She took Josephine up into a room that contained an old iron bed, a hideous fifties cabbage rose dressing table, an overstuffed armchair, a double wardrobe in beautiful glossy walnut, and not much room for anything else.

'If you'd like to undress and pop yourself into bed,' said the doctor, as she drew the curtains closed, 'I'll come back and have a look at you, I'll just go and get my toolbox.'

She punched the mattress on her way out. 'This old thing really is quite comfortable, believe it or not,' she said, and without another word left Josephine alone.

Josephine slipped out of her jacket and unbuttoned her blouse. There was something slightly strange about doing this here and now, she thought, as she stepped out of her skirt and hung it with the rest in the wardrobe; but she decided it was just being examined after dinner, after she'd got quite relaxed and actually slightly drunk. She supposed she'd assumed, if she'd thought about it at all, that they'd get the examination out of the way first, before the sociabilities. But Dr Shepard was nothing if not easygoing. Perhaps, thought Josephine idly, peeling off her tights, that was why she needed a housekeeper.

She sat on the bed. It was rather comfortable. She began looking forward to bedtime.

She wondered whether she ought to leave her bra and panties on, or take them off. The other times Dr Shepard had examined her, it had been at her old surgery in town. There it was all helpful nurses with voluminous gowns to cover you up while you were waiting. You didn't bare an inch of flesh until the actual moment when the doctor wanted to look at it, and you covered it up again straight afterwards. It all seemed a bit of a bother, actually. And Dr Shepard had already said that about sleeping naked, hadn't she?

Josephine took off her bra. She took off her panties.

Then she did something that surprised her. She knelt on the armchair, pulled the curtain back from the window, and looked out into the night.

Anybody who'd been looking would have been sure to see her kneeling there. With the bedroom light on, they'd have seen her more clearly than she would have seen them. There was nobody, of course; only the cherry trees, moving restlessly in a wind that had sprung up from nowhere during the evening. It was only because there wouldn't be anybody out there that she did it, really, she told herself, showing herself at the window like that. But what was she looking for anyway? Some signal, some sign that everything was going to be all right? There was only her reflection, her heart-shaped face and full, firm breasts bared to the night. Through them she could see the cherry trees stirring the darkness with their leaves, the amber glow of a streetlamp rippling over them like the moon over water.

Josephine heard Dr Shepard coming and quickly dived beneath the sheets.

'Here we are then. Not cold, are you? I should think not,' said Dr Shepard, and whisked off the covers.

If she was surprised to see Josephine lying there naked already, she didn't show it. She simply put her stethoscope to her chest, palpated her breasts and her midriff, asked her to lift her knees and open her legs, then turned her over and listened to her back. She left her like that for a minute or two while she squeezed her shoulders, massaging away a tension Josephine didn't even know was there. It felt delicious to be pampered like that. Josephine had always found something slightly sexy in being handled with impersonal care by a professional. Even having her hair done was a gently sensual experience for her. Being massaged by Dr Shepard was something much, much more. Josephine hoped she'd go on and massage her all over. But she stopped suddenly, patted her briskly on the bottom, and said, in a low voice, 'There's nothing wrong with you, my girl.'

'Well, that's nice to know, at any rate,' said Josephine inanely as she slipped from the bed and past Dr Shepard to retrieve her clothes from the chair. She felt slightly unnerved, suddenly, she didn't know why. She thought she'd been close to losing her grip again for a moment, drifting away under Dr Shepard's hands to her private world where she was utterly alone and nothing was quite what it was supposed to be.

Behind her, Dr Shepard moved to the door, as if in answer to a knock Josephine had failed to hear. She opened it, and the housekeeper came in.

Josephine gasped. She grabbed the first piece of clothing she'd picked up, her bra, and held it absurdly over her breasts. She was horribly conscious that she hadn't even got her panties on yet. The two women had heard her gasp, and were both looking at her. She felt herself giving them a silly lopsided grin, the only defence she could muster. The housekeeper smiled back perfectly neutrally.

If Josephine thought this time Dr Shepard would apologise for her disregard, she was wrong. 'Don't worry, Josephine,' was all she said. 'There's nothing much Annabel hasn't seen. No secrets from Annabel,' she said. Clearly she thought Josephine was embarrassed over nothing at all.

'Can we find our young friend a nightie, do you think?' Dr Shepard asked her housekeeper.

'Oh, no, really,' said Josephine, 'it doesn't matter. I'd just as soon not. It is summer,' she said brightly, 'after all.'

She was busy putting her bra back on as she spoke, trying to hook it up behind her now that it was in place, unwilling to take it off again to turn it round.

Dr Shepard regarded her critically. 'Are you going to get dressed again?' she asked, in a tone that implied surprise.

'Oh... No, I suppose not,' said Josephine. 'What time is it? It must be time I was in bed, I suppose.'

'Well,' said Dr Shepard patiently, 'we won't be going to bed for a little while yet. I'm going to have a bath before bed. I always do. Wouldn't you like a bath, Josephine?'

'Oh, yes. Yes,' said Josephine, still off-balance.

'Well, no need to get dressed then,' said Dr Shepard heartily. 'Annabel here will run you a bath, and we'll go and see if she's left us any of that Cointreau. You can come downstairs as you are.'

The two women were looking at her expectantly. Josephine stared at them, wide-eyed.

She swallowed. 'All right,' she said.

Rather deliberately, she unhooked the clasp of her bra and took it off again. She stood before them, naked.

Dr Shepard turned to her housekeeper. 'Annabel,' she said, 'why don't you fetch our young friend a dressing gown?'

There was something in her voice that sounded like triumph, as if she'd just won some obscure point in a long-running debate with her companion. But then, thought Josephine as the two women went out and closed the bedroom door behind them, Dr Shepard said everything with emphasis, a kind of studied negligence. Still, there did seem to be something unspoken between those two: just an ordinary taciturn domestic understanding, probably, probably they'd been together for a long time; or ... Good heavens.

Josephine sat down on the bed, struck suddenly by what was staring her in the face.

Lesbians. They were lesbians.

'Gone off men, have you?' Dr Shepard had asked her downstairs.

Heavens, how had she answered? What had she said?

'We won't be going to bed for a little while,' Dr Shepard had said. *'Our young friend,'* she'd called her; twice she'd called her that. *'A juicy young woman like you.'*

Lesbians. Well, it was very fashionable now, with some women, feminist separatism, all that. Josephine didn't know any lesbians, though, or none that she knew about. When she was a girl at school, a girls' boarding school, there had been rumours. Some of them were true. She'd even played about with one of the other girls herself, an unhappy and unpopular girl called Maria who'd taken to hanging around the changing rooms when Josephine was there. Once after netball Josephine had lingered deliberately, to let Maria watch her. She was curious. She was a virgin. When all the other girls had gone, Maria had taken down her pants. They'd felt each other. Maria had wanted them to masturbate, but Josephine was scared. That had been years ago, though. *Years* ago.

What did they say about lesbians? There was always a dominant one and a submissive one. Lesbians of Dr Shepard's generation, anyway. They'd probably been together for years and years, like an old married couple. Dr Shepard the butch one, making her way in a man's profession in the forties, acquiring her protective colouration, her blunt talk and her sprawling posture, her legs stuck out in front of her as she sipped her Cointreau. And Annabel the good little housewife, keeping the place tidy and cooking dinner every night, always there in the background, sometimes seen, never heard.

There was a knock on the bedroom door.

Josephine, sitting on the bed, looked down at her nakedness in a helpless daze.

'Come in,' she said.

Annabel came in and handed her a great big quilted dressing gown: a man's size, it had to be.

Josephine smiled. It was a beautiful garment, one she'd have been pleased to wear at any time, though she'd have been grateful for anything to wear just now. 'Thank you,' she said.

'I'll run your bath, miss,' said Annabel. 'It takes a little while to get the old boiler cranked up. I'll come and tell you when it's ready for you.'

'Thank you, Annabel,' said Josephine.

The housekeeper went out.

Biting her lip to suppress a nervous laugh, Josephine pulled on the dressing gown. The luxurious old fabric felt delicious against her bare skin. The sleeves were much too long, and she turned them back before turning out the light and slipping barefoot from the room.

She was imagining things again, she told herself. Lesbians. It was hardly likely. But maybe it was. And she'd agreed to spend the night under their roof, and got into this ludicrous, intimate conversation about having baths and sleeping naked. She'd stood there and let them both look at her, look all they wanted.

What had she let herself in for?

2

The bathroom was large and old-fashioned, with pink lino on the floor and white tiles all around the walls. It was spotlessly clean and smelled faintly of disinfectant. Josephine found it reassuring. It reminded her of being in hospital, years ago when she was a little girl. She wondered whether to lock the door, and decided not to. What was there to conceal any more? She smiled to herself and swished the water around in the enormous claw-foot enamel tub. It was just right.

She got in, soaped herself languidly all over, and lay down staring up into the steam. She didn't remember when she'd last felt so comfortable. Her own flat had a small plastic bath the colour of primroses. She always used the shower anyway: in and out in ten minutes. She'd quite forgotten what it felt like to let herself down into deep, hot water and just lie there, half afloat.

Her fingers strayed between her soapy thighs, started to stroke her clitoris, round and round.

There was a knock at the door.

With a guilty start, Josephine snatched away her hand.

A voice called, 'May I come in?'

It was Dr Shepard.

'Yes,' Josephine called. Her voice sounded odd, echoing from the slick surfaces of the room. 'It's not locked,' she said, glad now she'd made the right decision.

Still, it felt very strange to be in the bath, with another woman old enough to be her mother sitting fully dressed on the edge of it, talking with her as if it were the most natural thing in the world. What if Dr Shepard really was a lesbian? Josephine wanted to cover herself again, but she decided that the best protection was to show that she didn't mind a bit these two old women wandering in and out on her while

11

she was naked; that it didn't mean a thing to her, least of all anything sexual.

'I'm going to give you a referral,' Dr Shepard told her. She was speaking more gently now than she had downstairs, as if she was telling Josephine something she thought she might not want to hear; as if she had finally realised that this was very personal stuff they were talking about, and Josephine was not an insensitive creature. 'They're very good, these people. Remind me to give you the phone number tomorrow before you go.'

She trailed her hand in the water just above Josephine's feet. Josephine didn't respond.

'You mean a psychiatrist, don't you?' she said calmly. She had never entertained the thought that she might one day have to see a psychiatrist. She had always felt vaguely sorry for people she knew who did, and vaguely superior to them too. Surely one should be able to control one's own life. Surely it was an admission of failure as a human being to have to turn to a professional for advice on how to live.

'Not exactly.' Dr Shepard stood up. 'But therapy, if you like. Something to help you get out of that corner. To help you open up a little, mentally and physically.'

Josephine sat up in the bath and sponged water over her face. 'That sounds formidable,' she said.

'Well,' said Dr Shepard with some of her previous asperity. 'You don't have to go, you know. I can't make you go.'

'It's for my own good,' said Josephine, with ironic emphasis.

'Of course,' Dr Shepard said.

Josephine felt a pang of guilt then. Complaining when Dr Shepard was being so kind to her, and before she even knew what she really did have in mind. It wasn't as if anyone was trying to lock her up, to have her committed.

'I am sorry,' she said, and meant it. 'I'm just not used to doing things I haven't planned. It's all rather new to me.'

'That's the idea,' said Dr Shepard. She opened the door. 'Good night, Josephine,' she said. 'Sleep well.'

Soon Josephine lay in bed, in the dark, listening. All she could hear was the wind in the cherry trees. There was not a sound in the house. Annabel and Dr Shepard must have gone to bed too. She wondered again whether they shared a bed. *'No secrets from Annabel.'* Why had Dr Shepard said that?

12

For an instant she had a mental image of a stout figure appearing at her bedroom door in the middle of the night, clad in a thin cotton nightdress and holding a candle, coming to get into bed with her. She turned over crossly, putting it out of her mind. There probably was something wrong with her, she told herself as she fell asleep: imagining sex everywhere like some Freudian case.

On the way into work in the morning, Josephine unfolded the piece of paper Dr Shepard had given her and looked at it again. It had a central London phone number on, and a name, Dr Hazel. He would be tall, she thought, with fair hair just beginning to recede over a high forehead. He would have little wrinkles at the corners of his eyes, and speak quietly and with clinical arrogance about Getting in Touch with Her Emotions. In the light of day Josephine was beginning to have doubts. What she had agreed to in Dr Shepard's house, was it only last night? − it was not what she'd wanted, not at all. It seemed suspect, unrealistic, here in the everyday world, where people crowded sullenly into the tube and ignored one another. That was how life was lived.

She put the piece of paper on her desk by the phone. She would ring the number and speak to Dr Hazel that afternoon.

But it was a busy day, and there were far more pressing things to do at three and four and five o'clock than indulge her own foibles. And busy days followed it, three and four and five of them. It wasn't until one particularly dreadful Monday morning when she'd already shouted at one of the secretaries and almost knocked over the glass of water she needed for her aspirins and it wasn't even ten-thirty yet, that her eye fell on the little slip of paper and it seemed, for that instant, like some kind of lifeline.

Josephine gave an irritable sigh and picked up the phone.

'Ms Morrow,' the young woman's voice said, 'yes, Doctor's been expecting you to call.' She had a nice voice, Josephine thought to herself. 'You're coming for a week at the country place, aren't you?'

'Am I?' said Josephine, suspiciously. 'Dr Shepard didn't say.' But inside she thought, Yes, please, take me away and lock me up.

'That's right,' the receptionist assured her. 'Doctor will need to see you for a check-up first, though. When can you pop in?'

'Not this week,' said Josephine, looking at her diary, crammed with unwelcome names and undesirable appointments.

'We could fit you in this time next week,' said the receptionist.

'All right,' said Josephine. 'Where are you?'

13

She scribbled the address on the paper under the phone number, and added: 'Mon 11'. Then she looked at the aspirins and at the glass of water, and pushed them aside.

One week, she thought.

The following Monday was hot. Josephine decided not to go in to the office at all. She phoned in and told them she'd be working at home, but not to phone her unless something urgent came up, and in any case not until the afternoon. Then she put on a loose summer top, skirt and sandals, expecting Dr Hazel would want to examine her, and took the tube and a taxi to the address she'd written down.

It was in a quiet backstreet near St Pancras, on the second floor, above the offices of an export agency and an amateur sports association. There was no nameplate at the door, so Josephine pressed the bell and walked up. At the top of the stairs she found a door with an opaque glass panel. She knocked and went in.

She found herself in a small room, entirely empty except for a desk with a telephone, an appointment book and a card file. There were two other doors, identical to the one she had just come through. On the wall between them was a poster, a painting of a figure in a pierrot suit, black skull cap and a little black mask. He was standing with his back to her, leaning negligently out over the railing of a balcony above a moonlit garden, but looking back over his shoulder, as if to see who was coming up behind him. He didn't look sad, the way pierrots in paintings usually do. He looked quizzical, as if he was making a daring suggestion, an invitation to a piece of mischief. It was a striking picture, but not exactly medical, somehow. Perhaps, thought Josephine, she should stop thinking of this in medical terms.

It was at that moment that one of the doors opened and a nurse came out, saying to someone in the room she was leaving: 'Very good, Doctor.'

She was a strikingly pretty woman in her late twenties, Josephine guessed, with fine red-gold hair twisted up into a severe bun behind her starched white cap. She gave Josephine a professional smile as she came towards her.

'Ms Morrow? Do come this way, please.'

She led Josephine not into the doctor's office, but into another room, an obvious waiting room, with canvas stacking chairs around the walls, and in the middle a low round table holding half a dozen old magazines and a vase of poppies.

'I was beginning to wonder if I'd come to the right place,' said Josephine.

'Yes, we are a bit hard to find,' said the nurse. 'But I'm sure you'll be glad you came.'

She said this as if in confidence; as if she knew what doubts Josephine had had.

'Doctor's busy at the moment,' the nurse went on, 'so perhaps you'd just like to slip your things off.'

'Here?' said Josephine, looking around the waiting room. There was no couch, not even a screen.

'If you would,' said the nurse. 'Oh, don't worry. There's nobody else coming in.' She smiled. She had a lovely smile. 'You'll find a gown on the back of the door,' she said, showing her. 'I'll be just outside.' And out she went.

Feeling rather strange to be undressing in what was by all appearances a public room, Josephine put down her handbag, took off all her clothes and quickly put on the gown. She sat with her clothes and her bag on a chair next to her and leafed through a limp colour supplement. She could hear nothing but the traffic in the main road, the shutting of a door somewhere on the floor below.

After a minute or two, without knocking, the nurse returned.

'All ready, are we?' she said. 'That's the way. If you'd like to follow me now.'

Josephine followed her through the front room to the other door, the one the nurse had appeared from. The nurse opened it for her.

To Josephine's surprise, this room was empty too, though here there was at least a couch with a screen around it, a desk with an untidy pile of books on, more books on the windowsill, and a washbasin in the corner. All the signs of a rather spartan doctor's surgery, in fact, except the doctor himself.

Josephine looked at the nurse, slightly puzzled, a question on her lips; but the nurse simply said, 'If you'd like to lie down, we'll be ready for you in just a minute now.'

Then she left her alone again.

Where was the doctor? He had been in here when Josephine arrived, so how had he managed to leave without her hearing him?

She told herself it was just her anxiety that made the whole scene seem slightly strange, as if there were something amiss. How was she to know, after all? She knew nothing of 'therapy', of what was usual or unusual.

15

No doubt Dr Hazel had simply slipped downstairs for a minute, for some reason. Probably he'd gone to the loo, she told herself.

She lay down on the couch and waited. Footsteps echoed up from the street outside. She wondered how long all this was going to take.

In another minute, the nurse came in, very brisk now. 'I'm so sorry to keep you waiting like this, Ms Morrow,' she said, coming to the couch. 'Dr Hazel's coming just now.'

She held out her hands, as if expecting Josephine to give her something. Josephine sat up, at a loss.

'If I could just have the gown now, Ms Morrow, if you don't mind,' she said pleasantly. 'You won't get cold, I promise. It's a lovely day, isn't it?'

'Yes,' said Josephine automatically. She looked at the nurse, then thinking once more that this really was not the sort of treatment she'd been expecting, if she'd been expecting anything at all, she untied the sash of the gown and slipped it from her shoulders.

'Here, let's help you with that,' said the nurse. Her hands were cool on Josephine's bare skin. Smiling, she took the gown from her and left her alone in the room once more, naked on the couch, not even a sheet to cover herself with, as if it was what she did every day, a dozen times a day, for every patient.

Perhaps it was a test. Perhaps her consultation would start with an assessment of how she responded to being treated like this. Uneasily she wondered how she was doing. Low on self-assertion, that was for sure.

Again she waited.

No one came.

Nothing happened at all.

There was a clock on the wall, a plain, institutional numbered dial. She waited three minutes. She waited five.

She was beginning to feel distinctly unsettled: not angry, not yet, but feeling the familiar tension start to rise. Was this what Dr Shepard had chosen for her? Was this any way to begin the therapy that was supposed to relieve her of irritability and depression?

Seven minutes went by.

I'll wait ten, Josephine thought, and then I'll give the nurse a call. No, I won't.

'Hello?' she called. 'Nurse?'

There was no reply.

16

'Nurse!'

Still nothing. Not even a footstep, the creak of a chair. Feeling odd and uncomfortable and distinctly vulnerable, Josephine got up from the couch and walked naked to the door. She pressed her ear against it.

Nothing.

She opened the door, standing well behind it and calling out 'Hello?'

Cautiously she put out her head. The outer room was deserted, just as it had been when she arrived. The door to the stairs was closed, and the door to the waiting room, where her clothes were.

Exasperated, she stepped back into the consulting room and looked around for something, anything, to cover herself with.

There was nothing.

She thought of Dr Shepard and Annabel, the casual way they'd treated her when she was naked. Medical nonchalance. Well, she said to herself, she's seen me once. And the doctor's going to see me.

If there is a doctor, she thought.

Irritated, she brushed the thought aside.

She stepped out of the door, into the outer office, and walked bare and barefoot across to the door of the waiting room.

She knocked on the glass.

'Hello?' she called a third time.

But there was no answer.

Josephine turned the handle and went inside.

Her clothes had gone.

So had her handbag.

She couldn't believe it. She looked around the room, but there was nowhere else they could have been put out of sight, no cupboard, not even under a chair.

'This is absurd,' she said aloud, and went back into the outer room.

There was no cupboard, only a drawer in the desk where the appointments book lay. The nurse must have taken her clothes and tidied them away. What a peculiar establishment this was.

Josephine opened the drawer.

There were clothes in there, white clothes, folded up.

For a moment, Josephine thought they were hers.

She took them out, unfolded them.

They were sports clothes, the sort of clothes a schoolgirl might wear

17

for gym: a small white T-shirt and a pair of white shorts, folded around a pair of white plimsolls. Inside each plimsoll was a white ankle sock.

The clothes were clean, washed and ironed, if not new. The plimsolls looked as if they had never been worn.

Looking at them, Josephine had an odd sensation in the pit of her stomach. She felt that this was indeed the beginning of something, some strange kind of psychological test, some maze she had stepped into and had to find her own way through.

She had read an article once in a colour supplement about initiative tests that Japanese firms set their aspiring executives, people who wanted to succeed, people they really wanted to test. They involved exactly this kind of thing: sending a group who didn't know each other to a remote island for an imaginary conference. One of the group was a mole, there to see how the others reacted when they realised that nothing had been organised and they were stuck there for two days without food or even shelter. At the time, she'd thought the magazine had been making it up. It sounded more like the scenario for a corny old murder mystery than a survival exercise.

Now that she was inside it, now that it was actually happening to her, it didn't feel like that at all. It felt like something altogether different, something Josephine didn't even have a name for.

Yet.

She found herself smiling.

'Therapy, if you like,' Dr Shepard had said. *'Something to help you open up a little.'*

So, it was a test, was it?

Well, it made a change from sitting in the office.

Now, then. How to pass the test. What was her objective? To get out of here and get home. And if she could do it in some way that showed she hadn't done it in desperation, but had walked out laughing, that would surely put her ahead, whatever they were looking for in their test.

Perhaps they were looking at her now.

Perhaps Dr Hazel was actually here somewhere, watching her to see what she did next.

She didn't mind. She didn't mind at all.

An insecure person would hurry up and try the clothes on, just for the minimal comfort of being dressed.

Josephine decided she would not be insecure.

18

She put the clothes back in the drawer.

As she did, her hand touched something at the back of the drawer. It felt like a box.

She pulled it out. It was quite heavy.

It was a box of dominoes.

She shook it and heard them rattle faintly. Curious, she opened the box and looked inside. Dominoes; nothing else.

She put the box back in the drawer with the clothes, pulled the chair out from the desk and sat down. The canvas felt strange on her bare bottom. She told herself to be glad it wasn't wicker.

Now what?

Casually, she flicked through the appointments book, hoping that there would be some clue there.

But there was nothing, just columns of names and dates and times.

Perhaps there would be something in the consulting room, among the books, or in the waiting room, pencilled in one of the magazines: the clue to the next stage of this weird treasure hunt.

Ten minutes later, she gave up searching for it. If it was there, it was too well hidden. The old magazines were simply that, innocent of any cryptic messages, while the books in the surgery were simply old junk, not even medical books, the sort of thing you could pick up by the armful at any Oxfam shop. When she saw that, Josephine was sure this wasn't a doctor's office of any kind. It was a front. Dr Hazel had never been here at all; he probably didn't even exist. There was just an actress pretending to be a nurse, with instructions to make her undress and then leave the building as quickly and quietly as possible. They'd probably told her it was a practical joke, a sort of lewd Candid Camera set-up.

Whoever they were.

Josephine wondered about the door to the stairs. She allowed herself to try the handle.

It wasn't locked. She felt immensely relieved to discover that.

So, she could walk out now. If she only had the nerve to skip downstairs naked and ask at one of the other offices for assistance.

She hopped up on the desk — I'll give them nonchalance, she thought — and sat there, carelessly swinging her bare legs, deliberately not looking at the telephone.

She should not be in too much of a hurry. She should pick up the receiver, dial coolly and correctly, and speak to —

Who?

The police?

Surely not. That would ruin their game, and her chances of winning it. The office? That would demonstrate loyalty, a sense of duty, but no flair or imagination. Dr Shepard, to demand an explanation? That would be pretty conventional too. A good friend? Who could she call upon to rescue her from a situation like this, from this situation?

She couldn't even come up with anyone to consider.

She suddenly felt a startling flash of sexual arousal. You are alone, naked, in an office. No one knows you are there. Who would you choose to entice to join you?

That would certainly be an imaginative and audacious response: to ring up a lover and have sex with him on 'Dr Hazel's' examination couch!

But she hadn't got a lover; not even an old boyfriend she could trust herself to do that to. There was only Larry, her ex-husband, and nothing on earth would make her ever call him again. There wasn't even anyone in the department she wanted to seduce.

Well, then, whoever was in the offices downstairs. It didn't matter who, just a man, or preferably a boy, she could bring upstairs and offer herself to in exchange for clothes and her taxi fare. But then she'd have to go downstairs to find him, and plainly the idea was to use the phone, to make them come to her.

Whoever they were. Whoever the hell she could get up here.

Suddenly she thought: the sandwich boy. The boy who always brought the sandwich orders into the office at lunchtime. He wasn't exactly desirable, but he was nobody, she could play whatever game she liked with him and come out of it scot-free. Who'd ever believe him if he told them? They'd be more likely to fire him. She even knew the number of the catering firm, which was more than she could say for Dr Shepard's.

She could ring them now, and place a lavish order; offer them a bonus, say, for coming so far out of their area; and ask for the boy in person. Rodney, his name was.

Rodney!

Josephine gave a chuckle. All right, Dr Hazel, she thought: let's see you score this one on your personality profiles.

She reached out her hand to pick up the phone.

It rang.

|3|

Josephine nearly jumped out of her skin. She grabbed at the phone, then stopped short.

This proved they were watching her. They waited until they could see she'd made up her mind what to do, and then they rang the phone. And when a phone rang she, being an obedient and predictable person, would answer it at once.

Let them wait, she thought. Let them see me sitting here on the desk with nothing on, looking at the phone and listening to it ring.

It certainly made a racket in the empty room. Josephine stretched and looked around. She noticed the pierrot poster again, noticed the challenging eyes smiling from behind their mask.

Then, deciding her point had been made, she turned and coolly picked up the phone.

'Ms Morrow?' said a voice, a man's voice. At least they weren't going to play around pretending to be patients calling to make an appointment with Dr Hazel.

'That's right,' said Josephine.

'You're to come down straight away,' said the voice. 'The course starts tonight.'

'Tonight?' said Josephine. 'But I haven't a thing to wear.'

'Your clothes are in the desk,' he said, as if he hadn't even noticed the joke. She thought he had a faint accent: not German; Dutch, was it?

'They aren't, you know,' she said.

There was a slight pause, and Josephine suddenly felt he was about to hang up. That certainly wouldn't earn her any points for mastering the situation, so to keep him talking she said, 'That's not Dr Hazel, by any chance, is it?'

The pause continued. Then, as if echoing her, he said, 'That's right.'

21

'Where are you?' Josephine asked. 'I can't see you anywhere. I do think you might have the decency to put in an appearance when a new patient comes to see you. But then I see you're a very busy man,' she went on, turning the page of the appointments book and hoping he could hear it rustle.

'You will see me. Tonight. At Estwych.'

'Where?'

'We'll come and get you,' he said.

'Now?'

'There's a taxicab waiting,' he said, brusquely. 'Get dressed and go downstairs.'

Josephine began to doubt her interpretation. What if this really was Dr Hazel, and the whole thing was some bizarre concatenation of errors and misunderstandings? What if it wasn't a test at all, and that was only another one of her peculiar self-deceptions, like imagining Dr Shepard having some unnatural relationship with her housekeeper?

'Your nurse took my bag,' she said, and added slightly desperately, 'and all my clothes....'

The phone purred at her.

Josephine swore. She put the phone down very gently. She opened the desk drawer again, and took out the clothes. The only clothes she had. The clothes she'd have to wear to walk out of here.

Estwych, he had said. Wherever that was. The country place. A residential clinic or something. She looked at the clothes in her hand.

'Perhaps they'll have a tennis court,' she said aloud.

She lifted her foot up onto the desk and held one of the gymshoes beside it. It looked a bit small.

She realised she was just stalling, daydreaming, reluctant to make a move now her precious initiative had been snatched away from her.

She got off the desk and pulled the T-shirt over her head.

It was tight. Very tight. Her breasts strained against the thin white fabric. You could see her nipples, as clear as anything.

The shirt was very short. When she'd crammed herself into the shorts, she found the shirt would only just tuck in. Meanwhile the shorts themselves were threatening to split at the seam. She would have to go very carefully, not make any sudden movements, and definitely not bend over. It was all she could do to reach her feet, sitting on the desk again and drawing her knees up, to put on the socks, which fitted, and the shoes, which only just did.

22

There was a pattern to this now, Josephine thought as she took one last look around the abandoned surgery for anything, anything at all that might be useful on the journey. She was being exposed. Her body was being displayed to casual strangers in a way she found alarming, and, if she was honest, just a little bit thrilling. Dr Shepard and her housekeeper had had her naked between them with no trouble at all. The nurse, if she really was a nurse, had managed it in a twinkling. Normally she never wore anything that was the slightest bit risqué. Larry had never liked her to flaunt her body, and since she'd been working she'd made sure to dress very soberly. She would have been embarrassed to turn up in some of the things the high-fliers wore.

Then suddenly she remembered.

She remembered something she'd done when she was seventeen, eighteen maybe; something she hadn't thought of for years.

She'd gone on holiday with two friends, seeing Europe, and they'd got stuck at Orly. There'd been some trouble, a strike or a bomb scare, and they'd had to hang around in the departure lounge for several hours. It was hot that day too. The sun came blazing through the glass panels in the roof, and the café had run out of cold drinks. The lounge was packed to overflowing with hot, tired, irritable people, each guarding their carry-on bags. Josephine and her friends had managed to get two seats between them. They took it in turns to sit and stand while they waited and wondered if they'd ever get away.

Josephine had wandered a little way off and found a low ledge to perch on in a corner between the moulding of a litter bin and the wall. Precariously she had lowered her bottom onto it and squatted there, leaning back against the wall with her knees up and her feet drawn back under her, out of the aisle. It was far from comfortable, but it was a change from standing up.

Moments later, looking dazedly around between the pushchairs and backpacks, she'd noticed an elderly man sitting several yards away. Tucked away there in her corner, he was the only person in the room who could look directly at her, and he was. He was pretending to read a magazine, but he was looking at her. She had her knees slightly apart to balance on the ledge, and Josephine realised he could see right up her dress.

At any other time she would probably have made that a reason to abandon her perch, stand up and go and rejoin her friends. But for some reason, being on holiday, in a foreign place where no one knew

23

her, in the relative safety of a crowded room, the idea that this distinguished-looking man in his blue suit and chequered cravat was looking at her panties made her suddenly quite excited.

Trying not to let him know she'd spotted him, she turned sideways and looked up at the glass overhead, as if watching for planes. Bracing herself against the bin, she spread her knees a little further.

Glancing secretly at her observer to see what effect this had, she was delighted to see him shifting in his hard airport seat and making a furtive rearrangement in his lap. She knew what that meant. He had an erection! She had given him a hard-on! Josephine felt quite dizzy with glee.

It was then that she did it. She went quite mad.

She got up from her corner, gave her skirt a flick to straighten it, and without looking at the man, made her way through the crowd to the *dames*.

She even had to queue. Well, it passed the time. More than once she almost came to her senses and went back into the lounge, but a spirit of erotic mischief made her persevere.

When her turn came, she locked herself in the stall, pulled down her panties and squatted on the low pedestal. It was no use, she was so tense she couldn't even pee. She stood up, trod on the flush pedal, and then, instead of pulling her panties up, stepped out of them, picked them up and stuffed them in her handbag. Out of her handbag she took her sunglasses. She put them on.

Then she went back out into the lounge.

She was hoping no one would have taken her uninviting corner, and they hadn't. Just as she'd done before, she lowered herself into position, but this time keeping her knees together.

Protected by the sunglasses, she looked through the crowd of bored and restless travellers.

The man was still there, reading his magazine.

She waited until she was sure he'd noticed her return. Then, surreptitiously hitching up her skirt an inch or two at the hips, she parted her legs.

She saw him shift in his seat, holding his magazine up in front of him and covertly staring over the top of its glossy pages. She knew now he could see between her bare brown legs to the sunlit nest of her pubic hair. Why was she doing it? Why expose herself to the impersonal gaze of a total stranger, a man almost old enough to be her grandfather? Josephine didn't know. It was the heat, it was something in the dry and overladen air. Whatever it was, she had felt herself growing moist at the sight of him, his eyes feasting on her most intimate parts.

She had no desire to meet him, or even to catch his eye. If he'd stood up and walked towards her she'd have fled. But mentally she saluted him. She imagined him, later, masturbating urgently to the memory of the *mademoiselle* with the bare crotch, the parted, sun-kissed thighs. The splash of his semen would be a tribute to her, payment enough for her simple revelation. She recalled again now that wave of pleasurable feeling, and knew it was a secret kind of power.

She looked around the deserted office. She looked at the pierrot on the wall. He was leaning on the railing of his balcony, looking back at her through the little eyeholes of his mask. Are you coming? he seemed to be asking her. Do you dare?

I dare, she thought. She went to the door. Quietly she turned the handle and stepped out onto the stairs.

She hadn't noticed on the way up how much the stairs creaked at every step. Now she kept to the outside of the tread as she walked down on tiptoe, hoping very much she wouldn't meet anybody. She wondered if she'd have to walk to the taxi, if anyone on the street would notice her.

She passed the sports association office. Someone inside was typing slowly at a manual typewriter. She thought she could hear a radio, the brainless burble of a disc jockey. She passed the door and went on down.

Just as she reached the door of the export agency, just as she thought she was past it and safe, what she was dreading happened. The door opened and a man came out.

He was a thin, middle-aged clerkish type in a grey suit, complete with waistcoat and tightly knotted tie, though it must have been stifling in his office. He was reading a sheet of paper. He turned to come up the stairs, glanced up and saw her, a figure from a pornographic fantasy, a curvy blonde crammed into the clothes of a little girl, descending the stairs towards him.

'Afternoon,' he muttered, and looking back at his paper, stood aside to let her go by.

Josephine went down the remaining stairs with a grin on her face and elation in her heart. He hadn't noticed her! She wasn't so conspicuous after all. Or else she was, and he was so shocked, poor, repressed, mousy little clerk, that he hadn't even dared to stare.

Or else, she thought, he was just a nice man, a polite, old-fashioned man, one who would never ever take advantage of a woman, even to the extent of a stare.

Or else he was used to it. It happened every day, half-naked women creeping down from Dr Hazel's surgery with their breasts bursting out of tiny T-shirts and harrassed expressions on their faces.

Perhaps he was Dr Hazel. Perhaps he was the one who'd been watching her all along, through his secret periscope.

Josephine found her shirt had come untucked at the back, flapping open to reveal a generous area of bare skin. Tucking it in again, she stepped out into the sunlight.

|4|

There was no taxi in sight. She had looked up and down the street. Now she leaned against the wall, trying to look nonchalant, feeling the stare of every passer-by appraise her body. A passing car honked joyfully. A man leaned out of the window of a van and gave her the old short-arm sign, yelling something lustful and derisive. Elderly pedestrians and mothers trailing children looked shocked, looked away.

Josephine surveyed them all from under half-closed eyelids. The sun was hot on her skin. The shorts hurt where the elastic squeezed her waist.

Josephine found she didn't care about the leers, the affronted stares. No one will dare lay a finger on me, she told herself, not in broad daylight. She hoped it was true.

Several minutes passed, slowly. A pack of boys went past, hooting and jeering. The bolder ones hung about, circling her like dogs around a tempting piece of meat. She stared at them coolly and one by one, they swirled away, laughing and shouting to cover their embarrassment.

Where was the bloody taxi? No doctor at the surgery, no taxi in the street. They were trying to disorient her. It was part of the test. She pretended she was someone else. She was a character in a film. They could all look at her, but no one could touch her.

But what would happen if the film went on? If the taxi didn't turn up?

At that moment a taxi appeared around the corner.

Josephine looked up in sudden hope. She shaded her eyes, watching it approach.

It was just a black taxicab, like any other. It pulled in at the kerb, and the driver stuck his head out of the open window.

'Josephine Morrow?' he asked.

27

'Yes!' she said in some relief, stepping away from the wall. The driver was a burly, broad-faced young man with wild curly red hair and a gold earring. His nose was flat and broad, and looked as if it had been spread across his face. He had on a pair of plastic sunglasses that completely concealed his eyes, and a sports shirt striped vivid green and white like a corporation deckchair. A jungle of red hair flourished from the open neck, cascaded down his muscular forearms.

He grinned at Josephine, as every member of the male sex had been doing since she set foot outside. He looked at her over his glasses. His eyes were as green as bottles. He fixed her with a look of surprising power as he reached back and, without looking, opened the passenger door.

'Get in,' he said.

Josephine had never been told what to do by a taxi driver before. Perhaps he wasn't really a taxi driver. Perhaps *he* was Dr Hazel. He was quite attractive, really, in an animal sort of way.

She bent, very conscious of her straining shorts, and climbed into the cab.

She caught his eye in the mirror. He was watching her body move as she sat down.

'Are we going to Estwych?' she asked him through the sliding panel.

'To where?' he said.

He pulled out into the traffic.

'Estwych,' she repeated loudly.

'No, love,' he said.

She felt a moment of panic. 'Hold on, she told herself. This is more disorientation.

'Dr Hazel said you were taking me to a place called Estwych.'

He frowned as if he couldn't hear her over the noise of the engine. 'Dr Who?'

'Dr Hazel,' she repeated, firmly.

Hold your horses,' he said. 'One thing at a time.'

She willed herself not to lose her temper. Perhaps they wanted her to lose her temper with this stupid man.

She lay back and relaxed. She was completely in their hands anyway. There was nothing she could do, except prove that none of their calculated indignities could upset her.

She was sure he was still looking at her in the mirror as he drove, though she couldn't see his eyes for the sunglasses. Well, let him look.

Let him get a good look.

She slid down in her seat, letting her legs fall apart a little way. To hell with it, she thought. She gave him a slow smile.

Meanwhile, another part of herself was scolding her furiously. Don't make trouble. If you make trouble, you won't get through this. Sit up! Cross your legs! What do you think you're doing?

And the other part of her answered: I don't know. For once in my life, I don't know.

It must be an adventure.

'This Estwych,' she said after a while. 'I don't know if it's a town, or a village, a farm or something, or even just a building.'

'Nor do I, love,' he said, and began to whistle very loudly and very discouragingly.

She lay back and closed her eyes. Nonchalance, she thought. If she took no notice of him, he would see he wasn't bothering her.

Taxis were something of a luxury for Josephine, usually. She didn't earn enough to take taxis except on special occasions. And this was a special occasion, even if it was all wrapped in mystery. Or perhaps because it was. Perhaps that was Dr Shepard's idea, and Dr Hazel's. To take her out of herself.

Perhaps it was nothing more sinister than a mystery tour.

It was nice to just sit and be driven somewhere, she decided. It was better than being poked around in a doctor's surgery, she thought, which was what she'd expected to be happening by now. It was better than sitting in the office. Adventures didn't happen sitting around in offices.

After some minutes she opened her eyes. They were on a motorway. They were heading out of the city. Estwych, the country place. They were obviously going there, whatever the driver said.

At the moment he wasn't saying anything. She wasn't going to try to talk to him again. If he fancied a conversation, let him start one.

He didn't. He didn't say anything at all. Sometimes he whistled. Once he began to sing, in a loud tuneless voice, but he didn't sing more than a couple of lines before he subsided into silence again.

If he was trying to make her nervous, he'd have to do better than that. Josephine felt drowsy from the heat and the motion and the boredom.

'Here we are,' said the cabby suddenly.

Josephine sat up, blinking. What time was it? How long had they been driving?

29

She looked out of the window.

They were pulling in at a large, rambling country inn, set back from the road behind tall hedges.

She must have fallen asleep after all, she realised.

'Is this it?' she asked stupidly. 'Is this Estwych?'

'No, love,' he said. 'This is the Green Man.'

He pointed to a sign high up on a post above the hedge.

'Where are we?' she insisted.

'Whittingtry,' he said.

The name meant nothing to her.

He pulled up right outside the door, which was standing propped open in the heat. He reached back and opened the passenger door for her again. He had left the engine idling.

'You're expected,' he said again.

'Thank you,' said Josephine, trying to sound nonchalant.

He grinned at her, looking like a troll that had found a straying rambler and stolen his sunglasses. Josephine saw he had a gold tooth to go with his gold earring.

She went inside the inn.

Inside the air was cool and everything was utterly normal. There was anonymous modernised rural décor, horse brasses and hunting prints. Josephine heard conversations stop as she passed the open door of the public bar. She had almost forgotten what she looked like. Everything was utterly normal except her.

The young man at reception affected to take no notice of what she looked like. Josephine gave her name. There was a room booked for her. 'Room number eleven. Top of the stairs and to the right. No luggage, madam?'

'No.' She wanted to ease her shorts where they were sticking between her buttocks, but she couldn't with the clerk's eyes on her. 'Who booked my room, can you tell me?' she asked. 'Was it a Dr Hazel?'

'I'm afraid I wasn't on duty, madam,' he said.

'Well, wouldn't he have signed something?'

'Not necessarily, madam.'

As he handed her her key, she noticed a local map under glass on the counter top. An idea came to her.

'I'm looking for a place called Estwych,' she said, taking the key. 'I don't suppose you know anywhere of that name around here?'

'Estwych, madam?' He shook his head. 'Not around here, no.'

So there was still a journey ahead of her.

Assuming Estwych existed at all.

'Madam?'

The clerk was holding out a padded envelope. It had her name on.

'The gentleman left this for you.'

Josephine took it. It was rather heavy. Whatever was inside it gave a muffled clink.

Trying unsuccessfully to look as if it was something she'd been expecting, Josephine started to break the seal. Then a sixth sense suddenly made her change her mind.

'Thank you,' she said, and went upstairs, the envelope unopened under her arm.

She found her room and locked herself in. Glancing briefly around, she was deeply gratified to see the room boasted an *en suite* bathroom. If she couldn't eat or change her clothes, at least she could shower.

But first, the mystery gift.

She sat on the bed, turning the envelope in her hand and looking at her name, *Josephine Morrow*, written in fibre-tip by an energetic, hurried hand.

Dr Hazel's hand? Somehow she doubted it. If there really was a Dr Hazel at the source of all this, he hadn't done anything at all for himself so far.

Josephine broke the seal, upended the envelope, and tipped the contents out into her lap. When she saw what they were, she was grateful for the premonition that had stopped her opening it downstairs.

There were three things. A black silk scarf. A pair of shiny metal handcuffs. And a note. *'Shower. Do not dress. Wait in your room.'*

Josephine was getting used to being ordered around, just as she was getting used to walking about in discomfort and half-naked, but it still felt strange to be instructed anonymously in writing to do what she had been longing to do anyway.

The scarf and the handcuffs felt cool on her hot bare thighs: the soft, pliant coolness of silk and the hard, firm chill of steel. She picked them up, inspected them cursorily and put them on the bed with the empty envelope. This affair was growing more and more like a detective story. What was she supposed to deduce from these latest clues? The identity of the sinister Dr Hazel? The awesome secret of Estwych? Or

31

was she, perhaps, the suspect for some hitherto undisclosed crime? Why had Dr Hazel and his nurse disappeared from the St Pancras surgery? It would be quite logical, the way today had been going so far, that next a posse of hefty policemen would break down the door of the hotel room and charge Josephine with murdering them both. The handcuffs were open. It had not escaped her that there was no key.

She looked again at the note. The handwriting was the same as the handwriting on the outside of the envelope, a vigorous scrawl. It told her nothing. Josephine dropped it on the bed with the other things.

She went over to the window, opened it wide and leaned out, breathing the warm, succulent scents of a perfect summer's day in the English countryside. She watched the birds darting through the clear air, flitting here and there like her thoughts. She felt she was getting light-headed from fatigue, lack of food, travelling, the most peculiar mental and physical ordeals. Quite likely none of this was real. It was all some gigantic paranoid delusion. She had gone quite mad, dressed herself in these ridiculous clothes and deserted her home and her work to ride off into the unknown, convinced she was taking part in some secret therapeutic exercise. Dr Hazel would turn out to be a man in a white coat. Estwych would be the name of his private nursing home. That would just about make sense. Nothing else did.

Josephine kicked off her plimsolls, tight as they were, without undoing the laces. She tore off the dank, sweaty ankle socks, yanked down her shorts and struggled out of her T-shirt. Leaving all her clothes to lie where they fell, she strode into the bathroom and turned on the shower.

She showered and showered, first in hot water with plenty of rich, soapy lather, and afterwards in a blast of icy cold that shocked her back into life. The hotel towels were thick and deep-piled. There were three in the bathroom. She used them all. Then, snugly wrapped in the largest, she padded back into the bedroom. There was a full-length mirror on the built-in wardrobe. Josephine took off her towel and looked herself over. The only trace of what she had been through so far was a thick red line around her belly where the elastic of the shorts had cut into her. Below, her pubic hair lay curled in a soft damp slick.

Her stomach rumbled. She wondered who she was waiting for now, and whether they would take her to lunch. Probably not. '*Do not dress,*' the note said. Well, that was all right by Josephine. She had no very great desire to put the sweaty sports clothes back on. She supposed they would have some other demeaning costume for her.

'*Wait*,' said the note. Very well, she would. And while she was waiting, she would have something to eat.

She picked up the phone and, after consulting the typewritten list of numbers fixed neatly on the wall above, dialled reception.

'This is Ms Morrow in room eleven. Are you still serving lunch? Good. I wonder if you could have me something sent up. What's on the menu?'

She paused, listening. 'Mm-hm ,' she said. 'Mm-hm. Mm, well, is the camembert ripe? Yes, French bread, please. And the watercress and walnut salad sounds intriguing. Um, apple pie and cream, and a cup of black coffee. Oh, and a glass of dry white wine. Yes, that would be fine. Will you put all that on my bill, please? Excellent. Thank you so much.'

Josephine lay down on the bed, feeling better already.

In no time at all there was a knock on the door. 'Come in,' she called, and dashed into the bathroom. She turned the bath tap on full.

'Room service, madam,' called a voice. 'Your lunch.'

'Oh, thank you.' she said, raising her voice above the gushing water. 'Just leave it there, would you?' Then, her ear pressed to the door, she waited until she heard the bedroom door close before rushing out and falling on the food like a starving creature.

She ate hurriedly, telling herself to slow down and avoid indigestion, but conscious that whoever or whatever she was waiting for might overtake her before she got to the coffee. But all was well, including the watercress and walnut salad.

Finally laying down her fork, she said aloud, 'I must come here again.' She wiped her mouth, and dabbed a spot of cream she'd spilled, in her haste, on her right breast.

Sitting back refreshed and replete, she considered her position. There was nothing like a good lunch, and a glass of wine, for raising the spirits.

Nothing too horrible had happened after all. If at any point she'd decided she'd had enough adventure, if she'd truly wanted to call it off, she could have done. She could have done something, even if she wasn't quite sure what. Nobody had been holding a gun to her head, that was the point. They'd tried to humiliate her and she'd taken no

33

notice. That would surely stand her in good stead with Dr Hazel, whenever she eventually came face to face with him.

The scarf and the handcuffs she would not think about for the moment.

Interrupting Josephine's reverie of self-congratulation, the phone rang.

Startled, Josephine sat bolt upright, staring at it.

It rang again.

Feeling suddenly absurdly vulnerable, Josephine slid from the bed, grabbing the discarded bathtowel with one hand, fumbling the handset off the phone with the other.

'Hello?'

'Ms Morrow?'

'Of course,' she said, clutching the towel to her breasts, angry as much with herself for being rattled as with this false courtesy.

'Dr Hazel presents his compliments, Ms Morrow.' It was a woman's voice, and Japanese. 'He hopes you enjoyed your lunch.'

So they knew what she had done.

'Thank him very much from me,' said Josephine. 'Tell him he must let me return the favour one of these days.'

The woman laughed, delicately. It was the first time any of them had acknowledged one of her defensive witticisms.

'You have the package,' the voice went on. It wasn't a question. 'We'll be with you in a couple of minutes. We're looking forward very much to meeting you.'

There was a pause.

'Not half as much as I am to meeting Dr Hazel,' said Josephine belatedly; and almost missed what the woman said next.

'You must put on the blindfold.'

'What?' said Josephine, but she had rung off.

Josephine set the receiver back on the rest. She was trembling, breathing fast and shallow, her good mood scattered and gone. The scarf, a blindfold. She picked it up. They wanted her to sit naked and blind in a hotel room, awaiting their pleasure.

She couldn't do it. She wouldn't do it.

She put it down. She wrapped the towel around her properly, tucking the end in above her breasts as she sat on the bed, facing the door.

Her legs were trembling. Her heart was beating like mad.

34

She strained her ears for footsteps, but couldn't hear a sound.

She panicked, scrabbling for the scarf, frantically folding it lengthwise and wrapping it around her head, covering her eyes.

Just as she knotted it at the back, there was a knock at the door. Josephine opened her mouth, but nothing came out.

The knock was repeated, more sharply.

'Come in,' croaked Josephine.

She heard the sound of the door opening, and people coming into the room. She couldn't tell how many. Bravely she got to her feet and turned her sightless face towards them.

'You're dressed,' said a voice, a man's voice. She thought she had heard it somewhere before. 'You were told not to dress.'

She couldn't just sit there and say nothing. 'It's only a towel,' she said. 'I was getting cold, waiting,' she lied.

The man ignored her. 'Obedience is all-important,' he said. 'Absolute obedience is the law.'

Josephine's throat seized up. She contained a shudder. She would not be afraid, she would not. Even so, something blocked her anger too, stopped her from snatching off the blindfold and confronting them: some dim yearning towards whatever was at the end of this, beyond the meaningless instructions and elusive menace: revelation, or reward, or satisfaction – something nameless and formless to her yet, but Josephine knew deep inside, that she would never forgive herself if she gave up before the finish.

She could hang on. They wouldn't drive her mad.

She heard the clink of metal. One of them was behind her, picking up the handcuffs.

'Clasp your hands behind your back,' said the man.

'Why?' said Josephine. 'What for?' But she was weakening. As soon as they were out of her mouth, she wished the words unsaid.

She knew what for.

'Obedience is the law,' repeated the man, as calmly as before. 'Disobedience is punished.'

All right, Josephine Morrow, said Josephine silently to herself. Either this is some weirdo zombie cult who are going to carve you into pieces in an English country hotel room on a peaceful summer afternoon with the sun shining and swallows on the wing. Or else this is all charade, a kinky kind of play-acting psychotherapy that's twisting your mind in knots to hand back to you whole and new at the end of the week. Or else it's something else again. Something else. Do you want to go home now, back to the office and the flat and the telly and the supermarket and take Valium and masturbate for the rest of your life?

Or are you coming with me?

She clasped her hands behind her back, and felt the cool touch of someone else's hands, a woman's hands, she was sure, and the cold steel of the handcuffs fastened about her wrists. She heard one lock click shut, and then the other.

'Take off the towel,' said the man. Josephine was bewildered for a moment. How could she take the towel off with her hands locked together? But he was speaking to his partner, the woman. The woman on the phone, the Japanese, Josephine supposed, as she felt those cool hands now briefly brush the slopes of her breasts and the loosened towel drop to the floor behind her.

The man stepped forward. She could feel him standing over her. She could hear him breathing, breathing deep and easy, not excited, as he took hold of her breasts.

She gasped. He cupped her breasts in his hands, rubbing his thumbs across her nipples, not gently. He squeezed her, pressing her breasts down, then up, rubbing them slowly and hard against her chest.

It took her breath away. No one but Dr Shepard had laid hands on her naked body since she had expelled Larry from her bed. No one had handled her like that before ever.

The man released her.

'Turn around,' he said.

She turned, shuffling around, unsure in her shock and blindness which way she was facing.

'Bend over,' he told her.

She knew then where she had heard his voice before. He was the man who had phoned her at the surgery, the man with the continental accent who had said he was Dr Hazel.

Feeling terribly vulnerable with her hands trapped behind her, expecting to overbalance any moment, Josephine bent over. Then she felt hands come up and grasp her shoulders, pulling her down, and she fell forward, feeling the bedspread under her face and breasts, but under her stomach and hips the lap of the woman who had sat down to receive her and was now wrapping her arms around her, one across her back, the other under her stomach, encircling her to hold her down.

She knew what was going to happen in the second that it did.

The first slap fell on her upturned buttocks, a jolting, stinging pain that made her jerk in the woman's grip and cry out with surprise. The second fell, the third. It was the man spanking her, she knew: hard, lazy blows with his open hand on her defenceless bottom; and the woman his companion was holding her down for him.

Josephine had never been spanked: not as a girl at home or at school. She had known girls who had been beaten at school, very few. The housemistress would have beaten her, and Maria too, if they had been caught together in the changing room; but they were not caught, and Josephine had never been beaten. The pain of it was extraordinary, far more than she could ever have imagined. She kicked and shouted. When she shouted, he smacked her harder. She struggled; but the woman was strong.

He smacked her again, and she kicked out again. She felt her foot connecting with his leg, the fabric of a suit, flesh and bone beneath. Then, while the man continued to spank her, she felt the woman slide one of her legs out from under her and set it across the backs of her knees, holding her in a scissor grip. Josephine's left hip pressed into the woman's crotch as the woman crossed her feet, pinning Josephine's legs between her thighs. Josephine could feel her hip crushing the cloth of the woman's skirt up between her legs, feel the warmth of a bare thigh on the back of her own thigh, then the slinky rasp of a nylon stocking behind her knees; and she could feel the man's hand, spanking her again and again, on her left buttock, on her right, and now across the cleft between.

'Stop it!' she cried.

It stopped then, though whether because she had cried out or not, she didn't know. She lay there gasping, as much from shock as from pain. Her bottom was blazing.

She felt the woman release her, extricate herself lithely from beneath her. She lay face down on the bed, still cuffed and blindfolded, and heard the pair of them making brisk, soft sounds, as though they were straightening their clothes.

'There'll be a car shortly,' said the man, conversationally, no trace in his voice of anger or even exertion, as there came the sound of the door opening, then closing.

'Wait!' cried Josephine.

But she was alone again.

She struggled to her feet, wrenching for the first time at the handcuffs. They hurt her wrists, though nothing like as much as her bottom was hurting. Fumbling desperately with them, she felt something give under the pressure of her finger and click back again at once, like a spring. She felt for it again, and pressed it more firmly.

The cuff sprang open.

She pulled her hand free, snatched off the blindfold, holding her other hand up in front of her face.

They were toy handcuffs. They had no key because they had no locks. They opened with the touch of a lever.

This made Josephine oddly angry, that she had been tricked with toy handcuffs. Being held down between somebody's thighs and spanked like a little girl was one thing; but being tricked was another. Fiercely she pulled off the remaining handcuff and threw them clattering on the floor. Then, careless now that she was naked, she rushed to the bedroom door, tore it open, and stared wildly down the corridor.

'Doctor!' she shouted. 'Doctor Hazel!'

They'd gone.

Slowly Josephine turned back into the room, rubbing her abused bottom as she shut the door. She was stinging as if she'd sat on a fire. Yet she suspected either of them could have hit her very much harder if they'd wanted to. And their manner as they arrived and then as they left: impersonal, even brusquely business-like.

Who were these people? Was that Dr Hazel? Was this how he liked to greet his new patients?

Josephine realised then that she was staring stupidly at something her visitors had left behind: a white bundle on the dressing table.

She picked it up and unfolded it.

It was a clean white T-shirt, white shorts, and a pair of white ankle socks.

As she was staring at them, not knowing whether to laugh or cry, and still with one hand rubbing her bottom, the phone rang again.

She put down the clothes and picked up the phone.

It was the superior young man at reception. 'Your car, madam,' he said.

|5|

'You again.'

'Sheer coincidence,' the cabby said, with his gold-spotted grin. He reached out of the window and opened the passenger door for her.

Josephine hesitated, suspiciously.

'You're taking me to Estwych this time.'

'That's right, love.'

'You didn't know where it was just now.'

'You learn something new every day,' he told her. 'Get in, then,' he said.

Resignedly, Josephine climbed into the cab and sat down gingerly. She hoped he wouldn't notice her wince as her tender bottom met the seat cushion, but she saw he was watching her in his mirror. She wondered if he knew what had happened to her; how many times he had done this drive, with how many passengers.

'How did you like the Green Man?' he asked as he turned the cab onto the main road.

'The food was delicious,' she said.

'So they say,' he said. 'So they say. And what about the service?'

It was her turn not to answer.

When the receptionist had called to tell her her car had arrived, Josephine had said, 'Ask him to wait, please. I'll be down in a couple of minutes.' After putting the phone down, she'd spent the first half-minute clutching her bottom until some of the fire had subsided. They could have given her time to recover, she thought fiercely. But no, they were determined to keep her off-balance, never knowing quite what was going to happen next, or when. And each time they pushed her a bit further: deceiving her, stealing her clothes and her handbag, humiliating her in public, making her put on a blindfold, punishing her. Were they seeing how much she could take before her patience ran out and she snapped?

She thought for a moment of picking up the telephone and calling the man at reception, asking him to call the police, then stalling until they arrived and she could turn in Dr Hazel's escort. She had a case, didn't she? Did a spanking count as assault? Of course it did. They only had to look at her bottom.

Josephine backed up to the mirror and looked over her shoulder. Her bottom was one ragged flush of bright red. She twisted round, craning her neck to look at her right buttock. There were handprints all over it. You could see the individual fingermarks where Dr Hazel had smacked her, as clear as anything. Well, she wasn't going to show *that* to any policeman, or policewoman either.

And the rest of her story: would she tell them that? How she'd played along with him, left the surgery without complaint and got into the taxi without a murmur, let them handcuff her and strip her and then bent over for her spanking, all before she'd decided to call out? How would that sound in court?

No. No police. She knew now she was far beyond the world of police and solicitors and charges of assault; deep in another world that, confusingly, resembled in every detail the world she had always lived in. Only the rules were different. *'Obedience is the law,'* Dr Hazel had said.

She pulled on the clean clothes her visitors had left for her: the T-shirt that strangled her breasts, the shorts that were not exactly what she'd have chosen to put on a sore bottom, the little white socks and the familiar plimsolls. She noticed they'd taken away her laundry — how thoughtful of them — but left the black silk blindfold and handcuffs. Well, she didn't want them either, so she left them where they lay, and went downstairs to the car.

She looked out of the taxi window at the passing scenery. Surreptitiously she slipped her hand beneath her, palm upwards, gently feeling her bottom. Much of the pain had subsided now, leaving what was mostly a warm, tingling sensation. If she'd been asked, she would have had to admit it was not actually unpleasant: more like the soreness in your legs after a long, tiring walk, or the way she'd felt when she'd been once taken a full sauna and massage in Stockholm, battered and blissful.

She very much hoped she wouldn't be asked.

'You can open your window, you know,' said the driver. 'If you'd care to.'

Josephine opened the window. Sunlight poured in on her face, her bare arms and thighs. The air was full of the scent of flowers, the rich sap in the trees, the green vibrance of the grass.

The lane wound on, up and down. There wasn't any traffic. Josephine saw sheep in the fields, wild flowers on the banks, a distant tractor clambering up the hillside at an incredible angle.

The taxi slowed down, and pulled off the road into the entrance of a field.

'Why are we stopping?' Josephine asked.

'A little local custom,' the driver said.

He turned in his seat and leaned in at the little window.

'Did you bring your scarf?' he asked.

'What?'

'Dr Hazel said you'd have a black scarf with you. Have you not got it?'

'No,' said Josephine. 'I left it at the hotel. Nobody said I should –' She stopped.

A chill feeling came into her stomach. She felt her breathing quicken.

'Dear oh dear,' he said softly. 'Well, we must improvise, then, mustn't we?'

'Must we?' asked Josephine.

The cabby opened his door. 'We must,' he said.

He came and opened her door.

'Out you come,' he said, and took her hand gently, helping her out of the cab.

She stood on the dry earth, squinting in the bright sunlight. She heard the sound of crows, calling in the trees. They sounded very far away.

The driver, on the other hand, was very close. Very close indeed.

Suddenly she was conscious of the power of him, his sheer physical size. The chest that protruded so hairily from the green and white shirt was the shape of a barrel; and those arms had never got to that size just by turning the wheel of a car.

Josephine tried to contain her trembling, to keep it in. Nothing on earth would have made her reveal how much he was intimidating her.

'You've nothing on you, I suppose,' he said mildly.

'Only what I stand up in,' she said.

He fingered his earring, looking her up and down.

She took the chance to appraise him: his squashed profile, his wild hair, the strength in his back and shoulders. His mouth looked nice. The warm smell of him. Suddenly she realised that what she was feeling was not just fear. It was desire.

Not her type. Not her type at all. But all the same...

'We'll have to have something,' he said, interrupting her sunstruck reverie. He pointed a finger at her. 'Take your shirt off,' he said.

Josephine breathed in sharply, staring at him. It was as if he'd read her mind. Could he do that? Had she fallen into the hands of some gang of superhumans with the power to read the minds of ordinary humans?

'Come on now,' he said, quite gently.

Josephine felt herself colouring.

'I —'

He was looking left and right along the lane. 'No one'll see,' he said, obviously. 'Here,' he said, stepping away from her and gesturing beyond the cab to the field, 'you could nip in there and duck down behind the hedge if you'd rather.'

After what she'd been through already today, his concern for her modesty was more humiliating than the challenge. Josephine stayed where she was. She crossed her arms, took hold of the bottom of the T-shirt and pulled it up, over her face, tugging its narrow neck painfully over her head. Her breasts fell free, bouncing on her chest.

She pulled her arms out of the sleeves. Mutely she handed him the T-shirt.

He produced a penknife from his trouser pocket.

Josephine stood there beside the road, her arms folded over her breasts, while he swiftly cut a broad strip from the bottom of the shirt. Then he gave it back to her.

She pulled it over her head again. It had never been her size. Now it barely covered her breasts.

Barely was the word, she thought, stupidly.

She stood and let him slip the loop of white cotton fabric over her head and pull it tight around her eyes. She felt his capable hands knotting the surplus behind her head.

Supposing a car comes along now, she thought. What will they think we're up to?

42

What *are* we up to?

He was standing close behind her. She felt his breath on her neck. 'Now tell me honestly,' he murmured. 'Can you see anything?'

The material was thin. Josephine could see light and shadow, no details.

'No,' she said.

He came and stood in front of her. He was a dim shape, filling her field of view.

'Can you see my face?' he asked her.

'No,' she said. 'No, I can't. I can see the stripes of your shirt, just about. And if I had to guess, I'd say you probably had red hair.'

He made a movement with his hand across his face, and leaned nearer her.

'And what colour are my eyes?' he asked, softly.

'Green,' said Josephine. She understood he had taken off his sunglasses.

'Can you see that?' he asked, a warning in his voice.

'No,' she said. 'I saw them before.'

She relaxed, strangely, now he had covered her eyes. It calmed her, as once when in her teens, hitch-hiking, she had got into a car with a man who drove dangerously fast to impress her. She was not impressed, but she knew there was nothing she could do to make him slow down. So she found herself putting her fate completely in his hands.

This man, this taxi driver, if that was what he really was: he had lied to her, he had misled her, but it didn't matter. That was all part of the normal world. In this world, where it made perfect sense for her to be standing half-naked and blindfolded in the middle of nowhere, here she was, trusting him. It was like walking a tightrope, step by step, and whatever else he said or did, he wouldn't let her fall.

He kissed her.

She stood very still and passive, receiving his kiss. His mouth was warm, his lips firm, moist, not wet. His tongue brushed between her lips, hovered an instant, withdrew.

'Is that a local custom too?' she asked.

'No,' he said. 'That was me exceeding my instructions. You're just such a lovely woman.'

Josephine felt a small, steady flame of pleasure and yearning in her breast. 'I don't normally dress like this,' she pointed out, her voice shaking a little.

43

'You should,' he said. He was still very near. 'You look so nice like that. Put your hands behind your back,' he said.

She did.

'Look down,' he told her. 'Bow your head.'

Submissively, she bowed.

'Oh yes,' he said. 'Especially like that. My imagination's working overtime,' he murmured, close to her ear. 'You'd better get back in.'

He helped her through the door, into the seat: a hand at her elbow, nothing personal at all. But his touch made her heart beat faster.

'Mind your head,' he said. 'I hope he appreciates what I'm bringing him, this Dr Hazel of yours.'

Josephine sank back in the upholstery. It was hot and sticky under her bare thighs. She heard him climb in the driver's seat and slam his door. He started the cab and they moved back onto the road.

'How do you come to know him anyway?' he asked.

'Dr Hazel?' she said. 'I don't.'

'Then how is it you're coming to see him?'

Josephine thought about it; about Dr Shepard; the appointment, the nurse. She had an impulse to tell him everything, to see how he reacted. But she held back. 'It's a long story,' she said.

'Oh good,' he said. 'I like long stories.'

Even above the engine she could hear in his voice what sort of long stories he liked.

Suddenly she realised it didn't matter what she said; not in this world.

'Well,' she heard herself say, 'it was a sort of dare. From this friend of mine. Because of what happened to her.'

'A friend,' he repeated.

'Yes,' said Josephine.

'What's her name,' he asked, 'this friend?'

'Maria,' said Josephine. 'Maria Coroni.'

'That's nice, I like that,' said the cabby. They were motoring along slowly, round bend after bend. 'I like the name Maria,' he said. 'What happened to her?'

In an instant the whole story was clear in her mind, bright and vivid as a film.

'If I tell you,' said Josephine, 'you must promise not to tell anyone else.'

'Not a soul,' he said. 'I promise.'

44

'Well,' said Josephine, 'my friend —'

'Maria,' said the cabby.

'Yes,' said Josephine. 'Maria went to see her doctor. Not an ordinary doctor, a therapist. Called Dr Lamb. Maria was feeling depressed, she'd split up with her boyfriend, and she wasn't seeing anybody else. She told me she'd gone right off men. When any man showed an interest in her, she gave him the brush-off straight away. But that didn't stop her feeling lonely and unwanted. So she went to see Dr Lamb.

'Now Dr Lamb was very polite, and very gentle. He didn't ask her any embarrassing questions. But he was so nice, and so polite, she found herself wanting to tell him everything. And she told him how, since she'd split up with her boyfriend, she'd started — playing with herself.'

'That doesn't sound so bad,' said the driver. 'That sounds all right to me. Tell me about that,' he said.

'About Maria?' said Josephine. 'My friend Maria, playing with herself?'

'I'd like to hear about that,' said the driver, while the taxi bounced along the road.

'All right,' said Josephine. 'What she told me is, she comes home, after work. She's been shopping, she's carrying bags of shopping; and she comes home to her empty house, in the dark. She's all alone there. She knows she'll be alone all evening, just like every other evening, and she'll cook her dinner and eat it alone, and then she'll go to bed alone. And she said, Maria said: suddenly she doesn't feel like cooking at all. She isn't even hungry. But what she is instead is very, very horny.'

It felt strange, just saying the word, for the first time in her adult life, probably, and to a strange man, a man she fancied. She said it again.

'Horny. And what she does is this. She goes into the kitchen, without turning the light on, not turning any lights on anywhere; and she dumps her shopping on the table; and then she goes into the lounge, still in the dark, and sits in her favourite chair. Still with her coat on, and her shoes. The curtains are still open. There are people walking past in the street outside, coming home from work; but they can't see in because she's sitting there in the dark. She sprawls in the chair with her legs apart, and she unbuttons her coat and lets it fall open. Then she pulls her skirt up to her waist, and reaches into her panties.'

The cab tilted upwards, climbing a hill. Josephine wriggled on the sticky upholstery. Be bold, she thought. Don't draw back now.

'She strokes herself until she's wet,' she said. 'She starts dripping on the seat of the chair, and she has to get up and get a tissue to put under herself. She strokes harder and harder, faster and faster, until her fingers are soaked. Her pubic hair is all wet and matted. The curls stick up in little spikes. Her lips open. Her clitoris swells up. She arches her back and presses her shoulders against the chair, lifting herself right up out of the seat. Her legs are taut. They tremble. She slips a finger, her middle finger, into her vagina, and rubs her clitoris with her thumb.'

'What does she think about,' asked the cabby mildly, 'while she's at it?'

'She thinks about men,' said Josephine.

'But she's fed up with men.'

'She said she isn't fed up with thinking about them. She thinks about her boyfriend, and how when they were in Spain, on holiday, they went down naked to the beach at night and made love on the sand. She thinks about the young men they saw there, swimming and sunbathing, and how beautiful and brown they were. She imagines them coming up out of the sea like mermen, to watch her and her boyfriend make love. Sometimes, she thinks about other women watching her. Sometimes they join in.

'She told Dr Lamb all this, she said, without really meaning to, and he wasn't shocked or embarrassed at all. He told her she really ought to talk to his colleague, Dr. Hazel.

'And he made her an appointment.

'She had to go to a clinic in a back street somewhere around St Pancras. It was upstairs in one of those buildings that are all split up into offices. There was a nurse, quite a young one, in a starched white uniform. The nurse said Dr Hazel was busy but he'd be ready for her soon. And then she told her to take her clothes off.'

'Just like that?'

'Yes! Right there in the waiting room. "Take all your clothes off," the nurse said, "and give them to me." She stood there smiling, holding out her hand for Maria's clothes.'

'And what did your friend think of that, then?'

'Oh, Maria didn't mind. She's game for anything, Maria. You can't outface Maria. She thought it was a bit odd, but she didn't mind doing it. I mean, she was there to see the doctor. And you know, I wouldn't be a bit surprised if Maria didn't mind at all. I mean, a nice young nurse: Maria probably fancied her, if I know Maria! So she took her clothes off.'

'Tell me,' said the driver.

'She took off her coat, and her shoes. The nurse took the coat and went and hung it on the back of a chair, and put the shoes together under the chair. Then Maria took off her sweatshirt, pulled it over her head, and gave that to the nurse. Then she undid the buttons of her shirt, and untucked it from her skirt. She stood there with it hanging open while she undid the cuffs; and the nurse stood there waiting for it.

'Maria took off her shirt and gave it to the nurse. Then she reached behind her and unhooked her bra. And she slipped that off and gave it to her too.

'She felt a bit funny, standing there topless like that. She wondered what would happen if somebody came in, another patient come to see Dr Hazel. She wondered if the nurse would turn round and tell them to undress too. But she didn't stop. She unbuttoned the waistband of her skirt, and opened the zip.

'She took the skirt off. And she gave it to the nurse, and the nurse took it away.'

'What was she wearing under the skirt?'

'She was wearing a half-slip, and she took that off. Under that she was wearing tights.'

'Not stockings?' asked the cabby.

'It might have been stockings,' said Josephine.

'I think it was,' said the cabby.

'Do you know,' said Josephine, 'I think you're right. I've just remembered, she was definitely wearing stockings. And a suspender belt. She said so.

'So she undid the suspenders, and rolled down her stockings, very carefully, so as not to snag them; and she pulled them off and gave them to the nurse. And she gave her the suspender belt too.

'And that just left her standing there in her panties.

' "You can keep those on, if you'd rather," said the nurse.

'But Maria said, no, it was all or nothing. And she took a deep breath, and took down her panties. She gave her panties to the nurse. As the nurse took them, she gave Maria a secretive sort of smile, as if that had really been a little test, and Maria had just passed it.

47

'So there was Maria, with nothing on, and there was the nurse, with all her clothes.'

'And then the nurse started taking her clothes off, I suppose,' said the cabby.

Josephine thought about it. 'No,' she said.

'I'm sure she did, you know,' said the cabby.

'No she didn't,' said Josephine firmly. 'She just said, "Come this way," and she led Maria into a little consulting room with a couch. "Dr Hazel won't be long," she said, and she went out and shut the door.

'But Dr Hazel was a long time. He was a very long time. In fact, Dr Hazel never arrived at all!'

'So she never saw Dr Hazel after all?'

'No!'

'What a very mysterious gentleman he is, to be sure,' said the cabby complacently. 'So tell me,' he said, 'what did she do, your friend?'

'Maria,' said Josephine.

'Yes,' he said. 'Maria.'

'She waited and waited. There wasn't a sound. When she began to wonder what was happening out there, she called out for the nurse. But the nurse didn't come. So Maria looked round for something to cover herself up with. And do you know, there wasn't a thing in the room she could use.'

'Sheets on the couch,' he said, briskly.

'Not even a sheet on the couch,' said Josephine. 'So she tiptoed to the door, and opened it, and looked out, and there was nobody there. The office was empty.

'She looked for her clothes, but they were gone. Even her coat and shoes had gone. She looked all round the room, but there was nothing but a desk, a chair, a book of appointments, and a telephone. She looked in the next room, but it was empty. There was no Dr Hazel, not anywhere.

'She was stuck there, with no clothes, and no way of getting home.'

'So what did she do, your friend?'

'She phoned me,' said Josephine. 'Are we nearly there yet?'

'Now that depends,' he said.

'On what?'

'On the rest of the story,' he said.

Carefully Josephine lifted her feet and sat round sideways, with her head in one corner of the cab and her feet up on the seat. The cab negotiated another bend.

'What are you doing?' asked the driver.

'Getting comfortable,' she said.

'It is a long story, then,' he said.

'Not really,' she said. 'There's not much more.'

'Are you comfortable now?' asked the cabby.

'Just about,' said Josephine.

'Go on, then,' he said. 'She phoned you, and what did you do?'

'Well, I didn't believe her at first.'

'I bet you didn't,' he said, sympathetically.

'But then I thought, it's Maria, it's probably true. If it can happen to anyone, its Maria. So I grabbed some spare clothes and I went off to see if I could find the office. She'd given me directions, roughly, but she couldn't remember the exact address. She'd had it written down on a piece of paper, and the nurse had even taken her handbag!'

'What a thing to happen,' mused the cabby. 'So did you find the office?'

'Eventually,' said Josephine. 'There wasn't a sign on the door or anything, so I tiptoed upstairs, hoping I'd come to the right place, and wondering what I'd say if somebody asked me where I was going. But I got to the door at the top of the stairs, and I knocked, and quietly I said, "Maria?" And then the door opened, and there she was, Maria, standing there with nothing on. She was so glad to see me, she flung her arms around me and gave me a big hug. Then she just grabbed the bag of clothes and started getting dressed.

'I was a bit sorry about that,' Josephine said. 'I was quite enjoying it. Enjoying Maria with no clothes on, hugging me.

' "Any sign of Dr Hazel, then?" I asked her. "No," Maria said.

'I wanted to think of a way to delay her getting dressed; but that would have been unfair. So I let her get dressed, and then, just as we were leaving, the phone rang.

' "You answer it," she said. Whoever it was, she didn't want to talk to them. So I said, "Hello? Dr Hazel's surgery?", just like a receptionist; and this man's voice said, "Miss Coroni," just like that, because he thought I was Maria.

'So I said. "No, actually, this is Ms Morrow, who is this speaking, please?" I said, "Is this Dr Hazel?" '

'And was it?'

'He wouldn't say. But I'm sure it was. He spoke with a bit of an accent, a European accent. He said, "What are you doing in my office?" "I want to see you," I said. "I want to know what you mean by doing this to my friend."

'He was very cool. He said, "If you want to see me, you'd better make an appointment." "Oh, yes," I said, "like Miss Coroni did, I suppose." "That's right," he said. "And will I have to take all my clothes off in the waiting room too?" I said.

'Well, when Maria heard me say that, she just let out this scream of laughter and ran out of the door, down the stairs. She couldn't stand it.

'And Dr Hazel said, "That's right." He said I was to take off my clothes straight away, and tell him when I'd done it.

'So I did. I took off all my clothes.'

'Tell me,' said the cabby.

'Oh, *you* know,' said Josephine.

|6|

The car drove on and on.

'I took off everything and stood there naked in Dr Hazel's office,' she said. 'I picked up the phone again. I said, "All right, I've taken all my clothes off, now what?"'

' "I'll call you a taxi," he said.'

' "Where to?" I said.'

' "Estwych," he said.'

' "Can I get dressed now?" I asked him.'

' "Yes," he said. "Your clothes are in the drawer," he said. And he rang off!'

'So I looked in the drawer.'

'And what did you find?' asked the driver.

'These clothes,' said Josephine.

'So what did you do then?'

'I put them on. And I came downstairs to wait for you.'

'Your friend had gone, I suppose?' he said.

'Oh yes,' said Josephine. 'Quite gone. No sign of her.'

'Good friend, is she?'

'We were at school together,' said Josephine.

'At school? A girl's boarding school, was it?' he asked.

She could tell by the way he asked that he hoped it was. She could cope with that.

'Well, yes, it was, as a matter of fact.'

'And did you get up to some tricks there, then?' he asked.

'Well, yes, we did, as a matter of fact,' said Josephine. She stretched and yawned.

'I hope it's not boring for you,' said the cabby politely.

'Oh, no,' she said.

In fact, she felt quite strange. She'd always been good at making up

51

stories. Especially dirty ones. They used to do it at school, making up whoppers about the staff and telling them to the rest of the dorm, after lights out. The other girls had always said Josephine was best at it. Being blindfolded in the back of a taxi, telling dirty stories to a sexy stranger, she remembered that power she'd enjoyed. She was feeling careless and giddy, and slightly aroused. And she knew now the sort of thing he would enjoy.

'How far is it now?' she asked.

'I should think,' he said slowly, 'just about long enough for you to tell me about you and Maria, at your girls' boarding school. I should think,' he said again, 'by the time you've told me all about that, we should be just about there.'

'What do you want to know?' she asked.

'Did you wear a uniform?' he asked.

'Oh, yes,' she said. 'Grey gymslips and blue jumpers. White blouses and white knee socks. Black shoes with a button and a strap.'

'And navy blue knickers, was it?' he asked, idly.

'They were all right,' said Josephine, reflectively. 'They were warm. They kept your bottom warm on cold days. The bigger girls were allowed to wear white, but I kept mine. I *liked* my navy blue knickers,' she said.

'Were you a big girl, then?'

'Well, of course, eventually,' she said. 'All little girls grow into big girls eventually.'

'I suppose they do,' he said. 'I suppose they do. And what about Maria? Was she a big girl too?'

'She was,' said Josephine. 'She's a couple of years younger than me, but she's quite plump. Quite a big girl. She had breasts before I did.'

'Did you see them?' he asked.

'When we were at school? Yes, I did. I saw all of her. Every little bit of her.

'Everybody used to have showers together, after games. The big girls didn't have much to do with the little girls, none of us did, but I knew Maria had a crush on me because when I came in from hockey and she was changing, she'd always slow down and hang around so that we'd both be in the showers at the same time. So one day I slowed down too, and when everybody else was dressed and gone, there were just me and Maria there. Alone.

'Her eyes were on me every second while I took my games things off. I took everything off. I stood there, completely nude, getting my towel out of my locker, and then I turned and gave Maria a little smile over my shoulder. She was sitting there on the bench, taking off her socks. She was still wearing her knickers.'

'Nothing else,' said the cabby.

'Not a thing but her navy blue knickers and her white games socks,' Josephine said. 'I paused a moment, and then she stood up. She dropped her eyes then and didn't look at me. She just bent and took her knickers off.

'I went into the showers, and I already had the water running and was soaping myself when she came in. We didn't say anything, we just stood there, having our showers.

'Then I said, "Isn't it a nuisance, how there's always a bit of your back you can't quite reach?"

'And Maria said, "I'll do it for you. If you like."

'She came paddling over to me on the wet tiles. I gave her my soap and turned my back. She soaped my back for me, very carefully.'

' "Oh, Maria, that does feel nice," I said. "You are an angel."

' "I'll do the rest for you," she said. "If you like."

'And she knelt down in the shower, with the water pouring all over her, and soaped my back down to my bottom, and then she soaped my bottom.

'She said. "Do you want me to do between your legs?"

' "That would be lovely, Maria," I said.

'And it was. She soaped me from the back, and then she came round and soaped me from the front. Then I lay down on the floor and opened my legs, and Maria knelt between them and soaped the inside of my thighs, and up into my crotch. She lathered my pubic hair, and then she soaped my labia, and I opened up and she soaped my vagina, and ran the soap backwards and forwards between my vagina and my bottom, and round and round my clitoris.'

'Did you come?' asked the cabby.

'I came several times,' said Josephine. 'I stroked my nipples while Maria soaped my clit, and I came very nicely.'

'And did you soap her then?'

'Do you know, I didn't,' said Josephine.

'And why didn't you?'

'I don't know. I suppose because I was a senior and she was only a junior. I suppose I thought it was all right a senior letting a junior have a crush on her and feel her up in the showers and make her come, but I couldn't possibly have done the same for her.

'So I let her do it herself. And I watched.

'Maria ran the soap between her legs and she cried out. She made little sobbing cries. I hadn't made a sound. I was too worried we'd be caught.

' "Maria!" I said. "Shh! Someone'll hear!"

'But Maria didn't care. She worked herself up into a frenzy. She slid over on the tiles, and I was so excited I fell down on top of her, and she took my hand and rubbed it over her breast while she frigged away with the tiny little bit that was left of the soap.

'I let her do that, with my hand. I thought, as long as it wasn't me doing it, it was all all right.

'When Maria came, she arched her back and heaved herself right up off the floor. She made a strangled noise deep in her throat, and she came so violently I was scared. I thought she'd do herself an injury. But afterwards we both just lay there, panting. And when I got up and turned the water off, Maria came over all sweet and soppy, and started telling me that she wouldn't care if we had got caught, and if we had got punished. She said she'd take any punishment, even the cane, for me. I was the most beautiful girl in the school, and she loved my body, and she loved me. She asked if she could kiss me. I said no. I thought that was going too far. She said could she kiss my breasts, then, and I said no. Then she said could she kiss my bottom, and I gave in. I turned round and bent forward with my hands on my knees, and Maria knelt behind me and clasped my thighs with her arms, and kissed my bottom.

'Then all the other girls came in.

'They'd noticed how Maria was eyeing me up while I was changing, and that I was going along with it. They'd only pretended to go away. Three or four of them had stayed behind, hiding behind the lockers, and had listened and peeked through the curtain while we were in the showers. They'd seen the whole thing.

'They were horrible to us. They were particularly horrible to Maria, because she wasn't very popular, and they enjoyed finding her in the wrong. Other girls used to feel each other up, it happened all the time, but doing it with Maria Coroni was just disgusting, they said. They wouldn't let us out of the showers. They pinned us in a corner and slapped us and flicked us with wet towels.

'Then they made us get dressed, and took us to the housemistress.

'The housemistress was Mrs Maple. She was an old-fashioned woman with old-fashioned ideas. She was horrified to hear that two of her girls had been caught playing with each other's bodies in the showers. The fact that it was a junior and a senior only made it worse. She didn't want to know any of the details, she just lectured us for ages, made us stand there in our gymslips and look her in the eye while she told us what filthy, despicable, sinful little lesbians we were, and how we deserved to be very seriously punished.

'Then she opened the drawer of her desk and took out the strap.

'I was a good girl. I'd never had the strap. I'd never even seen it before.

'Maria had. She knew the strap. When Mrs Maple told her to fetch a chair, she knew which one to fetch, and where to put it, in the middle of the carpet, in front of the desk. Then she stood behind it, rather stiffly with her arms by her sides, like a soldier standing to attention.

'Mrs Maple stood up. She came round the desk, carrying the strap. "Bend over, Coroni," she said.

'Maria knew exactly what to do. She bent over the back of the chair and got hold of the seat. She held her head up while Mrs Maple came round behind her, looking at me across the room. Her face was white. But she didn't really look afraid; she looked resigned. As if she thought that there would be a price to pay for the pleasure we'd had in the showers, and now this was it.

'Then she let her head fall forward.

'I thought Mrs Maple would send me out of the room, but she didn't. She stood behind Maria with the strap in her hands, and she said since we'd sinned together, we would be punished together.

' "Come here, Morrow," she said.

'I went over to her.

'She pointed at Maria's bottom. "Lift your girlfriend's gymslip," she told me. She said it like that, with a sneer when she said *girlfriend*.

'I took hold of the skirt of Maria's gymslip and folded it back over her waist. She was wearing her navy blue knickers. Her bottom looked very plump in them. I felt sorry for her.

' "There's another chair," she said, "in that corner there. Fetch it."

'I looked. I could see the chair she meant. It had a pile of papers on it.

'I was so flustered I couldn't think what to do. I went over to the chair.

55

"It's got papers on it, Mrs Maple," I said.

' "Take the papers off and put them on the *floor*," she said impatiently. "Stupid girl."

'I moved the papers. I picked up the chair and brought it over to where she pointed, and set it down next to the one Maria was bending over.

'I looked at Mrs Maple.

' "Well?" she said. She lashed out with the strap and struck the seat of the chair. The noise was horrible. Dust flew up in a big cloud.

' "*Bend over, Morrow*," said Mrs Maple.

'I was feeling very stupid and very scared. I bent over next to Maria, the way I'd seen her do, and got hold of the seat of the chair.

'Mrs Maple stood behind and betwen us. "Lift your skirt," she said to me.

'I reached behind me, took hold of the skirt of my gymslip, and pulled it up above my bottom.

'Maria was very close beside me. My arm was touching her arm. She hadn't lifted her head since Mrs Maple had started speaking to me. I sneaked a sideways look at her, but her eyes were closed. I looked down at the seat of the chair. It had a sort of herringbone material on it, brown and grey. I wondered if I should close my eyes too, or if it would be braver to keep them open.

'Then I heard the strap come down, and Maria cried out.

'We were so close, I felt the shock of the blow. I gasped.

'Then Mrs Maple lifted the strap and brought it down on me.

'The pain was fierce, but the shock was worse. I gave a loud wail and I couldn't help it, my hands flew to the seat of my knickers.

'Mrs Maple stopped.

' "Remove your hands, Morrow," she said, in an icy voice.

'I bit my lip. Shakily I brought my hands back to the seat of the chair. I gripped it tightly.

'She strapped Maria again. The strap sounded louder this time, if anything, but Maria didn't make a sound.

'Mrs Maple strapped me again.

'The first stroke had been quite high across my buttocks. The second was lower, straight across the crown of my bottom. I couldn't help it, I yelled again. But I kept hold of the chair.

'We got three strokes, four, five. It seemed we'd been bending over there forever, side by side, with Mrs Maple strapping our bottoms. I'd quite forgotten what we'd done, how we'd come to be there. I sneaked another look at Maria. Her eyes were still shut, her face screwed up, and she was biting her lips, determined not to cry out again.

'I cried out every time, and I even let go of the chair a couple more times, though I managed to keep my hands away from my bottom.

'It didn't feel like a strap, a foot and a half of soft leather. It felt like a board she was hitting us with. And the strokes were getting further down each time, so each one fell less on our knickers and more on the bare skin at the top of our thighs. By the sixth she was strapping the backs of our legs.

'After six, she let us get up,. We stood up, very stiffly, and I clutched my bottom, I was hissing through my teeth at the pain.

' "You can go, Coroni," Miss Maple said. "Morrow, you stay behind."

'Why did she want me to stay behind? I had no idea, but it made me feel worse, if that was possible.

'Maria went out, whiter than ever, without a word. I saw her give me a forlorn glance as she shut the door. I remembered what she'd told me in the shower. I knew she'd have taken the whole punishment if she could have saved me. I felt like a really feeble specimen compared with her.

'And now it was just me and Mrs Maple.

'She'd gone back behind her desk again, and shut the strap away in her drawer. She looked at me with contempt. "Stand up straight, girl," she commanded. "Pull your skirt down."

'With difficulty I prised my hands away from my stinging bottom and straightened my skirt. I tried to compose myself. At least I hadn't burst into tears, I thought.

'I stood up straight, hands behind my back and faced Mrs Maple across her desk.

' "Morrow, girls like you disgust me," she said. "Do you hear? You disgust me!"

'She looked at me with loathing.

' "Coroni is a junior," she went on, "and frankly rather a stupid girl. But you, Morrow: you are a senior. Your offence is much more grave. I've no doubt you led her on."

'There was nothing I could say to that.

' "Your offence is more grave, and your punishment will be more severe," she went on.

57

'I didn't understand what she was saying.

' "You will take a caning," she said.

'I gaped at her in horror.

' "Four strokes," she said. "On the bare bottom."

'I was dizzy, I was numb, I was almost in tears. Four of the cane! On top of a strapping! And bare — that was unheard of. Nobody ever got the cane on the bare bottom. We thought there was a law against it. There probably was. But when I tried to plead with her, Mrs Maple simply shook her head and said: "What do you think your parents will say when I write and tell them their daughter is a lesbian?"

'Was I a lesbian? I didn't know. What else could you possibly call it, two girls masturbating together in the shower? I imagined my father's baffled anger. I imagined my mother's pained expression. She too would be disgusted. They would never forgive me, never. And that was a horror I couldn't bear.

' "After you've taken four strokes of the cane," she said, "without your knickers, then I may reconsider. If the offence is not repeated, I may decide it was an aberration. I may decide that there is no need to inform your parents of their daughter's depraved behaviour."

'I understood then. Mrs Maple *wasn't* allowed to cane one of her girls on the bare bottom. But she wanted to. She wanted to so much she was prepared to blackmail me for it.

'She went to a cupboard and returned holding a cane.

'She flexed it between her hands.

' "Bend over, please, Morrow," she said.

'Stiffly, I bent over the chair.

'I heard Mrs Maple's footsteps approach until she stood behind me again.

' "Lift your skirt," she commanded.

'I lifted my skirt out of the way once more.

'Then I felt her hands at the elastic of my knickers. Still burning from the strap, I felt her pull the elastic out and draw my knickers down onto my thighs.

'Bare, hot and throbbing, I yielded my bottom to the cane.

'I heard it come hissing down, and strike like white fire, with a jolt that nearly knocked me across the back of the chair.

'Then I really did burst into tears.'

'Did you wet yourself?' asked the taxi driver.

Josephine fell silent. She lay back on the hot upholstery, secure

58

behind her blindfold of torn white cotton. She didn't know how to reply.

'I hear a good many girls wet themselves the first time they have the cane,' said the taxi driver. 'A good many boys do too.'

He spoke as if it was an ordinary matter of complete indifference, like what the weather had been like, or what day of the week it was.

She couldn't tell what he wanted her to say.

'Do you think I might have done?' she asked, in a low voice.

'It's hard to say,' he said. 'A brave young woman like you.'

'I did,' said Josephine. 'I wet myself. I wasn't going to tell you,' she said.

'You must tell me everything,' he said.

There was a pause while Josephine gathered her thoughts. What happened next? What would the housemistress have done then?

'It really made Mrs Maple mad,' she said. 'If I'd disgusted her before, the sight and smell of pee running down my leg onto her carpet made her mad with rage. She lashed me harder, and I screamed. I tried to get up. She pounced on me, pushing me down, holding me with her left hand while she lashed me again with her right. I couldn't feel my bottom for the pain. I think I hardly felt the last stroke, it was fire on top of fire.

'But then it was over, and she came to her senses. She rushed and got a box of tissues, and started mopping the carpet, and dabbing at my

thighs where I'd wet myself. She rubbed a tissue in between my legs.

'She was groping between my legs just like Maria had done.

'I was so shocked, so amazed, I stopped crying. I started to get up from the chair, fumbling between my legs to take the tissue away from her. I caught her eye. She looked bewildered, confused, almost as shocked as me. She snatched her hand away and went round behind her desk, to sit in her chair and pat her hair.

' "I hope you've learned your lesson, Morrow," she said coldly. "Pull up your underwear and go."

'My bottom was blazing, throbbing. It felt twice its proper size. I couldn't face putting my knickers back on. I took them off. I stood up with them in my hand and put them in my pocket as I gingerly settled my gymslip back into place. I let Mrs Maple see me do it. I thought, You can't touch me now. Not now. I know you.

'And she didn't say a word.'

The taxi jolted. Josephine sat up, grabbed blindly for something to hold on to. She was sure they were leaving the road, driving over rough ground.

At that moment, they stopped.

'Are we there?' she asked.

'No,' he said.

Her heart started to hammer.

'Why are you stopping?' she asked.

'Time to pay your fare,' he said.

'**M**y fare?' said Josephine. 'I haven't got any money. The nurse took my handbag. I mean, Maria's handbag. Maria...' The cabby turned off the engine.

'You don't need money,' he said.

She heard him open the door and get out of the car. She heard him open her door.

Blind, she looked up into the brightness.

'Are you going to do what I think you're going to do?' she asked him.

'That depends,' he said, very reasonably, 'what you think I'm going to do.'

'I think you're going to spank me,' said Josephine. She felt a sinking feeling in the pit of her stomach. Making up stories about it was one thing. Actually going through it again was another.

'Why?' he said. 'Do you think you need a spanking?'

'No!' said Josephine. She'd told him her stories to get him excited. It wasn't a spanking she'd been asking for. She couldn't imagine wanting that, especially not from someone you fancied.

She realised she couldn't feel any trace now of the spanking the doctor given her at the Green Man; none at all.

'I'm counting on you,' he said, seriously. It seemed a strange thing to say. It reminded her that this was all some crazy kind of test. The cabby was on her side. He fancied her too. He'd said he liked her looking submissive. Men like that liked to spank women's bottoms.

Perhaps it was her fault after all, for getting him excited.

'I'm counting on you being a good girl,' he said.

'I'm not a girl,' Josephine said sharply. 'Just because I let you treat me like one, that doesn't mean I am one.'

'I'm sorry,' said the cabby. 'I do apologise.' He sounded sincere. 'Out you come,' he said. She felt him take her hand.

Awkwardly Josephine got out of the cab. She felt hard, dry earth under her feet. She stood up in the sun. She smelled petrol, the hot car, the scent of greenery. A little breeze licked her midriff, where the cut shirt exposed it.

The cabby held her hands in his. He led her forward, several paces across the hard earth.

'When you take a ride, you have to pay,' he said, seriously.

'But we haven't gone anywhere yet!' Josephine objected.

'Oh, but we have. We've gone a long, long way.'

She could hear he meant it.

'You can't take a long ride not meaning to pay for it,' he said, gravely.

'I didn't hire you!' said Josephine. She didn't like standing there with him holding her hands like this. She shrugged, crossly. 'Dr Hazel hired you. Let him pay.'

'Dr Hazel, is it?' said the cabby. 'Now I thought it was you wanted to see him. About your friend.'

'Maria,' said Josephine.

'About your friend Maria,' he said.

She stood waiting in the sunlight. It was warm on her face, her arms, the small of her back, her legs.

'Take them down, then.'

He let go of her hands. Josephine shuddered. She felt the last of her self-confidence shred and whirl away.

'My shorts?' she said, procrastinating.

'Your shorts,' he said.

She put her hands on the tight elastic.

'I'd rather see where I am first,' she said, in a small, tight voice.

'No,' he said.

Still she hesitated.

'Is there anyone watching?' she asked.

'No,' he said.

'Would you tell me if there was?'

'No,' he said.

She heard a tiny, metallic sound. 'Will you take them off now,' he asked, 'or will I do it for you?'

She realised the sound was him opening his penknife again.

'I was only asking,' she said, and she pulled her shorts down.

'Right off,' he said.

Her shorts around her thighs, Josephine reached out blindly

around her with both hands but found nothing to lean on. She didn't dare move from her spot. Carefully she reached down, bending her knees. She got hold of the shorts again, lowered them to the ground and stepped out of them.

She stood up.

She heard him step toward her.

His warm, strong hands closed on her bare bottom.

She shuddered again with tension.

'Not cold, are you?' he asked, conversationally.

Josephine shook her head, not trusting herself to speak.

'We'll soon warm you up,' he said.

Josephine felt a violent aversion suddenly. 'Please,' she said. 'Don't play with me. Just spank me, please, if you're going to.'

'That sounds nice,' he said. She could hear the desire, the passion in his voice. 'Say that again.'

'Spank me!' she said. 'Please!'

His hands left her again. He moved back a pace. 'Take your shirt off,' he said.

'Oh!'

Petulantly, Josephine dragged the shirt over her head and flung it to the ground. The blindfold came off with it. She was standing naked but for her ankle socks and plimsolls. They were in a bare, tilled field, behind a clump of trees. There was no one in sight.

'There goes your blindfold,' remarked the cabby, sadly. He was standing slightly to one side of her, in arm's reach. The taxi was parked behind him, a little way off. Its doors were open on the driver's side. 'I suppose you didn't bring your handcuffs either, did you?' he said.

'No.'

'You were supposed to bring your handcuffs.'

She looked at him beseechingly. 'You won't need them,' she said.

Without warning, he reached out and smacked her right leg, smacked her on the back of the thigh.

Caught unawares, Josephine found herself buckling at the knee. She clapped a hand to the place he'd struck her, stumbling, almost falling down.

'That's for not bringing your scarf,' he said. 'Turn round. Face about.'

Josephine winced. She stood upright, panting from the adrenalin, knowing what was to come.

She made the turn.

She stood firm for the second smack. It fell on the back of her other leg.

'That's for not bringing your handcuffs,' he said.

Gasping, her legs stinging, she hobbled away, reaching for her clothes.

'Where are you going?' he called.

She looked at him.

'I haven't taken the fare yet,' he said.

He went to the taxi, climbed into the back, sat on the passenger seat where she had been sitting.

Josephine left her clothes in the dirt and went to him. She bent over his knee, leaning into the cab, holding her face up off the hot upholstery.

'That's the way,' he said, gently.

He spanked her, the second spanking she'd had today, the second in her life. It was nothing like the first.

At the Green Man, Dr Hazel and his assistant had been swift and brutal. They'd taken her by surprise, pinning her down as she struggled, and the doctor slapped her hard and fast. That was the way she'd assumed all spankings happened. Unless they were cold and cruel like in her story about Maria and Mrs. Maple.

She'd been taking a short cut through a children's playground once, and seen a young mother lose her temper with her little boy. Ignoring Josephine as she approached between the swings, the woman had grabbed the little boy under the arms and dumped him face down across her lap, lifting her right hand and walloping him immediately on the seat of his bright green shorts, three times, four. It hadn't taken more than that many seconds. She'd been yelling at him all the while, her face grim and angry. She'd dumped him on the ground again, and Josephine had glimpsed his face as she walked quickly by, trying to pretend she hadn't seen anything. It was red with rage and shock, his mouth a perfect round O. He just stood there, quivering, unable for a moment even to scream.

That was a spanking: a swift, brutal retribution, intended to hurt and humiliate a little child out of some petty disobedience.

The cabby's spanking was not like that at all.

He didn't pin her down. He rested his left hand lightly on her bare back, and put his right hand, just as lightly, on her bottom. It was as

64

if he was measuring her, taking possession of her. He was taking her obedience for granted. (She remembered Dr Hazel saying: 'At Estwych, absolute obedience is the law.' But she wasn't at Estwych yet. Or was she?) Physically, it was perfectly possible for her to have got up again off his lap.

But she stayed there.

Waiting.

He stroked the cheeks of her bottom. He stroked her thighs, where he'd smacked her.

He started to pat her bottom, all over, rhythmically, very softly. She waited.

The pats became harder, slower.

There was a pause then, in the rhythm, the briefest of pauses.

And then he smacked her.

He smacked her on the right buttock, right in the middle.

It wasn't a hard smack, but it wasn't a pat now. It stung, just a little.

He matched it with another smack on the left. It was just the same.

He smacked her again on the right, a little higher, and then at once again, a little lower, a little harder. And repeated it the other side.

Josephine sighed. She shifted on his lap. She felt tension leaving her. She was relaxing.

She could hardly credit it. She was naked, over a stranger's knee, having her bottom smacked, and she was not only permitting it, tolerating it: she was accepting it. She could feel how he was measuring out her spanking, working methodically up and down and across her bottom, quite slowly, so that each smack landed and stung and burned down into her before the next landed, in a different place. It was as if each smack was a challenge, an invitation: could she take another? Another? A little harder? How about there? and *here*?

That one made her gasp.

He moved his left hand, sliding it a little way across her back and down her right side. Now it was more of a light hold on her, like a lover's: still no restraint, but an inch or two more intimacy.

He went on spanking her.

It began to hurt.

But it wasn't a violent pain, not a pain that threatened to wound her. It was more like the pain of strenuous exercise, like cannoning around the netball court at school, forcing her aching muscles to give up that one more ounce of energy that might mean another net. An acceptable pain. She thought again of the sauna in Sweden: the pain she paid for, because it was going to do her good.

The smacks fell harder now. She was gasping at every one, feeling it call a response from her that she gave, grudgingly, because she wanted to be strong and suffer in silence. She didn't want to give him the satisfaction of knowing he was hurting her. But he was, now and she cried out.

He paused.

She knew, somehow, it was a pause; that it wasn't finished. And that he knew it too; knew what she was going through, over his knee.

He was something of an expert at this, she realised.

She opened her eyes and looked down at the shiny seat of the taxi, an inch below her nose. She remembered in the story how she'd said she looked at the pattern of the chair seat while she was waiting for the cane.

Her bottom throbbed.

'Do you collect many fares this way?' she asked him.

He laughed. A soft, happy laugh. He was happy, doing this to her.

For goodness' sake, she thought, in a sudden moment of panic, how much will you let them do to you because it makes them happy?

'I think I've paid my fare,' she said. Her voice came out sharp and high.

'Oh, you've paid your fare all right,' said the cabby.

Hope leapt in her.

'Can I get up then?'

Why didn't she just get up, if she wanted to? He wasn't stopping her. Why did she ask permission?

She really was relaxed, she realised with astonishment. Her limbs were all limp, like waking up on a Sunday morning in a warm bed, conscious but floating just below the surface of sleep, completely unable to move.

He laid his right hand lightly on her bottom again. He didn't move his left hand.

'You've paid your fare,' he said again, 'but I think you need a little more.'

'Why?' she said. 'What for?' His tone disturbed her; it came too close to what she was suspecting, fearing, beginning to feel.

'For telling such dreadful fibs,' he said.

He smacked her again, twice.

She cried out. 'But they were for you!'

'Were they now?' he said, as if this was another fib, but he was prepared to overlook it, to be patient with her. 'Then this is for you.'

He spanked her several more times. The intimacy was gone, the peculiar sensation of participating in something sensuous utterly vanished. Josephine lay there, gritting her teeth, as the cabby's big hand rose and fell on her bottom. She put up with it. That was all, she told herself, crossly.

When he'd finished spanking her, he helped her off his knee. He held her lightly, suggested she lie face down somewhere for a while until she recovered. Josephine, clutching her abused bottom, was aware there was nowhere to lie but on the seat of the taxi, which was hot and uncomfortable, or on the ground, in the dirt. To get away from him, to reassert herself, stiffly and without a word she went over to where her clothes lay, on the ground. She picked them up and put them on. They were tight, sweaty, streaked now with dirt. There was grit inside them that she couldn't shake free. No matter if this spanking had been nothing like Dr Hazel's at the Green Man, her sore bottom was just the same.

And the infuriating, humiliating shorts hurt.

The taxi driver lay back in the back of his cab, his arms behind his head. With his sunglasses, it was hard to tell whether he was watching her dress or not. He looked pleased with himself. She had felt his erection as she climbed off his lap. She no longer felt any inclination to touch it, to fondle it.

'Here,' he called.

She looked.

He was holding up a strip of something white, dangling it in the listless breeze.

The strip he'd cut from her shirt. Her blindfold.

'Again?' said Josephine.

'We're not there yet,' he pointed out.

She came back to the cab and stood looking in at him. 'It feels as if we are,' she said. 'It feels as if we've been there for quite some time.'

He didn't take this up. He shrugged, as if it was all the same to him. 'Dr Hazel's orders,' he said.

She gestured brusquely. 'Get out,' she said. 'Let me get in.'

He obliged. When she was settled, uncomfortably, back in her seat, he beckoned and she bowed her head, letting him tie the strip of cotton across her eyes.

They drove on.

'The last time I brought someone this way,' he said suddenly, 'the last fare I had for Estwych —'

'I thought you'd never heard of it,' objected Josephine rudely.

He revved the engine. 'What?'

'Nothing,' she said, sullenly.

'She was Japanese,' he said.

Suddenly Josephine was all ears. The woman at the Green Man, Dr Hazel's assistant; she was Japanese, Josephine was sure of it.

'Would you like to hear?' asked the cabby.

'Tell me,' said Josephine.

'I took her to the hotel, same as you,' he said.

This made Josephine instantly suspicious, for some reason. 'Was she wearing shorts two sizes too small as well?' she asked, ironically.

'Oh no,' he said, all innocence. 'She was very smart. Very smart, she was. In an expensive suit, very dashing, very smart. Dark blue, it was, and scarlet red, with fine embroidery on it. Skinny-looking birds sitting on vines. Looked as if it might have been made of silk. She had black stockings, and a little black leather handbag on a long thin strap. And a round hat with a little veil.'

Of course, Josephine thought, there was no reason for his story to be any more true than hers had been. He was probably telling her about some woman he'd seen on TV, some old film with Gary Grant and sexy orientals in Shanghai.

'She said her name was Suriko. Or no, she said to call her that. As if her real name was something else, you know? But down here, she wanted to be called Suriko.'

Again for some unknown reason, that reversed Josephine's opinion. Why would he make that up? Why give her a name at all? She didn't know his name, even though he knew hers. She decided she wanted to keep it that way. It was like a little corner of power she still had over him: that he was, after all, just another anonymous man who drove a taxi.

'I took her to the Green Man,' he said. 'As I came away, there was a tractor in the road, so I had to wait a bit, coming out of the forecourt there. I looked in the door, and I saw her at the reception there. The man was giving her a package.'

Well, that much was familiar.

'Later I got the call, to go and pick her up at the Green Man and bring her to Estwych. Just like you!' he said. 'So I went to the hotel, and gave her name at the reception, and went back and sat in the cab to wait.

'She came out. There was a man with her.'

'Dr Hazel, I presume,' said Josephine.

'Well, I wouldn't know,' said the driver. They turned a corner. 'But I don't think it was. I don't think this was a doctor anybody.'

He didn't say why.

'He was a youngish man, tall, very dark. Sort of Italian-looking, d'you know what I mean? He was helping our Suriko out of the building, walking very close with her, with his arm around her from behind like she needed help. She was looking down at the ground. She had both her hands behind her back. This young man was supporting her. And I noticed he was carrying her handbag.'

'Handcuffs,' said Josephine.

'What say?'

Josephine felt very tired, and sore. 'She was wearing handcuffs,' she said.

'Now that was very clever of you,' said the cabby admiringly.

'Not really,' she muttered.

'She was indeed. And I thought to myself, Oh my goodness, I thought: the police. This Suriko was a wanted woman, and here he was, the policeman, bringing her in.

'This man helps her into the back of the cab, and settled her there, just where you're sitting now. He sits down beside her and shuts the door. She doesn't look up, doesn't look at me, doesn't say a word. "Where to, sir?" I say, expecting him to say, the police station. But no, Estwych, he says, just like the call. So I drive out into the road, and off we go.

'In a little I'm looking in my mirror, and I see this young man undoing the lady's jacket. Undoing Suriko's jacket, he was. And when I looked again, he'd got it open and he was pushing it down her arms, and her not resisting, as if maybe she wanted him to do that; or else it was the handcuffs, and she knew whatever she did he was determined to take off her jacket, and by golly he would.

'So I took another look in the mirror, just a little peek, like, and I see that underneath the jacket she hasn't got a blouse on, not any kind of blouse. All I can see is this shiny black thing she's wearing; and

69

when the cab gives a little jolt, she bounces on the seat a little there, and I see it's a kind of corset affair. It goes round her body, and at the side there are all these straps, holding it on. All shiny black. Looks like that plastic, what do you call it, PCV.'

'PVC,' said Josephine.

'That's the stuff,' agreed the cabby. 'So then this feller, he reaches behind Suriko on the seat, and he unlocks the handcuffs. I see him help her off with the jacket, and she pulls her arms out and brings them forward, puts her hands in her lap, and she's sitting there in her hat and this corset, rubbing her wrists. Do they make your wrists hurt, those things?'

Josephine thought about the handcuffs. 'They're not very comfortable,' she said.

'Well, I tell you, nor was Suriko, because after that he had her up on the seat and he was taking her skirt off, pulling it right off her, in the back of my cab! I saw she was wearing black stockings, that were fastened to the bottom of the corset. And she had little red panties on. The same scarlet red as the skirt. And little boots with spiky heels, did I say that?

'Well, next the man is at her corset, and I think he's undoing these straps at the side. I think, Goodness gracious, if he isn't going to strip her stark naked in the back of the cab. But he doesn't take the corset off. He pulls these straps out sideways, and then he makes Suriko slip her arms under them some way. And next time I look I see he's got her arms strapped to her sides at the elbows, and her hands sticking out in front of her all helpless as she lies there on the seat, her legs up over his lap.

'And he's doing something at her neck. That's when her hat falls off, and all her hair falls down. Long hair she had, so black it looked blue, the way it does. It must have been pinned up some way with the pin that held the hat, and it all falls down around her face, and she's helpless to reach up and brush it out of her eyes there. But now it's in the young man's way, and he pushes it out of the way, her lovely hair, not carefully at all, just as if it was some kind of old thing that was a nuisance. He pushes it away, and I see what he's doing is putting a collar on her. A black collar with silver studs, and silver chains coming off it, swinging down over her shoulders and dangling against the edge of the seat.

'Black cuffs. They've got black cuffs on the end, these chains, and when he's got her collar fixed, then he takes these cuffs and he starts buckling them round her wrists. As if she's not completely helpless already, poor thing! The cuffs are on her wrists, but there's still something flapping off them, I can't see what.

'She says something then. I can't hear, what for the engine, for she says it very quietly. And he nods, the young man, and reaches into the pocket of his smart Italian suit, and he pulls out a black scarf. And he ties it round her eyes.

'Then I'm driving along, and I look in the mirror again, and I see now he's at her corset again, and he's undoing more buckles, more straps. And he has her bend her legs and lift her knees up to her chest. Then he feeds these straps round behind her knees, and buckles those on. Then he brings her hands round on their chains until they're up against the sides of her legs, and I see the black parts that I saw flapping before from the cuffs on her wrists are more cuffs, joined on to those, and these ones go round her ankles. She's got her hands chained up to her neck, and her ankles chained to her hands, and the whole of her tied up with the straps of this corset. And she's blindfolded, like you, only more, because hers is with the black scarf.

'She can't move a bit. Not a bit.'

'And you saw all this in the mirror?' asked Josephine. 'While you were driving along these narrow country roads?' They were, at that moment, driving down what felt like a very narrow bumpy track. Josephine heard bushes brush both sides of the cab as they descended.

'Every bit of it,' he agreed, enthusiastically.

'It's a wonder you didn't have an accident,' she said.

'So then we get to the house there, and I pull up, and get out. I open the door for them, because I'm thinking, here's Suriko all tied up like a parcel, and he's going to need some help lifting her out of the back of the cab. I open the door, and there she is, lying on his lap, all tied up in black PCV with her spiky heels sticking in the air. And I'm looking straight at her bottom, at her bright red panties straining tight over the cheeks of her bottom. A beautiful bottom, she had.'

'I suppose then the young man said they hadn't any money, and asked if you'd like to give her a spanking instead,' said Josephine.

'No,' said the cab driver curiously. 'No, he didn't. Whatever gave you that idea?'

He stopped the cab.

71

'Here we are,' he said. 'This is Estwych.'

Josephine heard the sound of water flowing. She heard him get out of the cab and open her door.

He helped her out, to stand on what felt like flagstones.

She was here. At last she was here, wherever she was.

She didn't want to be here at all.

His hands were warm on her bare arms. 'You'll be all right here,' he said. 'Believe me. They'll take care of you. Hey. Hey, Josephine.'

Automatically she turned to face him, though she couldn't see him. It was the first time he'd called her by name.

'Did I take care of you, or not?'

She couldn't answer.

He patted her on the bottom, and released her to her fate. She heard him walk away, get into his cab, start the engine. He called something to her, something she couldn't make out.

'What?' she called back. Impatiently, she tore off the flimsy blindfold.

She was standing on the doorstep of an old half-timbered house. It stood among trees, on the bank of a river.

'Ring the bell,' called the cabby again.

Josephine looked round. The cab was turning, going back up the track. She caught sight of the driver through the window: his red hair, his violent green and white shirt, the glint of his earring, or was it the low sun flaring off his cheap plastic sunglasses?

Absurdly, she didn't want him to go. She felt like calling him back.

But he was gone.

And she was here.

There was an old-fashioned black iron bell-pull. She got hold of it and gave it a tug.

At once the door opened.

A familiar figure was standing there smiling.

It was Annabel the housekeeper.

'Hello, Miss Morrow,' she said. 'Welcome to Estwych.'

72

8

Suddenly Josephine was back in the real world.

'Annabel?' she said, disoriented. 'What are you doing here?' She looked past her, into a hall full of antique furniture. 'Is Dr Shepard here?'

'No, miss,' Annabel said. 'I work for Dr Hazel sometimes too.'

Josephine felt a great relief sweep over her at the sight of the stout little woman smiling on the doorstep.

'Thank goodness for that,' she said.

'Well, come along in, Miss Morrow,' said Annabel. She barely glanced at her scanty attire, seeming not a bit put out by it. Perhaps she thought it was a new summer fashion. 'You've not brought any luggage, have you, miss?'

'No,' said Josephine, wondering how she was going to explain. 'I –'

'Oh, that's quite all right, miss,' said the housekeeper as she shut the heavy oak door. 'We've everything you'll need here.'

'Is Dr Hazel here? I must see him.'

Annabel turned her face away slightly. 'Not yet,' she said. 'Dr Hazel will be arriving later.'

Josephine looked at her surroundings.

The hall was lit by soft wall-lights in little fringed lampshades, to compensate for the tiny windows, which were leaded in a traditional old diamond pattern. Everything around her seemed traditional and old, in fact: the grandfather clock, the framed prints of hunting scenes, the Jacobean chairs standing against the wall. The air smelled of ancient timber and wax polish. In an alcove, on a small table blackened with age, lay a leather-bound ledger complete with fountain pen.

All in all, it looked like the entrance to an expensive club or a country hotel: restful, discreet, a haven of old-world charm and civilisation. There stood Annabel in her long lavender dress and button boots, the very incarnation of service and courtesy; and there behind her, crossing the hall, was a maid in black dress, white apron and a little white cap, carrying a decanter and glasses on a brass tray. Did Josephine's eyes deceive her, or did she even bob a tiny curtsey as she scurried by?

Annabel clasped her hands together and inclined her head. 'Have you had a tiring journey, Miss Morrow?'

'Very,' said Josephine.

Perhaps, she hoped, there would be no need to say any more than that. At least until she met Dr Hazel and found out whether he was really responsible for everything that had happened to her; or whether, as she was beginning now to suspect, she'd been the victim of some sort of elaborate practical joke. Medical students, she thought belatedly. She remembered some of the outrages perpetrated by trainee medics on rag weeks. The cab driver; the couple at the Green Man; the nurse: they were all in it together.

No wonder they'd kept her blindfolded. And the cab driver, in his ridiculous sunglasses: he didn't want her to be able to recognize him again.

She felt herself blushing to think what a fool she'd let them make of her. And that story she'd told him. *'Please spank me,'* she heard herself saying again. Her bottom was still tender now, as she stood here in the hall at Estwych, while he was undoubtedly off somewhere, back to the Green Man to tell the other two, the Japanese woman and her boyfriend, how he'd got on. They'd be having a great laugh at her expense. Josephine just hoped they hadn't got any photos or tapes of her while they were at it. Surreptitiously, she rubbed her bottom.

Annabel was at the table in the alcove, running her finger down the columns of the ledger. 'Let's get you settled in, then, Miss Morrow, shall we?' she said, pencilling something in and taking a key from the drawer in the table. 'I've put you in Room 3, it's a very nice room. You'll find everything you need, as I say. If not, you can always ring the bell. Shall I get a maid to show you the way?'

'Oh, no need,' said Josephine. 'I'm sure I can find it.'

'Up the stairs and to your left,' Annabel said. 'Numbers are on the doors.'

She held out the key, dangling from a round black tag. Josephine took it.

'Shall I send you up a pot of tea, Miss Morrow?' asked Annabel.

'Oh, that would be wonderful,' said Josephine sincerely.

She felt very conscious, as she crossed the hall, that she was still half naked. She smiled at the housekeeper and set off upstairs.

There was a hush about the place: not a sound from any of the rooms she passed as she crossed the landing. Probably all the rest of the — what should she call them? Patients? Guests? Clients? Residents? *Inmates?* Probably they were all sleeping, anyway, or downstairs in the lounge, waiting for Dr Hazel to arrive and the week to begin. She wondered who they would be, and what sort of therapy Dr Hazel really practised.

Perhaps her gauntlet of humiliations and punishments had been intended after all, had been part of the treatment, and this genteel luxury was the reward for survivors.

Josephine remembered her original idea, that this was some sort of initiative test, like the one Japanese firms sent their executives on. Japanese, she thought suddenly. The woman at the Green Man: she was Japanese. The one the cab driver had made up the story about. Unless that was coincidence. The things she'd been through today, they could have been the kind of things the Japanese did on their tests, to sort out the people who were really committed to coming here from the ones who were just indulging themselves and hoping to be pampered.

In a moment of panic, she realised she didn't know anything. This had been the strangest, most frightening day of her life, and she had no idea what any of it *meant*. Was she winning? Losing? *What were they doing to her?*

She stood with her head bowed, resting on the door of Number 3. Hold on, she told herself, breathing hard. You're just panicking because they've taken the pressure off. You won't get anywhere by falling apart now. Don't let them see you fall apart.

The lock turned smoothly and silently. Josephine opened the door and went in.

Annabel was right, thought Josephine. Room 3 was very nice. The ceiling was low, and criss-crossed by stout black beams. The floor was obviously original, it undulated like the waves of the sea. There was a big double bed, a table beside it, a wardrobe across the room and a comfortable-looking old armchair under the window. A simple fireplace, with a large grey and white pot standing in the spotless grate. Candles on the mantelpiece, and a towelling-handled bell rope hanging nearby.

She took the key out of the lock and closed the door. She went over to the window to look at the view, and put the key on the sill, where she wouldn't lose it. She was always anxious about forgetting her key in hotels. As she laid it down, a design engraved on the key fob caught her eye. She picked it up and examined it. It was a little mask, the sort they called a domino. Where had she seen that before, today?

The view from her window was beautiful. On the left there was a big green tree rising up from thick, dense bushes. An oak? An ash? Josephine didn't know. It was a lovely tree, anyway. Beyond it, a soft green meadow curved up the gentle slope of the hill, to a wooden fence and another line of trees. There were flowers in the meadow, Josephine could see: little dots of gold, still bright in the lengthening shadows. Buttercups, were they? And others, even tinier, that were bright mauve or blue. On the hill the grass was long and tangled with spiky gorse bushes. Beyond, the fields and trees stretched away into a misty blue distance, with not another building in sight. Dr Hazel had found a beautiful spot for his clinic.

There was a second door in her room, in the wall beside the wardrobe. Before Josephine could open it, there was a knock at the outer door.

'Come in,' she called.

It was the maid, with her tea.

'Goodness, that was quick,' said Josephine. She looked around. 'Put it down on the table, would you, please.'

The girl obeyed. 'Are you happy with the room, ma'am?' she asked, obviously having been instructed to.

'I've hardly finished looking round yet,' said Josephine, with her hand on the handle of the second door, 'but I think it's lovely. Is this the bathroom?'

'Yes, ma'am.'

'Oh, good,' said Josephine, opening it. 'I'm dying for a shower.'

Inside was a bathroom as modern and convenient as the bedroom was quaint and old-fashioned. Thick white towels were piled on a heated towel rail. There was a shower head over the bath, with a curtain running round. Josephine stood for a moment silently clutching her bottom, flexing her knees, willing the pain away. Then she turned the shower tap, and hot water sprang instantly from the sprinkler in a powerful stream.

76

'If you let me have your clothes, ma'am, I'll take them for the wash,' she heard the maid say.

'Oh thank you,' said Josephine. 'Thank you very much.'

Relieved to be rid of the horrible things at last, she stripped off the T-shirt and shorts at once, and kicked off the plimsolls and the socks, which were damp and disgusting. She wrapped herself in a towel, bundled up the clothes, and stepped back out into the bedroom to hand them to the maid.

'These aren't my clothes,' she found herself saying. 'Somebody gave me these to wear. It was a sort of joke.'

Blank-faced, the maid took them. 'Yes, ma'am,' she said, automatically.

'Oh, look,' said Josephine, having second thoughts, 'the T-shirt. I really don't think you should bother with it. With washing it, I mean. It's no good. It's torn already.'

'Yes, ma'am,' said the maid.

'You might as well throw it away,' said Josephine.

'Yes, ma'am,' said the maid.

In the bathroom, the shower hissed on, invitingly. Josephine turned to go back to it.

'Oh, I'm sorry,' she said, suddenly realising. 'I haven't got anything else with me! I, er, left in such a hurry I didn't have time to pack.'

The maid, just like Annabel, was too well trained to show any surprise; or else she seemed to think this was perfectly normal. Perhaps it was perfectly normal, where Dr Hazel's clients were concerned. 'Your clothes are in the wardrobe, ma'am,' said the maid.

'My *clothes*? Are you sure?'

'Yes, ma'am,' said the maid; and clearly this *was* perfectly normal. Where else would a resident's clothes be?

'Thank goodness for that,' said Josephine again. Was that why the nurse had made off with her clothes: to bring them ahead, while she travelled in the skimpy sports gear? If she had the nerve. And she had. Here she was, and her clothes were here too.

'I hope she brought my handbag,' said Josephine.

The maid nodded. 'There's a bag in there, ma'am,' she said.

'Oh, good,' said Josephine feelingly. She was longing to get into the shower. 'That's all right, then.'

'Yes, ma'am. Will there be anything else, ma'am?'

'No thank you,' said Josephine. 'Thank you very much,' she said.

The maid went out and shut the door.

Josephine dropped the bath towel on the floor and, for the second time that afternoon, stepped into a warm and welcome shower. It felt good on her sweaty back and thighs, and she soaped and soaped at her sore bottom. She wondered if she had bruises. She felt a sudden spasm of anger at them, at herself. Hold on, she thought. You're doing all right, only you've had a very confusing and stressful day. Just relax now, and hold on until you see Dr Hazel. Don't go to pieces.

She thought of the story she'd told the cabby, about her and Maria Coroni. Where on earth had that come from? It made her want to laugh now. Her little encounter with Maria Coroni hadn't been anywhere near as voluptuous as she'd managed to make it sound. Truth to tell, it had been furtive, dismal. Josephine had been so timid, so afraid they'd get caught, she hadn't had time to feel turned on by what they were doing.

She wondered what had happened to Maria, and where she was now. Probably married to a stockbroker and living in Rome, with an enormous family.

Josephine turned the water down a little. She soaped her thighs, and between her thighs. Slowly and intently she ran the corner of the soap up through her pubic hair. She felt light-headed, between laughter and tears. She sniffed.

Part of her story had been almost true. Only it was her that came back home alone to an empty flat and sat playing with herself in the lounge with the curtains open and all the lights off.

Josephine remembered her tea.

She turned off the shower, wrapped herself in two big towels, and padded out of the bathroom, across the wavy floor to the table by the bed. Through the thick carpet, her feet made no sound on the floor. In fact she still hadn't heard a single sound from anywhere else in the building since she arrived.

Suddenly her heart sank. Maybe it was another trap. Like the fake clinic in St Pancras. Here she was, naked again, in another strange place, with no evidence there was anyone else at all in the rest of the building.

Josephine suddenly had the awful feeling that she would come out of her room, go downstairs, and find the whole place deserted.

No, she was being stupid. Her clothes were in the wardrobe, the girl had said. And Annabel was here. Annabel wasn't a madcap medical student. She wan't a practical joker. She was a solid and dependable member of the old-fashioned servant class, and she wouldn't be putting up with any nonsense from so-called nurses and taxi drivers.

The tea tray was a complete service: a little two-cup teapot (with real leaves, not a bag: she checked); a jug of hot water and one of milk; a cup and saucer of fine white china with a thin line of dark blue all around the rim; and a little bowl of white sugar with a crested spoon. Whatever else it was, then, Estwych wasn't one of these terrible health farms where they made you live on lettuce leaves and lemon juice.

If she hadn't heard a sound from anyone else in the building, that just went to show what a restful, uneventful place this really was. It was quiet in the country. She just wasn't used to it yet. They often had really thick walls, anyway, these ancient houses.

She poured a cup of tea; added milk and sugar to the cup and water to the pot; then still steaming and draped in a towel she sat on the bed, and sipped her tea. It was delicious.

She dried her hair slowly and meditatively with the other towel while she drank her tea.

From the bed she could look across and see out of the window. There were a couple of tiny clouds drifting slowly from right to left, tinted a peachy pink by the setting sun. They were moving so slowly they were still in view when Josephine finished her tea and turned to the table to pour herself a second cup.

She added the milk and sugar, stirred it, and put the spoon down in the saucer. She sat back against the pillows again, letting the towel fall open so that the steam could escape from her body as she dried. She rested the china teacup carefully on her stomach. She toyed with the spoon, and looked at its enamelled crest.

It wasn't a crest. It was a little motif, shaped like a figure of eight. Josephine looked closer.

It was a mask. A domino mask.

A domino on the spoon, and a domino on the keyring.

A picture of a pierrot in a domino on the wall of Dr Hazel's so-called surgery. And a box of dominoes, the other kind of dominoes, in the drawer of the desk behind the clothes.

Josephine shut her eyes. She took a deep breath. Then she set the teacup carefully but firmly down on the tray, and got off the bed, leaving the towel behind.

Naked, she padded across the silent floor to the wardrobe.

She opened the door.

Inside there was nothing except a pair of ankle boots with spike heels, and a small black leather handbag hanging by a narrow shoulder strap from a hook on the back of the door.

Josephine's heart began to beat very fast.

With great misgivings, she took down the bag and opened it.

Inside was a little bundle of black nylon and black leather.

Josephine took it out of the bag. She sat on the bed and took the bundle apart in her lap. There were four things in it.

A pair of sheer black stockings, with seams.

A narrow black suspender belt, almost severe in its simplicity, but trimmed with the very slightest line of lace.

And a black leather collar, like a dog collar, but big enough to go snugly round her neck. It fastened at the back with a buckle, and at the front it had a shiny silver ring mounted on it.

Her clothes.

She looked at them for a second or two. She didn't put them on.

Instead she stuffed them back into the tiny handbag.

They wouldn't go back in. They had been very carefully packed before, there was only just room for them; and now they wouldn't go back in.

Josephine abandoned them, leaving them on the bed. She snatched up the bath towel, wrapped it around her, and tucked the end in as securely as she could over her breasts. She marched to the door; back to the window sill to get her key; then back to the door and out along the landing to the stairs, then down the stairs to the hall.

There was still no one around.

Josephine reached the front door and had her hand on the handle before Annabel said: 'And where do you think you're going, Miss Morrow?'

|9|

W here was she going? Out into the lane, to start walking back to London, barefoot and draped in a bath towel?

Josephine held on to the door handle, but didn't make any further attempt to turn it. Her head sagged. Her damp hair straggled against the polished wood of the door.

'Now come along, Miss Morrow,' said Annabel sternly. 'Dr Hazel will be here soon.'

'Good,' said Josephine tonelessly. 'I want to see Dr Hazel.'

'Then I suggest you go straight back upstairs and get dressed, miss,' said Annabel.

Josephine turned and looked at her, clasping the towel over her breasts.

'I will,' she said. 'I'd love to. But I haven't got any clothes.'

'Your clothes are in the wardrobe,' said Annabel. 'In your room.'

'No, they're not,' said Josephine.

'Please don't argue with me, miss,' said Annabel firmly. 'They are.'

Josephine looked her in the eye. 'Do you know what there is, hanging in that wardrobe?'

Annabel looked straight back up at her. 'Yes, miss,' she said. 'I do. And I suggest you go and put them on at once, before Dr Hazel arrives and finds you wandering around like this. Look at you. It won't do. It won't do at all. Anyone would think this was some sort of mental home, to look at you.'

Josephine leaned back against the solid, comforting wooden door.

'Annabel,' she said. 'Annabel, I think I'm going mad.'

For reply, the housekeeper took a firm grip of Josephine's forearm. 'That's quite enough of that, thank you, Miss Morrow,' she said.

Josephine looked down in surprise at Annabel's hand.

'Annabel! Let go, you're hurting me.'

81

Annabel ignored her.

'You're to come upstairs at once,' she said.

'Annabel! Let go, please!'

Josephine tried to prise away her grip. She couldn't budge a single finger. Clearly, the little woman's bulk was not all fat.

'Upstairs I said, and upstairs I meant!'

'But I — Ow! Annabel!'

The housekeeper's eyes looked very fierce now. 'You're at Estwych now, Miss Morrow,' she said. 'At Estwych! Remember that!'

She pulled on Josephine's arm and brought her face up as close as she could to Josephine's. 'At Estwych absolute obedience is the law,' she said.

Then she turned her head to shout along the hall.

'Janet!'

Silent in her little black slippers, the maid appeared. She regarded the tableau without surprise; with no particular expression at all, in fact.

'Janet,' said Annabel, 'Miss Morrow is going back to her room now. She's to get dressed. Will you take her back there, please, and see that she does?'

'Yes, Mrs Taylor,' said Janet.

'And will you see that she stays there until I come, Janet.'

'Yes, Mrs Taylor,' said Janet.

Defeated, Josephine trod heavily back upstairs, following the girl in the black dress along the landing and down the corridor to Room 3.

At the door, the maid turned.

'Have you got the key, ma'am?'

'It's not locked,' said Josephine.

Janet turned the handle and opened the door.

Josephine followed her in.

While Janet shut the door behind them, Josephine went over to the table by the bed and looked at the teapot.

'I was just going to pour myself another cup of tea,' she said.

'Mrs Taylor says you're to put your things on, ma'am,' Janet objected.

'I know,' said Josephine. 'I heard.'

She took the lid off the teapot, picked up the spoon with the domino design and stirred the tea. Still clutching the towel about her, she poured some tea into her cup, added milk, stirred it, picked it up and

82

took a mouthful.

She grimaced.

'Stewed,' she said.

'Mrs Taylor says —' said Janet.

'I know,' said Josephine. 'I know what Mrs Taylor said. Is there a phone here? A telephone?'

The girl shook her head. To look at her you'd think she'd never heard the word before.

'No, of course not,' said Josephine.

She looked at the things on the bed. They were spilling out of the little bag where she'd tried to stuff them back in. She picked up one of the stockings, let it run over her fingers and fall back to the bed.

'Is this Dr Hazel's idea of clothes?' she asked.

'I don't know, ma'am,' said Janet.

'Does everyone here wear these?'

'No, ma'am.'

'Where are my clothes? *My* clothes?'

'I don't know, ma'am,' said the maid blankly. 'Mrs Taylor says you're to —'

'I know, Janet, I know.'

Josephine came away from the bed, stood in the middle of the floor, facing the little maid. She unfastened the twist that held the bath towel around her body; let it fall to the floor.

She looked at Janet, watching her keenly.

'Is this what you want to see?' she asked.

The maid didn't answer. There was still no expression on her face.

There was a knock at the door.

'Who is it?' called Josephine.

The handle turned. The door opened. Annabel came in.

Josephine stood there, her hands on her hips, facing the door.

Annabel gave her one scornful glance, then turned on the hapless maid.

'I thought I told you to make sure she got dressed.'

'I did, I told her, Mrs Taylor, but she wouldn't.'

Annabel disregarded this entirely. 'I told you to see to it. Didn't I?'

'But Mrs Taylor —'

'Didn't I, Janet?'

Janet dropped her eyes. 'Yes, Mrs Taylor,' she whispered.

'Fetch a stool,' ordered the housekeeper.

Janet bobbed a curtsey, and hurried from the room.

'Annabel —' said Josephine, coming forward.

The housekeeper waved her away. 'Put those things on,' she said.

Janet returned from somewhere, struggling with a broad padded stool, like the stool of a parlour piano. She set it down in front of the door and stood away from it.

Annabel took her seat.

She made a brusque gesture.

The maid turned her back to her, scooping up her long black dress and layer on layer of creamy petticoats at the back. Soon she had hoisted them clear of her drawers, which were as old-fashioned as the rest of her dress: loose, made of coarse yellowed linen, and fastened with buttons at the side.

She started to struggle with the buttons. Her skirts were in the way, she couldn't see. Annabel slapped her hand away, and unfastened the buttons herself.

As the housekeeper opened the back flap of the drawers and bared the cheeks of her skinny, white bottom, Janet looked round at her with a look expectant and beseeching and forlorn, all at once.

'Annabel, you can't —' said Josephine.

'Are you dressed yet, Miss Morrow?' asked Annabel, not looking at her.

'Annabel, it's my fault! All right? Is that what you want? It's all my fault!'

Still the stout little woman didn't look at her. 'I'll expect to find you dressed and ready when I've finished here,' she said.

She sat back, pulling Janet by the arm.

Janet, unresisting, lay face down across her knee.

Josephine pulled the tangled accessories from the bag and separated them again. She took up the suspender belt and wrapped it around her hips.

Annabel gave Janet a smack on the bottom.

Josephine gathered up the stocking in her hands and, setting one foot up on the bed, slipped the stocking onto her foot.

Annabel smacked the little maid again, and again, and again.

Janet began to whimper. She was, what, fifteen, Josephine estimated. Perhaps a small sixteen.

She drew the stocking up her leg, smoothing out the twists and wrinkles, and turning over the top, fastened it to the dangling suspenders.

Annabel tipped the maid further over her knee, almost spilling her on the floor. Janet threw out her hands to catch herself as Annabel gave her two meaty slaps right across the underhang of her bottom. She yelped aloud.

Josephine drew on the second stocking, and fastened that too.

By this time Janet's bottom was an unsightly, blotchy mess of pink and white. She moaned and sobbed, jerking her head and kicking her feet as her spanking continued.

Josephine took the collar from the bed and put it around her neck. She worked out the way to fasten it, with difficulty, under her chin, and then turned it so the buckle was to the back, the silver ring in front.

She supposed that was the way to wear it.

'I'm ready,' she said loudly.

Annabel looked at her swiftly.

'Boots,' she said. 'In the wardrobe.'

And she resumed spanking the crying Janet until Josephine had fetched out the black leather boots, put them on and stood tottering upright in them.

'Now,' said Josephine.

At once, Annabel stopped spanking Janet and set her on her feet.

Janet was crying loudly, rubbing her bottom, rubbing her face, then rubbing her bottom again.

Looking at her, Josephine felt a strange, abstract kind of guilt. She had caused her to be punished. She had brought it on her, half-knowing it would happen. Yet at the same time, she knew on another level, she had passed another test. Annabel had set this one for her, giving the maid an unmanageable task, but actually putting it into Josephine's hands to choose whether she succeeded at it or not. As she watched, dispassionately, the young girl's misery subside, she knew that despite that, or somehow, perhaps, because of it, her decision had been the right one. Janet's spanking had been a demonstration: of what? Josephine almost understood: then it was gone again.

'Get out,' said Annabel to the maid. 'Be about your duties.'

Janet jumped, snivelled, wiped her eyes and nose on her sleeve. She groped for the buttons on her dangling drawers.

'Get out!' cried the housekeeper.

Holding her dress up with both hands, Janet ran for the door, and

85

out of the room.

'That was cruel,' said Josephine forcefully.

Annabel looked her up and down, obviously approving of what she saw.

'It's never wasted,' she observed.

'It wasn't her fault,' said Josephine.

'No,' mused Annabel. She rubbed her chin.

She spread her legs, leaning forward on the stool. She slapped her knees loudly, looking up at Josephine as she stood there, naked collared and stockinged.

'And what are we to do with you?' she asked, loudly and cheerfully. Her old eyes sparkled.

'Are you asking me?' said Josephine quietly.

'No, miss. Not yet. No, I think I know what's to be done with you.'

She looked at the palm of her right hand, inspecting it as if she expected to find it damaged from smacking Janet's bottom.

'I think it's time you were introduced to the hairbrush,' she said.

She pointed to the bathroom.

Josephine felt the familiar cold draught in the pit of her stomach. Unsteady on the narrow heels, she walked into the bathroom and looked on the shelf above the basin.

There was a hairbrush there, soft bristle set in a long wooden oval with a thoughtfully curved handle.

She picked it up and looked at it.

Then she took it into the bedroom.

Annabel held out her hand. 'Bring it here,' she said.

Josephine brought it to her.

Annabel took it in her right hand, slapped the back of it into the palm of her left.

'Bend over my knee, Miss Morrow,' she said.

Josephine went around and bent forward, over the housekeeper's knee.

'I see someone's been seeing to you already,' said the housekeeper.

She spanked Josephine with the back of the hairbrush. She spanked her across her knee, as if she were a child, a little girl, like the maid Janet, being punished for her failure to comply with the impossible and incomprehensible demands of the grown-up world.

In a sense, reflected Josephine as she winced and jerked under the brush, that was what she was. And, like a child, she let herself be spanked, but resisted it too, reaching backwards with the only protection she had, putting her own right hand in the way, between her bottom and the brush.

Annabel put down the brush. She seized Josephine's wrist firmly in her right hand. With her left she dragged Josephine's left arm out from where it was pinned under her. She crossed the two hands in the small of her back, and bore down on the wrists with her left hand, immobilizing them.

'We'll have cuffs for you later,' she promised Josephine.

Then she took up the brush again and resumed spanking Josephine's bottom.

It was not like her first spanking, in the room at the Green Man, which had been violent and alarming; nor like her second, in the taxi, which had been considerate and oddly sensual. This one was a piece of business, a routine act whose whole justification was itself. The law of Estwych was obedience, and Josephine was required to be obedient to the back of the brush that Annabel whacked down with such rigid, unerring accuracy on her buttocks, her flanks, the backs of her thighs. It was a rhythmical spanking, like the taxi driver's, but faster and more mechanical than his, each stroke coming down with the same force, wherever it landed and when; however she gasped and bucked and cried.

'Shout all you like, miss,' Annabel told her: not vindictively, but strangely sympathetically, as if this was another house rule she would be required to observe. Josephine's immediate impulse was to bite her lip, not to give Annabel the satisfaction; but this was the last flicker of antagonism she felt. All she could feel now was the pain, the scratchy wool of Annabel's dress under her thighs and stomach, the pressure on her wrists, holding her under. She forgot the collar, the stockings and suspenders; she forgot the absurd things she had been trying to tell herself minutes before, about students and practical jokes, about executives and initiative tests. Here, in this world, things were altogether simpler. The executive was the one who wielded the brush. The student was the one across her knee, learning a lesson that was the simplest and most complicated imaginable.

To obey. To obey completely, and without question.

At last it was over. Josephine found herself lying on the bed, the covers in disarray. She had been clutching herself and crying pitifully; she didn't know how long. 'You'll wait here for the doctor,' Annabel had told her.

Josephine waited.

The agony in her bottom subsided to a dull ache. She was sure now it was bruised and swollen, but when she crawled off the bed, kicked off the ridiculous boots and limped into the bathroom to examine herself, over her shoulder, in the full-length mirror, she saw only an inflamed mess of dull red, already beginning to fade.

More for the sake of form than anything else, she tried the door to the corridor. It was locked. Annabel had taken the key with the domino tag.

It was dark now. Josephine lay in the dark. There was a cord by her head for the light switch, but she did not pull it. She did not draw the curtains to shut out the black and starlit country night; nor did she light any of the candles.

For the first time she heard sounds, the intermittent sounds of the other guests at Estwych, footsteps in the corridor and going down the stairs, the murmur of brief, civilized conversations.

A while later, there was a knock at the door.

'Who is it?' called Josephine, her voice rusty from crying.

'Dinner, ma'am,' said a young voice. There was the sound of a key in the lock.

The door opened. Light spilled into the room from the corridor. In came Janet, carefully bearing a laden tray.

'Oh Janet...'

Josephine sat up, automatically trying to cover herself with the counterpane. Then she realised what she was doing and dropped her hand.

The maid said, 'Shall I put the light on for you, ma'am?'

'All right,' Josephine said.

Josephine blinked as the light came on. She looked at the tray, with its covered dishes. The room was full of the smell of meat and wine. She was very hungry.

She watched the young girl move the tea tray from the bedside table, replacing it with the dinner tray. She seemed absolutely calm, the good servant, absorbed in her work.

Suddenly Josephine reached out and touched her arm.

'Janet, I – '

The girl turned her head and looked at her. Her face was quiet, her complexion fair, a sprinkle of butterscotch freckles beneath pale eyes with lashes so fine they were almost invisible.

Josephine could see her breathing.

'I'm sorry,' she said. 'I really — '

A puzzled expression came into Janet's eyes. For an instant Josephine thought the girl didn't know what she meant. Then she recognised it as concern, concern for her in her turmoil of guilt and regret.

'It's all right, ma'am', said Janet.

'But — '

'It's all right, ma'am, really it is. It's all right.'

'But I — '

Janet stood there by the bed, the tea tray in her hands, looking down patiently as she was required to do, at the naked woman.

In the face of such self-possession, Josephine didn't know what she had been about to say. She fell back, dissatisfied, on the pillows.

Janet looked around the room.

'Shall I draw the curtains, ma'am?'

'If you like...'

Janet stood, unmoving.

'Yes, yes, Janet, do please draw the curtains.'

'And tidy up for you a bit?'

The maid went around shutting the wardrobe door where Josephine had left it open, straightening the room's few pieces of furniture. She picked up the stool the housekeeper had sent her for and took it out.

Josephine lifted a starched napkin and discovered a glass of red wine. She brought it to her lips and look a sip. It was exquisite.

The maid came back in. She bent and picked up something from the floor.

It was the hairbrush.

She went and put it back in the bathroom.

'I'll be saying goodnight, then, ma'am,' she said, picking up the tray again.

'Is Dr Hazel here?' Josephine asked

'Not yet, ma'am. The doctor will be here soon.'

'Can you — I don't suppose you can leave me the key, can you?'

'No, ma'am.' The maid made to leave.

'Janet?'

'Yes, ma'am?'

Her patience was automatic and infinite.

'Thank you, Janet.'

'Yes, ma'am. Good night, ma'am.'

'Good night, Janet.'

Left alone, Josephine finished her dinner, just as she was, sitting on the bed in her stockings and her collar. Afterwards she took them off, slipped naked beneath the covers and fell fast asleep.

She dreamed she was at a fairground, climbing the helter skelter. She could tell the hard rough texture of the coconut mat in her hand. The tower seemed to go up forever, past landings and harshly-lit corridors where official figures in grey suits with huge padded shoulders stood arguing over folded newspapers. In front of her as she climbed was a creature; sometimes it was a young child, a girl of six or seven with blonde hair in pigtails; sometimes it was a black and white terrier, or a scuttling, panting thing with too many legs. It dawdled until she came up behind it, then squealed and fled, giggling.

Suddenly she woke up, with a bright light in her eyes and no idea where she was. A figure was standing over her, a tall man, shining a torch in her face.

'I hear you've been asking to see me,' he said. His voice was deep, quietly authoritative, like the voice of a professional confidant.

'Dr Hazel?'

'Yes.'

|10|

Josephine raised herself up on one elbow, shading her eyes from the dazzling beam.

'Don't...'

The man turned the beam on the wall, located the cord for the light switch and leaned over her to take hold of it. Josephine covered herself with the sheet. She caught the scent of a cosmetic, aftershave, something very sleek and expensive.

Above the bed a reading light came on. The man switched off his torch and pocketed it.

'I'm sorry,' he said, sitting down uninvited on her bed. 'You were sleeping very soundly.'

Josephine's mouth felt parched and clothy. Her head was muzzy.

'The wine,' she said. 'They put something in it.'

She gestured to the red-stained glass on the tray.

The man cocked an eyebrow. 'Something in it?' he repeated. He sounded slightly cautious, as though he thought she was deluded and needed humouring.

'Drug...' said Josephine. She felt absolutely exhausted, unable to come to properly.

The man picked up the glass, held it under his nose and sniffed like a connoisseur, keeping a quizzical eye on her all the while. She was sure he was humouring her, and giving her a chance to take a better look at him as her eyes gradually focused.

He was tall, mid-thirties, with the white-gold hair, broad cheekbones and bland features of a Scandinavian. He was wearing a beautiful suit in pale grey with a very fine blue chalkstripe, and an open-necked shirt of deep chartreuse. When he smiled, and put down the glass without offering a comment, he revealed a double row of small, perfectly even teeth.

'I'm sorry I couldn't keep our appointment in London,' he said. 'Something came up. No doubt Jackie explained it to you.'

'Jackie? Was that the woman who was pretending to be a nurse?'

'She's my nurse, yes.'

'No,' said Josephine, feeling a little stronger now. 'Jackie didn't explain a thing.'

'Oh, no? I'm sorry,' he said, with another professional smile. 'Anyway, I'm Dr Hazel, yes. And you're Josephine Morrow, whom my good friend Dr Shepard told me about.'

He held out his hand.

'Welcome to Estwych,' he said. 'I'm pleased to meet you.'

Josephine didn't take his hand. She didn't let go of the bedcovers.

'We've met,' she said.

Dr Hazel gave her the very slightest of frowns, as if he was slightly puzzled by what she said but most interested to have it explained.

'Is that so?'

'Yesterday. In Whittingtry.'

Dr Hazel shook his head, frowning more markedly now, and looked down at his hands as if trying to think of a polite way to contradict her.

He raised his eyes to meet hers again.

'Whittingtry?' he said. He was making out the name was unfamiliar to him.

'That's right,' said Josephine. 'Could you get me a glass of water, please?'

He got to his feet. 'Shall I ring for a maid?' he asked.

'No,' she said. 'No. Just a glass of water. From the bathroom. Please.'

He turned and went into the bathroom. Josephine heard the water running. He came out with a glass of water, and brought it to her.

'Thank you.'

She held on to the bedclothes with one hand, took the water with the other. She sipped it, took a deeper drink.

'You came to see me in Whittingtry, at a hotel called the Green Man,' she said. 'Yesterday afternoon.' She wondered, then, how long she'd been asleep. The night was as deathly quiet here as the day. 'What time is it?'

Dr Hazel shot his cuff and glanced at a rolled gold wristwatch. 'Almost two,' he said, as if mildly surprised to discover it himself. He sat down again beside her as she drank her water.

'You must be mistaken, Miss Morrow,' he said. 'I know of Whittingtry, yes, but I've never been there. Certainly not yesterday.'

She said, 'Your driver took me there.'

'My driver?'

'The man who drives your taxi.'

Dr Hazel shook his head. He looked genuinely bemused. 'I haven't got a driver,' he said gently. 'Did he say he was my driver?'

'First of all he claimed he didn't know you, but he knew my name. He said he'd been sent to pick me up. He took me to this inn, the Green Man.'

'He said I'd sent him?'

'No,' said Josephine. This was beginning to sound convoluted and pedantic. It was making less sense to her every moment, and she wished she'd never begun. She felt foolish, trying to recount this man's devious schemes to himself.

'He said he'd never heard of Estwych. But later he said he had, and he brought me here,' she said, looking at him directly and accusingly.

'Oh dear, oh dear,' he said. His impersonation of professional concern was perfect.

'Miss Morrow,' he said. 'Josephine. Will you please tell me what has been going on while my back has been turned?'

She did.

It was all she had to use against him, her clear knowledge of everything that had happened to her so far. She felt, at that moment, naked and vulnerable in bed, that her only defence against this suave and manipulative trickster was to assert the very sense of clarity that he and his organisation appeared to be trying to destroy in her.

He listened, politely. He looked thoughtful when she told him about the two people who had come to her room at the Green Man, and asked questions about them. Without offering any comment, he gave the decided impression that he had no idea who they had been, or why the man had been impersonating him; though he left it quite open that she had, perhaps, made a mistake. To a blindfold victim under duress one man with a foreign accent, a man of few words anyway, may easily be mistaken for another. He looked shocked, then grave when he heard about her maltreatments. Throughout he managed to convey the feeling that he believed completely in her suffering, and was sorry for her; but that her story was so bizarre he would have to keep an open mind about what had actually happened to her and why, at least until he had some other evidence.

At last he sighed and shook his head.

'My dear,' he said, 'it seems you've been the victim of a particularly elaborate and painful practical joke.' His voice was soothing, reassuring. 'Let me say at once I have no idea who any of these people were, except of course for Jackie, if it *was* Jackie who neglected you so brutally at my office, and Annabel, Mrs Taylor, who is a most trusted and valuable member of my team. I must confess I have trouble recognising her in the portrait you give of her. Never have I known her to be anything other than kind and infinitely forbearing with her domestic staff. And to attack a patient!'

So, thought Josephine, she was a patient.

Dr Hazel shook his head again.

'I can only wonder whether you perhaps have encountered yet another impostor, claiming to be Mrs Taylor.'

'Wake her up and ask her,' said Josephine.

'I should have no hesitation in doing so,' he said. 'None at all. But unfortunately she is not here. She has returned to her home in Hampstead, and will not be back until the evening.'

He struggled, looking at Josephine with an expression both humorous and perplexed. He started towards the bell-rope again.

'The maid: Janet, you say?'

'No,' said Josephine, 'don't.'

She was weakening. She was beginning to believe him. They were all true, all her fears. How could she have been so stupid?

'May I ask one thing?' asked Dr Hazel. 'Will you let me assess the extent of the assault?'

He laid his hand on hers. 'Will you permit me to examine you?'

Josephine sighed. She dropped the bedclothes.

As she uncovered herself, she watched Dr Hazel's face. She saw nothing there but professional objectivity. He pulled the covers to the foot of the bed, exposing her at full length, then indicated with one hand that she should roll over on her tummy.

Touching her gently with cool, dry hands, he examined her bottom and thighs. She heard his breathing, smooth and even.

'This must be very sore,' he said.

'It was,' she agreed. 'It's not so bad now.'

He went on lightly palpating her tender flesh.

'Is it bruised?' she asked him.

'Fortunately, no,' he said. 'At least not yet.'

His voice was tight with restrained emotion. Suddenly she realised he was angry. 'But we must do something for this,' he went on, 'without delay. Ms Morrow, I must admit that when you started to speak I did not altogether believe my ears. It is, you must admit, an outrageous story. Outrageous,' he repeated, sternly. 'I cannot tell you how sorry I am that you have been so grievously humiliated and assaulted. I am angry that a client of mine should be physically abused under my roof and in my name. No doubt you wish to call the police and get an investigation under way as quickly as possible.'

At that moment, Josephine realised she wanted no such thing. She had already been through the idea of calling the police, more than once, and rejected it firmly. Nothing would induce her to extend the embarrassment, prolong the agony. Nothing would make her risk any of this turning up in the papers.

'Actually, I'd rather not, doctor,' she said.

'But you must!' he protested.

'I'd rather leave it in your hands,' she told him. 'If you want to call them in and investigate your staff, I'd rather you kept me out of it, if you don't mind. I don't mind. I don't want any scandal. All I really want is to sleep. In the morning I'll want some clothes. And then I'll want to go home.'

'You are being most forbearing,' the doctor said. 'You are a most admirable example of the self-possessed young woman of today.'

For some reason, that was more embarrassing than the whole ordeal of showing him the marks of her spankings. Josephine grabbed the covers and rolled over, pulling them up over her and looking at him as she lay back on the pillow.

'Please,' he said. 'You must let me treat you. A soothing cream for the pain, and an ointment to bring out any bruising.'

'I'm fine,' she said. 'It's all right. A good night's sleep is all I need.'

He shook his head. 'I warn you,' he said mildly, 'if you don't get some medication on that inflammation now, you will be stiff and sore for days. I can help you. I can relieve that. But you must come at once. Please.'

Reluctantly she sat up in bed, covering her breasts with the blankets again.

'I haven't got anything to wear,' she said, 'except that lot.'

She nodded at the little pile of lingerie and leather on the floor by the bed. Dr Hazel barely glanced at it. He didn't react. She supposed he hadn't registered what was lying there. She didn't feel like insisting he look at it properly. It would only start him off about the police again.

'There's a robe in the wardrobe,' he told her.

'No, there isn't,' she said.

Dr Hazel went over to the wardrobe and opened the door. He reached inside. Josephine heard the click of a hanger against the rail. Dr Hazel drew out a light green dressing gown, a short one.

'That wasn't there before,' said Josephine.

He made no reply. He just stood there, holding out the gown.

Josephine gave another sigh. If he was so concerned for her, he should bring it and give it to her. But she was too tired to care.

Naked, she slipped out of bed and went over to take the robe from him. Instead he took it from the hanger himself and held it out for her to slip her arms into the sleeves. Josephine pulled it closed in front and tied the sash. It was very short, but comfortable, and reassuring.

'I don't suppose there's a pair of slippers in there too, is there?' she asked.

He opened the door again, gesturing for her to look.

Inside the wardrobe were all her clothes, everything the nurse had taken away from her at the clinic: her white top and skirt, hanging on hangers. Her bra and panties were folded up on the floor of the wardrobe. She took them out and unfolded them. They had been laundered, washed and ironed.

She turned and looked at Dr Hazel, holding her underwear in her hand.

'Do you want to get dressed?' he asked her. 'There's no need, but of course, if it would make you more comfortable...'

Josephine shook her head and put the things back in the wardrobe.

'I can't see my sandals anywhere,' she said.

'I'm sorry,' he said. 'I'll ask Jackie in the morning.'

All Josephine wanted was to go back to sleep, and to catch the first train home in the morning. But he was adamant and wouldn't hear of not doing something for her tonight. And he was right, she was stiffening up.

'Come down to the dispensary,' he said. 'I can put something on that will ease the ache.'

|11|

Barefoot on the soft carpet, hugging the green robe tight about her, Josephine followed Dr Hazel out of Room 3 and along the corridor. The lights were glowing dimly on reduced power. He led her not to the main staircase but the other way, to a door at the end of the corridor, which he opened and shone his torch through. Josephine saw a narrow stone staircase leading down into darkness.

She looked at him questioningly.

'I'm afraid the lights seem not to be working,' he said, flipping a wall switch up and down and tutting to himself. 'This is all most unsatisfactory. Things are clearly getting out of hand here in my absence. I shall telephone Mrs Taylor at seven o'clock, Ms Morrow, please believe me.'

He put out his hand to help her.

'It's all right,' she said. 'I can manage.'

Dr Hazel led the way, shining his torch on the steps.

'There will be light further down,' he said.

She didn't ask how he knew. She kept close behind him. The stone was cold beneath her feet.

They went down one darkened flight, turned a corner and went down another, then a third. The walls were plain, cold stone.

Josephine didn't like this. 'Is the dispensary in the cellar?'

'That's right,' he said, not pausing or turning round. 'Many medicines must be kept cool, you know.'

'I suppose so,' she said. She lingered on the stairs.

'Come along, Ms Morrow,' said Dr Hazel, not turning.

'I'm tired,' she said. 'I think I'll just go back to bed.'

Dr Hazel turned then and smiled up at her. His face looked sinister in the torchlight. 'No, Ms Morrow,' he said. 'You will not. You will come with me.'

Josephine turned and started back up the stairs.

At once he was upon her, holding her by the elbows. He spoke softly into her ear. 'No, Ms Morrow,' he said. 'You are in Estwych now, and must obey me. At Estwych,' he said, 'obedience is the law.'

It was true. It was all true. And Dr Hazel was in on it too.

He put his hand on the back of her neck and turned her head to face him. 'You will learn,' he promised her. Then he kissed her mouth.

She struggled, but he held her tight. His lips were warm and moved upon hers with great assurance. His tongue probed between her lips and found the tip of her tongue. He pushed her back, firmly, against the wall of the stairs and kissed her. He pressed his body against hers, naked beneath the thin dressing gown. She lifted her hands and laid them on his chest, as if to push him away, to push him downstairs; but she did not push.

Josephine felt the sensual warmth of his questing tongue, the hard stone of the wall at her back. Her heart was beating, beating like a drum.

Dr Hazel pulled back, still keeping one hand behind her head.

They looked at each other in the torchlight.

'You have come very far,' he said, 'and learned many things.'

Dumb, rapt, she stared at him like a bird at a snake.

'You are ready for the next lesson,' he said.

She tried to break away. 'No — '

'Yes,' he said. His voice echoed in the stone passage.

He kept one hand lightly gripping the back of her neck as she went before him down the stairs.

'Not much further,' he said.

At the foot of the stairs the passage, low-ceilinged and floored with hard-packed dirt, led away to the right, deep under the house. Everything was damp and very cold. Josephine wondered if they might even be beneath the river. They walked along by the light of the torch past stacked old furniture, barrels and trunks, bales of mildewed paper. More than once she heard the scuttling of tiny clawed feet, somewhere out of sight.

Ahead was a doorway filled with firelight. The heavy door of old black oak stood open.

'Inside,' Dr Hazel instructed her.

She went in. Dr Hazel followed her, and the door slammed heavily shut behind them.

The cellar was a dungeon, broad and low, cavernous and full of shadows. The light was the light of a brazier glowing fitfully in the centre of the earthen floor. There were people standing around it, dark apparatus standing all around, and hanging from the walls. There was a smell of sweat, of smoke and damp.

Josephine looked across the fire and saw a short, stout woman wearing a lavender dress and brown boots.

'Annabel,' she said.

'Hello, Miss Morrow,' said Annabel.

'You're supposed to be in Hampstead,' Josephine said. She heard herself, trying to make light of this nightmare, trying to keep away the fear.

'Perhaps we are in Hampstead, Josephine,' said Dr Hazel. His voice sounded flat in the cellar. 'Perhaps Hampstead is in Estwych.'

Josephine shivered.

She saw the housekeeper was holding something in her hand, a stick of wood with rags wrapped round it. She dipped the rag into the brazier. It caught immediately. Annabel held it out and a young woman in the familiar black and white maid's uniform took it from her.

It was Janet. She gave no sign of recognising Josephine. Holding the blazing torch well away from herself, she went across the dungeon, firelight dancing all around her little form, to climb up on a stool and set the torch in a bracket on the wall.

Annabel meanwhile lit another torch, and another. A second maid, a black girl no older than Janet, took them and went further off to set them in a black iron stand that looked hundreds of years old. The black girl was not introduced.

In the spreading torchlight, Josephine could see now. She could see everything.

There was a pillory, a hinged plank across the top of a pole, with holes for a victim to put their head and hands through, and a fat iron padlock to lock it tight. There was a tilted slab of wood so old and stained it was almost black: at the bottom were irons for the feet and at the top, a pair of manacles attached to a roller that could be turned, slowly and inexorably, by a great spoked wheel like a windlass. There was a gruesome shape that looked like a woman made of ancient iron, hinged at one side and open at the other to show, within, an array of thoughtfully positioned spikes. On the walls hung knives, whips, flails, tongs.

Everywhere there were chains: hanging in loops from the ceiling

99

or piled at the feet of the machines like slumbering iron snakes.

'No!' said Josephine again, turning to Dr Hazel shaking her head in fear. 'I – I can't – '

Dr Hazel seized her by the elbows, turning her to face the fire. She struggled, tried to pull away, but Annabel was upon her, lifting her arm and bringing it down.

There was a swish and an echoing crack, and pain seared Josephine's bare thighs. Her legs gave way, and she fell to the ground, crying out. Annabel stood over her, a short whip of braided leather in her hand.

'You must not speak, Josephine,' said Dr Hazel. 'Very soon all your questions will be answered. Only now you must be obedient, and not speak.'

Gasping for breath, lying on the floor with her thighs on fire, Josephine could not disobey.

Dr Hazel snapped his fingers. The maids came hurrying to him and began to strip off his clothes. While Janet untied his shoes and removed them one after the other, the black girl took his jacket and expertly unbuttoned his shirt. Underneath he wore a tight sleeveless tunic of black leather. It shone darkly in the firelight. Janet unzipped his fly and pulled his trousers down. Josephine saw that the tunic ended at the waist. Beneath he was wearing a complicated kind of jock strap, with a codpiece that had chased silver fastenings. As he turned, one hand resting his weight on the head of the crouching Janet to slip his feet into the long black boots the black maid had fetched for him, Josephine saw that at the back the jock strap was merely a single thong that rose between his buttocks, leaving them bare.

Josephine tried to rise.

'Don't get up, Miss Morrow,' Annabel advised her. 'There's no need.'

Without instruction, the maids came to where she lay and lifted her to her knees. They stripped off the green gown, laying her body bare. They they drew her hands out in front of her, crossed them at the wrist, and snapped a heavy pair of black iron handcuffs on her.

She knelt there, naked and restrained, while Janet buckled a leather collar about her neck. No one spoke. Josephine heard the women's breathing, soft and even, the rustling of Janet's petticoats, the crackling of the fire.

Dr Hazel and Annabel now came forward and stood over her. From the black maid Dr Hazel took a pair of leather bands and fastened them about his wrists, looking as if he was about to perform some strenuous activity.

Josephine was sure now what it would be.

Her mouth dry, her head dazed from sleep and the wine, from disorientation and fear, she knelt and watched Dr Hazel slip something over his face.

It was a slender black mask: a domino.

At a signal, the maids each took one of Josephine's arms and lifted her to her feet. Leaving Janet to lead her forward a yard or two, the black girl went off to the far side of the cellar and started to operate a wheel on the wall.

Janet pressed Josephine's shoulder, making her kneel down again. Meanwhile, above her head, something squealed, regularly and rhythmically.

In dread she looked up. She saw a chain running along the ceiling to a pulley, which was turning as the maid turned the wheel, lowering a length of chain towards her head.

Gently Janet pulled Josephine's arms, drawing them up over her head.

'No!' cried Josephine, struggling.

Annabel lashed her again with the whip, catching her across the shoulders.

Again she cried out, squeezing her eyes shut and arching her back with the pain. Encumbered as she was, she would have fallen on her face if the maid hadn't supported her.

Numbly, the stripes across her thighs and back burning, she felt her cuffs padlocked to the end of the chain. Then the maid at the wheel began to turn it back the other way, and Josephine was slowly drawn upwards by her hands. The huge cuffs supported her wrists as she was pulled, first to her feet, then up on tiptoe. The pulley squeaked and squealed.

Dr Hazel made a signal, and the squealing stopped.

Josephine hung by her hands, her toes touching the floor just enough to share the weight. She felt as if her arms were going to pull out of their sockets.

Dr Hazel came and stood before her.

He smiled a narrow smile.

The firelight flickered on his face as he contemplated her helpless body.

101

When he spoke, it was to Annabel.

'Has the slave been prepared?'

'Yes, sir,' said Annabel quietly. 'She has learned to bend to the hand, and to the brush.' The housekeeper spoke as if the doctor had not himself examined Josephine's marks, a few minutes before. She spoke as if to another man entirely.

'Does she understand?' he asked.

Annabel looked up at Josephine. Her kindly face was changed by the torchlight. She seemd intent, almost predatory.

'Not yet, sir,' said Annabel. 'That will come.'

Dr Hazel dismissed her with one hand. Josephine heard the whisper of her skirt as she stepped two paces away.

The man in the mask stood for a moment regarding her, his hands on his hips. He stood motionless, a statue of cruelty in his costume, the black leather tunic, wristbands, boots and mask. And Annabel completed the image by putting the whip into his outstretched hand.

'I shall advise you to turn around, my dear,' Dr Hazel went on. 'Since this is your first formal encounter with the whip, I shall try to confine my attentions to your back, your buttocks and thighs. If you spin around too much on the chain, I fear I may catch you once or twice in more sensitive areas. Will you turn now, please?'

But Josephine was unable to move, even to tear her eyes away from the masked man with the whip.

Dr Hazel clicked his tongue. 'Dawn, Janet,' he called. 'Position the slave.'

The maids hurried forward and, holding Josephine by the hips and thighs, spun her around again so her back was to her tormentor. Their hands were warm on her cold skin.

Her mouth trembled. She felt a flood of words threatening to burst out, pleading, begging them to release her.

But she knew if she uttered so much as a syllable, she was lost. She bit her lip and screwed shut her eyes.

As if he had read her mind, Dr Hazel continued suavely, 'Later perhaps you will be permitted a gag. But tonight – tonight you must learn how to howl and scream and beg.'

Josephine stiffened.

'Oh yes, my dear,' he went on, detecting her movement, 'you will beg. And you will scream, I promise you that. Scream all you wish, my dear: no one will hear you.'

She heard him step towards her, his boots loud on the hard-packed earth.

'Your treatment will consist of ten strokes, Ms Morrow,' he said. 'This is the first.'

Whikk!

It fell diagonally down her back, from her right shoulder to her waist. It was like an electric shock, so fierce and so sudden that her mind hardly registered it at first, while her heart stopped and her body spasmed and kicked. Then, an instant later, the pain came surging up her spine and every nerve of her back screamed aloud in her head.

She bit down on her tongue, desperate to deny him the satisfaction of hearing his promise fulfilled.

The lash fell again, from left to right, making an exact cross with the first stroke. Josephine felt her eyes starting to tear. She would not cry out. She wouldn't.

The third stroke.

'*Aaahh!*' she cried.

It had come sooner than the second, catching her off guard, falling horizontally across her waist. Her entire back was numb, tingling, numb again. He whipped her again, moving down to the swell of her buttocks, whipping her from left to right, and from right to left. She dangled at the end of her chain like a maltreated puppet, and as the whip caught her from the left, so she swung a little way to the left as if to meet it. Then it came again from the right, and back she swung that way, helpless as a doll.

How many strokes had she had now? Dazed, she had lost count. Her arms were shrieking to be freed, her heart was thudding in her breast, and to her horror tears were coursing down her cheeks. When he hit her again, she heard herself scream aloud. How could he do this to her, rouse her from her bed and trick her with his talk of ointments and care? They would find her. They would come after her and rescue her from this prison.

Who would?

Nobody.

To her horror, Josephine felt herself spinning round.

She flailed with her feet, trying desperately to halt her spin. It was useless, her own momentum was against her. She glimpsed Dr Hazel, the whip curling back over his shoulder from his upraised hand.

'No, no!' she cried. She begged. She heard her own voice calling

103

out, pleading with him to stop. She tried to swing back out of his reach but she had no leverage. Then she tried and tried to swing herself further around, to turn her back to him when that hateful whip fell again.

It fell. It caught her across her right flank, lashing down upon her right buttock and down her thigh. She jerked and squealed on her chain.

Then she saw, through the thickening smoke of the fires and the mist of her tears, that it was over. Dr Hazel was handing the whip back to Annabel. The black maid, Dawn, was down on her knees before him. She was deftly handling the straps and buckles of his costume, quickly unfastening his jock strap.

As Josephine hung before them, burning and sobbing, she saw the young girl's expert fingers slip Dr Hazel's cock from its concealment. It was long, circumcised, with a purple tip, and straining erect. Dr Hazel was smiling distantly at Josephine over Dawn's head. Dawn was slipping his cock into her mouth.

She seemed to be doing it perfectly willingly, as if it were an everyday duty of hers, to suck the doctor's cock, while Annabel the house-keeper and Janet stood placidly by.

Josephine hung her head, exhausted, her sobs abating. Through a mist of fiery pain she heard Dr Hazel grunt with pleasure as Dawn's tongue found a tender spot. She heard him hiss through his teeth.

As if involuntarily, not knowing why she did, Josephine lifted her head again to look. The doctor stood, legs braced wide apart, gripping his fingers tight in the tangle of Dawn's black curls. He stood there, gasping and snarling and muttering foul-sounding words in a foreign language as the maid worked away at him, her face bobbing at his crotch.

Josephine averted her face and spun slowly away on her chain. But as she did so, Annabel gave a sign and the other maid stepped forward and prevented her, standing behind her and holding on to her aching legs. She stood and held Josephine so that she faced squarely the grim tableau before her. Evidently Dr Hazel wished to have the tear-filled eyes of his victim upon him as he climaxed, thrusting himself deep into the mouth of the gulping girl.

It was soon done.

Scarcely was the last guttural shout of triumph out of him than Dr Hazel thrust his young fellatrix brusquely aside and came striding up

104

to Josephine. His cock shivered and dripped.

Swaying, almost fainting from her ordeal, Josephine turned her head away again, pulling against Janet's grip. But she had no strength left.

Dr Hazel reached up with one hand and grasped her chin, making her look at him, at his moist and shrivelling organ. Then he dipped his other hand between her legs.

Josephine gasped.

Smiling a satiated smile, Dr Hazel withdrew his fingers from her crotch and held them up for her to see.

They were wet.

He lifted them to her nose. She smelled the familiar smell of herself, of her own body when she was aroused. It was the scent that clung to her fingers every time she masturbated. Yet she felt nothing. She was bewildered, horrified.

Dr Hazel let go her chin and Josephine's head fell forward. She couldn't hold it up any longer. The ferocious stinging of the whip had died already to a deep and painful throbbing, and the circulation in her arms felt as if it had stopped for good.

'She's nearly ready,' Josephine heard Annabel say complacently, as if she were a turkey trussed for roasting, or a baby learning to crawl.

Josephine heard their footsteps moving away across the torture chamber.

They were leaving her. They were going away and leaving her dangling there, whipped, forsaken and alone.

She lifted her head.

'Dr Hazel!' she cried. Her voice echoed through the growing murk. She heard the tall man laugh. 'I'm not Dr Hazel,' he said.

He said it chidingly, almost gently, as if he were disappointed in her for ever believing him.

Then they took a torch each and went out. The great oak door boomed shut behind them with the finality of a deserted tomb.

One by one, the last fires guttered and went out.

|12|

It was an hour before she thought to try the handcuffs.

By pushing down with her feet until she was on tiptoe, and straining upwards, she could just reach the catches of the handcuffs with the tip of her index finger.

They weren't locked. They were toy handcuffs, like the pair they had put on her at the hotel that afternoon. They closed with a spring-loaded catch.

Groaning aloud, Josephine managed to flick the left cuff open. Suddenly released, she fell to the floor, a mass of pins and needles and aching, punished flesh. The chain swung, creaking into silence overhead.

She lay there for a minute, panting in the dark. Then she pulled herself together and got to her feet.

They'd taken the gown away. Every time she took her clothes off, someone took them away.

She padded to the door, grabbed the heavy ring-shaped handle and twisted it, expecting it to be locked.

It wasn't.

She heaved it open. Naked and shivering, she hurried out into the corridor.

She came to the stairs and started up them, her stiff legs and aching back complaining at every step.

In the darkness she blundered along an upstairs corridor, searching for a light switch. For all her groping along the walls, her fingers couldn't find anything but pictures, horse brasses, heavy wooden beams thick with cold paint. Everything was silent, everyone asleep.

Josephine turned a corner. By moonlight through a window she could see another landing, and a flight of stairs leading up.

This wasn't the way back to her room. She'd taken a wrong turning somewhere.

She turned back into the darkness, looking for the passage she'd missed.

There was a bar of light under one of the doors. Number 9.

Who lived in there? Annabel? The blond man who had whipped her? One of the infinitely obliging maids?

Josephine leaned one hand on the wall. She wanted to knock on the door. But she couldn't. She couldn't make herself to do it. Still she must have made some sound, for the next thing that happened was, the door opened slightly, and a face looked out into the hallway.

The shaft of light was dim, but it fell straight on Josephine's face and on her naked body.

She made no attempt to cover herself. Let them look.

The figure standing in the doorway was a young woman in a nurse's uniform. Starched cap, starched white apron, pinstriped short-sleeved dress, black nylons and lace-up shoes. She had a little watch pinned to the breast of her apron.

'Hello, Ms Morrow,' she said softly.

Josephine recognised her then. But she couldn't speak. She leaned on the doorframe, her knees giving way.

The nurse reached out her hand. 'For goodness' sake,' she said. 'Come in the warm.'

She caught hold of Josephine under the arms, pulling her body to her gently but firmly, supporting her weight. In a daze, Josephine thought how scrubbed and clean she smelt. Her fingernails were neatly trimmed. Her red-gold hair was pulled back in a neat bun and fastened with hairgrips.

She carried Josephine into the room.

Once inside she shifted her grip, putting an arm around Josephine's back. Josephine stiffened, cried out in pain.

The nurse said, 'Hush, now.'

She pushed the door to with her free hand and guided Josephine to the bed. It was a double bed, covered in a cheap Indian print bedspread. Josephine sank onto it, lying on her side, her knees drawn up, trembling.

As the nurse went back to close the door, Josephine looked vaguely at her surroundings. The light was dim: a single lamp at the bedside was the only light she had on.

The room was much like number 3, though it looked as if it had been occupied for some time. There seemed to be a lot of furniture:

a pair of armchairs, a wardrobe, an ironing board, a table pushed back against one wall. Everything was strewn with magazines and clothes, pairs of tights and cassette cases in a cheerful jumble. The wardrobe door was open, with a dress hanging over it and a bulging plastic carrier bag hanging from the doorknob. At the foot of the bed was a tiny TV sharing a sewing table with a large floppy green plant in a bright ceramic pot. The TV was on, the sound turned low. John Mills was standing on the bridge of a warship, holding a pair of binoculars and saying something to a scared-looking rating.

The nurse went to the TV and turned it off.

She stood by the bed, her clean white hands folded. Josephine looked up at her.

'He said he was Dr Hazel,' she said.

'Who did?'

'Tall man,' Josephine said. 'Blond.' She closed her eyes, saw his face again rushing towards her in the darkness on the stairs. 'And Annabel, and — the maid, she — '

She saw the man in his torturer's costume, his hand crushing a handful of the black girl's hair as her mouth worked busily at his swollen groin.

Her own groin had been wet, seeping with inexplicable desire.

She jerked her head backwards on the pillow, gazing up at the nurse, a white vision in the gentle light. Her womb pulsed within her in time to the throbbing of her stripes.

'Sven,' the nurse said. 'He likes to make his mark quickly.'

Her voice was measured and low.

More intently she asked, 'Did he give you anything?'

'He — ' Josephine's voice caught. She was fighting tears. 'He whipped me.'

'Nothing else?' said the nurse. 'Open your hands,' she commanded.

Josephine was holding her hands clenched tight between her thighs. Stiffly she drew them out, opened them.

The nurse took them in her own cool hands, looked to see if she was holding anything.

'What — ' Josephine began to ask.

'Doesn't matter,' she said quickly.

She put a hand on Josephine's shoulder. Josephine winced, rolled forward, her face in the pillow, her back exposed to the nurse's mild, forgiving gaze.

The nurse put one knee up on the bed.

She leaned over Josephine, examining her. Her fingertips traced the line of a weal and Josephine stiffened, catching her breath.

She felt the fingers travel down to her bottom, stroking the dull burning flesh as though to draw out the heat of all her punishments.

The nurse asked, 'Who else?'

'Who?'

'Someone else has been seeing to you.'

'Annabel...'

'Not the cane,' the nurse observed.

'No, she – '

To say the word was more humiliating than anything so far.

'She spanked me,' Josephine whispered.

The tears came then.

Heedless, she wept into the crisp white pillows.

'Oh, hush now, hush,' the nurse said.

She bent her head very close. She murmured in Josephine's ear.

'You can tell me.'

Josephine twisted her head round, looked up into shining green eyes. She blinked. Tears ran from her eyes, back into her hair.

'With a brush,' she said.

'Did you disobey?'

'I – '

'Were you – ' she asked it with firm deliberation. 'Disobedient?'

With the side of her finger she wiped a tear from Josephine's face.

'Yes,' whispered Josephine. 'I wouldn't put on the – '

The nurse was waiting.

'The clothes,' said Josephine. Ridiculously, she felt herself blushing.

The nurse shifted on the bed, kneeling up on both knees, sitting back on her calves, close to Josephine's side. 'And before that?' she asked, assuredly. 'Before the brush? Was there someone else?'

'In the cab ... the driver ...'

Confessing, the tension left her chest. She felt empty, washed up on a strand of pain. But she was not deserted, not alone. She looked up at the nurse in the soft light, seeing the spray of freckles on her downy cheeks, the wisps of fine copper hair that escaped from under her starched cap. Her breasts were a comforting swell beneath her white apron. Josephine's heart was still hammering as this gentle, confident young woman stroked her skin.

109

'Were you disobedient?' the nurse asked again. The word was warm and powerful on her lips and she lingered on it as she spoke.

'I told him stories,' said Josephine. She remembered. She felt foolish. She shut her eyes. Tears squeezed between the lids. 'I'd left the handcuffs ... the blindfold.'

'Left them where?'

Josephine looked at her uncertainly. 'At the hotel.'

'Ah. And what happened there? At the hotel?'

'They said I shouldn't have put the towel on.'

'Who said?'

'The man, Sven. I think. He had a woman with him.'

'Twice already,' said the nurse. 'He likes you,' she said, suggestively. She spoke in the tones of a lover teasing a lover.

She sat on the bed, shifting close to Josephine. She reached out a hand towards her, as if about to take hold of her right breast.

Alarmed, apprehensive, Josephine tensed, turning half onto her back, gripping the mattress with both hands.

'We all like you, Josephine,' said the nurse, smiling a smile of purest, saddest love.

She patted Josephine's shoulder with her hand, fingers spread widely. For a moment, her wrist brushed Josephine's nipple: the merest touch.

Josephine froze. Warmth plunged inside her, twisting down through her hollowness, piercing from her nipple to her womb, seeking out her innermost part.

The nurse lifted her head, looking Josephine in the face with an expression of mischievous apprehension.

'Do you understand yet?' she asked keenly, as if it were a great hoax, a joke with a cryptic punchline. 'Do you understand now?'

'No,' moaned Josephine, understanding nothing. She felt herself weeping again.

'Don't be sad,' said the nurse then, kindly. 'Dr Hazel will be here soon.'

'There really is a Dr Hazel?'

The nurse nodded her lovely head. 'Believe me,' she said.

'Can I?' Josephine asked dully.

'This is Estwych,' said the nurse. 'You can believe what you like — as long as you obey the law.'

She drew a finger along one of the marks Sven had put there with

110

his whip, down Josephine's back to her bottom.

Josephine shivered. Her tears stopped. She felt as light as a cork, bobbing on a high tide of fear and longing and despair.

'What would you like?' asked the nurse.

'Like?' said Josephine.

'Yes. If you could have anything in the world right now, what would you like? Would you like to go home?'

'No,' said Josephine. She could hear them both breathing.

She thought again of the man called Sven, pressing her against the wall, kissing her against her will. Why did he lash her? Why did it excite him? Why had she been wet? What did Annabel mean, saying she was 'nearly ready'?

'It can stop whenever you choose, you see,' the nurse was saying. 'All you have to do is put your clothes on and go home. They're in your wardrobe.'

Joephine remembered. 'Did you put them there?' she asked.

'That's right,' said the nurse. 'Would you like to go back to your room now?'

She asked it with her mischievous look again, as if she was only teasing.

'No,' said Josephine. Her voice was small.

Timidly she lifted her hand, unsure what she was going to do, what she was reaching for.

Before Josephine could complete the motion, the nurse had slipped down from the bed. She was walking away, out of Josephine's view. Josephine heard the whisper of her nylons and her starched cotton skirt as she crossed the silent room. Her senses were all alert, her back was crawling with ragged fire. She was trapped in a body she no longer understood. Her will had been disconnected. She could not move.

She heard the nurse open a door and switch on a light. She heard her shoes walking on lino; heard the click of a spring catch as she opened a cupboard; heard the scrape of glass pots on wood.

She waited.

The nurse turned the light off and came out of the bathroom.

She walked back to the bed. Josephine saw she was holding a small jar with something white in it.

'On your tummy,' she told Josephine. With professional deftness, she whisked off the lid of the jar.

'What are you — '

111

'This will help,' she said.

Josephine stared at her. 'That's what Sven said,' she told her. 'Then he took me downstairs and whipped me.'

'I'm not Sven. I'm not going to whip you,' said the nurse, dabbing the fingers of her right hand in the cream. 'Promise.'

Josephine turned over and the nurse patted cream on her back. 'Not tonight,' she said.

Josephine hissed. 'It stings.'

'Doesn't it just.' She could hear the smile. 'It feels better in a minute,' the nurse said.

She rubbed the salve in smooth, slow, firm strokes diagonally down Josephine's back.

Josephine murmured wordlessly, her face pressed into the pillow. The sting flared and broadened and dulled, dying away, and she began to feel a wonderful sense of coolness and release.

She felt the nurse working her way down the weal where the whip had caught her turning. The expert fingers followed it as it curled around her hip.

'They saw to you well,' she said. There was admiration, even envy in her voice.

'Did they?'

Josephine remembered her thought about the taxi man when he was spanking her, that he was an expert.

'They did. You're a lucky girl.'

'I'm not a girl,' Josephine said.

'You are,' said the nurse warmly. 'Inside.'

'No,' said Josephine.

'Are you not?' said the nurse, conversationally. Her hand moved up over the small of Josephine's back and down. She began slowly to spread the cream on her bottom.

'I think that's the worst, the whip,' she said. 'Especially the first time. It feels worse the first time, because you're new and you've no idea what's happening.'

She smacked Josephine's left thigh lightly, twice.

'Open your legs a bit.'

Shifting on the coarse cotton spread, Josephine complied.

The nurse's hand slipped sweetly and softly down the crack of her bottom and into her crotch. The cream tingled as it found the sensitive pucker of Josephine's anus and brushed the lips of her vulva. Then the deep coolness began to spread.

'Aaahh...' she sighed.

'Is that nice?'

'Mmm...'

Josephine closed her eyes. She felt the mattress move as the nurse put her weight on the bed. She was kneeling up beside her again, soothing the pain smouldering in her thighs and running her smooth hands down the backs of her legs.

Josephine opened her eyes. She turned her head to look at the nurse.

'Jackie,' she said. 'He said your name was Jackie. Sven. Or was that another lie?'

'No,' the nurse said. 'That's my name. Jacqueline. Everyone calls me Jackie.'

'Tell me about Dr Hazel,' said Josephine.

Jackie sat back on her heels, taking her hand from Josephine's thigh.

'Please don't stop,' Josephine said.

'I'm just getting some more cream,' said Jackie, pasting another stinging, cooling daub on the underside of Josephine's right buttock. 'You'll meet Dr Hazel in the morning,' she said.

'What will he do to me?'

'Oh, nothing.'

She rubbed in the cream, round and round and round. It was definitely working. Josephine could feel the relief — more than relief, pleasure.

'Not unless you really want it,' Jackie said.

Josephine felt a tiny thrill of fear.

'You can have anything here,' Jackie said softly, 'as long as you obey the law.'

She ran her knuckles very lightly up Josephine's spine, her hand crossing the marks of the whip like a train crossing the tracks: cold and hot and cold and hot.

Josephine moaned.

'It's confusing when you're new,' said Jackie. 'I remember.'

Josephine turned her head on the pillow. She looked at the kneeling nurse in the soft light of the bedroom. 'Do you?'

'Oh yes.'

'What happened to you?' Josephine asked.

113

|13|

Jackie told her: 'My mum and dad never laid a finger on me. They didn't think it was right. At least, my ma didn't, and she wouldn't have let my dad hit me if he'd tried. I never had a spanking till I went to stay with my Uncle Gilbert and Auntie Joan when I was nine. Uncle Gil put me across his knee and smacked me on the seat of my pants for spilling my milk. I was so shocked I didn't even think to cry.

'Auntie Joan made an awful fuss of me afterwards, cuddling me and telling me everything was all right now. I think she gave me a peppermint! But after that, every time I went to stay with them, they always managed to find some reason to take my knickers down and spank me. It was always, Jacqueline, I told you to make your bed; Jacqueline, you left the bathroom heater on. What did I tell you, girl? Come here, over my knee. Later it was: Jacqueline, your skirt's too short. Come here. Bend over.

'The funny thing was, I never told at home. I think my dad knew what was going on, but he never said. I think he thought it was probably good for me. I wasn't a naughty child, perhaps he thought that was why. Gil and Joan couldn't have children, it was like I was there to make up for it. Four or five times a year I went to stay, a weekend, sometimes a week or more. I liked going there, I was fond of them. I didn't mind the spankings.

'They made a special thing of it, quite a performance. I had to go and put the proper clothes on, a blouse and a skirt, or a dress, never jeans. And clean knickers. Every time, clean knickers. They had a special stool for me to bend over. They'd both be there, and I'd have to stand and look solemn while they gave me a little lecture. Then Auntie Joan would pat the seat of the stool and look at me meaningfully. "Come here, Jacqueline. Let's have you over here for your Uncle Gil."

114

'I'd bend over the stool and catch hold of the legs while Auntie Joan folded back my skirt and pulled down my knickers. She'd look inside to see they were clean. Then she'd pat me and say, "Are you all right, dear? All right, Gilbert, I think she's ready now." And he'd be taking off his slipper ... I tried not to shout, though the louder I shouted, the more fuss Auntie Joan would make of me afterwards. It was quite a game.

'The thing was, when I went away to start training, I quite missed all that. It was so regimented at the college, like an old-fashioned girls' school. But we didn't have the cane! We were being taught to be responsible, grown-up individuals. But really it was more like the army or something. Bells, lining up in queues, going to assemblies, report meetings — hurry up here, there and everywhere.

'Anyway. I was in a hostel. That was later, I was seventeen, eighteen maybe. I was sharing with a girl called Nicola. Nicola Reynolds. We were both a bit untidy, but we just made each other worse. I'd think, Oh, let her pick it up. And she'd be thinking, Oh, I'm not going to pick that up, let Jackie do it. And the next thing we knew, there'd be a surprise inspection and we'd be in trouble.

'You had to get so many points for hygiene and conduct, besides all your class work and going on the wards. When you did something wrong the warden would report you to the sister, and the sister would discipline you. If it was serious, she'd report you to Matron.

'Nicola and I were up before Sister. It was the umpteenth time. But this time Dr McAllan was there. He was smashing, Dr McAllan. We reckoned he and Sister had a thing going. He was thirty, maybe; he looked a bit like Sean Connery. Very dark, very sexy. A sexy little smile he had. He was smiling to himself, sitting there in his armchair watching us squirm. Yes Sister, no, Sister, sorry, Sister.

' "I don't know what I'm to do with you," Sister said.

'Then Dr McAllan spoke up. "Smack their bottoms for them, Sister," he said. "I would."

'That really woke me up. I hadn't heard that since years before, staying with Auntie Joan. I looked at Dr McAllan with my mouth open.

'But if I thought that was a surprise, what he said next bowled me over. Dr McAllen said, "I've smacked Nurse Reynolds's bottom for her once already, haven't I, Nurse?"

'I was amazed. I looked at Nicola. She was looking at the floor, looking as if she wished it would open up and swallow her. Her cheeks were bright pink.

115

' "Haven't I, Nurse Reynolds?" he said again.

' "Yes, doctor," she whispered.

'Well, you could have knocked me down with a feather, I swear you could.

' "Well, Nurse?" said Dr McAllan. "Must I do it again?"

'I saw Nicola duck a quick look up at him. Then she sort of shuffled towards him.

'That amused him greatly. "Good heavens, not here, girl!" he said. "In the gym,' he said, and he looked at his watch. "Shall we say five o'clock?"

'Nicola stepped back. She looked at the floor again. She wouldn't look at me.

'Sister did, though. She looked at me like I'd just crawled out from under a stone. "What about the other one, doctor?" she said. "Will you take care of her too?"

'Dr McAllan looked at me with his little smile. "I'd be delighted," he said.

'I swear I felt my knees going. I nearly fainted on the spot.

'Sister squared up the report book on her desk and leaned forward, planting her elbows and clasping her hands together. "I'll give you a choice," she said to us. "Dr McAllan at five o'clock this afternoon, or a mention in Matron's book."

'Nicola and I looked at each other for the first time. She had a sort of frozen look on her face, I couldn't tell what she was really thinking. I suppose I probably looked much the same.

'She brushed her hair away from her face and said something, something in a little murmur no one could properly hear.

' "What was that, Nurse Reynolds?" said Dr McAllan loudly. "Speak up, girl!"

' "It was my fault," said Nicola, dropping her hand and sticking her chin out like a soldier. "I'm the untidy one." She looked aside at me. "Not Jackie," she said.

'Dr McAllan looked hugely amused by this. "So you want to take both punishments yourself, eh, Nurse?"

'Nicola glanced at me again and nodded.

'I noticed Dr McAllan glance at me too, but he said, "That's all right by me if it's all right by Sister."

'I'd already imagined it in lurid detail. Me dropping my knickers and going over Dr McAllan's lap. His strong left arm going round my

116

waist, his strong right hand coming down on my bare bottom.

'I spoke up. "No," I said. "I'll be there, at five."

' "Both of you, then. Splendid," said Dr McAllan.

'Well, I grabbed hold of Nicola as soon as we got out of the office. "What does he do to you?" I said. "You never told me." She was dead embarrassed. She didn't want to talk about it. "You'll find out," she said.

'The gym was in the basement, it was where they did physiotherapy. We were there at five, on the dot, in our best uniforms. "He treats you just like a little baby," Nicola said as we went down in the lift. She was angry, and embarrassed, but she'd nerved herself up for it. "At least it gets it over with quick," she said.

'She knocked on the door, and there was Dr McAllan. He had a rugby shirt on and track suit trousers. He looked very cool, very stern. He said good afternoon, very formal, then he said, "Nurse Reynolds. Please come in." He held the door open, and Nicola patted her cap and strode in. Dr McAllan looked me straight in the eye and gave me a special smile. Then he closed the door. I was left there in the corridor, nervous as a kitten I was. There was nobody about. I put my hand up my skirt and touched myself. And I pressed my ear to the door.

'It didn't take long. I couldn't hear any words, but soon I heard — smack! smack! smack! Ten or twelve I think he gave her, and then she came out again, red in the face. She gave me a wild look and stalked off down the corridor like a child in a temper. She wasn't hanging around to listen to me get mine!

'Dr McAllan called me. I went in. It was quite a large room, the physio gym, with all the equipment. Wall bars and a little vaulting horse, some weights and a medicine ball. A little office for the therapists to use. I stood there in the middle of the floor, my arms by my sides, my heart pounding like a steam engine. He didn't bother telling me off. He just looked me in the eye. "Are you ready, Nurse?" he said.

' "Yes, doctor," I said, in a little whisper. I could hardly speak.

'He nodded at the wall bars. "Go and get hold of the bottom bar," he said.

'I went over to the wall and bent over. The bottom bar was about four inches off the floor. I caught hold of it. I stood absolutely still — legs straight, bottom taut.

'Dr McAllan came up behind me. I heard his gymshoes squeak on

117

the polished floor. I didn't look round. He lifted the skirt of my uniform and tucked it up. He started tugging my tights down. He said, "Do the regulations allow you to wear tights?"

' "Yes, doctor," I said.

' "In future you'll wear stockings and suspenders," he said. He was being very calm, very matter-of-fact, as if he had authority to decide what underwear I put on.

'Then he took down my knickers.

'I could feel the sticky wet patch in my knickers, I knew he'd see it. I thought, what would Uncle Gilbert and Auntie Joan have said? And what would Dr McAllan say?

'Well, Dr McAllan didn't say anything, just took hold of my hips and lined me up. "Legs apart, nurse," he said. I shifted my legs. I knew he was looking right in my crotch, seeing how eager and wet I was. He didn't say anything. He started to smack me.

'It wasn't that hard. Uncle Gil had smacked me harder, sometimes. But it was loud. Every time he smacked my bottom the sound echoed around the empty gym like a whipcrack. I bit my lip and tried not to cry out.

'Then he started playing with me himself. He started fingering me.

'He'd smack my bottom, and then he'd stroke me between the legs and run his finger up between my lips and back between my cheeks and play with my anus, and spread my juices around, just brushing my clit ever so lightly with the tip of his finger until I was gasping and begging, no, no, I don't know what I was saying. And then he'd start spanking me again.

'Then he made me kneel down in front of him. He made a sign that I was to take down his trousers.

'So then I thought, this is it. My bottom was tingling, my insides were churning, I was so excited I was panting like a bitch. I got hold of the elastic of his trousers and I pulled them down. He wasn't wearing anything underneath. I was amazed, he didn't even have an erection. There was me so hot and dripping with it, all running down my legs and he was still so cool. I thought, how does he control himself?

'Then he told me to kiss his thighs, and in his crotch, between his thighs, and fondle his balls. He told me to kiss his cock, and I did. Then he said to take the head of it in my mouth, just the head, and lick it until it was stiff.

'I'd never had a man's cock in my mouth before. It was so salty. And

118

I was nuzzling it and licking it, and it was getting bigger and harder. He started to groan, I thought he was going to come straight away. I was thinking, do I let him come in my mouth? Do I? Will he be angry if I take my mouth away when he comes? I didn't know what it would be like, having a man come in your mouth, I didn't know whether it would be nice. I didn't know much!

'But he had his hand on my head and he pushed me away and took hold of his cock himself. He was rubbing it, I knelt there on the floor looking up at him, waiting for him to tell me what to do next.

'He didn't smile. He still looked very stern. That made me just melt. I'd have done anything for him.

'He told me to go down on all fours with my legs apart, facing away from him, and he told me to play with myself. I didn't need telling twice. I went down on the floor and reached back between my thighs and started rubbing my clit. I gasped and moaned, I put it all on a bit for him, playing it up, and I was wondering all the while how I looked to him with my red bottom sticking up in the air and my hand at my crotch, rubbing away for all I was worth.

'He soon let me know what he thought. I glanced around and saw he was taking his clothes off. He was standing there with nothing on. He had a leather belt in his hand.

'I let out a gasp. He was holding the buckle and winding the belt around his hand, leaving a long end dangling. He came towards me. I moaned and rubbed myself harder and harder. He lifted up the belt.

'Jesus, that stung! He let me have four good ones, right across the backside, and didn't I yell?

'Then he told me to get up and go and bend over the vaulting horse, because he was going to give me a good leathering. And he did.

'Jesus, it hurt. But oh, as soon as the shock of each stroke was over and there was the fire burning in me, oh, that felt good. I'd never felt so good.

'And then as I lay there draped over the horse, clutching myself and moaning, gasping, he dropped the belt and grabbed me by the hips, and he thrust right into me. And that felt best of all.

'He had one knee up beside me, pressing against the horse, and his cock rammed right inside me. He was pulling me to him as he pounded away at me, crushing my blazing backside against his hip. I was seeing stars, I really was. I had my head down, was clawing at the floor and shouting at him, and he was banging away. Then I came.

119

It was so high and clear and cool I couldn't even feel the pain in my bottom for a minute. It was a minute that seemed to go on and on forever.

'I felt him come, throbbing inside me, and he fell forward, lying on my back, squashing me to the leather top of the horse. We were all sweaty. I still had all my clothes on. He pulled out of me, and stood up, leaning on the horse with one hand resting lightly on my back. I just lay there spent and gasping. Jesus, I was sore.

'He made me fetch tissues from the physio's office and clean us both up. His penis was all soft and dribbling. I wiped it gently, and I squatted down and wiped my crotch. He watched me. While I wiped myself he asked me whether I'd been punished before, and I told him about my aunt and uncle. He made me tell him everything.

'He was so masterful, even standing there in the gym with no clothes on. "Get dressed," he said. "Go back to your duties."

'Luckily Nicola had an evening off, and I didn't see her to speak to until the next day. I didn't want to tell her what we'd done, Dr McAllan and me. Wild horses wouldn't have dragged it out of me. And when I saw Dr McAllan next, on the wards, he was so cool, just his usual self, with his little smile and his sexy dark eyes. I was getting wet just from the sight of him. I felt myself blushing, I couldn't look at him.

'Then one day I had a note from Sister. I was to pack an overnight bag and report to the side gate. Dr McAllan was there, in his old green MG. "Get in," he said. I asked him where we were going. He told me, "You're going to be tested." I didn't know what he meant. I felt frightened but very excited, the way I had in the gym.

'As he drove away, he told me to pull up my skirt. I thought he wanted to check I was wearing stockings. I was, I'd changed over since he told me, hoping he might stop me in the corridor one day and inspect me. This was the first time he had. He barely glanced, and he drove on.

'I sat there in the car with my skirt up. I was so excited, but frustrated. I asked Dr McAllan if he wanted me to do anything else. I put my hand on his thigh.

'He knocked my hand away. He told me to tuck my skirt in my belt so it would stay up. He sounded cross.

'He hardly spoke to me after that. He blindfolded me for the last few miles, he said I wasn't to see where we were going. I don't know what people thought, this MG whizzing past with a doctor and nurse and the nurse with a blindfold over her eyes.

'At last the car stopped. He told me not to move. I heard him get out and slam the door, heard him walk away and ring a doorbell.

'I could hear water. It sounded like a river.

'A woman greeted him, called him doctor. He called her Annabel. They had a murmured conversation, I could only hear part of it. He said I was to be tested. He was handing me over to her. She sounded as if he'd told her all about me.

'I heard the car door open. It felt so strange, sitting there in the car with my skirt up and my eyes covered while a strange woman inspected me. I nearly jumped out of my skin when she touched my shoulder.

' "Come along, miss," said Annabel. Her voice sounded like one of the older nurses at the hospital. "Let's get you started."

'She led me indoors and upstairs. When she took my blindfold off I was in here. There was Annabel, in a long black dress with an apron over it, and a maid with my bag. I hadn't even known the maid was there. I felt so self-conscious, being there with my skirt tucked up around my waist, in a strange place with two strange women. I started to ask questions.

'Annabel told me to be quiet and take my clothes off. She told the maid to go and run a bath, and she stood there and watched me undress. Then she sent the maid away.

'She took me in the bathroom and bathed me. She asked me all about my aunt and uncle, what they'd done and hadn't done. I was mortified. He'd told her! He'd told her everything! I had to lie there in the bath with Annabel soaping me all over, sponging my breasts and my back, and then my bottom and between my legs, and all the while she kept asking, "Did they ever put a collar on you? Did they ever discipline you with the back of a hairbrush? After discipline, did you masturbate?"

'She dried me off with a big towel. She wouldn't let me do anything myself. She asked me, "Was Dr McAllan the first man to enter you during discipline?"

'I felt myself blushing. I said he was.

'She brought me back in here. She told me my clothes were in the wardrobe. She told me to put them on.

'There was a collar, a suspender belt, a pair of black stockings and a pair of black leather boots with heels.

'Annabel stood at the door with her hands folded and watched me put them on.

'Then she took me downstairs, just as I was, into the dining room. There was a maid there with a black leather briefcase.

'Annabel led me to the head of the table. She pulled the chair out and turned it round, and bent me right over the back of it, with my bare bottom towards the table.

'I heard her open the case and take some things out. I heard them clink in her hands.

'She put a chain around my wrists. It was cold. She chained my wrists to the front legs of the chair, and my ankles to the back legs. Then I felt her push something through my legs from behind. It felt like a leather belt.

'She left me there, with the belt hanging between my legs, over the back of the chair.

' "The others will be down shortly," she said.'

|14|

'WOuld you like a drink?'

Josephine lay on her stomach, her head turned sideways on the pillow. Rarely had she felt more relaxed, more alert. It was as if a new sense had opened up in her body.

'I'd like some gin,' said the nurse. 'How about you?'

'Yes,' said Josephine. 'Yes please.'

She looked up at her in the dim light.

'Was all that true?' she said.

'Every word of it,' said Jackie. She sat back on her heels again, her knees spread, making a taut lap in her uniform dress.

'How do you feel now, Ms Morrow?' she asked, professionally.

'All right,' said Josephine.

There was a catch in her voice.

'Not in pain now?'

'No.'

She really wasn't. There was a quiet burning sensation where the whip had marked her, but she couldn't have called it pain. Jackie had taken all that away with her ointment, and her hands, and her story.

Jackie stepped down off the bed, smoothing her dress, lifting an automatic hand to check her cap was in place. Josephine felt a sudden pang of distress, not wanting her to leave. Jackie must have sensed it. 'Just a minute, dear,' she said.

She went into the bathroom again. Josephine heard water running, briefly. Then Jackie was approaching with something small and shiny in her hand. She was shaking it up and down.

'On your back now,' she said gently. 'I want to take your temperature.'

Obediently Josephine rolled over. The burn of the whip flared as her back came into contact with the sheets, then subsided again. She opened her mouth.

123

Jackie came to the bed. She shook her head slightly.

'Open your legs,' she said.

Josephine spread her legs.

Her crotch was hot, her vulva soft and moist.

Jackie nodded approval. With deft fingers she slipped the thermometer into Josephine's vagina.

She could feel it there, cold for an instant, then warm. A tiny shudder of pleasure ran through her loins.

Jackie looked down with a smile of amusement. She reached down and brushed Josephine's fringe from her damp forehead.

Josephine said, 'Are you really a nurse?'

'If you want me to be,' said Jackie.

She turned her hand and ran the back of her fingers down Josephine's cheek, down her neck, letting her knuckles stray down between her breasts. Helplessly Josephine felt her body respond, her pelvis rising up from the bed as if to thrust against the little thermometer.

Jackie left her lying there and went over to the table. She crouched down and reached underneath it. Josephine saw the white fabric of her skirt tighten along her thigh.

She stood up with two tumblers in her hand and a bottle of gin in the crook of her arm. Coming back to the bed she sat down beside Josephine, stood the glasses on the bedside table and poured gin in them. 'I haven't any tonic,' she said gravely, 'or even any ice. I'm sorry.'

Her knees still spread, Josephine inched gingerly up the bed, trying not to disturb the thermometer. She reclined against the pillows and took her glass from Jackie. She drank. The raw spirit was a chemical on her tongue, a fire in her throat. It was like a new drug, a secret potion that would change her into something not human, a creature of quicksilver and chemical fire. She grimaced at the violent taste, drawing back her lips and sighing with fierce delight. She drained her glass.

The planes of the room, the face and form of Jackie sipping her gin and watching her tenderly, shifted subtly into new configurations. She felt the pores of her skin open, the hairs in her nostrils stir as Jackie bent over her again.

Jackie said, 'I think you're done.'

She slipped the thermometer from Josephine's richly oozing slit, drawing a string of silver mucus after it, and held it up to the light. Reading it, she raised her eyebrows and gave a small chuckle.

124

'What does it say?'

'It says you'll survive,' said Jackie. Then, catching Josephine's eye, she dipped the little glass tube into her glass like a swizzle stick, and stirred her drink with it.

'Antiseptic,' she said, 'gin.'

She took the thermometer from the glass and tapped it on the rim, shaking the last drops off. The clink of glass on glass rang distinctly in the silent bedroom.

Jackie lifted the glass to her lips and took a sip. She licked her lips, twitching her eyebrows suggestively.

The light of the lamp showed the soft down on her cheek, the glistening of her steady eyes.

Josephine pressed her greasy back against the pillows. Her heart was racing. Her breathing was fast and shallow. She was naked and fragile and defenceless. She took a large swallow of gin. Perhaps this was not happening. Perhaps it was a hallucination of alcohol on top of stress, disturbed sleep, pain and shock. Perhaps there was a drug in her glass again, or in the ointment. Fear fought with longing in her breast.

'Can I stay tonight?' she asked. 'Here, with you?'

Jackie looked down at her hands. She didn't want to reply. Josephine wondered what she'd said wrong.

'I don't want to be alone,' she said; and it was true.

Jackie looked up at her from under lowered brows. She smiled her mischievous smile.

'All right,' she whispered. 'But don't tell anyone.'

'No, no, of course...'

Jackie patted her hand: a reassuring, sexless gesture. She swung her legs to the floor and stood up, finishing the gin in her glass. She went into the bathroom and closed the door behind her.

Josephine put her glass down as gently as she could on the bedside table. She lay on the bed and listened to the quiet slither of cloth, the running of water. There was the rhythmic sound of Jackie brushing her teeth. Josephine switched out the bedside lamp. She climbed up and slid down in between the sheets.

The curtains were still open. While Jackie had been talking, the moon had come up above the trees and now it was shining directly in at the window, laying a lattice of shadow and cold silver light across the bed.

125

A woman, thought Josephine to herself. A woman's body.

She thought of Annabel and Dr Shepard, and then, at once, of Maria in the changing room at school. She frowned, pushing the memory away. Jackie's story was of a man, Dr McAllan. She had shared a room with another woman, not a bed.

The sheets were cotton crisp with starch, like Jackie's uniform. Josephine lay down flat and pulled the sheet up until it covered her breasts. She wondered if it would be safer to turn over and pretend to be asleep. She looked at the bathroom door, a black rectangle outlined in seeping yellow light.

At that moment, the light went out.

She heard rather than saw the door open. A shape came into the room, barefoot, silent as it came across the carpet to the bed. Josephine saw Jackie by moonlight, wearing a brief nightdress with a pattern of what she thought were little flowers. Her long hair was down now, sliding lightly across her shoulders as she put one foot up to climb into bed.

Josephine glimpsed a cave, a valley of black shadow between her thighs. Then Jackie was in bed, close beside her.

'Did you like my little story?' asked Jackie.

'Yes...' said Josephine.

Clumsily she put her arm across Jackie's body.

Jackie drew closer, snuggling up against her.

Josephine hugged her. An electric thrill of triumph sang through her bones.

'Did it excite you?' Jackie asked.

Josephine sniffed. There were tears in her eyes again. 'Yes,' she whispered. 'Yes!'

Hearing or sensing the tears, Jackie lifted her head. 'What's wrong?' she asked gently. 'Are you not happy?'

'I don't know,' Josephine said. Her voice sounded strange to her in the dark, feathery and high. 'I think I'm afraid.'

'I'll look after you,' said Jackie, patting Josephine's stomach. 'You're safe now, tonight,' she promised.

Josephine sighed. Longing filled her.

She drew her hand across Jackie's back, caressing her.

She drew it across Jackie's arm, and laid it gently on her breast.

She felt Jackie catch her breath.

Then Jackie's voice in the dark asked: 'Will you tell me a story now?'

126

Josephine stirred, distracted. 'It wouldn't be true.'

'It doesn't matter.'

But Josephine said, 'It does. It does.'

She took her hand from Jackie's breast, levered herself up on one elbow and reached for her glass. She could see it beside the bed like a glass of liquid silver in the moonlight. She brought it carefully to her mouth and took a sip.

'I'm tired of fantasies,' she said. 'Tired of stories.'

She offered the glass to Jackie. She saw Jackie lift her head and open her mouth. Josephine thought, I shall spill it; but the gin had given her courage and she set the glass to Jackie's lips and tilted it so a little of the drink ran into her mouth. She felt Jackie swallow.

She took another sip herself and put the glass aside again. She leaned over Jackie. Her arms were like wings, carrying her across the crumpled moonlit landscape of the bed.

'I want you,' she said.

Jackie let herself be embraced. She did not respond.

'It was me took your clothes away this morning,' she whispered.

What on earth did that have to do with anything?

'I don't care,' said Josephine.

It seemed weeks ago, and worlds away.

Jackie said, 'My uncle Gil would have smacked my legs for a trick like that.'

Josephine held her close.

'I forgive you,' she said.

She brought her face close to Jackie's and kissed her on the mouth. A shudder surged in her belly.

Growing bolder, Josephine fondled Jackie's breasts through the fabric of her nightdress. She brought her knees up and rubbed the inside of her thigh up along Jackie's thigh, feeling the cloth ride up between them, feeling the smoothness of Jackie's skin, the jutting corner of the hip under her thigh.

She kissed Jackie's face, her hair, her cheek. She was breathing hard now with relief and desire. She dipped her face between Jackie's head and shoulder, kissing Jackie's neck and rubbing her cheek against her shoulders. The nightdress was cool cotton, soft, not starched.

Josephine drew back her head, looking searchingly at Jackie in the moonlight. She seemed to have become completely passive, limp and

127

unresisting in Josephine's arms. Josephine freed her right hand and stroked the hair back from Jackie's face.

'Are you all right?' she murmured.

Jackie made a small, soft sound, a wordless assent.

Josephine buried her face in Jackie's neck, nuzzling her throat, her hands roaming around her body. She reached down to caress her leg, ran her hand around the back of her thigh, pressing it between her bottom and the bed.

It was just like being with a man, and yet not like it at all. Larry was hairy; his body was all hard muscled shapes unprotected by fat; he had never been so inert, so sensitive. The gin percolated through Josephine's nerve ends and into her brain, and evaporated in a cool white flare. She was so tense now with sex and urgency she could not feel the drink at all. Her nerves were crystalline, her head was transparent. She was one with the moonlight, inside and out. Jackie's body smelt of soap and warm milk. Her pores breathed liquid joy.

Josephine slipped her hand between Jackie's legs.

Jackie gasped, bowing forward in the bed, hunching her shoulders as though something had pierced straight through her womb, pinning her to the bed.

Her crotch was dewy with the first trickle of desire.

Josephine kisssed her, pressing her tongue between her teeth and into her mouth. She took her hand from her crotch and ran it up over her stomach, rubbing her pubic hair against the bone with the heel of her hand. She reached up under Jackie's nightdress for her breasts, and ran her fingers over her nipples.

The moonlight made Jackie's face the face of a strange creature, a child of the stars, of something other than flesh. But it was flesh under Josephine's hand, warm tender flesh.

She kissed Jackie's forehead. She plucked at the nightdress.

'Take it off,' she said.

Jackie sat up in bed. Josephine drew away to give her room as she worked the nightdress up and over her head, and flung it away into the dark, lost, unheeded.

Jackie lay down again. Josephine stroked her breasts. She rubbed her cheek against them. She thought of Sven, at the hotel, handling her breasts as if they were his to do with as he liked. Was it the truth?

She raised her head to look at Jackie's breasts in the mysterious light. When had she ever seen an adult woman's breasts, bare and free?

128

'What's that?' she asked.

'What?'

There was a mark between Jackie's breasts, a dark design on her white skin. 'This,' said Josephine, touching the mark with one finger, slipping the other hand behind the small of Jackie's back.

Lying on her back, Jackie looked along her nose to see where Josephine was stroking her, as if she did not know what could be drawn there, in between her breasts. She put her finger where Josephine's was.

There was quite enough light to make it out. It was a tattoo, the same design as was on the key tag, and the handle of the spoon. The domino mask.

'What is it?'

'It means I belong here,' said Jackie.

Suddenly she ran the back of her fingers through Josephine's wet crotch, slicked them up through her pubic hair, making her gasp. She darted her head up and took Josephine's nipple into her mouth.

The room funnelled away to infinity. Josephine had never felt such a jolt of passion and power.

Josephine rolled over on her back, Jackie in her arms. Jackie wriggled. She straddled Josephine with her slim legs. Josephine let go of her waist and slipped her left hand into Jackie's crotch again. She was hot now and dripping.

Josephine probed tentative fingers into the crack. Jackie squirmed, sighing. Josephine found the tight pucker of her anus, the elastic wet slit of her vagina. Jackie came up on top of her on her elbows and knees, and Josephine slid her forefinger tentatively up between the open lips to the tense bump of her clitoris. Jackie moaned. She came alive in Josephine's hands. She collapsed and lay against her, one leg thrown up and over her, her mouth seeking Josephine's mouth, her hand pressing Josephine's hand harder against the bud of her desire, rubbing Josephine's wet fingers up and down, up and down.

Josephine's silver wings unfurled again. Jackie's body was a strange land, a plane of being. Where skin met skin new nerves blossomed and fused. They drank each other, pressed their groins into each other's face. They gasped and crooned and flew. Jackie licked Josephine while a high wind rose and rose inside her. Jackie's hair was everywhere; Josephine held a fistful of it in her left hand and caressed Jackie's bottom with her right. The cleft between her buttocks was

running with sweat and fluid. Then Jackie's thighs were clasped tight
either side of her head, tighter, tighter, threatening to crush her head
as she gasped and tongued at Jackie's quivering clitoris. Josephine
could feel every stripe the whip had made cutting her back like a knife
of steel. She was standing up from the bed on her shoulders and heels.

Everything blazed up in silver fire and melted.

They lay in each other's arms, breast to breast, their hearts
thudding. The bed was a bed of fire. They panted into one another's
hair.

Josephine drifted. She dreamed she was floating in a sea as warm
as a bath, her feet on a level with her head. The seawater was deep
turquoise, and the sun blazed from a turquoise sky, uninterrupted by
the white ice-cream clouds that writhed and boiled in the blue.

She came back to herself. 'Dr McAllan,' she heard herself say.

'Who?'

'In your story. He was Dr Hazel, wasn't he?'

Jackie didn't reply. Josephine felt her take hold of her right hand
and draw it down until it rested on her bottom.

'Go to sleep,' Jackie said. 'It's late.'

|15|

Josephine woke up from a dream of childhood. She had to go back to school, into a new dormitory. But she had all her adult belongings with her, her clothes and shoes, kitchen equipment and everything from the broom cupboard, and only a tiny locker beside her bed to keep it all in.

She woke and remembered that she wasn't at school; then that she wasn't at home; then that she was in Jackie's bed. She was lying on her side.

She opened her eyes. It was broad day. Jackie was curled up with her back to her, nude and warm.

Josephine slipped her hand between Jackie and the sheets, laying it gently on Jackie's stomach. It was warm and firm. It rose and fell softly with her breathing. Jackie didn't wake.

Josephine rolled on her back.

There was a woman standing at the foot of the bed, beside the TV and the floppy plant.

She was a Japanese woman. She was looking down at them. She looked displeased.

Josephine jumped, with a gasp that woke Jackie. Jackie turned on her back and gazed dazedly into the room.

When the woman saw Jackie was awake, she began to scold them.

'What do you think you are doing?'

Her voice was tight, clipped, her accent aristocratic English,

Jackie sat up in bed, the covers falling from her breasts.

Josephine, alarmed and at a disadvantage, sat up too, more slowly, holding the sheet up at her throat. Her back was sore. She remembered Sven, his whip.

Jackie was blinking, unable to speak.

The woman was short, her body angular. The planes of her face

131

were rigid with disdain. She stood with her legs apart, elbows out, the backs of her wrists resting on her hips. On one arm a cascade of bracelets and bangles rattled, clashing together.

She was wearing a short dress in deep metallic pink that left her arms and legs bare. When she moved, coming around Josephine's side of the bed, the stiff fabric of the dress rustled audibly.

She shot out a hand and snatched the sheet away, exposing Josephine's breasts. Josephine clutched an arm across herself.

The woman demanded: 'Where is her tattoo?'

Jackie, distressed, ran a hand through the tangle of her fine gold hair. 'Suriko – '

Josephine gathered the bedclothes up, covering herself again.

'You have broken the rule,' said Suriko implacably. Her voice was very loud. 'She is not ready. She has no tattoo.'

Jackie started to plead with her. 'Suriko, she's ready, she is, it's just...'

Suriko drew something from her pocket, something small and black. She threw it on the bed. It fell face up.

It was a domino: double one.

Jackie saw it and fell silent at once.

Josephine turned to Jackie. 'Jackie, who is she? What's that for?'

Suriko stared haughtily at her. 'Be silent,' she snapped. She told Jackie: 'Keep her quiet.'

To Josephine's dismay, Jackie complied, turning to her with a quick look and gesture that told her to obey. She seemed to have become completely docile. She reached out a slim hand and took the domino from the crumpled bedspread.

'Come to the attic at midday,' commanded Suriko, 'for your punishment.'

She turned on her heel and strode from the room.

Baffled, Josephine confronted Jackie as the door closed. 'She can't punish you for sleeping with me!'

'She can,' said Jackie quietly. 'She can. She's right, it's my fault, I shouldn't have led you on.'

She toyed with the domino, twirling it sadly between her fingers. Josephine looked at it. There had been a box of dominoes in the desk at Dr Hazel's London surgery. 'What does it mean?'

'Whoever gives you the domino,' said Jackie, 'they're your master or mistress for that day. They can call upon you at any time, to do anything. You must obey them unquestioningly.'

She set the tip of her finger between Josephine's breasts, on the place where her own tattoo was.

'If you haven't the tattoo, you're everybody's slave. And nobody's lover.'

She bent and kissed the place, a light, dry kiss.

'We broke the rule.'

Then she put her arms around Josephine and clasped her to her breasts. 'Will you come at twelve and watch my punishment? It'll be easier for me, having you there.'

Josephine's heart quickened. 'All right,' she said. Her voice was unsteady.

Kissing her on the lips, Jackie released her and got out of bed. Josephine pushed back the covers, looking down at herself.

'What can I wear?' she asked, unsure.

'Your clothes are in your wardrobe,' said Jackie, disappearing into the bathroom.

Josephine had forgotten.

Jackie had left the bathroom door open. Bemused, Josephine followed her in. She was sitting on the toilet. Josephine could hear her stream splashing in the bowl.

Jackie smiled up at her. 'How's your back?' she asked.

'It's fine.'

'Well, that's something.'

Jackie tore off two sheets of paper. She spread her legs and wiped herself briskly.

'You must go,' she said.

'Like this?'

'Keep your eyes on the floor,' Jackie advised, 'and your hands behind your back. Remember, when they see you've no tattoo, you're fair game.'

She stood up and flushed the toilet, began to run water into the basin.

'Will you come at twelve?' she asked again.

'Yes,' said Josephine.

Preoccupied, she closed the door marked 9 behind her. She glanced along the corridor. It all looked quite different by daylight. Naked, she walked silently on the soft carpet, remembering to keep her eyes down. Turning the corner she found herself in her own corridor. No one was about.

Her door was unlocked. She went in. Her breakfast was sitting on a tray on the bedside table, under a clean cloth of whitest linen.

She showered and dried herself, then sat on the bed wrapped in a towel. Breakfast was lavish, all perfectly cooked, and piping hot.

Absolute obedience, she thought. The Estwych law. And that was how they worked it, with the tattoo and the dominoes. Suriko said she wasn't ready, Jackie said she was. Because she hadn't got a tattoo, they could treat her like a slave, for their own pleasure. She wasn't even worth a domino.

When would she get her tattoo? Was there still another test she had to pass? Dr Hazel, she thought. It all depended on Dr Hazel. When would he come? Or was he here already, pretending to be someone else, secretly watching her?

She thought of Jackie: Jackie in her uniform, Jackie last night in bed, Jackie this morning in the bathroom. Suriko was going to punish Jackie. To her amazement she realised she was jealous of Jackie. She parted her legs, touched herself lightly, shuddered.

The day was already well advanced. The sun was high, and streaming in through the little panes of the windows. Josephine wanted to go out and laze naked in the sunshine. But she didn't want to meet anyone. Not Sven, not Suriko — no one.

She crossed to the mantelpiece and rang the bell.

A maid appeared, one she hadn't seen before. She wasn't at all disconcerted that Josephine was standing by the hearth carelessly draped in a towel.

'You can take the tray,' Josephine told her.

'Yes, ma'am. Will there be anything else, ma'am?'

'You can tell Dr Hazel I'm still waiting to see him,' she said.

The maid hesitated, then ducked her head. 'Yes, ma'am.'

When she'd gone, Josephine went to the wardrobe. She opened it.

Her clothes had disappeared again. Inside were the same things as before: the net stockings, the suspender belt, the collar, the spike-heeled boots. Josephine took a deep breath. She took them out. She held one of the stockings to her face, running its mesh up and down her cheek. She went and leaned on the windowsill, opened the window, looked out at the tree. The rich air of summer washed in, swept sensuously over her.

She lay and waited for Dr Hazel.

No one came.

At ten to twelve, she rose and put on her clothes. She left her room and found a staircase that led up to the top of the house. The steps were bare, old wood, unpolished. They creaked beneath her as she climbed.

At the top was a low door, hanging askew in its frame. Josephine pushed it open and went in.

She found herself in a dark attic full of cobwebs and old junk.

It was hot, the air stale and oppressive. Glancing around in the dusty light she saw a rocking horse, a big glass dome full of stuffed birds, an old wind-up gramophone with a horn, a golfing bag, a listing card table, a dressmaker's dummy.

They were all there, watching her.

Annabel was sitting in a big old armchair. She had a black wool suit on and a double row of pearls. She looked quite at her ease, less like a housekeeper, more like the lady of the manor. Her chair was covered in a dustsheet. Her hands were clasped in her lap.

Sven was sitting on the arm of her chair. He was wearing a long white coat and black trousers with a sharp crease. His fair hair had been smeared back over his scalp, dark with grease. He had a little pair of glasses on, the lenses round and tinted so his eyes could not be seen.

Suriko had changed her clothes. She was dressed to go riding. She had a red coat, black jodhpurs, thigh boots of shiny leather. She stood beside the rocking horse, swaying it gently back and forth with one gloved hand.

Josephine whirled round.

Behind her sat the cabby, straddling an old kitchen chair turned back to front. He too looked very different. He was wearing a flat black cap with a peak, black leather trousers and a black leather waistcoat, no shirt. He still had his sunglasses on, and his gold earring. There was a gold chain hanging in the hair on his chest. She supposed there was a tattoo there, overgrown with red hair. He had bound her hands and bandaged her eyes and spanked her. She did not know his name.

Two maids were in attendance: the one who had taken away her breakfast tray, and Dawn, who had sucked Sven's cock and let him spurt his seed deep in her mouth.

Jackie was not there.

Disoriented, Josephine stood looking around the group.

Nobody moved or spoke. The only sound was the squeak of the springs of the horse, rocking to and fro, to and fro.

Josephine noticed the dressmaker's dummy was wearing a black leather bra and panties, with heart-shaped holes where the nipples and the crotch would have been.

Seeing that, Josephine remembered. She lowered her eyes, looking at the sharp toes of her shiny boots. She clasped her hands behind her.

Sven spoke.

'Her presentation is commendable,' he said, drawling. He seemed to be congratulating Annabel, as if she were in charge.

'Doesn't she look fine, though?' agreed the cabby softly.

His chair creaked as he shifted his weight.

Josephine felt the blood rising in her face. She willed herself not to look up. Her head was pounding, her breathing short and shallow. She felt as if any moment she might float off the floor.

She heard the rocking horse fall still. There was the sound of boot-heels on the bare wooden floor.

'She was disobedient,' observed Suriko.

'On the contrary,' said the cabby, not raising his voice. 'I'm sure she was very obedient indeed.'

He chuckled.

Sven laughed loudly and coarsely.

Suriko resumed her walk. She came close to Josephine.

Josephine could smell leather and wax and felt.

'Not ready,' Suriko declared.

Josephine heard the chink of metal, felt Suriko's fingers at her collar. She gazed at her boots. Cold metal links brushed her bare shoulders. A chain fell into her view. She felt the weight of it, hanging from the ring on her collar. Suriko was holding the other end.

Suriko led her, stumbling on her heels, into the angle of the roof. Josephine tried to keep her eyes turned down. She felt the chain being fastened to a rafter. She was standing hunched, the slope of the roof on the back of her neck, a foot of chain holding her to the rafter. Suriko was forcing her elbows together behind her back, pulling her shoulders back uncomfortably so that her breasts stood out. She felt the sweat break out, on her forehead and cheeks. Her jaw was damp where it rested on her chest.

They came to handle her. The red-haired hands of the cabby took

136

hold of her breasts and squeezed them. Josephine gasped.

'She looks ready,' he said.

'Not until Dr Hazel says so.'

That was Annabel. Josephine noticed how much more commanding her tone had become, as if she was not the servant but the mistress of the house.

Sven grasped her by the shoulder, turning her about. The chain tightened, pulling on her collar. He was examining her whipmarks. She could tell he was pleased.

'The slave knows me already,' he boasted.

He pulled on her hips suddenly, grabbed her by the buttocks and forced them apart, regardless how she writhed and squirmed. He pushed a finger painfully into her anus.

'Before the week is out her arse will know the length of my cock!'

Abruptly he let go of the struggling Josephine. She stumbled, trying to balance on the unfamiliar heels with her hands behind her. Unable to keep her eyes on the floor, she threw up her head. Sven and the cabby were kissing, demonstratively, roughly, lasciviously. Josephine caught a glimpse and dropped her eyes at once. She was hot. Her head was spinning. Her heart was beating fit to burst.

She felt the cabby ruffle her hair, ungently, commenting on its beauty. Then he spoke in her ear, wetly, loud enough for them all to hear.

'I want to come in your hair,' he said, his voice deep with passion.

Suriko laughed and stamped her boot. She pinched Josephine painfully on the leg. 'Her thighs are perfect for the crop,' she announced. 'I shall make her squeal. I shall hear her beg for my cunt against her mouth.'

The door opened and everyone fell silent.

Josephine risked a glance.

It was Jackie. She was in her uniform.

From the corner of her eye she saw them all make a concerted movement. They were all putting on domino masks; like the pierrot in the picture at the surgery.

Suriko pulled a pair of handcuffs from her jacket pocket and stepped forward to put them on Jackie.

Josephine wanted to look, to catch Jackie's eye. She dropped her gaze. She heard everyone resume their seats. It was a kind of tribunal, she realised.

'Jacqueline,' said Suriko sharply, 'you are charged with taking this slave, this novice, into your bed. You are charged with taking pleasure with her.' She laughed, lasciviously.

'Plead,' said Sven, brusquely.

'Plead,' said the cabby.

'Plead,' said Suriko.

Annabel did not speak.

Jackie's voice was intent and low.

'Guilty,' she said.

'Plead!' they all said, urgently.

In the moment of silence that followed, Josephine could hear the rustle of Jackie's starched uniform. She imagined Jackie raising her head, looking Suriko in the eye.

'I beg for punishment,' said Jackie.

She heard someone give a deep sigh of longing anticipation.

'Your sentence is the strap,' said Suriko. 'Fifty strokes.'

'Another fifty,' said Sven. His voice came taut and clear.

Josephine thought she heard Jackie gasp.

'Strip,' said Annabel. Josephine heard Suriko go to Jackie and release her from the cuffs.

She screwed her eyes up tight, swallowing, fighting herself.

The cabby's warm hand landed on the back of her head, ruffling her hair again.

'Does she want to watch?' he said, amused. 'Does she?'

Josephine gave a shuddering nod.

They laughed at her.

'Let her watch,' he said. 'Let her watch her girlfriend's punishment.'

Startled, she looked up into his face. He had taken off his glasses. Behind his mask his eyes were green and mysterious. He grinned and scratched his belly lazily. He cuffed her head, and went back to his old chair.

Josephine looked at Jackie. Their eyes met. Jackie's face was pale, her cheeks bright spots of pink. She ran her eyes down Josephine's pinioned body.

She stripped.

She stepped out of her shoes. She reached behind her neck, pulled the halter of her apron up and over her head, then reached behind again to untie the strings and unfastened her uniform. Apron and dress fell swishing forward into her arms, and she climbed out of them,

138

letting them fall to the floor.

Everyone was motionless, watching, their arms folded, masks on their faces.

Jackie stood before them in her little white cap, bra and panties, suspenders and seamed black stockings. Her brassière was white, cut low. Her breasts were like pears, long slender pears balanced in the white cups. They fattened as she leaned forward to unfasten her suspenders. Balancing unaided, she lifted one knee and then the other, placing each foot on the other shin and deftly rolling down her stockings. One after the other, she wriggled them off her feet. She stood up straight, barefoot on the rough boards, reached behind her a third time and unhooked her brassière. She slipped the straps from her shoulders. It fell silently at her feet.

Josephine's lips ached for her long pink nipples.

Jackie threw away her suspender belt. She slid her thumbs inside the waistband of her panties and, bending slightly, pulled them down, down to her thighs, her knees, and lifting each foot in turn, stepped out of them.

She put her hands behind her back, and the cabby came forward and cuffed them together.

Josephine heard a rattle. It was Suriko at the golf bag.

Looking around, Josephine saw what she had not noticed before, that the bag was full not of golf clubs but of canes, riding crops, animal whips, a bundle of twigs she knew must be birch.

Suriko was drawing out a long strap of thick leather.

Suddenly Josephine heard herself crying out: 'It wasn't her fault! It wasn't!'

She shook her head vigorously.

They were all staring at her curiously.

'It was my fault!' she begged them. 'Punish me! Punish me! Oh, punish me, not her!'

They all exchanged a swift glance. Something relaxed in the room, though the air was as tense as ever.

The two naked women stared into each other's eyes.

Josephine's confession hung in the air.

Nothing had been said. They had come to an agreement. 'We shall punish both of you,' said Suriko, in a tone that sounded like a warning; as if there were still time for her to change her mind. 'It will be no less for Jackie if you share it.'

Josephine thought then of Jackie's story, of Nicola offering to take both punishments. The story had been a fantasy, not true. And yet it was.

She pulled forward on her chain, hollowing her back, thrusting her breasts out defiantly.

'Let me share it!' she cried.

Ceremoniously they released Josephine's chain and brought her face to face with Jackie, breast to breast. In the slave boots, Josephine was the taller.

With leather belts the maids bound them to one another at waist and knee. Annabel chained their collars together, snicking a little padlock closed on one end of the chain. Josephine felt their sweat, mingling betwen their squeezed breasts. She smelt again the odour she had drunk so freely of last night. She stared longingly into Jackie's moist green eyes. When they kissed there was a warm murmur of approval. Sven was reaching up and slipping the free end of the chain over a hook in the roof.

Josephine bent her knees to press her crotch against Jackie's. She felt weak. They were all holding straps now, standing around them in a circle.

As the first blow fell, Josephine thought: The cabby is Dr Hazel.

|16|

The black cab was waiting at the top of the drive. Its driver was waiting too, leaning on the bonnet in his sunglasses, a white shirt and shorts. I know you now, said Josephine to herself. She came up the rutted path between the trees, picking her way, taking her time.

She had no tattoo. She was everyone's.

The maid had woken her, opening the curtains. 'Another lovely day, miss.' There had been a tray, croissants and tea. And a piece of paper, folded.

Josephine felt confused, sore, hugely refreshed. She didn't remember going to bed. She remembered heat, pain, leather straps and chains, fierce tongues, hot quims and urgent penises. She remembered tears, the taste of a vagina.

The maid was standing by her bed, telling her something. 'A light breakfast.'

She thought she had slept forever, and never so deeply, so well.

'Sorry?' she said, blinking, rubbing her eyes.

'Before your game.'

The maid gave her the note.

Beautiful Ms Morrow –
Will you do me the honour of being my partner at tennis today?

It was signed, simply, 'Roy'.

An alarm began to sound faintly inside her head. She came wider awake. 'Who is Roy?'

'The gentleman in number 1,' said the maid.

'Red hair?' asked Josephine.

The maid grinned broadly, as though she thought she had been the intermediary in a lovers' tryst. 'That's the gentleman,' she said, admiringly.

He's Roy Hazel, then, thought Josephine to herself; nor is he just

141

a cab driver. This is it. This is my test, and if I pass I get my tattoo. I hope I don't have to beat him at tennis, she thought.

'Your outfit's in the wardrobe,' the maid said, inevitably.

There wasn't a pocket in the tennis skirt, so Josephine had tucked the note in the waist of her knickers, which were white like the skirt and the shirt and the ankle socks and shoes. At least the tennis gear fitted.

The day was beginning to be hot, the sun splashing down through the leaves. She felt the edge of the folded paper rub her tender bottom, moving when she moved. It was already moist from her sweat.

'You look adorable,' said the cabby, opening the door of his cab.

'You must be Roy,' said Josephine. 'I don't think we've been introduced.'

He had been energetic with the strap, never missing his mark as she and Jackie spun helplessly on their chain. After, she had clutched his buttocks and he her hair as they thrust and bucked together on the dusty floor.

He smirked. They shook hands.

He produced a long white silk scarf from his pocket and flicked it lightly in the air.

'Remember?' he said.

She smiled. She turned about and let him tie it around her eyes.

He nuzzled her ear affectionately. 'Can you see anything at all now?'

'Only the future,' she said.

He chuckled.

They drove up the bumpy lane and turned onto a road.

Josephine lay back in a universe of cool white silk, She heard the sound of a car, passing them; another; another. It was hard to remember there were other people in the world. It was hard to believe that nearby other people were getting up, cooking lunch, walking dogs, reading Sunday papers.

She and he did not tell each other stories.

They went down a bumpy lane.

'How's your tennis?' he asked.

'Appalling,' she said.

There was a tiny hollow of apprehension in her stomach.

Win? Or lose? What was he looking for?

He stopped. She heard the creak of the handbrake.

'You can take that off now,' he said.

'The blindfold?' she said, surprised.

'Hard to play with that on,' he said gently.

She pulled it off her head.

They were parked on the grass verge of a narrow lane, beside a tall hedge. Above the hedge wire fencing went up another few feet.

Josephine opened the door and swung her bare legs outside. From behind the hedge came the regular knock of ball on racquet, the scuffle of feet on asphalt, muted cries of enjoyment and laughing protest.

She got out of the cab.

An elderly couple walked by, the man in white flannels, blazer and cravat and a shapeless old fishing hat, the woman in a pale blue dess with a white cardigan over her shoulders. They smiled at Roy and Josephine. The man lifted his hat.

'Morning.'

'Hello,' Josephine murmured. She looked to Roy, suddenly shy, embarrassed at being out in public. She didn't want to meet anyone else. She no longer knew how to respond.

Courteously Roy took her arm and steered her around the hedge, into the club. She glanced nervously at the people playing in the courts on either side of the path. They looked like ordinary young people playing tennis. There was a King Charles spaniel trotting about in a preoccupied way, nosing at stray tennis balls.

Beyond the courts they came to a small wooden clubhouse, with elaborate green gables and a painted weathervane. Roy leaned in over the sill of a half-door.

'Morning, Roy!' said a voice inside.

'Morning, Trevor.'

Trevor was a gangling teenage boy with Brylcreemed hair and wire-rimmed glasses. He beamed amiably at Josephine.

'This is Ms Morrow,' said Roy.

'Pleased to meet you, Ms Morrow,' said Trevor.

'Josephine, it is, actually,' said Roy, calmly. 'You don't mind if Trevor here calls you Josephine, do you, now?'

'Of course not,' said Josephine. Her voice sounded brittle and false. In fact she minded deeply. Being introduced to anyone outside Estwych now was a deeper, more disturbing violation than anything they might do to her body.

'Josephine's from London. She's staying with us at the house for a day or two,' Roy continued, nonchalantly.

Josephine looked at him uncertainly. She could see his hairy chest in the opening of his shirt, his gold chain bright in the sunlight.

'That's right,' she said inanely.

'In fact you're here for the week, aren't you Josephine, that's right, isn't it?'

'Yes,' she said, feeling stupid and betrayed.

'How do you like it down here in Estwych, Josephine?' Trevor asked her.

'Oh, it's very nice,' she said weakly. 'It's lovely.'

'We think so,' said Trevor, grinning at her.

Josephine held her breath. She would have run naked through fire rather than have him ask what she was doing in the village.

She looked away, back at the courts. A couple had just finished their game and were leaving, whistling the spaniel after them. Trevor handed Roy and Josephine their equipment and bade them good luck. He told Josephine it was nice meeting her.

Then they were on the court.

Roy was bouncing a ball with his racquet, stretching, jumping.

There were couple of women playing on the next court, a few yards away through the wire. One of them had buck teeth and gave a piercing whinny of a laugh every time she missed a shot. Josephine turned her back. The sun was in her eyes. Why was she feeling so nervous, so suspicious?

They warmed up, knocking easy lobs back and forth to each other across the net.

Josephine started to relax.

'Shall we play now?' called Roy loudly.

'All right,' she said, confidence returning.

And won the first game.

He had power and size, but he was far from nimble. On a good rally she got him trapped up at the net, lurching left and right, and soon wore him out.

The second went to deuce twice. He was red in the face and complaining loudly about her more erratic shots. Josephine was sweating freely, and breathing hard. Sometimes, on the ones she had to reach for, she could feel dimly where the straps had fallen across her back. Was it only yesterday afternoon? She supposed the exercise had worked the soreness out of her bottom and thighs. She was starting to enjoy herself.

She won the second.

'That was easy!' she said, laughing, taunting him, as they met at the net.

'Is that right?' he said. 'Shall I stop making it easy for you, then?'

His smile made her forget where she was, forget the other players, her nerves, her fears of getting this test, whatever it was, wrong, and failing to earn her tattoo. She wanted him again.

'If you can,' she said. He was so easy to make fun of, he was a big teddy bear.

His eyes were green as grass. His gold tooth flashed in the sun.

He won the next game and the next. She fought back, but he took the set. In the second she won one game.

Then he wiped her out.

She stood bent over with her hands on her knees, sobbing for breath.

'Best of five?' he suggested.

She tried to stand. Her sides were aching, her ankles, her calves, her shoulders. She had run around more, and more uselessly, in the last thirty minutes than in the last fifteen years.

Her head was throbbing in the sunlight. Should she accept? Concede defeat?

'I don't know what you want!'

She became aware the women on the next court had stopped playing and were looking at her.

He came close to her, leaned over the net.

'Have you had enough?' he asked, mild concern in his voice.

'What are the stakes?' she said.

He pursed his lips. 'Now, you should have asked that before we started, shouldn't you?'

He reached over and took the racquet from under her arm, patted her gently on the back.

'Take a shower,' he said. He pointed to a door in the clubhouse. 'I'll give these to young Trevor.'

Defeated, dejected, Josephine went into the ladies' locker room. It was empty. There was a rack of towels at one end, a partitioned shower stall at the other. Used towels lay, sad, damp and neglected, on the floor. The lockers were uniform grey steel, with a wooden bench in between.

Josephine sat and hung her head, pulling bad-temperedly at her

145

laces. He hadn't told her the terms of the test. She knew she had failed, whatever it was, win or endure. He had called it off. She had no chance, no appeal. She peeled off her socks.

'Damn. Damn!'

He had been playing with her. It wasn't a game, it was like a cat with a mouse. She was anybody's.

She dragged her shirt violently over her head. Braless, her breasts pulled free.

She remembered Jackie's breasts, squeezed tight against her own.

She stripped down her shorts and knickers. A damp, crumpled piece of paper fell to the floor.

She ignored it. She took a towel and went into the shower.

The water was hot. There was a large bar of white soap. Josephine lathered herself all over.

There had been an easy shot at the very end of the last game, well within her reach. She could have returned it easily if it hadn't been for his hustler game. She'd got overconfident, worn herself out too soon, and he'd eaten her up. The shower was hissing loudly. She didn't hear the pad of bare feet until he was upon her.

A hand fell on her shoulder.

She jumped, cried out in shock, whirled around.

It was Roy, naked. He smiled, pulled her to him.

As he came into the spray, the water sluiced his chest hair, plastering it against his skin. She could see his tattoo. 'What —?'

'My prize,' he said.

He was pulling her by the left arm with his left hand, sideways on to him. He let go of her arm and reached it across her back, gripping her by the right arm and forcing her to bend forward.

'Roy! Not here!'

He took no notice.

In a spray of soapsuds and water, his great broad hand landed on her bottom. She struggled, protesting. The water poured down over them both. His great hand rose and fell, rose and fell. Recoiling, gasping, she slipped and went down on one knee on the tiles, falling against him. His penis was erect. Flailing, she caught her hand on it.

He grunted loudly with pleasure.

He had remembered the story she had told him, about Maria in the shower.

146

Far more frightened of discovery than of him, she begged, 'Stop it, Roy, stop it! Wait till we get back...'

But he was on the floor with her now, sliding wet flesh against wet flesh in the soap and the steam, sitting under the shower and hauling her across his lap. He walloped her determinedly, the way Annabel had whacked her with the hairbrush.

He manhandled her to the floor again, positioning her in a crouch on all fours, her knees spread, her bottom in the air. She realised he was moving round to take her from behind.

Half laughing, half scared, she resisted. 'Not here! Someone will come!' She pulled away, struggled upright. The nosy women, surely they would be in any minute.

His hair was dark brown, slicked down to his heavy skull. His erection was like a thick club. She knew the length and thickness of it. She knew its taste. She shook her head fierce and fast. 'No, Roy, no!' She was almost shouting.

He reached for her with one hand. She ducked out of his way. He reached past her, into the soap dish. He pulled out something, something small and black. With a hungry growl he threw it in the water at her feet.

It was a domino.

Double two.

Josephine was electrified. She was rubbing her bottom, sniffing the water that had run up her nose. She dashed water from her eyes, stared at him with wild surprise.

Suddenly she was full of adrenalin. It was as if the miserable tennis match, the ordeal in the attic, had never been. She bent from the waist, scrabbling for the wet domino. It slipped from her wet fingers, spinning across the floor. Before she could retrieve it, he was upon her.

With a savage spank he sent her sprawling out of the falling spray, dived after her, on top of her. He wrestled her to him, hauled her by her hips, dragging her back onto all fours. Obedient now, she spread herself for him, bottom up, digging her soapy fingers into her slit, moaning as his hand landed again and again on her throbbing bottom. He heaved himself into position between her taut thighs and thrust. The blunt head of his penis shoved at the swelling lips of her quim. Then, with sweet and savage force, he was inside her.

Josephine cried aloud. Her fingernails scraped frantically at the tiles.

Thudding into her, Roy continued to spank her, now the left buttock, now the right, smacking her flanks as if she were a recalcitrant steed. She sobbed, grinding her bottom into his lap, fighting with him now against the flesh, not knowing if it were his flesh or her own, only that it was to be stirred, goaded, slapped into ecstasy, into submission. She gritted her teeth, squealing as he clawed her shoulders, sliding with him across the floor, rolling into the pelting shower again, coming in a great surge.

Swiftly and brutally he pulled out of her. He crawled over her back. He weighed down hard on her. She writhed, twisting out from being squashed under him. His erection was violent red and glistening with her juices. He snagged her shoulder as she came out of the arch of his thighs, pulled her head towards his crotch.

He sat against the wall. On her stomach between his thighs, heaving herself up on her arms, she tongued his cock. The shower fell on her back like tropical rain. He seized a sudden handful of her hair, pulling it, making her cry aloud. She felt him convulse against her scalp.

She lay there feeling violated and ecstatic.

Roy rose, shaggy and soaked. His eyes were wise and delighted. He made a noise like a crow of triumph, and bending over her, gave her a slobbering kiss. His sagging penis trailed a line of semen down her face. Then, with a bound, he was gone.

Josephine tried to rise; failed. She knelt in the shower, soaping herself wearily again, all over. Her bottom stung. She gave her hair a soap shampoo.

The water washed away his seed. She thought she heard it gurgle in the plughole.

When Josephine stepped out of the shower with a towel about her, there was a maid in a black dress and white apron picking up the wet towels from the floor.

Josephine halted in surprise, and stared.

So they had maids here too

The maid flashed her a look, bobbed a curtsey and whisked away. It was Janet, the maid Annabel had spanked in her room.

'Janet! Wait!'

But she was gone.

Josephine looked for her tennis clothes.

They had vanished.

She tried the grey lockers.

They all opened. They were all empty.

A strange suspicion growing in her mind, Josephine limped naked and barefoot out of the locker room, and out of the building.

Cautiously, she peered around the corner of the wall.

The place was deserted. The tennis courts were silent, their nets lowered. The trees whispered in the breeze and fell still.

Everyone had vanished. Even the dog.

Bolder now, Josephine found the gentlemen's locker room, knocked on the door, went in.

There was no one there. Roy had disappeared too.

Beginning to panic, Josephine started to run along the path, back between the courts, around the end of the high hedge.

The taxi had gone. The road was deserted.

She went irresolutely back to the clubhouse, looking for a phone. She found one, in a deserted clubroom, and picked it up. Who could she call? No one. She held the receiver to her ear. It was dead.

Josephine left the clubhouse and padded back along the path to the road, back along the road the way they had come. Before she had gone a hundred yards she realised she could hear the river. Before she had gone another hundred, she saw a tree she recognised, looming over the hedge.

It was the tree outside her bedroom window.

There was a gate in the hedge. She opened it and let herself into the grounds.

They had never left the house. The tennis courts were behind the house, screened on all sides by vegetation.

Naked, she limped up the path, and in by a garden door. There was an antique green sports car parked under a tree, but no sign of anyone about.

Up in Room 3 there was another tray, with a hot dish, salad, fruit trifle and a chilled half-bottle of Chablis.

And an envelope.

The envelope knocked against a dishcover as she picked it up. It had something heavy inside.

She tore it open and shook the contents onto the bed.

There was a domino.

A double three. And a note.

Rest now. Tomorrow you are mine.

It was from Sven.

|17|

Standing on the grass verge at the bus-stop where Roy had dropped her, Josephine sweltered in the hazy sunshine. Though there was no prospect of rain, she was wearing a full-length mac in black poplin with a minute line of scarlet trim. Under the mac she had a broad black suspender belt on, black stockings, and boots. Nothing else, not even her collar. Roy had kept her blindfold when he let her out of the taxi.

Annabel had given her a pound. 'That'll take you to Houghton Hill and back.'

'Can't Roy take me?'

'Only as far as the bus stop.'

In Houghton Hill, she was to go shopping.

There had been another note. The writing was the same. *'Go to Wheatley's. Bring back a riding crop.'*

Without money. Obviously she was going to have to steal it. She felt a lurch of alarm and excitement. She had never, never stolen from a shop before. What would happen if they caught her?

At least this journey was real. She got on the old brown and cream bus and paid her fare, took a seat with some care, and watched the fields and trees roll steadily by the window. She attracted some odd looks in her unseasonable coat. Josephine hid a small smile of excitement. What would they have said if they knew she was naked under it? Josephine hardly cared. The other passengers were like beings from another world, extras in her film. She was the star.

She was pleased and proud to have been accepted. Roy wouldn't admit he was Dr Hazel, but obviously she had passed his test after all. Roy might have given her a domino because he felt sorry for her. Sven never would.

The bus rolled up Houghton Hill and stopped in the old market

150

square. She didn't have to ask for Wheatley's, she could see it as soon as she got off the bus, on the other side of the road. It was large enough. A gold-painted sign over the door read: *Outfitters to the gentry*.

Josephine crossed over and looked in the window. Two elegant plaster dummies in wellingtons and shooting jackets smiled vacantly into a hamper overflowing with picnic crockery. In the corner a stuffed pheasant stared stiffly out at the passers-by. The other window was full of fishing gear, rods and nets and flies.

Josephine opened the door and went in.

It was cool and dim inside. Browsing families were examining sunhats and Aertex shirts. An old gentleman identical to the man who'd greeted her yesterday outside the tennis courts was fingering a pair of silver hip flasks.

Josephine walked boldly up to an assistant. 'Do you sell riding crops?' she asked, haughtily.

He didn't blink. 'Downstairs, madam.'

There they were, in racks and glass cases, in an alcove of their own: walking sticks and shooting sticks, umbrellas for the city, for golf, for the handbag, cues and clubs and racquets and canes — and riding crops. There was an assistant, a sallow young man standing with his folded hands resting on the glass top of a display counter. Josephine smiled at him.

He smiled at her. 'May I help you, madam?'

She looked him straight in the eye. 'I want a riding crop,' she said.

'Certainly, madam.' He came out of his place and led her to a glass cabinet in the corner. 'These are leather, this one is bone, and this, this is a new lightweight steel shank ...'

There were brown ones, black ones, tan ones; ones with a loop for the wrist, others with decorative tassels. There were crops with handles of soapstone and ivory, tortoiseshell too, plastic imitations surely.

Josephine interrupted the sales talk. 'Could you open it for me?'

'Certainly, madam.' The young man fished a bunch of keys on a chain out of his pocket, selected one and unlocked the cabinet.

Josephine fingered the crops. They looked fierce and strange. She bent closer, wondering if they were locked in in any way.

'May I?' she said.

He assented.

She lifted one from its support, took it out and hefted it in her hand,

151

asking his opinion, swishing it experimentally through the air. As she did so she looked around. There was no one about. She pursed her lips, shook her head, hung the crop back in place. She stroked a second, hesitated over a third. She gave a cough. She coughed again, excusing herself, coughing helplessly.

The assistant hovered, concerned.

'Could you – water?' she got out, still coughing. 'Water!'

She could have sworn there was suspicion in his eyes, but he nodded, murmuring, and walked briskly away, out of the alcove and out of sight.

Josephine opened her coat with one hand, plucked a crop from the end of the line with the other. As quickly as she could she slipped the crop through her suspender belt. It was sleek and cool against her thigh. Her coat would cover it, the crop's angled handle would stop it from falling straight through onto the floor.

She felt her heart was beating loud enough to hear.

She pulled another crop from the case and pushed the door to. She could hear the footsteps of the salesman returning. She took the second crop and laid it on the counter, flashing him a brilliant smile as he returned with water in a paper cup.

'I'm so sorry,' she told him. 'So silly of me.'

'Not at all, madam.'

He presented the water. She thanked him graciously, patted her chest, cleared her throat effortfully and drank. He went round to his own side of the counter.

Her pantomime over, Josephine directed his attention to the crop on the counter. 'How much is this one?'

He told her.

'Could you write that down for me?' The lofty manner came easily to her, though she had been afraid she would shake and spill the cup. She realised this was hardly any different from the way she treated secretaries and shop assistants every day in the real world, as if they were inferior species. Well, she thought to herself, so they were. The elect had a domino mask tattooed on their chests.

The salesman held out a slip of paper to her. 'Thank you so much.' She put it in her pocket. 'Is that the time? Goodness, I must go. Goodbye.'

And away she walked, quickly, towards the stairs, aiming herself straight at the open door, the street, sunlight and freedom.

A hand fell on her arm.

Josephine turned, her eyebrows raised imperiously. It was a stout woman in her fifties in a smart suit.

It was Annabel. Josephine had seen her across the shop floor from behind, looking at luggage, and had taken no notice of her, thinking she was a customer.

'Would you step this way, madam?' Annabel said, in a voice that was quiet and polite, but firm as a new steel-shank crop.

Josephine had no choice.

Annabel took her into an office with MANAGER painted on the door.

She shut the door behind them. The room was empty.

'I'm sorry, madam, but would you open your coat, please?'

Josephine took a deep breath.

She untied the belt, unfastened the buttons, and opened the coat.

Annabel did not blink at the sight of her bare breasts, her naked crotch. Expressionlessly, she stepped forward, reached out and took hold of the handle of the crop, protruding above Josephine's suspender belt. Not meeting Josephine's eyes, she drew it free. Josephine felt the length of it slide up her thigh and over her pelvis.

Annabel turned and laid the crop on the manager's desk.

Josephine pulled her coat closed and tied the belt again. She did not button it up.

Outside the window, a pigeon was cooing softly, evocatively.

Annabel picked up the manager's phone. 'Is Mr Breimer there?' she asked, her voice neutral, businesslike. 'Could you ask him to come in now, please?'

Disoriented, Josephine looked around her. The office was real. Certainly the shop was real. It was not like the tennis courts. It was a real shop, in a real town.

So what was Annabel doing here?

The fact that it was Annabel frightened her more than if it had been any of the others. Annabel had betrayed her. Annabel was two people already. Suppose she was a third? Suppose this was some elaborate trap? Was she going to turn her in?

Josephine knew one thing, and that was that she must never, ever, ask.

Could she bribe this manager, Mr Breimer? Weren't her breasts magnificent, her body desirable, the heady promise of the mound

153

between her thighs quite irresistible? The old Josephine would never have thought of her body in that way, but now she knew it was so.

There was a footstep outside.

Annabel glanced towards the door.

The handle turned.

Josephine turned to face the door, already loosening her belt again.

The door opened and Sven walked in.

He wore a silky summerweight suit in dove grey with the finest charcoal stripe, a cream shirt and a tie the colour of ox's blood. His hair was perfectly combed. His eyes considered her without recognition.

'*Tomorrow you are mine.*'

With the slightest motion of his sharp chin, he indicated her coat.

With a dramatic gesture, Josephine opened it, throwing it back off her shoulders. It slid from her back, hanging from her elbows.

Sven's eyes flickered across her body.

Then he looked at the crop on the desk.

Joephine thought he would use it, but no. He went around the desk and opened a drawer. From it he drew a small whip with several thongs, and laid it lightly on the desktop beside the crop, with no more regard than if it had been a ballpoint pen.

'A wise selection, madam,' he said, touching the crop with the very tip of a manicured forefinger. 'One of our finest lines.'

Josephine looked into his eyes, confronting him across the desk. She breathed in deeply, feeling her breasts rise and swell.

Annabel was still in the room. She had gone over to the door and closed it, softly. Josephine heard the key turn in the lock. She thought at first Annabel had gone, but then she was aware of her still standing there, silently watching.

Sven picked up the whip.

'This is called a martinet,' he said, running the thongs lightly through his fingers. 'We recommend it highly for the discipline of slaves.'

He slid the tips of his fingers smoothly down the handle, a comprehensively obscene and erotic gesture.

'You will take the crop back to Suriko,' he told her.

Josephine lifted her chin, stood as tall as she could. She was thinking about Annabel. Annabel had been present last time Sven had taken command of her. Why was that?

Suddenly she knew. Annabel was Dr Hazel. Could Dr Hazel be a woman? It hadn't occured to her. Could a woman be so cruel? Suriko was...

At a gesture from Sven, Annabel came forward and relieved Josephine of her coat.

At Sven's direction, Josephine went to the bookcase and took out three large heavy ledgers, one after the other, and put them in a pile on the desktop, at the edges. Naked she stood against the desk. On tiptoe in her boots, her pubic mound brushed the spine of the top ledger.

She bent over the desk, reaching out and grasping the sides to anchor herself. Her nipples were pressed hard against the polished wood.

Sven lifted her hips, positioning her bottom on the pile of books. She knew without being told to stretch her legs out behind her, heels up, toes only on the floor. He was slipping the edge of his hand between her thighs, testing her readiness.

She knew he would find his hand wet when he drew it out.

The martinet stung her. It stung like nothing she had felt so far. It spread as it landed, catching her in half a dozen places. It stung and pricked. It felt more like wire than leather.

By the third she could tell the strokes apart only by the slight swishing as the tails of the whip cut down through the air. Sven was whisking her very lightly, with hardly a tenth of the power he had put behind the lashing he had given her on her first night. Yet her bottom shimmered and tingled with biting fire. She gasped and jerked against the desktop, throwing back her head, clinging on for dear life.

The fire grew. Her bottom pulsed with fire. She could not tell if he was still whipping her or not. She was panting, kicking her feet. The ledgers were sliding under her.

She felt Sven press down on the small of her back with his left hand. The whip cut her again. She cried out. Again. Her eyes were tight shut. Again. She was staring into the dark molten fire at the Earth's core.

He stopped whipping her. He smacked her thighs, pushing them peremptorily apart. Josephine raised her head, blinking a sudden flow of tears, looking around.

Sven was unzipping his fly.

He pulled out his cock.

It was erect in his hand, stretching towards her between his thumb and forefinger as though it could scent her. She could feel the sticky puddle forming beneath her on the ledger, oozing between her thighs. Looking back over her shoulder, she opened her legs wide.

Annabel came over from her post by the door. She had a jar in her hand, a jar of Vaseline. She took off its lid and began to plaster it thickly on Sven's erect penis. When he was well coated, she thrust a greasy gob of it up Josephine's anus.

Josephine felt as if she was about to shit violently and uncontrollably. She cried out. Annabel, unconcerned, kept slathering the Vaseline into her. Josephine pressed her face against the desktop, her eyes tight shut. She told herself she was not really going to shit, her bottom didn't know what was happening to it.

Then Annabel's hand was gone.

Sven leaned in between Josephine's legs. He supported her knees, one in each hand. His erection was a dull weight pressing into the cleft of her shivering bottom.

Josephine clung to the desk as he laid hands on her again, lifting her hips, sliding the length of his cock into her quim. He was hot. She cried out. His hot cock pierced through her womb, through her belly, her heart, up into her brain. She was shouting incoherently, the muscles of her vagina squeezing and grinding down on him. He was fucking her, standing up, over his desk, or whoever's desk it truly was. He was fully clothed. The zip of his fly sawed at her groin; the cloth of his jacket chafed the cheeks of her bottom, not so silkily now. Her bottom throbbed from the whip, her head was still full of molten rock, but she was aloft, in free-fall, flying.

Then he was out of her again.

She knew what was coming.

He thrust into her anus.

It felt like a poker. She shouted. He screwed himself into her with a glutinous, shuddering motion. She felt her anus clutch him. She could not breathe. The fire of the whip went spiralling up her spine. She heard herself sob. The ledgers slid out from beneath her, banging loudly on the floor one after the other. Sven was bending over her, almost lying on her back. He threw one arm up across her shoulders, grabbing hold of the far edge of the desk. She could hardly move. He was on top of her, inside her, he had flayed her and gathered her to him, invading her completely, filling her bones and her veins and the pores of her skin with himself. He shoved at her with brutal, short strokes. She could hear him snorting in her ear.

156

She came in a chain of multiple climaxes, like a firework that showers amber, then crimson, then white. She was drooling, chewing at the desktop, giving guttural shouts of animal passion, demanding more. As she squirmed he came, heaving himself into her bottom in great liquid jolts. She felt him throb in her down to panting silence.

He rose, ponderously.

They were still joined together.

Josephine could hear the bird, cooing outside the window; the murmur of traffic in the street beyond. Her bottom raged. Her heart was still.

He explored her aching flesh with casual hands. Then she heard a soft sound, felt cloth between her legs. He was shrinking, withdrawing into a handkerchief.

She lay there, indifferent.

Men finished so quickly.

|18|

The maid's name was Lorna. She rubbed salve methodically into Josephine's bottom and thighs. Lorna did not think Suriko was cruel.

'She keeps us on our toes,' she admitted.

Josephine lay naked on the bed, her head pillowed on her arms, Lorna pressed lightly on Josephine's flesh with both hands, rubbing in slow circles, in opposite directions. She was restoring Josephine, polishing her like a treasure, an heirloom, a fine piece of furniture.

'When she's here, we have to watch it,' said Lorna.

'What about Dr Hazel?' asked Josephine, dreamily, 'When will Dr Hazel be here?'

'Soon, miss. Any day now, Mrs Taylor says.'

Josephine shifted on the bed. 'I must have made a mistake, then.' She opened her legs slightly.

'What was that, miss?'

'I thought perhaps Dr Hazel was here already.'

Lorna's hands slid sweetly down the outside of Josephine's thighs, and up the inside.

'Oh no, miss.'

Josephine raised her head, looking along the length of her back. There didn't seem to be much damage, considering the amount of punishment she'd taken. She was in the hands of experts. She supposed you could become an expert, if you were dedicated enough, if you practised regularly. There would be books you could read.

Either that or her punishments had not been so severe after all.

'How do I look, Lorna?'

'Very nice, miss.'

Josephine leaned up on her left elbow, reaching out with her right hand, taking Lorna by the wrist. She rolled over on her back, bringing her knees together, then letting them fall open. She looked at Lorna, her eyebrows raised in a wordless question.

Lorna's arm was limp, passive.

'There's no marks on your front, miss,' she said, gravely.

'Aren't there, Lorna? Even so...'

'No, miss.' The maid detached Josephine's hand. She stepped back half a pace from the bed, straightening her cap.

Josephine drew her left hand up the line of her ribcage, cupping her breast and letting it loll out from under her hand, while she twisted slightly on the sheet. With her right hand she teased out a curl of her pubic hair.

'I thought you might...'

'Oh no, miss,' Lorna said. She wiped salve off her fingers into a tissue. 'We can't do that,' she explained.

Josephine reflected. 'What about if I commanded you to, Lorna?'

'No, miss,' she said again. She looked steadily at Josephine's breasts. 'You haven't got your tattoo yet, miss.'

She screwed the lid back on the ointment and went away.

Josephine got up. She was bored; a little frustrated. When would Dr Hazel come? When would they open the circle and let her in?

There had been no note with her breakfast. She decided to put on whatever clothes they had provided for her today and go downstairs. She would meet someone. Something would happen. If not, she could go and make a nuisance of herself on the tennis courts.

She opened the wardrobe; and stopped, staring inside.

On the shelf was a pile of clean underclothes, panties, bra, slip, tights: her own. She could tell without looking. Her good suit was hanging on the rail. Set neatly beneath were her best summer shoes, buffed up to a much brighter shine than she could ever impart.

Josephine was startled. This time these were not the things she'd been wearing when she arrived. She fingered the clothes, checking them. Perhaps they were very cunning fakes. No, they were real. What would have been the point of faking them? They'd been and taken them from her flat. They had her key, they had her handbag.

Slowly she began to dress. She hooked up her bra, stepped into her panties and pulled them up.

The idea of one of them, any of them, walking casually into her flat, going through her clothes, sorting out her underwear; it was particularly disturbing.

She remembered, vividly, the sensation she had had over Sven's desk the day before, that he had filled her full, that there was no part of her being that had not been invaded by him. It was more than that. There was no part of her world that was beyond them. They were there. Perhaps they had always been there, watching her, waiting.

Waiting until she was ready.

She was ready. But was she? She was determined. She buttoned her blouse and pulled on her skirt. If they could still surprise her like this, was she ready?

Would she ever stop feeling that this was a particularly bewildering, exhilarating dream?

Josephine bent down and took out her shoes.

There was something behind them, propped up against the back of the wardrobe.

She took it out. It was a file: the kind she used every day in the office. The label read: 'Domino Ltd.'

It was in her writing.

She stroked the words with the tip of her finger, as though she thought they might not be real and might brush off.

They were real, and they were in her writing. Yet she knew she had never written those words on a file.

Inside were papers, photocopies of letters with her signature on, letters from other firms, scraps from telephone notepads with scribbled messages, underlined, decorated with arrows, exclamation marks and doodles. There was a costing sheet from accounts, someone had altered the figures with a red pen. Everything in there was utterly normal, utterly familiar, yet she had never seen any of it before. She recognised nothing, nothing except the rectangular black stone in the corner at the bottom. A domino. Double four.

Josephine sat down on the end of the bed to read through the documents.

She had barely decided which to look at first when there was a knock at the door.

'Come,' she called.

It was Lorna the maid.

'The meeting's ready for you, miss.'

'Meeting, Lorna? What meeting?'

For the first time she wondered then: could the *maid* be Dr Hazel? Lorna herself; or Janet, or Dawn. What better disguise could there be for the master than a servant?

'In the library, miss. They said to say they were ready for your report.'

In the library they were all present, Annabel, Suriko, Roy, Jackie and Sven. They were all wearing executive suits and sitting around a large oval table with notepads and glasses in front of them. Venetian blinds were lowered over the windows. The sun spilled in across the table and the plum-coloured carpet in measured stripes.

Annabel was presiding. She was wearing what she'd worn yesterday, as the store detective in Wheatley's. Yet she looked quite different. Her hair was different, was that it? No. Her face was different. She said, 'Thank you for coming, Ms Morrow.'

She said it coolly, as if it were a reproach.

The seat nearest Josephine, at the foot of the table, was empty. She moved to sit down in it, facing Annabel.

Annabel continued. 'We're ready to have your report now.'

'My report,' repeated Josephine.

'On the Japanese deal.'

Josephine sat down, pulled her chair in to the table. She looked around. On her left Sven was toying with an expensive pen, tapping it silently on the table and running his fingers down it, picking it up by the bottom and letting it swing round between his finger and thumb, doing it again. On her right was Roy. He was just smiling complacently at her, his arms folded.

Josephine raised her eyebrows.

'The Japanese deal,' she said flatly.

She looked at Suriko, sitting on the chairwoman's right.

Suriko was wearing a high-collared jacket, a blouse of brilliant turquoise and a very aggressive pair of glasses. She stared stonily down the table at Josephine. Josephine heard someone give an aggrieved sigh. Was it Annabel, who was looking at her over the top of a document she was holding up, as if interrupted while reading it? Or Jackie, who was looking at her watch and writing quickly in a spiral notebook?

'We should be very careful of the Japanese deal,' Josephine said.

Suriko frowned. Her carmine lips pouted.

'But we're all ready to proceed,' pointed out Sven, as if talking gently to a stubborn child, presenting it with an unarguable state of affairs.

'We might proceed,' said Josephine. 'That might be an option.'

She looked around the table. She saw Roy leaning back in his chair. He was grinning at her now.

'Perhaps we should go over the details of the Japanese deal,' said Josephine.

'Please do,' said Annabel, emphatically.

Josephine opened her file and started to scan quickly through the papers they had left her. While she did so she kept speaking. 'The Japanese figures are very impressive,' she said. 'They certainly have a commanding initiative here. In fact you could say they have the competition at their feet. But their terms are extremely –' she caught Suriko's eye.

'Aggressive,' she said. 'I'm not sure we should put ourselves completely in their hands at this point. Not until they've given us something more to go on.'

This didn't please them. Annabel was shaking her head slowly, looking down at the papers in front of her, squaring them between her hands and tapping them on the table, as if it was Josephine she really wanted to sort out. Sven was holding his fancy pen up lengthwise between his thumb and first two fingers, pressing on it as though he was trying to snap it in half.

'You do realise, Ms Morrow,' he said, 'that you are the only person around this table who's holding up this remarkable and very promising opportunity?'

Josephine lowered her eyes, then looked up at him. 'Has there been a vote?' she asked. 'You might have waited.'

He ignored her. 'Madam chair,' he said, 'this woman ...' He flung out a dramatic hand in Josephine's direction, without looking at her. 'This woman is the sole and simple reason we have not been able to proceed.'

'It's all her fault, all right,' said Roy roundly, still grinning his head off.

Annabel looked round the table. 'Are we all agreed on that?'

Heads nodded, raised fingers and pens signalled assent. Only Jackie kept on taking her minutes, not meeting Josephine's eye.

'Ms Morrow,' said Annabel, resting her elbows on the table and steepling her hands in front of her. 'Are you ready to respect the decision of this meeting?'

Josephine felt a familiar hammering sensation in her chest. She looked down at the papers in her hands, then up at the chair again.

162

'If I'm not?' she asked quietly.

'We'll outvote you!' warned Roy, merrily.

Josephine sat back and folded her arms. There was nothing in the file that was going to be any help at all.

'I might resign,' she said placidly.

'No, you won't, Miss Morrow,' Annabel said, positively. She spoke directly at Josephine, looking her in the eye. 'You wouldn't,' she told her.

'A sample of the merchandise,' said Suriko. She clapped her hands smartly, twice.

Janet the maid came in. She was carrying the riding crop Josephine had tried to steal from Wheatley's. She was carrying it in two hands, raised in front of her. She deposited it on the table before Suriko.

Suriko picked it up at once, ignoring her.

'This is a sample,' she said. 'With the board's permission, I propose that this would be an excellent occasion to demonstrate its qualities.'

She flexed the crop, grimly.

Annabel looked inquiringly around the table. No one spoke or moved. 'Carry on, Ms Suriko,' she said. 'You have our attention.'

Suriko rose. She tapped the palm of her left hand twice with the crop. She gazed at Josephine.

'Stand up, please,' she said.

Josephine did not move.

Suriko looked at Sven and Roy. 'Perhaps the gentlemen either side of Ms Morrow would like to assist her.'

The gentlemen did not wait for any further instruction. Lithely they were up and on her, taking an arm each and lifting her to her feet. Josephine did not resist them.

Suriko came round the table towards her. Her skirt was very tight. 'We will be more comfortable without our jackets,' Suriko said, taking hers off. Roy at once helped Josephine out of hers, taking the opportunity to brush his hand across her breast. He hung the jacket on the back of her chair.

'Her skirt?' asked Sven.

Josephine pulled her arm free. 'I'm perfectly capable of taking my own skirt off, thank you, Mr Breimer,' she said.

The men stood back from her and watched. All eyes were on her as she unzipped her skirt, lowered it and stepped out of it. Then she handed it to Sven. He took it, not without surprise. He looked at her;

163

then at once he folded it with care and hung it across her jacket.

'You may lift your slip,' Suriko said, 'and take down your panties.'

Josephine did so. She stood there displaying herself to them, holding her slip bunched up to her stomach, her panties down to her knees.

She hoped she was not shaking.

'You may bend over the table,' said Suriko.

Attentively, Roy moved her file, her notepad and water glass out of the way. Sven moved her chair.

Josephine lay down, her hips on the edge of the table, her feet out behind her. She felt the sunlight on her face. Where she lay she could see the sun directly through the slats of the blind. She closed her eyes and waited.

She could scarcely hear Suriko's approach across the carpet.

Then she felt her lay the cold crop across her bottom, just resting it there a moment, as though she was measuring her swing.

'Shall we vote on it, Madam Chair?' asked Suriko loudly across Josephine's back.

'One stroke per vote,' said Annabel. 'All those in favour?' There was a stirring, a shift in seats and raising of hands.

'Carried unanimously,' said Annabel. 'Please proceed.'

Josephine heard the sharp swish of the crop rising, then the briefest of pauses, then the sharper swish as it fell.

It split her like lightning. She screamed aloud, terrifying herself with her own scream. Her hands flew to her buttocks; she tried to roll aside, out of the way.

They waited an instant. Then Sven and Roy took her arms and spread her out again.

'No! No!' The prospect of even a second stroke of that horrific pain was more than she could bear.

It came.

It came and she screamed again.

And survived.

She was panting, squealing, tugging her arms. The two men held her firmly down on her face, on the table top.

Now she was sure they had cut her. She would be broken and bruised for a month. Every nerve in her bottom was shrieking its agony. She was kicking, bucking up and down, anything to relieve that terrible, maddening pain.

164

Suriko lifted her hand.

The third stroke fell.

It came in lower than the others, across the fleshy underhang of her bottom, straight across her anus. She hardly knew that it had come, it hurt so much that for a breath she could not feel it, could not feel anything. The sensation was so great, so utterly breath-taking, her body did not know that it was pain.

Then it knew.

Josephine howled. She heard herself pleading.

She felt Suriko's cool fingers test her flesh.

'Two more,' said the Japanese woman. 'The thighs.'

'No – no – *aaaahh!*'

Her left leg was mangled, broken, smashed into pieces.

She struggled to lift her head. 'No more!'

But as she shouted the last stroke fell, and she was crippled for life. Her legs flailed uselessly behind her, like the tail of a stranded seal. Her bottom was swollen to five times its normal size. It was pounding with drums of fire. She tore her hands from the loosening grip of Roy and Sven and clasped them to her lacerated flesh.

It felt better, worse, worse, better clutching herself and rolling from side to side on the table. She was aware of them all watching her. She was aware of Suriko, standing there with the crop in her hand, a smile of pure pleasure in her eyes, a smile still modestly restrained from her lips.

Gradually Josephine regained control. She fought down a sob, breathed deeply for a few seconds while the pain started to go down. It was less than total now. She felt it soften around the edges.

In the centre, it burned on and on.

Josephine tried to stand up. The men were at her elbows again, supporting her as she came upright. She ignored them. She was amazed to find she still had legs. The pain jolted and redoubled as she moved. Her shocked muscles refused to support her. She leaned on the back of her chair.

She nodded to Suriko, then turned to Annabel, watching impassively as ever.

'Thank you, Madam Chair,' she said, as well as she could. 'I stand corrected.'

And with that, her legs gave way altogether and she collapsed sprawling on the floor behind her seat.

She looked up and saw Suriko looking down at her.

'Perhaps you would like to remind Ms Morrow,' Annabel was saying, 'of the way we do business here.'

'With your permission, Madam Chair,' said Suriko crisply. She took off her glasses. She stood between Josephine's legs. She pulled up her tight skirt.

Beneath she was wearing crotchless tights. A fierce bush of wiry black hair bristled from a hole where the gusset should have been. Josephine could see that the hair was moist, glistening.

Suriko crouched down on the floor between Josephine's thighs. She knelt, she bowed. Her brilliant mouth was an inch from Josephine's vagina.

She put out a long, slender, pink tongue.

The tip of Suriko's tongue soothed Josephine's labia. They softened and swelled and dilated.

The tip of Suriko's tongue found the tip of Josephine's desire.

The members of the board of Domino Ltd. watched this piece of procedure with great interest.

Now Josephine felt the beginning of a feeling that made sense of the pain.

The sensation softened and swelled and dilated. It was warm and wet. It made her shiver. Her screaming nerve ends flowered and spun. She still hurt terribly, but the hurt was only the root of a magnificent thrill that was flourishing in her flesh. She sighed. She lifted her legs and squeezed Surkio's sleek head betwen her thighs. Her thighs were on fire again, but there was something at the heart of the fire, something wild and wicked.

She was glad it was Suriko, as the ecstasy started to flutter and beat its wings in the fire. Men were all very well. But only women really knew.

She didn't mind that everyone was watching them. Perhaps it meant this really was the final, the final, the final spiral, the final tongue, the final murmurous inspiration, the final needle of desire, oh, aah, the final *test*.

Is it you, Suriko? she asked silently as she clawed the carpet with her hands. Are *you* Dr Hazel? Now that I wear your mark, will you give me my tattoo?

Suriko sucked and nibbled. Josephine gasped. She gripped Suriko's head with her angry thighs.

|19|

Josephine lunched alone as usual, out on the lawn above the river.
Afterwards she lay there, naked, face down in the grass, gently
toasting her stripes in the sun.

From time to time she fingered them, hissing softly to herself
between her teeth.

She heard someone walking quietly towards her through the grass.
She did not lift her head.

The person crouched down beside Josephine and kissed the top
of her head. Josephine did not move.

Whoever it was picked up Josephine's suntan lotion and took off the
cap. Josephine heard the squelching noise as the tube was squeezed.

She felt a soft hand spread the lotion across her bottom. She
stiffened, caught her breath. Her weals burned, then cooled.

Not Lorna, she thought to herself. None of the maids, nor Annabel.
A woman, for sure. Suriko, extending her claim?

Josephine guessed. She opened her eyes. It was Jackie.

'That's nice,' she said.

They kissed.

Jackie was stooping over her in a white tulle shirt and billowing white
harem pants. Beneath she was wearing nothing, that was clear. Her
soft red hair was down on her shoulders.

'Why don't you join me?' suggested Josephine. She reached up for
the drawstring of the pants.

But Jackie prevented her. 'My skin,' she said. 'I burn terribly.'

'So do I,' said Josephine. 'Terribly.'

Jackie smiled, slightly. She traced Josephine's marks. 'It's not so
bad,' she said.

Josephine rolled over on her side, trying to hug her. 'Yes it is,' she
said feelingly. 'I burn and burn and burn...'

Jackie evaded her. She squatted on her heels. She was wearing a floppy cotton sunhat and huge round sunglasses. She untied the loosened knot at her waist and retied it. 'Don't plan anything for this evening,' she said, incongruously.

Josephine screwed up her eyes against the sun. 'Don't?' she said.

'No,' said Jackie. She looked around as if to see whether anyone else was in earshot. 'I'm taking you out to dinner,' she said.

Josephine was surprised, pleased, wary.

'Is that allowed?' she asked.

Jackie settled the string of her trousers around her waist, running her hands around her back. When she brought them forward again, there was a domino in one.

'It's commanded,' she said.

Double five.

Josephine was delighted. She took it.

'What shall I wear?' she asked.

'Any little thing that takes your fancy.'

That evening, at dusk, the wardrobe yielded a pair of washed-out purple moleskin trousers, a white T-shirt and a loose top in an improbable orange tartan. Doubtful, Josephine put them on. They were not what she would ever have considered wearing, but they looked marvellous. In the pocket of the top was a necklace of huge wooden beads. She put it on and posed in front of the mirror, combing down her hair, then ruffling it up again.

She heard a car horn outside and hurried downstairs.

Jackie had changed into a demure sundress, white with oranges and lemons, and a yellow cardigan. She was at the wheel of an old sports car, an MG, bottle green.

'Come on,' she called as Josephine appeared.

Josephine got into the car, pulled on an awkwardly-fitted seatbelt. 'This is like Dr McAllan's, isn't it?'

'Who?'

'The doctor who brought you here,' said Josephine. 'You said he had a car like this.'

'He gave it me,' said Jackie, offhand.

Josephine looked askance at her, but she was concentrating on pulling out. It was impossible to tell anything from her expression.

Jackie drove up the road to the corner, then stopped, the engine idling. She was looking for something in her handbag. 'Here,' she said.

It was a scarf; a blindfold. Josephine bowed her head and let Jackie fasten it around her eyes, knotting it at the back of her head. Then she drove off into the gathering gloom, driving fast.

She drove for ten minutes or so, turning often round bends or corners, Josephine couldn't tell. Then she pulled off the road and stopped. Josephine could hear the river.

Taking off the scarf, she found herself in a pub car park. Dinner was a pint and a shepherd's pie. Josephine had never tasted anything so delicious.

They ate at a rough wood table in the garden. Moths fluttered frenziedly at the electric lanterns.

Jackie was three-quarters of the way down her pint in no time. Josephine was still thinking about Jackie being a nurse. She frowned. 'You drink and drive?' she said.

'Only here. There's no traffic on these roads.'

Josephine reached across the table and stroked her cheek, tucking a fine tress of hair behind her ear.

'What are you?' she asked softly. 'Really, I mean. In real life.'

'This is real life,' Jackie said.

'Is it a rule?' Josephine asked. 'That you mustn't discuss it?' She could imagine that.

'This is real,' Jackie repeated. 'I mean it.'

She looked away, out of the oasis of yellow light, towards the dark river gurgling between its banks. She seemed restless.

She finished her drink. Josephine indicated the rest of hers, she'd had enough. Jackie shook her head.

'Shall we go?' suggested Josephine.

Jackie covered Josephine's hands with her own. As they rose, she kissed her searchingly. Josephine felt suddenly very self-conscious, kissing another woman on the mouth in a public place. No one seemed to be looking.

Back in the car, Jackie blindfolded her again. 'I don't know why you bother,' said Josephine.

'Dr Hazel's orders. Until you get your tattoo.'

The beer had been good, and strong. Josephine never drank beer normally. She felt bolder behind the blindfold, as she had before, in Roy's taxi. 'Shall I tell you what I think? I think you're Dr Hazel. I think that was your clinic I came to in London.'

There was no answer.

'It makes no difference, blindfolding me. I could find the house.'

'How?'

'I'd just ask for the village. And then I'd look along the river. The village isn't that big, I know that.'

'It is,' maintained Jackie seriously. 'The village is enormous.'

Josephine laughed dismissively. But Jackie was not to be swayed. 'Sometimes Estwych is everywhere,' she said.

Josephine wriggled on the rigid old upholstery. The wooden bench had been harsh on her sore bottom. 'Be gentle with me tonight,' she said.

They went upstairs to Room 3, Josephine's room. A maid brought them a bottle of gin and four lengths of soft white rope. Jackie stripped Josephine, laid her down on her back, tied her wrists and ankles to the corners of the bed, and licked gin out of her cleavage, her navel, the hollow of her throat. She poured gin into Josephine's pubic hair and sucked it lingeringly out again. Time stood still.

Lips kissed lips.

Afterwards, lying with Jackie in her arms, her face buried in her hair, Josephine felt expansive, self-indulgent. She complained. 'I'm always the victim.'

'Obedience is the law,' said Jackie. 'Obedience under all conditions. Obedience to the domino master. If I were to tell you to run out naked into the street and give yourself to the first man you see, you'd do it. You'd have to.'

'You told me,' said Josephine, 'that until I got a tattoo I would be everybody's slave and nobody's lover. Since then, everyone has had me.'

Jackie lifted her head and looked into Josephine's eyes in the darkness. 'Since when?'

'Since in the attic. When I asked them to let me share your punishment.'

Jackie said nothing.

Josephine thought about it. 'Was that the test? I thought we were waiting for Dr Hazel. Jackie, tell me! Tell me! I don't understand...' Josephine could hear her own voice, whining, she knew she was being childish. 'You said it was a rule...'

'Do you not understand yet?' Jackie laid her hand sympathetically on Josephine's cheek. 'We *make* the rules. *We* do.'

Josephine thought about that. She reached out and put on the bedside lamp. Then she rolled out from under Jackie's weight and got out of bed.

The night was as hot as the day. The country stars startled the night above the trees.

Josephine went over to the mantelpiece. They were all still there, lying in a row, neat as wooden soldiers: the double three Sven had sent her; the double four from the Domino Ltd. file; the double five Jackie had given her that afternoon. The only one missing was Roy's double two, the one that had skidded away from her wet fingers in the shower. She picked up the double five and brought it to the bed. With a cautious smile, she handed it back to Jackie.

Jackie smiled too.

'Congratulations,' she murmured.

She looked up expectantly, cradling the domino in her hand.

Josephine's mind was empty. A moment ago she had been full of plans and fantasies; now she could think of nothing. She sat on the bed. She drew Jackie to her and kissed her, to avoid having to speak to her. Then she kissed her again.

'What now?' Jackie asked.

Josephine couldn't quite believe they had got there. Any moment something would happen, someone would come in, Suriko, Annabel, Sven, and take it all away from her. Dr Hazel would come and forbid it.

She shuddered, laughing self-consciously. 'You say something,' she said.

Jackie was still fully dressed.

'Would you like me to lift my skirt?' she said.

Josephine's mouth was dry. She tried to speak, and couldn't. She looked for the bottle but couldn't find it.

'Would you like me to lift my skirt, Josie?'

No one ever called her Josie. She'd never thought she liked it. But on Jackie's lips it sounded different. Perhaps she was Josie now.

'Yes,' she said, hoarsely. 'Do that.'

Jackie stood up.

She put her hands to her thighs and took hold of her sundress. She drew it up to her hips, to her waist. Underneath she was wearing white stockings and suspenders. Her panties were a pale colour, indistinguishable in the dark.

Josephine's heart leapt.

Jackie's voice came quietly, disembodied in the gloom.

171

'Are you going to punish me, Josie? Are you going to smack my legs?'

Josephine nodded. She was tense. She didn't trust herself to speak. 'Sit up, then.'

Josephine sat up on the bed. Jackie lifted her knee, placed it on the bed beside her. She hiked her skirt up behind, up above her bottom. Deliberately she reached to unfasten her suspenders.

Josephine watched as she rolled down the top of her stocking to the knee. Her thigh was white, her skin smooth and unmarked. It seemed to fill the circle of lamplight. She offered Josephine her fair white thigh. Her knee touched Josephine's hip.

'I mark very well, I should say,' Jackie said softly.

Josephine lifted her hand.

She looked at Jackie's legs parted before her, the neat, light-coloured panties revealed beneath the gathered skirt, the fabric of them stretched at the crotch. There was a fringe of fine hair, red-gold, escaping from the hem around the mound of her pubis. Josephine could smell the odour of her sex. She fell back, dizzy, against the headboard. Her weals hurt.

'I can't!'

Jackie stroked her head. 'Are we taking you too fast?'

'Yes.'

'Would you like me to strip? Shall I take all my clothes off?'

Josephine shook her head. Her neck muscles ached with tension. She breathed deep, gulping air into her body.

She put her hand on Jackie's bottom. Her voice trembled. 'Come here over my knee,' she said.

Jackie got up beside her, kneeling upright on the bed. Then she leaned forward, bending over on hands and knees, making herself a bridge across Josephine's thighs.

Her hair fell down around her head. She was dappled with freckles in the lamplight, all down her neck and shoulders, spilling down the back of her dress.

She lowered herself gently until she lay over Josephine's lap, stretched out across the bed. Her face was turned away. Josephine could see only the back of her head. She stroked her glorious wild red hair. Somehow that made it easier, not to see her face. Made it possible.

She pulled Jackie's dress up as far as it would go, halfway up her back.

'I'm going to take your knickers down now, Jacqueline,' she said.
Did she sound stern?

Jackie did not move or speak.

Josephine took the elastic of Jackie's panties between finger and thumb of each hand. She stretched the waistband out and pulled it back and down.

The freckles ran on down her back, all the way to her bottom.

Josephine took a deep breath and lifted her hand and before she could change her mind, smacked her.

It sounded very loud. The soft flesh bounced beneath her hand. Was that too hard?

She smacked her again, the other side.

Where the first smack had fallen, she could see a white print of her hand, with all the fingers clear. She lifted her hand and saw another one beneath it. The pale outlines were rapidly filling in a delicate shade of pink.

Again she smacked her, again.

Still she made no sound.

Josephine thought of Roy, when he had spanked her. She wished she knew how to do this, how hard, how fast, how many: how you could tell. She remembered feeling his hand moving around her bottom, never falling in the same place twice running. He had smacked her all over: on the swell of her buttocks, on both sides, above and below. He had smacked her thighs.

She smacked Jackie low down, where the bulge of her bottom curved in to the tops of her thighs.

Jackie gasped.

'Too hard?' murmured Josephine.

Jackie shook her head. Still she didn't look around.

Josephine smacked her again, in the same place the other side of the dark soft cleft.

Jackie's legs kicked and straightened.

Josephine smacked her again and again. She was falling into a rhythm now, slow and lazy. She was lifting her hand higher, bringing it down with more feeling. The white skin under her hand was a mass of indistinct blotches, pale pink at the edges rising towards red in the middle. Her hand was stinging.

Jackie lifted her head. She clung to the edge of the mattress. 'Oh!' she cried. 'Oh!' Her cries were cries of passion and relief. She arched her back. She ground her pelvis against Josephine's thigh. Josephine felt the hair rasping her skin, the moisture seeping through the hair.

She slipped her left arm around Jackie's waist, turning her bottom towards her as she smacked and smacked and smacked her. Jackie cried out, writhing on her lap.

Josephine planted her left hand firmly on Jackie's left buttock. The skin was hot to the touch.

Jackie spun around again, crouching astride Josephine's body, nuzzling between her thighs. Her red bottom bounced in Josephine's face. Josephine could see the marks of her fingers. She had done that. She had.

Josephine laid her cheek against Jackie's bottom. 'Will you ever forgive me?' she asked.

'Never,' said Jackie.

She lowered her head and nibbled Josephine's swollen clitoris.

|20|

On Friday they took her for a picnic.

They went upstream in a couple of rowing boats. Sven and Suriko rowed Annabel, Roy rowed Jackie and Josephine. They rowed to an island in the river and ate bread and cheese with wine in a meadow beneath a bank where rabbits darted, alarmed, unable to adjust to the presence of other animals in their field. Sven stripped off and went swimming, crawling slow, tireless back and forth across the bend of the river. Roy was in shorts, and Suriko in a bathing suit that plunged in front to reveal her tattoo. They waded out together, toying with each other and laughing. Jackie went in too, her sundress tucked up in her knickers. She stayed in the shallows, where it was shady.

Apprehensive at first, Josephine kept expecting someone to claim her, but no one did. How many more dominoes were there? Did you need one to play? After a while, she realised they knew. They knew things had changed between her and Jackie. They were letting her rest after her boardroom drama. They were waiting for her now.

She could not do anything with everyone there. Inhibition and desire went all the way down, layer on layer like the skins of an onion. She undressed and lay in the sun. Her stripes were purple now, less swollen, less ridged. Annabel came out of the shade and slathered lotion on her until she felt like a sardine.

The long afternoon declined. Jackie came out of the river and kissed her. She stroked Josephine's nipples, trying to arouse her; but Josephine was passive. She was away, engrossed in a dream of a childhood she had never had, that she had only read about in books, of infinitely long and uneventful summers on tranquil riverbanks.

Roy bellowed. There was a sudden flurry of violence in the water. Sven had surfaced under him and thrust a handful of sodden water-weed into his shorts. Meanwhile Annabel had Suriko over the stern of one of the wallowing boats. She was switching her with a handful of willow for some imaginary misdeed.

If Josephine wasn't going to provide their entertainment, they would make their own.

Later clouds gathered, stealing the sun. She shivered, and rose. Jackie helped her on with her flimsy clothes. She smoothed the gusset of her pale blue panties into the cleft of her buttocks. Josephine slapped her hands away. She was too solicitous. Josephine felt irritable, dissatisfied with herself – as though she had failed in some way. Another discreet and invisible test. Something had been expected of her and she had done nothing. It made it worse that nobody seemed to mind. She felt she should have seized upon some unnamed opportunity, and brought everyone to their feet.

They loaded things into the boats and climbed aboard. As Roy pushed their boat out into the stream, Josephine looked back and glimpsed a flurry of movement in the bushes. Black dresses, white aprons. Black flesh, and white. The maids had been there, watching from concealment, having a holiday of their own. Half naked figures pounced on an unfinished bottle of wine.

Josephine looked at Annabel in the other boat, but her eyes were closed, her placid face tilted to the feeble remains of the sunshine.

Later, alone in her room, Josephine heard the sound of laughter, voices. She heard a car drive away.

She did not want company. She took a long shower and towelled herself dry in front of the mirror. She examined the marks of her cropping. Even those would fade, Annabel said, leaving no scar. She stroked the valley between her breasts where her tattoo would be. She was lonely suddenly. Yet she would not leave her room.

No one brought her any dinner. It was as if they had all forgotten about her, gone away without telling her. She had a fantasy of summoning the maids and spanking them until they cried. She took her hand from the bell rope and straightened the dominoes on the mantelpiece, adjusting them minutely with the tip of her finger. Her discontent was her own, and not to be put upon anyone.

She wished she could have the afternoon back again. She saw herself on her own in the wood, chained to a tree, her clothes in tatters. One by one they came to her, striding or skulking through the bushes. Her body was theirs, infinitely yielding and resilient. She sobbed and laughed as they used her.

She got out of bed and went to the wardrobe. Her slave clothes were there. She put on her collar and went back to bed. She masturbated and slept.

Next morning Annabel surprised her, bringing in her breakfast.

'Another beautiful day, Miss Morrow.'

Josephine lounged naked in her collar, drowsy, spreading honey unenthusiastically on a slice of toast.

'Is Dr Hazel here yet?'

'Won't be long now, Miss Morrow,' Annabel said.

Josephine's eyes prickled with sudden anger. 'You're always saying that!' She threw down the toast, knocking over her empty teacup. 'The week's almost over,' she complained.

Annabel looked at her intelligently. 'Are you sore, Miss Morrow? Shall I fetch the ointment?'

'Yes. No. Annabel...'

Annabel sat on the bed. 'What is it, Miss Morrow?' she said gently.

'I don't like this,' said Josephine miserably. She fingered her collar. 'I don't like waiting. I don't like not knowing what's happening.'

'You only have to ask,' said Annabel.

'I don't *want* to ask!'

Annabel reached into the pocket of her apron and pulled out a domino. She put it in Josephine's hand and closed her fingers over it.

'I was going to give it to you this afternoon,' she said. 'I'm busy until after lunch.'

Josephine stared at her, not understanding.

She looked at the domino in her hand. It was the double one.

'From you?' she said.

'I'll see you in the study at two o'clock sharp,' Annabel said. 'For your lessons.'

The double one. Something had happened between Annabel and Jackie. Josephine's self-pity vanished, consumed in a flare of jealousy. She fought the impulse to stifle it. She could be angry. She could. Knowing there would be lessons in the afternoon.

Energised, she poured herself tea, moving vigorously. Annabel, smiling, got up to leave.

'Annabel?' said Josephine, her mouth full of toast. 'Could you get me a penknife, please?'

177

'I'll send one up for you.'

Janet the maid brought Josephine shorts and thick socks, walking shoes, a bra and knickers and a khaki shirt with pockets and straps and tabs and buckles. She looked like a game warden. She knocked on the door of Room 1.

Roy was lazing in bed. He was surprised to see her. She could hear the shower running. She supposed it was Sven.

Roy fingered his earring. 'What can I do for you, Josephine?' he asked courteously.

'I'm free until after lunch. I want to go for a walk.'

He didn't mention blindfolds and nor did she. They walked along the river, crossed a bridge and went up into fields where cows stood solemnly chewing, eyeing them suspiciously. Somewhere a dog barked, but they saw no one.

The path wound through an old coppice. Josephine took out her knife and cut a switch from a stand of willow.

Roy watched, amused. 'D'you think you might need that this afternoon?'

'No,' she said. 'This morning.'

She took his hand and led him off the path, winding between the trees. She talked to him. She reminded him of the lies he had told her. He had said he didn't know where Estwych was. He had kissed her without instruction or permission. He had given her two spankings, one after the other, when she should have had only one.

They had come to a stop. He took off his sunglasses and faced her, his hands behind his back. In the dappled light beneath the trees his face was open and still in a way she hadn't seen before. She put her hands on his warm, broad chest and stood on tiptoe to kiss his soft lips. Then she fumbled in the pocket over her left breast.

'Here,' she said, and gave him the double three.

He took her hand, and kissed her fingertips lightly, reverently, before taking the domino and tucking it in his own shirt pocket.

Josephine tapped the switch against the side of her leg. She slashed it into a bush.

'Turn round,' she said.

He turned, docile as a great ox.

'Bare your bottom,' she said.

He dropped his shorts, eased down his underpants.

His bottom was as broad and massive as the rest of him. Dark red

178

hair sprouted from the cleft.

Josephine stepped forward in the grass, took a firm stand on the bumpy ground. He had spanked her in the open air, across his knee. 'Touch your toes,' she said; and as soon as he bent down, she whipped him with the switch

His skin was tough, but almost as fair as Jackie's. 'I mark very well,' Jackie had said, and she did; so did he. Violent red slashes appeared wherever Josephine brought the switch down. She delighted in them. It was nothing like spanking Jackie, though. Nothing so intimate and sensuous. It was like a game, a test of strength and skill. He had had his turn, now it was hers.

She brought the switch up above her shoulder and leaned into her delivery. She lashed the underhang of his bottom. He cried out loudly. There was a clatter of wings as a startled pigeon flew out of a distant tree. She laughed, standing back with her hands on her hips, admiring her own handiwork. He laughed too, coming upright, looking round at her.

'Did I say you could get up?' she cried at the top of her voice. She thrashed his buttocks and legs. His penis was erect. Her crotch was moistening. His cries grew more frequent, hoarser.

She flung down the switch, pulling open the waistband of her shorts. She dragged down shorts and panties together, lay down in the grass on her back. Was this Estwych land? Would anyone come by? She didn't care. 'Here,' she commanded, as if he were a big dog. He rose, stiffly, and came to her, dropping on his knees between her parted thighs. She reached for him, clasped the buttocks she had flagellated. He winced, and she was glad of it. She pulled him down to her. His body was heavy and hot. He smelt of spicy deodorant and fresh hunger. She took his cock in her hand, rubbing it against her belly. He panted, raggedly. He thrust his hand between the buttons of her shirt and mauled her breast.

'Fuck me!' she shouted, surprising herself. 'Fuck me!'

Impatiently she dragged him into position, lifting her legs off the ground to help him in. He swore long and low and fervently. She could see in his eyes he was in a strange place, she was not cowed, she was not confused or contrite. She had whipped his bottom with a stinging stick. He would learn. She grabbed a handful of the hair on his chest, hoisting her hips against him, taking him in deep. Her eyes widened, she croaked with desire, her voice strangled in her throat. He grunted,

179

puffed and blew. His balls slapped against her bottom. He was her beast; and she was Queen of the Woods.

But in the wardrobe at half past one was a gymslip, and a white blouse, and a pair of shiny black round-toed shoes that fastened with a strap across the instep and a press-stud. There were white ankle socks, and thick cotton knickers of navy blue.

'What have you got there?' said Roy behind her. He had followed her up to her room, helpless as a hound. She turned on him, shouting and laughing.

'Get out! Out!'

He ran, ducking his head in mock dismay, pulling the door closed as a shoe bounced off the lintel.

Josephine stopped laughing. She looked again in the wardrobe. It was the uniform of her old school. How did they know? They knew everything. How did they get it? You could have anything you wanted. She did not want this. She hated it. But there was the domino, double one. And there was Annabel, waiting in the study. She showered hurriedly and dressed herself. She could be queen, or she could be child, she told herself. Or they could be her. The morning seemed a million years ago. She tied her tie. She examined herself in the mirror, and stuck out her tongue.

'Come in.'

'You sent for me, miss.'

'Mrs Taylor,' said Annabel.

'Yes, Mrs Taylor.'

Annabel was wearing a long brown dress with a brooch of paste diamonds at the throat, and a black academic gown with wide sleeves. She sat at a high desk, looking at the little girl who had come shuffling reluctantly in.

'Yes, Morrow. I sent for you. Stand up straight. Hands at your sides. You know why you're here.'

'No, Mrs Taylor.'

A flicker of displeasure crossed Annabel's face. She laid her hands flat on the lid of the desk.

'You're a dirty, immodest, wicked girl,' she said. 'What are you?'

Josephine struggled. 'I'm not, Mrs Taylor!'

Annabel slapped the desk loudly, making her jump. *'Don't answer back!'*

Josephine stood, trying not to shrug. She kept her hands down. She looked at the floor.

'What were you doing in the changing room with Maria Coroni?'

That genuinely shocked her. She gaped. He had told her! The story she had told Roy, he had told Annabel, told all of them, probably. She wished she had hit him harder.

Absurdly, she found herself blushing. She was sixteen. She and Maria had been reported to the housemistress. Somebody had seen them after all and she had never known.

'You're a filthy, despicable, sinful little lesbian,' said Annabel.

'I'm not! I'm not!'

Annabel leaned towards her over the top of the desk. 'Your girl-friend has told us everything,' she said. 'Are you telling me she was lying? Trying to get you into trouble?'

Josephine fell silent. She wasn't going to walk into that one. She looked at her shoes again.

'You're to see Dr Hazel,' said Annabel bluntly.

Taken by surprise again, Josephine looked up. Their eyes met.

'Now?' Josephine heard herself ask.

'When I've finished with you,' said Annabel.

She opened the desk and took out a strap.

'You know what to do, Morrow,' she said quietly.

Josephine looked around.

There was an upright wooden chair in the corner with a pile of books and papers on it.

She went over, picked them up and moved them to a side table where a bowl of flowers stood. The curtains were half closed, the after-noon sunshine spilling in a band across the floor. Josephine moved the chair into the sunlight. She stood behind it, then bent over the back, lifting the skirt of her gymslip as she lowered herself into position.

She heard Annabel stand up and approach. She hollowed her back. The strap fell across the seat of her knickers.

She closed her eyes.

The strap fell again, an inch lower.

Josephine concentrated on the strap.

It fell again, lower down the taut curve of her bottom.

She willed it to land, meeting it each time with her will.

The strap fell.

She knew now how to do this.

The strap fell.

Sometimes the pain was everything, sometimes it was nothing at all. This time it was irrelevant. She would pass through it and meet Dr Hazel.

The strap fell a last time.

Josephine did not move. She had not cried out, or even let slip a gasp of pain. Her bottom throbbed. She waited, bending over the back of the chair.

'The cane,' said Annabel.

Of course. She remembered her story, her silly story in the back of the taxi.

Would she have to wet herself? She would not do it.

Annabel went past her to a cupboard in the corner.

'You will take a caning,' she said. 'Four strokes on the bare bottom. Take down your knickers.'

Was that a change? In the story, had she taken them down herself or had she had Mrs Maple to do it?

She didn't hesitate. She reached behind her and pulled her knickers down around her thighs.

She heard Annabel give a sigh.

'What are you?' she asked.

'A lesbian,' she said.

The cane came swishing down. It was like the whip, but like the crop. It was infinitely thin. It was made of pain.

'What are you?' Annabel asked again.

'I had Roy,' Josephine confessed. 'In the wood.'

The cane came down.

'What are you?'

'Nothing!'

She bit back a cry as the cane came down.

'Who are you?'

'I'm Josephine — Morrow!'

The fourth stroke sent her jolting forward, almost tumbling head-first off the chair.

'Get up, Miss Morrow.'

Josephine got to her feet, leaning on the chair with one hand, rubbing her stinging bottom with the other. She looked at the woman who had beaten her.

'You must undress now, Miss Morrow,' said Annabel. She was

182

Annabel again. She was taking off her teacher's gown.

For a moment Josephine thought Annabel was about to strip off too, but she simply bundled the gown into the cupboard with the cane. Josephine pulled off her clothes. She stood naked, attentive, her hands clasped to her tingling bottom.

'It's you, Annabel,' she said. 'You're Dr Hazel.'

'Oh no, miss.'

Annabel opened the door of the study, and led the naked Josephine out into the hall.

'She's waiting for you,' she said.

|21|

Next door to the study was an unmarked room. Annabel knocked.

'Come in,' called a familiar voice.

Annabel opened the door and ushered Josephine in.

It was a sitting room, airily, sparsely furnished with a low suite upholstered in a natural repp. There was a black japanned coffee table with a tray of tea things on it. A chrome trolley of what looked like surgical equipment stood incongruously in the corner. The walls were mushroom, a huge round mirror in a sunburst frame on one, paintings on all the others. French windows stood ajar. A breeze from the garden stirred floor-length nets.

A woman got up from the couch, one hand outstretched to greet her, the remains of a large slice of cake in the other.

'Sorry I'm so late, Josephine, I couldn't get away.'

'Hello, Dr Shepard,' said Josephine.

Dr Shepard smiled, glancing up and down her body. 'Call me Hazel,' she said.

'Dr Hazel?'

'That's what they all call me. Come here, come and sit down.'

'No thank you,' said Josephine. Delicately she clasped her bottom.

Dr Shepard put her hand on Josephine's shoulder. 'Turn round,' she said.

Josephine turned. She lifted her hands.

'Excellent,' said Dr Shepard. 'I think you've had the lot now, haven't you?' Her voice was sympathetic and warm.

'I don't know,' said Josephine. 'I haven't had the slipper yet. And I used to know a boy who said his mum did it with a wooden spoon...'

'You can have anything you need, do you know that?' Dr Shepard turned Josephine around again and looked into her eyes. Her hand stayed resting on Josephine's shoulder. 'Anything at all, have they told you that? And there's only one rule.'

'Obedience,' said Josephine.

'Absolute obedience,' said Dr Shepard, nodding weightily. She dropped her hand, clasped it loosely in front of her with the fingers of the other hand. 'They say you've learnt that.'

'I do know it,' said Josephine feelingly.

Dr Shepard continued nodding, now with some emphasis. 'You do,' she said, scrutinizing her again. 'I've seen some of your tapes.'

'Tapes?'

'Some of them. The board meeting,' she said with a sudden grin. She chuckled. 'Bloody good!' she said.

She put the rest of the cake in her mouth and stooped down to the tea tray. 'Would you like a cup?'

'You said I can have anything I want,' said Josephine.

Dr Shepard, still bending, looked round at her vaguely. She was still chewing. 'What do you want, a whisky? Glass of wine? Champagne?'

'I want a tattoo,' said Josephine. Involuntarily, her glance flicked towards the trolley in the corner, and back to Dr Shepard.

Dr Shepard grunted. She poured tea, added a slice of lemon. She straightened, the cup in her hand. 'You're already doing everything there is! What do you want a tattoo for?'

'I want to belong,' said Josephine.

Dr Shepard glanced at Annabel, then back at Josephine. The women were both smiling. 'I knew you'd like it down here,' she said.

'I want to come back,' said Josephine.

'You will, Josephine, you will.'

Josephine turned to Annabel. 'Annabel, you won't let me in without a tattoo, will you?'

'No, miss,' said Annabel.

'Hazel,' said Josephine, insistently. 'Dr Hazel, please.'

'Oh for goodness sake!' Dr Shepard gulped two hasty mouthfuls of tea. 'Lie down there,' she said, pointing to the couch. She was smiling even more broadly now.

Annabel went and brought the trolley. There was electrical equipment on it too. Josephine didn't want to look at it. She looked at the painting on the wall above the fireplace. There were a group of melancholy pierrots sitting on a rustic seat, dwarfed by some improbably frilly shrubbery. One of them had a carnival mask with a beak. He

185

was playing a tiny guitar.

Dr Shepard swabbed the skin between Josephine's breast with cotton wool. The place went cold.

'Let me have a piece of cake,' said Josephine.

Annabel cut her one. Josephine held it close to her mouth and took quick bites out of it.

'Does it hurt?' she asked.

'Nothing hurts here,' said Dr Shepard. She had taken her jacket off. She was wearing a short-sleeved blouse. She bent low over Josephine's breasts, tracing a shape on the skin with something that buzzed. 'Very still now,' she murmured.

Josephine could hear voices in the garden, Suriko talking to Dawn, the voices receding as they moved away across the lawn.

She could hardly feel the needle going in. Then it felt hot, and hurt like an injection. She chewed her cake, very deliberately. This was not a kind of pain she could imagine enjoying.

Annabel mopped at her skin.

'How did you know?' Josephine asked.

'Know what, pet?'

'That it would be good for me. All this.'

'You wouldn't have got here otherwise,' said Dr Shepard, adjusting her ink flow. 'You'd have given up long before.'

'No, but how did you know in the first place? When I came to Hampstead?'

'I'm not often wrong,' was all she'd say.

In a while, she said Josephine could sit up.

'Is that it?' It looked sketchy.

'That's the outline. We'll fill it in the next time. Don't worry! It's perfectly valid.'

She shook an aerosol and sprayed it. An icy mist congealed, dried to a film. It was transparent and flexible, like a patch of thick polythene wrap. 'That'll last a couple of days if you don't pick it.'

'All right,' she said, rubbing it.

'Don't rub it either!'

'It feels funny.'

'How's your bottom?'

'Sore.'

'You'd forgotten about it, hadn't you?'

'Of course I hadn't. Would you like to examine me?'

'I already have,' smiled Dr Shepard broadly.

'Do it again,' She gestured to Annabel, standing to one side. 'Annabel. Come and help her.'

Dr Shepard turned off her equipment as Josephine lay down flat again on the couch. 'No secrets from Annabel,' she said.

'You fired me up,' Josephine said to Annabel, as she lifted her knees up to her chest, 'you can finish me off.'

She hooked one leg over the back of the couch.

'Both of you.'

She closed her eyes and relaxed. The two women pampered her. One stroked her hair, her breasts, nuzzled her face, caressed her shoulders, the insides of her elbows, her throat. The other soothed her burning thighs, and slipped a finger into her steadily moistening quim. Josephine felt a jolt of pleasure as the ball of the thumb rolled sweetly over her clitoris.

She came quick and hard, arching her back as Dr Shepard pinched her nipples. The moment she'd stopped pulsating, she sat up, pushing the women away.

'Right,' she said. 'Now then. Annabel.' She swayed on her feet, unsteady from pain and pleasure. Annabel reached to support her, but she caught herself with a hand on the back of the couch. 'Come with me,' she said, surprising them both.

She walked towards the door, opened it without a backward glance.

'Are you coming back?' Dr Shepard called after her.

'Maybe not,' said Josephine. She ran an agitated hand through her hair, then through her crotch. 'I don't know. I'll find you,' she said. 'Thank you for my tattoo,' she called, already halfway into the study.

Rooting among her abandoned clothes, she found what she was looking for. A domino. Double three. She stood up and and gave it to Annabel.

Annabel's eyes grew round. 'For me, miss?'

'That's right,' she said. She bent and picked up the cane. 'I'm going to take you over the back of that chair,' she said, pointing with the cane. 'Now. Pull your skirt up. Come on.'

Annabel's hands plucked at her brown dress, struggling to pull it up to her broad hips. 'Wouldn't you rather just spank me, miss, I mean you're not very practised — '

I'll give you practise,' said Josephine, lashing her with the cane. 'Come on! And your slip!'

187

Bending woefully over the chairback with many inarticulate complaints, Annabel finally succeeded in revealing a full pair of white drawers, the equivalent of the maids' but many a size larger. She was also wearing a white corset, with black stockings on straining suspenders. Josephine's fingers quickly discovered that the knicker buttons were in the same place as Janet's too.

Annabel's bottom was fat and white. The first cut of the cane left a livid diagonal streak up the right buttock. Annabel squealed, clapped her hand to the place.

It was not so easy either, Josephine realised. She had meant that one to land horizontally, straight across both sides.

She shortened her grip and lashed her on the other buttock.

Annabel wailed. She clung to herself with both hands for dear life. Her balance over the chair seemed extremely precarious.

'Do you want me to ring for the maids?' said Josephine sweetly. 'To hold you down?'

'No, miss — '

'Then take your hands away.'

Annabel did, and was rewarded with a third cut. She cried out huskily and clasped it with her hand again. That one had fallen higher than either of the others, Josephine saw. She must try to keep the rest low down. Avoiding Annabel's hand, she swung into the underhang, and was pleased to hear the cane land with a sharp *thwack*.

'Two more,' she said, taking a breather. Annabel quivered. 'Do you want me to put them on your thighs?' Josephine asked.

'Oh no, miss, please!'

'Then take your bloody hands away!'

Annabel's bottom was untidily streaked with pink and angry red. Josephine faintly remembered people at school talking about an evil housemistress who 'let the strokes cross'. There was quite a bit to learn, obviously. Oh well.

She brought the last two in fast and hard, almost catching Annabel's hand with the second as she brought it back to clutch the first.

'You're done,' Josephine said. She stepped back, running the length of the cane sensuously between finger and thumb. The wood was warm. 'Get up.'

Shakily Annabel rose. She stared at Josephine. Her face was white, apprehensive.

Josephine was suddenly acutely aware of her nakedness. She

wondered if Suriko or anyone could see her from the garden. She turned a degree or two in that direction, her legs astride, stroking her crotch.

'Thank me,' she said distantly.

Annabel ducked her head. 'Thank you,' she piped, breathlessly. 'Ms Morrow. Will that be all, miss?'

'You can go,' Josephine told her. Without another look at her she swept out of the room, still carrying the cane, leaving Annabel wincing, hauling up her tangled drawers.

Josephine knocked on the open sitting room door with her knuckles and walked straight in. Dr Shepard was there, looking amused. She had obviously been listening.

'No one's *ever* done that!' she said quietly, intently.

Josephine stood with her feet apart, swinging the cane. 'Not even you?'

Dr Shepard chuckled robustly. 'Come and have some tea,' she said.

Cautiously, Josephine sat down on the couch at her side. She lowered her head, squinting down at her tattoo.

'It's not very impressive,' she said. Dr Sheppard handed her a cup of tea. 'Thanks.'

'Annabel thinks it is. What is it, Annabel?'

The housekeeper had appeared at the door, fully-clothed, hovering uncertainly. She indicated the case. 'Shall I take that from you, Ms Morrow?'

'No thanks, Annabel. I may need it. I've got a domino left. Put something suitable in my wardrobe, would you?'

Dr Shepard gestured towards the window. 'Suriko is down by the river, I think,' she said, slurping her tea. 'With one of the maids. I shouldn't disturb them, if I were you.'

'It'll have to be Sven, then,' said Josephine.

'You are having fun, aren't you? said Dr Shepard admiringly.

Josephine reached out and clasped her hand, brought it to her crotch.

'You're dripping on the furniture,' commented Dr Shepard.

'Lick it up,' said Josephine.

'Oh, I'm too old – '

Josephine narrowed her eyes. 'Go on,' she said, persuasively. 'Dr Hazel. Let me see your tongue elevator.'

Slowly Dr Shepard got down on her knees and lapped between

Josephine's thighs. Josephine clasped her head affectionately, letting her own head loll back on her shoulders. Breathing hard, she looked lazily at the sunlit garden, smelled the scents of summer mingling warmly with the odours of her own desire.

'Enough,' she murmured.

Dr Shepard kissed her thigh. She was on all fours, looking up at her.

'I'll see you later,' Josephine promised.

She took her cane and went up to her room, moving lightly on the stairs. Her muscles were threatening to stiffen. She touched her toes fifteen times in front of the mirror, then smoothed some ointment on her bottom and down the backs of her thighs. She felt the familiar burn intensify and gradually cool.

In the wardrobe were a laced leather basque and stockings, a pair of long gloves, another of long boots, all in black. There was a collar with silver spikes and no ring.

Josephine laughed. She looked at it all with satisfaction.

Then she started to get dressed.

Folded in the palm of one of the gloves was a black velvet domino mask. It was lined with silk and fitted snugly around the head with silken elastic.

Josephine looked at herself in the mirror. The corset came down far enough in front not to snag the protective film over her tattoo. Her chest was sore. She tried not to touch it. She picked up her last domino and rang the bell. 'Lace me up,' she told the maid, Lorna. 'Then you can take this to Mr Breimer.'

'He's out, madam.'

'When he comes back.'

She eyed the maid contemplatively as she got down on her knees to buff up the boots.

'Tell me, Lorna, have you been good today?'

Large brown eyes looked up at her between thick black lashes.

'Yes, madam.'

'Have you done your duties properly? Correctly? Without fault?'

'Yes, madam.'

'You have no punishments owing to you?'

'No, madam.'

'When were you last punished, Lorna?'

'Yesterday, madam.'

'Any marks?'

'No, madam.'

'Show me.'

Unhesitatingly the girl hiked up her long black dress and unbuttoned her knickers. She turned and leaned forward, displaying her bottom to Josephine.

Her skin was sallow, rather matte and dry. Her bottom was neat and high. She was right, it was perfectly clear. It would be a pleasure to brighten it up for her.

'I think I'm going to have you across my knee anyway,' Josephine told her. 'I'm sure it won't be wasted.'

The maid wrinkled her nose, rubbed it with her hand. 'No, madam,' she said, impishly.

Dealing with Lorna took quite a while, especially when Josephine found that she had a need for the girl's tongue as well as her bottom. Lorna was not very skilful with her tongue. Some further correction became necessary.

It was already getting dark when Sven came to the door of Room 3, the domino in his hand.

'What's this?'

He contemplated Josephine in her costume. He was wearing his little black glasses, but she was sure he noticed her belt, and the coiled whip tucked into it. Nor would his eyes have missed her tattoo.

'My turn,' she said, 'to play.'

He looked harrassed. He ran a hand through his hair. It was sweaty and disordered. His shirt was rumpled and damp with perspiration. Seeing she would not take it back, he tucked the domino in his shirt pocket with a lop-sided smile.

'I've only just got in,' he said.

'I know,' she said. She ran a finger along the top edge of her mask. 'I've been waiting.'

'I've had a hard day.' He gestured, irritably, weakly. 'I'm tired...'

Josephine didn't move. She said, 'You got me out of bed, I remember. You told me you were Dr Hazel. You said you were going to help me.'

For the first time she had ever seen, he looked disconcerted. He took off his glasses and folded them, unfolded them. 'I'm going to have a shower,' he said, aggressively.

'Later,' said Josephine. 'You'll need it.'

He laughed awkwardly. He tried to kiss her, calling her lover. She

191

pushed his face away.

He lowered his head, touched one hand to his temple, as though trying to still hectic thoughts. 'This is not such a good idea,' he said, earnestly.

Josephine took no notice. 'Earlier you went on a good deal about obedience,' she said. She walked past him to the open door. 'Shall we go?'

'Go?'

'Downstairs.'

In her mind were handcuffs and chains, torches burning in the hot night. She vowed he would jerk his seed into the smoky air before he slept tonight, without benefit of hand or mouth or juicy quim. But first, he would scream.

'You remember the way,' she told him, pleasantly.

|22|

S he went to bed late and woke late. Her tattoo itched. She needed
  something to take her mind off it.

Dawn came to clear her breakfast tray.

'Where is Suriko, Dawn?'

'She went riding, madam.'

'Was she alone?'

'Yes, madam.'

Josephine had a shower. The marks Suriko had given her were
fading. She dressed sportily, in a short white tennis skirt, clean white
knickers, ankle socks and plimsolls, and a maroon Aertex shirt. Her
nipples peeked through the tiny holes in the fabric of the shirt.

She had an idea one of them would be after her today, her last day
at Estwych. That was not her idea. Rapidly she slipped down the back
stairs and found her way to the stable.

There were two stalls. One was empty. A brindle pony stood in the
other, chewing somnolently. It turned its head and raised its ears
suspiciously. Josephine patted and stroked its hindquarters. Its tail
twitched.

The stable was warm and dusty. The air smelt rich and comfortable.
Senior girls had gone riding at Josephine's school. She remembered
the mingled scent of wood and hay and leather and fresh manure. She
yawned. When would Suriko be back? On the walls various pieces of
equipment, iron and leather, hung from square-headed nails. They
were not all equestrian. Iron manacles and shackles hung from chains.
Josephine picked one up and let it go. It swung from side to side like
a pendulum, scraping against the wall. The pony snorted and pawed
the ground. It looked at her solemnly.

'Nice horse,' said Josephine. She yawned again. 'Excuse me,' she
said.

In the corner where the rakes and shovels and brooms stood was a small stack of straw bales, partly undone and scattered. Josephine sat down on them. The straw was not kind to her punished flesh, but she was tired. She fell asleep there, drifting in and out of dreams of waterfalls and staircases.

Hooves on the flagstones woke her. It was Suriko, coming home. She was dressed as she had been in the attic, in jodphurs and a riding coat, with a hard black hat. She was carrying the crop Josephine had taken from the shop in Houghton Hill. Her placid face showed no expression as she caught sight of Josephine reclining on the straw.

'I feel I owe you something,' said Josephine.

Her skirt had ridden up to her waist while she napped. She made no attempt to pull it down. She touched herself lazily and caught her breath. She breathed deep into the hollow of her belly, the kick of sudden desire.

Suriko stood before her, her legs astride, the crop held lightly between her kid-gloved hands.

'Give it to me,' she said.

'I can't. I haven't any dominoes left.'

'When one player has no dominoes left,' Suriko said, quietly, in her austere, melodious voice, 'the game is over.'

She led her horse, a trim black mare, into its stall and began to take off its harness.

Josephine sat up. She picked straw from her hair and clothes. She crossed her arms and pulled her shirt off over her head. Then she caressed herself, cupping her breasts and squeezing her nipples between finger and thumb. She remembered doing that at home — was it only a week ago? — stripping off in the hall of her flat and masturbating urgently and violently.

She went into the stall where Suriko was scooping oats into the manger. She went in alongside the horse so as not to alarm it.

'Fetch her a bucket,' said Suriko, glancing at her across the mare's back. 'There's a tap,' she said, 'out in the yard.'

Josephine found a galvanised iron bucket and went out in the sunshine. She ran water in from the tap, spilling some on herself. The cold water splashed out of the bucket and onto her breasts. She gasped. Her nipples stood up like soldiers.

With both hands she carried the bucket in to the mare. Weighed down, her upper arms squeezed her breasts together, making them

194

even more prominent.

Suriko was rubbing the horse down.

Josephine clanked the bucket heavily down on the floor. Suriko only had to step forward to reach it.

The horse started at the sound, pulling its neck out from under Suriko's hand, looking round to see what was happening.

Suriko held out her gloved hand.

'Here,' she said, indicating the bucket.

Josephine put her hands on her hips.

Suriko stared at her, at her nakedness, her eyes bright and hard.

'Give it to me,' she said again.

Josephine picked up the bucket. She held it up with one hand and slipped the other one underneath it, supporting it.

She threw the contents over Suriko.

The water caught her in the chest, splashing up into her face.

She cried out, swayed backwards by the force and shock. Her black hat fell off.

The horse whinnied unhappily.

Suriko stood dashing the water from her eyes, gasping like a stranded fish. Her fine clothes were completely drenched. The horse nuzzled her querulously. She pushed it away. It sniffed its wet side, snorted hard, began to lick itself.

Calmly, without a word, Suriko unbuttoned her red riding coat. She took off her dripping white blouse. Underneath she wore a bra of black net. Her skin was damp with water and perspiration.

She shook out her hair vigorously with stiff fingers and wiped her hands on her sodden trousers. She glanced at Josephine. Then she hooked the heel of her left riding boot under the partition and worked it off her foot.

Josephine felt the slow hammering of passion begin to pound in her chest, her temples.

Abruptly she turned away and left the stall. She went back and threw herself on the straw and waited.

She heard scuffling sounds, slithering, the knock of a second boot-heel on wood.

She waited.

In a moment Suriko came out of the stall, round the partition, approaching her. She was wearing a narrow black suspender belt that matched the bra, seamless black stockings, and a pair of minute black

195

knickers that were just a black triangle hugging her crotch. She was carrying the crop.

She flew at Josephine.

Josephine went sprawling on her back, Suriko on top of her.

Suriko was grabbing at her hair, lifting the crop up to strike. But Josephine's arms were longer, she lashed out and knocked it from her hand. It clattered against the partition and fell to the floor.

Now Suriko was grabbing handfuls of Josephine's hair with both hands, trying to bang her head against the stable wall. Josephine had one knee up in Suriko's midriff. She shoved with her shin, unsettling Suriko. They rolled over together in the straw, panting and gasping.

Josephine tried to throw her leg over Suriko, tried to get on top of her. Suriko suddenly let go her hair and made a claw of her hand, scratching at Josephine's cheek. Reflexively, Josephine jerked her head back just in time. She threw up a hand and caught Suriko's wrist. They struggled, locked. Suriko's body was warm and slick against Josephine's skin.

Josephine's bare breasts bounced painfully as she went down on her back again. Suriko ducked her head down, biting at them. She bit Josephine's right breast. Josephine squealed and brought her arm round, hitting Suriko under the chin with her elbow. Shouting, Suriko arched backwards, hurt. She had a hand to her jaw where Josephine's elbow had connected. Her eyes were wide, her nostrils wide, her teeth gleaming. She grabbed again for Josephine's hair, but Josephine was on top of her, trying to straddle her and sit on her. Dimly she could hear the horses snuffling nervously and banging against their stalls.

Suriko bucked up beneath her, throwing her off balance. She fell back on the floor, amid the dirt and spilt straw.

Suriko dived at her. With both hands she seized the front of Josephine's skimpy skirt as it flapped uselessly up over her thigh. She wrenched at it and tore it.

Josephine shouted, grabbing Suriko's bra and tugging. Suriko's face grimaced in pain as Josephine twisted the fabric tight between her little breasts. Suriko was still groping at Josephine's groin. She snagged Josephine's panties and tore them from her single-handed.

Josephine pulled out of her grip and got up on all fours, panting, her hair disarrayed, her skirt hanging in three pieces from its waistband. Suriko sat up against the bales, arms and legs spread. Her bra had skewed round, leaving her right breast bare.

Josephine sat up on her haunches. She was bigger than Suriko; she was rested. Suriko had been riding in the sun and doing who knew what else. She was tired and wet.

Josephine pointed dramatically to her unfinished tattoo. 'This is my domino!' she said. 'This!'

Suriko flew up at her again. But Josephine was ready for her this time. She braced herself on one leg, leaned sideways out of the thrust of Suriko's right arm. It felt lean and muscular in her grip: not like a man's flesh, but not like Jackie's either. Levering herself up and bearing down on Suriko, she twisted the woman's arm up behind her back.

Suriko squealed. She struck out at Josephine with her free hand, but Josephine was up, bending her over double. 'You have a fine bottom for the crop,' she said, spanking her hard.

Suriko yelled and fought, but Josephine dragged her to the wall where the chains hung. Limb by limb she locked her into place, spreadeagled, facing the wall. She left her there and went back into the mare's stall where Suriko's clothes lay.

She found what she was looking for. A domino. The double six.

She brought it back to the pinioned Suriko. Suriko was staring tearfully at her over her shoulder. Both her stockings were thickly laddered. One of her suspenders had given way. Josephine leaned up close to her, pressing her body against her back, bending her knees to rub her pelvis over Suriko's bottom. Suriko groaned between her teeth.

Josephine leaned over Suriko's shoulder and delicately tucked the domino into her bra. Then she reached down between their bodies and hauled down Suriko's panties.

Suriko wailed.

Josephine went and picked up the riding crop.

Suriko had ceased to struggle. She gazed apprehensively back at the straw- and manure-streaked woman with the tattered skirt flapping around her naked loins.

Josephine came close again and kissed her. She lifted the crop.

The first stroke came whipping down.

Suriko yelled, a full-throated yell.

An angry red line began to appear across her tight bottom.

Her chains rattled. She strained and pulled. The second stroke fell and she arched her back, hissing through her teeth. The third fell, and the wooden wall shook.

One of the horses neighed loudly in concern.

Josephine, panting, stepped back to examine her handiwork. Three fresh weals blazed across Suriko's bottom.

'No more,' Suriko pleaded. 'No more!'

'Two more, my love,' said Josephine, sweeping the hair back out of her eyes. 'Only two.'

But still her captive begged: 'No more! No more!'

She brought the crop lashing in low, aiming for the underhang of Suriko's little bottom. Suriko squealed, slamming her body against the wall as though she was trying to go straight through. Tackle shook on the nails where it hung.

Josephine came close in again, slipping her free arm around Suriko's waist. 'What would you do,' she murmured in her ear, 'to be let off the last one?'

'Anything!' sobbed Suriko. Her eyes were already red, her nose was running.

Josephine rubbed her mouth in Suriko's thick, sweaty hair.

'Nothing,' she said.

She stood back, feet astride, the fingers of her left hand spread on Suriko's shoulder, and with a vicious whip of her elbow, slammed the crop across Suriko's bottom.

Face contorted, lips drawn back in a snarl of pain, Suriko clawed at the wall.

Josephine dropped the crop.

A sparrow came fluttering in at the stable door and hopped about in the dirt, pecking at some crumbs of feed. The horses whickered to each other. The sun came squeezing through a high, small window, lighting the dust motes whirling in the air.

Josephine stood hugging Suriko, her mouth against the back of her neck. Suriko was trembling.

Josephine unfastened Suriko's arms, then her legs.

Shakily Suriko knelt unbidden at her feet. She kissed her plimsolls.

'Kiss me here,' ordered Josephine, pointing.

Suriko did. Unhesitatingly she buried her face in the moist spreading softness of Josephine's crotch.

Josephine hissed, arching her back. She twined her fingers in Suriko's hair. Suriko was more deft with her lips and tongue than the maid Lorna. Josephine's knees began to buckle and sway. They tumbled together into the straw.

Suriko was on her knees, parting her flaming buttocks with her hands. Josephine crouched behind her, pushing her face into Suriko's steaming cleft. The woman tasted like nothing, no one, she had ever tasted before, a sour reeking taste thick with salt. Suriko sobbed and cried out in Japanese, grinding her bottom into Josephine's face. Gently Josephine licked her wounds, making her squeal all over again.

Suriko lay in Josephine's arms. 'You are a powerful woman,' she said. 'Powerful.' She stroked Josephine's left breast slowly, sliding the nipple between her fingers. It began to come erect again. She fingered her own welts, gritting her teeth. Her eyes filled with tears again.

Josephine kissed them, licked them softly away.

There was a sound outside. Voices.

Dr Shepard appeared in the doorway, silhouetted against the sunlight. She was wearing a long Arab robe and a broad-brimmed, fraying straw hat.

'Anyone about?' she called.

Slowly the two women disentangled themselves and stood up, brushing straw off each other. Josephine in her socks and plimsolls, Suriko in the remains of her tattered lingerie, came out into the sunny yard.

They were all there, smiling as they watched them emerge from the stable. Sven and Roy were both wearing T-shirts, shorts and sunglasses. Roy had his arms folded across his barrel chest.

Jackie came forward, in her billowing harem pants and a clinging shirt of royal blue cotton. She had her hair tied back in a ponytail. Bracelets rattled on her wrists as she embraced Josephine.

After the hot, odorous body of Suriko, Jackie smelt fragrant and sweet.

'Did you whip her?' she asked, unnecessarily. Suriko was with the men. Sven was supporting her as she bent over, displaying her stripes. Josephine saw her looking back at her as she bent, as if she was reluctant to part from her.

Josephine looked at Jackie's open, smiling face, her lips parted questioningly. She had never been here before, at the centre of power and attention. She could not imagine how she had got here.

Jackie dipped her head and kissed the red teethmarks in Josephine's right breast.

She closed her eyes and kissed Jackie's mouth slowly, sliding her tongue between Jackie's teeth and circling it around Jackie's tongue.

She could hear the men murmuring appreciatively. After her orgasm with Suriko, she felt no lust, only a perfect quiescent satisfaction. But even as she framed the thought, Jackie's questing fingers slipped into the cleft of her bottom and she felt her appetite begin to stir again.

'Josephine,' said Dr Shepard.

Josephine surfaced, looking round, squinting against the sunlight.

'It's Sunday,' Dr Shepard said.

Josephine didn't know what she was talking about.

'Work tomorrow,' she said. 'Time to go home, Josephine.'

Josephine barely understood. She lingered, Jackie in her arms.

'Come on, Josephine,' said Dr Shepard loudly and imperiously. 'In you go and get dressed.'

'You'll find your clothes in your wardrobe, Miss Morrow,' said Annabel.

Reluctantly, the women let go of each other. Jackie was looking wistful. Dr Shepard raised a beckoning finger. Jackie went to her, and Dr Shepard and Annabel began to speak to her quietly. Would Josephine be allowed to see her again? In London? There was no way of knowing.

Saddened, Josephine passed along the line, kissing Annabel's cheek and Suriko's lips and saying goodbye. Annabel brushed straw from her back. Josephine stood passively a moment while the men, Roy lazily and Sven coolly, inspected her body, the marks she bore. Roy fondled her breasts. Sven thrust his hand between her thighs, clutching her vulva as though he would crush it. He put his lips close to her ear. 'You are the best of us all,' he said distinctly.

Josephine went to her room. Her clothes were back in the wardrobe. Her own clothes, bra and panties, her top and skirt. Her handbag and her sandals were there too this time.

She took a last shower, then dressed. In the mirror she brushed her hair. There was no sign of anything that had happened. She pressed the cloth of her top in between her breasts to see if her tattoo showed through, but her bra obscured it.

Have to get some new bras, she thought.

Suddenly she was depressed. She had nothing to take with her but her handbag. She went out of Room 3 without looking back.

The house was empty and quiet. Perhaps the maids had Sundays off. And everyone else was still outside in the sun. Were they leaving too? Did they live here or elsewhere? Who were they all really?

She went back out to the stable.

The yard was deserted.

Inside, the horses champed drowsily at their feed. Someone had picked up what was left of her clothes and Suriko's, and hung the crops on the wall.

Josephine went back outside. She wandered towards the tennis courts. There was no one there either.

She looked in the lane and saw the taxi there, waiting.

Josephine thought about riding back up to London with Roy. She imagined the journey would be complicated. There would be interruptions. Welcome interruptions, she was sure. Even so, she could not help feeling disappointed as she made her way up to the cab.

As she neared, the engine started up, rumbling and muttering. Josephine came up to the window of the cab and looked in.

Jackie was behind the wheel. She was wearing Roy's black peaked cap, black leather gauntlets, her revealing shirt, and very little else.

'Where to, ma'am?' she said.

Epilogue

She would not sleep. When at last he released her from bondage, she dozed a while in his arms. His touch had been sure and expert, his cock firm and unhesitant. She felt sticky and sore and relaxed. Her back and bottom throbbed drowsily.

She would not sleep. Francis would be back with the car at nine. Yet rest, even deep rest, was possible, even in restraint, even under severe discipline. The strap that stung and numbed also relieved and released. She did not understand that, but she knew it to be true. She rubbed her chin on her chest, feeling her collar press into her neck. She tightened her grip round the man, the stranger, the unknown master. She drew closer to him in the bed.

Absently he patted her back, her shoulder. He seemed distant, though he was so warm, his skin so smooth, his flesh so welcoming. She wondered if he had another duty to fulfil, another body to arouse and quieten. She did not know his name.

'Are you awake?' she asked.

'Mm.'

She reached for his shrunken genitals and caressed them. They were soft and wet. She teased his crinkly pubic hair between the tips of her fingers.

'I love you,' she said.

'You don't,' he said, amused.

'I do, I do, I do ...' She smothered her protest in his hair, his cheeks, his mouth. She kissed him with a kiss that rose up from the base of her spine and drew her soul forth with a grip of iron. His lips were strong and bore no questions. He cupped her tender bottom in his hands and she gasped and writhed. He had punished her body until she screamed and wept. He had worn the domino mask and ruled her with a strap, with a hairbrush across his knee like an errant school-

202

child, with a rod of wood. His discipline was severe and so gentle, so considerately cruel.

She fingered her collar. She wished he would padlock a chain to the ring in front and lead her through a hidden portal behind the walls of Estwych to a place where there was no time, no doubt, no need to wait and seek and wonder. A place where there was not even any law, only logic, and even a tattoo might count for nothing. She wished she could be extinguished in a blaze of some spiritual fire that the whip and the cock could only hint at, could only symbolize and crudely approximate. She stroked his crotch and murmured avowals and self-abnegations she hoped he would not hear.

'You don't love me,' he said, amused, scandalized. 'You don't even know me. I could leave your bed this minute and let another slip between the sheets, and you would not be perturbed at all.'

Josephine caressed his smooth, taut flanks. She wondered how he would be, under the strap. Would he jerk and cry out, or hiss between clenched teeth, or lie silent and aloof? If only she were staying to discover. But day would come, and with it time, and with that Francis and the Mercedes. Damn them, damn all loyal servants, observers of necessities and keepers of appointments.

Somewhere an owl called.

'I must get up,' she said, cuddling close to him.

'Must?' he murmured.

'I made a promise,' she said. 'To Annabel.' She kissed him, searchingly. 'Newcomers,' she explained.

'Ah.'

He flapped the bedsheets open, exposing her to the night. She protested, wriggling down beneath the sheets. She fondled his leg.

'I must get up,' she said again.

They kissed, deep and slow. His hands were on her breasts, between her thighs. She sighed. She told him with her mouth how supreme he was. She would stay with him, devoted to him, forever. She would rise and leave him any minute.

'I must go.'

Josephine got out of bed. The night was chilly after the heat of their encounters. Naked she padded quickly across the darkened room to the bellrope by the hearth, and gave it a tug.

She came back and sat on the bed, naked. She stroked her lover's hair.

'Of course,' she said, 'if you haven't finished with me.'

He groaned and buried his face. She laughed. There was a knock at the door.

'Enter.'

It was Lucy the maid. 'You rang, madam?'

'Yes, Lucy. Bring me some things.'

'Things, madam?'

'Yes, Lucy. There are some new arrivals, I hear.'

'Yes, madam. In Room 6.'

'I shall see them.'

'Very good, madam.'

She undressed and washed. She put on a long black robe that swept to the floor, with a high collar that stood up behind her neck, and sleeves wide and long enough her hands were hidden. On her fingers she wore rings of silver with black stones; on her wrists leather bands with silver embossing.

At the proper time, at the pull of a silver ring the robe would fall from her body. Beneath she wore a narrow black leather collar with a hanging fringe of imitation silver cat teeth; a black corset in a subtle pattern of diamonds differentiated only by a thread of silver in the weave; her sheer black stockings on dark crimson suspenders. Lucy the maid helped her on with a pair of black leather boots so glossy they reflected her willing hands. Josephine slipped her hand behind Lucy's neck and raised her face to kiss her on the mouth.

'Now you can pack my case,' she said.

The man lay back in the bed, sipping cognac. Josephine looked at his from across the room. She had dismissed him from her mind. Still he was good to look at. Under the firm embrace of her corset she could feel the sharp reminders of his slender hands. She looked at him in the light of the remaining candles, making him her mirror. In the serene admiration of his dark eyes, the precise curve of satisfaction in his lips, she could see her own glory.

She strode back to the bed, trying out the boots. She extended her hand to him.

'You may kiss my hand,' she said.

He understood. He set aside his glass and touched his lips, infinitely lightly, lingeringly, to her knuckles.

'Your Majesty,' he said, mockingly.

She took his domino from the mantelpiece, and slipped a domino mask over her eyes. Then she stepped out into the corridor and along to Room 6, on the other side of the house. Lucy came behind, carrying the attaché case.

'Set it down, Lucy,' said Josephine outside the door. 'You have done well. Tell Mrs Taylor I am pleased.'

Lucy bobbed a curtsey, her eyes cast down. Was she hiding a smile? Josephine would not notice. As the maid hurried away, skirts swishing softly in the silence of the night, Josephine knocked at the door.

'Come in,' called a voice. A young woman's voice.

Josephine picked up the case and went inside.

Room 6 was Victorian. Oriental rugs in layers over a carpet of sombre green. Damask curtains with a baubled fringe and fat silken cords. Gaslamps with tulip glasses of pastel pink. A huge wooden bed with an ornate headboard inlaid with ceramic and jet. A washstand big enough to dine off and a wardrobe that almost touched the ceiling. Mahogany chairs, upright, with flat horsehair cushions of tarnished gold. Armchairs deep enough to curl up and sleep in, facing a tiny black leaded grate where a coal fire burned low. Gilt candlesticks, china plates and ornaments, a mantel clock, silhouettes in frames, dried flowers under glass bells. Squat vases with metallic glazes bearing fleshy green plants. The thick scent of orchids.

A young man, slender and white-skinned, with a brush of red hair, knelt at the foot of the bed. He did not look up as Josephine came in. As she came near him, she saw he could not. An iron yoke weighed his shoulders down and pressed his head forward in a bow of perpetual submission. His hands were cuffed behind his back, the cuffs linked by a short chain to the shackles that restrained his feet. Another chain tethered him to the bed. He was blindfolded and naked. His cock was erect. Its circumcised tip glistened in the gaslight.

The woman's voice spoke from the bed.

'Hallo,' she said.

She was sitting on the bed with her bare feet drawn up under her. She made no move to get up.

Her face was small, with a bewitchingly sharp line to the nose and jaw. Her eyes were foxy, and slightly slant. Her hair was wavy, an undistinquished brown, cut so it hung just off her shoulders. Her hands on the counterpane looked small but strong, accustomed to work; her legs were short and chubby. She was wearing loose white lounging pyjamas in a soft ribbed material. Her breasts beneath the top were the size of apples. The vee of the neck showed a triangle of bare skin, pink with the sheen of youth and health. She was very young, surely scarcely into her twenties. She was the youngest person Josephine had ever seen at Estwych. Except for the maids.

Josephine remembered her. It was a maid she had met, a maid she had got into trouble on her very first day here, years before.

'Janet?'

The young woman smiled. It was not clear whether she recognised this masked, black-robed woman or not. What was clear was that she was very much at home here.

'We're here for the week,' she said cheerfully, as if this were some kind of holiday camp. She nodded at the man she had secured at the foot of her bed. 'I've brought him to get his tattoo.'

Josephine said only, 'That was presumptuous of you.'

She eased the bands on her wrists, flexing the muscles of her forearms. She took the domino from her sleeve and tossed it onto the counterpane. She gave a slight nod in the direction of the door.

'Fetch me my case,' she said.

Chastened, the young woman began to climb from the bed.

'Yes, mistress,' she said.

THE
NATIONAL FRONT

Martin Walker

Fontana/Collins

CONTENTS

Introduction

There are a number of differences between a journalist and a historian, but the most important one is that a journalist, simply by describing and commenting on events as they happen, has the power to influence them. This, doubtless to the detriment of the objective book I had hoped to write, and which the dons of Oxford and Harvard had trained me to write, has been my experience with the National Front. It was inevitable that a journalist on a national newspaper, writing and reporting and analysing regularly the affairs of the NF, would have this effect, if only because nobody else was doing the job.

The result was predictable. The NF is to produce its own lengthy account of its latest split, and it has already announced that the book will be dedicated to me. The NF has suggested that I am an agent of Israeli Intelligence – while my friends in the PLO will testify that I am an anti-Zionist, even though I volunteered for the Israeli war effort in 1967. The NF has suggested that I use a false name, and that I was born Blumenthal. This is nonsense. The NF avers that I am an enemy, a hostile, and they have ruled that no NF member should speak to me or communicate with me in any way. The NF went to a considerable expense in 1974 and 1975 to 'clean' their meeting halls and HQ of bugs which they suspected I had placed. The supporters of John Tyndall have alleged in writing that I was a key and shadowy figure in the internal debate and split which rent the NF into two separate parties in 1975. I can only say that I wish to heaven they were right. But they are not.

I oppose the National Front, the ideology they stand for, the policies they present and the poison they inject. Even so, I am enough of a democrat to accept that they have a right to make their points to the electorate, to hire public halls, and to stand for elections. If they win a British general election, then they are entitled to my respect. Looking at the current volatility of British politics, this is not necessarily a ludicrous proposition. Should they be elected, I fear that I would feel constrained to leave the country for my own safety. I have been physically threatened by several leading NF members. I have been plagued with late-night phone calls threatening to 'get me'. I have had a fire lit with my mail at the base of my door. Even my girlfriends have been threatened.

And yet I have been met with courtesy by a number of NF leaders. I have lunched, dined, drunk and talked to the small hours with some of them. One or two I now count as personal friends, and I cannot find it in my heart or my conscience to call them 'Fascists'. To understand this one has to accept the degree to which racism is institutionalized in this oldest of imperial nations, the way in which Disraeli consciously presented the imperial idea to the emergent working class as a bait to make them vote Conservative, and the way in which the concept of Empire has helped, psychologically, to compensate the English and Scottish working class from which I come to accept the horrors of being the guinea pigs for industrial society.

When John Kingsley Read tells me that he is sick and tired of the British elite being apologetic for the Empire, I have to agree, because his and my grandparents were also victims of an imperial system. When Roy Painter expresses his fury at the callous destruction of the working-class community of North London by architects, planners and Labour-controlled councils I have to agree, because the South Durham mining area I come from was also cut down by the planners of the National Coal Board. By destroying the relationship between the community and the Miners' Union, they opened the door to the crude union feudalism which Dan Smith and Andy Cunningham applied to rape the North-east – but that is another story. When Martin Webster tells me of his fear of walking certain streets in towns of our country, I understand. I fear those streets too. I lived in Moss Side, Manchester and I lived in the ghetto on 19th St NW in Washington DC and I made sure everyone in the block knew I was British, and even so it was unpleasant. When John Harrison-Broadley talks of the Second World War, and the Battle of Britain and fighting against the odds, I know what he means. My father and two uncles were in the RAF in the war, and when at the age of seventeen I took my private pilot's licence, my father solemnly gave me the log-book of the uncle who had died in the Pathfinder squadron over Turin. It was a key event, after the confrontations of adolescence, in my learning to love him and it moved me deeply.

The reader is entitled to know my prejudices, and my own political posture. I wish I was sure enough to describe them. To be brief, I vote Labour and doubt whether I could ever vote anything else; it would seem a betrayal of my upbringing, of my education as a scholarship kid who went to grammar schools and won a scholarship to Oxford because of the 1944 Education Act and the Welfare State, and of my father whose first political

8

memory is of throwing rocks at blacklegs in the General Strike. I despise nationalism, whether it be British, White Racist or Martian. I firmly believe that the human race, in 5,000 or 50,000 years will be a uniform coffee-colour with a pleasing tinge of yellow and I lustfully believe in accelerating the process. My Scottish friends warn me against English Nationalism; my McNeil mother would giggle.

I fear that I am polluted by the racism of my society. I recall the sense of shock I felt in Rhodesia, after working six months in South Africa, when I turned around in a bar and saw a black face that was not serving me. I fear to analyse the sense of culture shock I feel in Southall and Brixton, although I have been in love and lived with black women and shared my home for eighteen months with a black friend from the Bahamas who first stunned and then intrigued my National Front friends as we all argued into the night.

This book should speak for itself, as a reasonably objective account of the growth of a racialist party, its development, its leaders and its trials. I hope it is not a hatchet job; I am pleased that it is not a sociological tract. Readers, presumably, want to know how the NF grew and what happened during that growth. If NF loyalists, Trotskyists and ordinary voters can read and use it on that basis, I will be happy.

To think of National Front members as Fascists in the classic sense of the 1930s is silly. To think of them as party members in the sense of being dedicated or committed ideologues is to over-state the case. The membership of the NF is rather like a bath with both taps running and the plughole empty. Members pour in and pour out. Although some 20,000 people went through the NF in 1974, the stable membership was about 12,000, and the bulk of them did little more than vote, attend one or two rallies, the occasional branch meeting and canvass at election time.

The pattern of recruitment is fitful; floods of new members follow publicity for the NF at elections and by-elections, and the great surges have tended to come with a renewed focus of national interest on immigration. The arrival of the Ugandan Asians in 1972, for example, brought so much new support that the character of the Front began to change. New members, new talent from other parties, established local politicians with experience of local issues and campaigning all welled into a party which was still dominated by the old neo-Nazis and cranks who had been scrabbling in the gutter of racist politics for a generation.

I think it is important to understand the differences between the two kinds of NF members, the old loyalists and the new supporters who entered the NF when it was beginning to realize the possibility of becoming a real mass movement. The NF has been led, nominally at least, by men who cannot be simply dismissed by reference to prison convictions they were given ten and fifteen years ago. The Tyndalls and the Websters, veterans of Nazi parties and the schismatic days of the 1960s, still dominate the NF's administrative HQ and still play a key part on the National Directorate. But they are no longer in total control, and if the NF continues to expand, the power of these veterans will probably diminish further. Or as Roy Painter, leader of the populist group, said when John Tyndall lost the party chairmanship in October 1974: 'The NF is not a dirty word any more'.

Painter was overstating the case. The racialist roots and proposals of the NF manifesto still make it repugnant to me and to many other people. But as a Labour voter, I still support a party which deprived the Kenyan Asians of their British citizenship, which toughened the controls on immigration and which connives at a great deal of institutional racism in the trade unions. On matters of racism, no political party in Britain has clean hands.

The cynic could argue that the prejudices of the National Front are at least honestly presented, without concern for the liberal catchwords and pieties which successive British Governments have mouthed (and betrayed) in the past. Indeed, John Tyndall had no qualms about stating his opposition to inter-racial marriages in a TV interview in September 1974. And if the NF propaganda of recent months is any guide, the party has already recognized that it is so closely associated with firm opposition to coloured immigrants that this core of its message barely needs further labouring. Like George Wallace in his 1968 American election campaign, who mentioned school bussing, law and order, motherhood and nobody in the audience ever doubted that every single one of them meant 'Nigger'.

And if the NF hardly needs to stress the word immigration today, it is because this issue, like so many of the NF's wares, is one which operates on the very fringe of the human consciousness. Later in this book, I give an account of a private lecture Tyndall gave to an NF leadership training session. Tyndall talked at length about the role of the irrational in the NF's membership; he spoke most urgently of the need for the NF to appeal to 'the hidden forces of the human soul'. I know what the man means, and everybody who has studied Germany in the 1930s or seen a film by Leni Riefenstahl knows what he means, even though we cannot quantify his meaning for scholarly dissection.

Tyndall is talking of marches, of the sense of unity of columns with waving banners and the sound of men in step. He is talking of blind loyalties, of faiths that ignore reason and orders that are obeyed. It is an appeal to which we European savages are fairly vulnerable – we fought two European tribal wars about it in this century. One lesson we should have learned from the experience is that this native vulnerability of ours increases when the economy turns sour. Let inflation undermine the faith of the middle classes in their morsels of property, or let unemployment bring shame and insecurity to the respectable working class, and many people turn to what Enoch Powell once called 'the great simplicities'. Over 100,000 British voters have already put their faith into the 'great simplicities' of the NF even without a dramatic economic collapse. More to the point, they have voted for a party which is still dominated by men who were widely dismissed as criminals and lunatics ten years ago.

The National Front is a legal party, presenting a coherent and not unthoughtful party programme to the electors. It has developed a party organization which, if not national, is effective and significant in the bulk of our major urban areas. It is growing as a party; it has tried to take intelligent advantage of political events such as the campaign to remove Britain from the EEC. My own suspicion is that we are going to have to learn to live with it.

Some of the more thoughtful NF leaders suggest that the continued erosion of the two-party system in Britain is playing into their hands. They look at the style of Margaret Thatcher, new leader of the Conservative Party, and hope – with some reason – that her aggressively middle-class image will lead an increasing number of working-class Tory voters to shift to the NF. They suggest that increasing militancy in the trade unions gives NF recruiters an opportunity to win over the many non-militants on the shop floor. And they point to 20 per cent inflation and economic crisis when they argue that lower-middle-class insecurity has traditionally led to increased support for nationalist and authoritarian parties.

Will the NF grow or not? One can argue it either way. The European experience with the MSI and the NPD suggest that a nationalist, authoritarian party can rarely expect to get more than 10 per cent of the vote so long as the economy expands and the major political parties retain their influence. In Britain in 1977, those two vital qualifications no longer apply. In a period of crisis and uncertainty, a maverick party such as the NF could conceivably explode into power. We simply do not know the economic and social parameters which will shape their and our future – and I fear that the NF is reasonably well-equipped to take advantage of whatever political opportunities that future may yet offer them.

Martin Walker

Acknowledgements

In October 1974, the National Front issued this bulletin to its members:

> No co-operation, assistance, advice, information or comment – not matter what the subject or issue – may be given by any member of the National Front to Mr Martin Walker or to any other journalist suspected by members to be working for or on behalf of Mr Walker. Any questions from him must be replied to by use of the simple statement 'No Comment'. This ruling applies to all forms of attempted interviews by Mr Walker, be they 'on or off the record', 'informal', 'social' or whatever.

This directive from the Executive Council was declared 'in view of the quite clear malice which this man has for the National Front and the vendetta which he pursues against some leading members of the party'.

This book has been written in defiance of that ban, thanks in part to the readiness of several National Front members and officers to talk frankly and at length to me about the party's growth and structure. For obvious reasons it is impossible to name them here. But in the nine months that I was able to study the NF in detail before that ban was applied, I was met with courtesy and helpfulness by many of the party leaders, and I should like to thank Mr Roy Painter, Mr Martin Webster, Mr John Tyndall and Mr J. Kingsley Read for their assistance in this period.

I have used the libraries of the Press Association, the Wiener Library, the Institute of Race Relations, the *Morning Star*, the *Birmingham Post and Mail* and *Private Eye*, and have had access to the publications and researches of the Transport and General Workers' Union, the International Marxist Group, the Communist Party, the Association of Jewish Ex-Servicemen, the Institute of Jewish Affairs, the Monday Club and the Birmingham group, All Faiths for One Race. I am indebted to many friends and researchers in the media for their work and help, including Christopher Hitchens, Peter Chippindale, Gerry Gable and David Ashton.

I was granted interviews by Colin Jordan, John O'Brien, Dan

13

Harmston, Harold Soref, Rodney Legg, Rosine de Bounevialle and Mrs A. K. Chesterton. I also had the benefit of long discussions with Geoffrey Stewart-Smith, Jonathan Guinness and Martin Webster. My lectures to students at Edinburgh, Sussex, Warwick and Hull universities brought much new information and some welcome perspectives.

This book began when I was writing a column for the *Guardian*, without whose indulgence and support I could not have been accepted at so many group, branch and local planning meetings of the NF. The editor and trustees of the *Guardian*, and my colleagues there, have my deepest thanks.

In the course of my research, I have accumulated a wealth of knowledge about the far right in Britain; in particular I have compiled a card index of the names, addresses and backgrounds of many NF militants and organizers. All of this basic data is being presented to the Institute of Race Relations in London, where much of my research was done, and whose lovely people sustained me with affection, argument and coffee. I hope others will find this material of use. The book was mainly written at the home of my friends, John and Marjorie Brunner, in Somerset. They keep a writer's house and I love them dearly. Susan Morgan helped with the research, loved me and sustained me. I dedicate the book to my parents and to other anti-Fascists everywhere.

ONE

The Fascist Tradition in Britain

Few words have been as used and abused as 'Fascism'. The term has been devalued to the level of a generalized political insult. The National Front, for example, attacks its left-wing opponents as 'red Fascists', and the left attacks the 'liberal democracies' as Fascist. The word has become such an accepted label of abuse that it has now acquired a host of prefixes to enable us to blaze a few trails of meaning through the syntactic jungle. Proto-fascist, crypto-fascist, neo-fascist, state-fascist, quasi-fascist; the sub-groups go forth and multiply and do little to impose meaning on the confusion.

So we should try to begin at the beginning. Let us start with the premise that there are two kinds of society, totalitarian and pluralistic. The totalitarian society is a single-minded structure. It mobilizes all its resources under one authority to achieve one goal. Economy, education, military and medical establishments, religion and the media and the security forces are all focused upon one over-riding objective, whether it be upon national economic development, war, space exploration or the fulfilment of an ideology. All individual 'rights' are suspended before the higher purpose of the totalitarian will.

The pluralistic kind of society has agreed to permit its citizens to differ about the society's objectives, and the function of the state (leaving aside the class confrontations which may define its bounds) is to set the ground rules and hold the ring to permit various groups with various objectives to promote their different social programmes without altering the basic pluralistic quality of the state.

The totalitarians can themselves be sub-divided into a number of groups, but it is most convenient to think in terms of two: those who believe that the sacred entity of the nation itself requires protection and redemption as a prelude to national expansion and greater influence and power; and those who believe that the human race as a whole needs a single moral and political purpose, and that the greatest contribution the people can make is to become a totalitarian state with the objective of spreading the great moral purpose to the rest of the world. The first group we call Fascists, the second group we call Communists.

Both are children of crisis, and until real danger presents itself, the role of totalitarians in a plural society is a lowly one. Britain

15

is historically accustomed to one form or another of coalition government, which is the essence of pluralism. The two-party system of one loose coalition opposing another is a regular pattern in English history, whether we think in terms of the medieval monarchy against elements of the medieval aristocracy, the Roundheads versus the Cavaliers, the Whigs against the Tories of the late eighteenth century, the coalition of the landed interests against the industrial interests of the nineteenth century. The pattern is never precise, and the very looseness of the coalitions means that the two sides never fell into clearly-distinguished battle lines. There were peers inside the Liberal Party of 1906, and there was Jo Chamberlain, that archetypal Birmingham industrialist, in the ranks of the Conservatives. There was Disraeli, trying to rally the working and peasant classes to Toryism, and Lloyd George, trying to win them for the Liberals. But the working classes created their own new coalition with the socialist intelligentsia and the more ambitious (or realistic) Liberals and the two-party (or two-coalition) structure remained.

The great strength of the British pluralist system of channelling political allegiance into one of two wide coalitions is that many citizens who sympathize with totalitarian objectives are encouraged to stay within the political mainstream. Almost all the specific policies of the National Front can quite properly be held by members of the Conservative Party. On immigration, on defence policies, on the return of capital punishment and more stringent punishments for crimes of violence, on censorship and education policies, there is little that separates the National Front member from the right-wing Conservative. Similarly, the Labour Party can happily absorb Marxists, class war theorists and syndicalists. The coalitions are almost infinitely flexible. Britain, after all, has never seen a violent dispossession of its ruling class like the French revolution, nor has it suffered defeat and occupation by a foreign power. The great climacterics which create permanent and irreconcilable divisions between the ruling class and the revolutionaries, or between the patriots and the collaborators are foreign to the British political tradition.

The British Union of Fascists of Sir Oswald Mosley was an attempt to break through this tradition of political accommodation and gradual change. Mosley himself was a young man of vaulting ambition. He had returned from the trenches of the First World War to become a Conservative Member of Parliament. In subsequent elections he stood as an Independent Conservative, as an Independent, as a Labour candidate and then as a member of his own New Party: promotion and receptiveness to new ideas were too slow in the conventional parties, and Mosley resolved to create his own. Inevitably, his defection from the Labour Party provoked the hostility of the labour movement, which harassed his New Party campaign at its first electoral test, the Ashton-under-Lyne by-election of 1931. According to John Strachey, who was a New Party supporter, Mosley looked down with disgust at the angry and hostile mob which the labour movement had rallied against him. 'That is the crowd,' Mosley said, 'which has prevented anyone from doing anything in England since the war.' It was at that moment, concluded Strachey, that Mosley became a Fascist. The collapse of his New Party at the 1931 general election convinced him that he and his supporters could not take the conventional parliamentary route to power, just as the Labour Party's refusal instantly to adopt his imaginative plans to overcome unemployment had destroyed his faith in the capacity of the Labour coalition to react quickly and resolutely enough to national danger.

In 1932, with the New Party failure behind him, Mosley took Harold Nicolson to Italy, to study Mussolini's Fascism at first hand. Mosley had been attracted by a statement that Mussolini had made a month before he achieved (or was summoned to) power. The Italian had said 'Our programme is simple: we wish to govern Italy. It is not programmes that are wanting for the salvation of Italy but men and will power.'

The first decade of Mussolini passed with little attempt to create a classic doctrine or definition of Fascism. Mussolini was a pragmatic ruler and slapdash administrator who declared 'Fascism is not for export'. It was an Italian answer to an Italian crisis and not until that crisis was some years past, and the applause from other European nations rang in his ears, did Mussolini begin to evolve a cohesive, if not coherent, ideology. Mussolini had governed by the seat of his pants, guided in part by his early Socialism, in part by his instinctive and bombastic nationalism and above all – like most successful newspaper editors – by his flair for presentation and publicity.

The ideology which Mussolini finally defined was given the name of the 'Corporate State'. He defined it as 'A society working with the harmony and precision of the human body. Every interest and every individual is subordinated to the overriding purpose of the nation.' The great problem, of course, was to determine what the purpose of the nation was to be. Was it material prosperity for its citizens, or imperial expansion, or conquest of neighbours or what? At one time or another,

Mussolini declared the national purpose to be all of these. He was caught in the trap of extreme nationalism – once the nation has been forged into an efficient tool for the expression of the national will, it is very difficult not to let that tool be applied to the familiar human activity of asserting that will against neighbours.

Mosley saw no such source of determination in Britain. He had seen the indecision and caution with which the Labour Government reacted to his plans to counter unemployment. He had seen the irresolution of the British trade unions which led to the collapse of the General Strike of 1926 within a week. He had also seen the puny efforts of Miss Rotha Linton-Orman and General Walter Blakeney to build a British Fascisti in the 1920s. Their anti-internationalism and economic theories ('Communism is run by international Jews') were to be adopted by Mosley, by A. K. Chesterton and later by the National Front. But their movement had collapsed by 1928, with subscriptions collecting a mere £604 a year – against £6848 in 1925.

On 1 October 1932, Mosley launched the British Union of Fascists. He brought with him some of his old supporters from the New Party; Dr Robert Forgan as BUF Director of Organization; Eric Piercy, as commander of the Blackshirt defence force; W. E. D. Allen, who had been Unionist MP for West Belfast; F. M. Box who succeeded Forgan as Director of Organization and who had been a Conservative Party agent. Mosley's support within the Labour Movement attracted Independent Labour Party support; Wilfred Risdon, ILP Midlands organizer; John Beckett, ILP MP for Peckham and George Sutton, an ILP member who had been Mosley's secretary since 1920, all rallied to the BUF. From the British Fascisti came William Joyce, later to achieve notoriety as Lord Haw-Haw, and Neil Francis-Hawkins who brought with him the British Fascisti membership and subscription lists. And Alexander Raven Thomson, who was to remain loyal for twenty years, joined him from the Communist Party.

Although Mussolini had specifically warned him against building a para-military force in Britain, Mosley was convinced after the Ashton-under-Lyne by-election that he needed a corps of tough stewards to guarantee order at his meetings. Housed in BUF HQ, the Black House in Chelsea, they became something of a private standing army, comprising some 400 men, uniformed, equipped with armoured vehicles and truncheons and a tiny 'air force'.

By British standards, they were alarming, although they had

neither the numbers nor the organization of Hitler's *Sturmab-teilung* or Mussolini's *Squadristi*. But in March 1933, their methods of dealing with hecklers at a rally in Manchester's Free Trade Hall led to violent disorder and the police closed the meeting. Mosley had insisted at the beginning of the event that he did not want violence and stressed that the 140 Blackshirts were only scattered around the hall to ensure the right of free speech.

In 1933, the numbers of unemployed rose to almost three million, and the strains upon the democratic system were under-lined by the growth of Sir Stafford Cripps's Socialist League, which called for quasi-dictatorial powers for a Socialist Govern-ment. Lord Rothermere and those Conservatives whose ranks swelled the BUF meeting at the Albert Hall in April 1934 saw the BUF as a kind of ginger group for the Conservative Party. They did not share Mosley's concern to overthrow the British parliamentary system – they simply saw him as potentially its ablest and most determined defender against the threat of Socialism. By the middle of 1934, the violence of the BUF rally at Olympia and the general distaste for the brutalities of Hitler's Night of the Long Knives in Germany had combined with declining unemployment to cool Rothermere's Blackshirt ardour.

In a letter to Mosley late in June of 1934, Rothermere sug-gested that a movement calling itself Fascist would never succeed in Britain, that he could not support anti-semitism, that he could no more support dictatorship and that he did not agree that Britain's parliamentary institutions should be dismantled in favour of the corporate state. He stressed that he and his news-papers endorsed Mosley in the hope of building a BUF-Con-servative alliance against Socialism.

Mosley's inability to gain significant Conservative support, and the progressive improvement in Britain's economic position, put the BUF into a decline from which it never really recovered. Some of its key supporters, such as Dr Forgan, resigned rather than support a policy of anti-semitism. More were frightened away by the public outrage which greeted the Blackshirt brutalities at the Olympia rally. By 1935, the loss of BUF momentum was underlined by the closure of the Black House and the quiet disbanding of the Defence Force. The 20 BUF clubs around the country (which its enemies called barracks) were turned into bookshops and administrative centres and the focus of the BUF shifted away from quasi-military opposition to Red Revolution. A new constitution was published, written mainly by General J. F. C. Fuller, better known as one of

Britain's leading military historians and strategic thinkers. The emphasis turned more towards electoral politics, and the BUF campaigned during the 1935 general election not for its own candidates (although it had the previous year promised to fight 100 seats, it in fact contested none) but under the slogan 'Fascism next time'.

The renewed drive of the movement in 1936 was based on concentrating Fascist strength into one area, the East End of London, and in attempting to convince the public of its size, discipline and determination by ever more marches and rallies. The East End campaign was begun when every other strategy had failed. The uninterrupted surge to power had been checked in 1934. An attempt to build an industrial base in the cotton towns in 1935 was initially promising, after 20 new recruiting centres were opened in the north-west and Mosley promised to close competing cotton factories in India, ban cheap Japanese imports and 'deal with' the Jewish capitalists in London, but little of this support survived the recruiting drive. Nor did Mosley have much success with the winter campaign of 1935 to win support among small traders and shopkeepers with his promise to close the large chain stores.

But in the course of 1936, Mosley became for the Left a symbol of the Fascism which was becoming a clear threat to European peace. It was the year of Hitler's occupation of the Rhineland, the year of Italy's Imperial war in Ethiopia and the year of the outbreak of the Spanish Civil War. Anti-fascists mobilized in greater force than ever before to demonstrate against a BUF meeting in the Albert Hall in March, and were brutally charged and dispersed by the police.

This heralded a summer of political demonstrations, marches and violence that the police strained every nerve to contain. The overwhelming impression that comes from the reports of the Metropolitan Police Commissioner and the Cabinet minutes was that the BUF was seen simply as a threat to public order, and not as a potentially revolutionary force with ambition to overthrow the state. Certainly the tradition of common law, and the tradition of British pluralism, demanded that Mosley's supporters had a right to hold mass meetings and marches, and had a right to police protection against their opponents. In guaranteeing that right, the Metropolitan Police were worked into the ground in 1936.

Mosley's campaign in the East End was intensive – the police attended 536 meetings there in August, 603 in September and 647 in October. For the whole of October, 300 police reinforcements had to be drafted to the East End every day. Mosley was opposed by the Communist Party, by the Independent Labour Party, by some trade unions and by the organized Jewish community. The greatest confrontation came on 4 October in Cable Street; the anti-fascist organizations had publicized the date so well that a significant proportion of the estimated 100,000 people who crammed the surrounding streets had come as tourists rather than as demonstrators.

To guarantee the Fascists' right to march were 7000 police, including the entire mounted corps and an autogyro. While waiting for Mosley to join his 3000 assembled Fascists, the police held back the crowd and after some hard fighting, captured and dismantled a barricade in Cable Street. Mosley agreed to the request of Sir Philip Game, the Police Commissioner, that he divert his march. Game's annual report later stated that he had 'little doubt that serious rioting and bloodshed would have occurred had the march been allowed to take place'.

In the mythology of the British Left, this day of Cable Street has been elevated into a heroic, Verdun-like decision of the British working class to stop Fascism on the streets of London. It is a dangerous myth to uphold. There were four BUF meetings planned for that afternoon in the East End, and three of them continued without opposition. Mosley was to march in the East End again, and his supporters were to continue with some success to work and fight elections there until after the outbreak of war. The official police report on Fascist activity suggested that Mosley had gained 2000 recruits in the East End in the two months after the battle of Cable Street.

The Labour Party annual conference began the day after the battle, and demanded that the Government hold an enquiry into the disturbance, and introduce legislation which would protect free speech, but curb the militarization of politics, and incitement to racial strife. The Labour Movement, the Jewish community and local government authorities in East London all urged some form of legislation, and in November 1936, the text of a Bill which was to become the Public Order Act was published. It was not aimed at stopping Mosley or the BUF, but at the kind of methods which could be used by any political party whose activities rested on public marches and rallies. It banned the wearing of uniforms in public for political purposes, and prohibited para-military organizations which were designed to use force – or which 'aroused reasonable apprehension' that force might be used. It gave the chief of the local police the right to impose routes and conditions upon political marches if he

21

had grounds to fear disorder. The Act banned the presence of 'offensive weapons' at public demonstrations and gave the police powers to arrest disorderly counter-demonstrators.

It was an impartial Act, which has been used in recent times against Irish Republican demonstrators and against the Left, and it did not stop Mosley for the simple reason that it was not designed for such a purpose. Its object was to preserve public order. Mosley continued to wear a black shirt under a suit and continued to march.

Mosley and his men marched in Kentish Town in July, without serious opposition, and in South London in October. The police having cleared a path through counter-demonstrators, Mosley was able to begin his speech 'Brother Fascists, we have passed'. And he retained considerable support in the East End, where his candidates polled an average 18 per cent of the votes in the local elections for Bethnal Green, Stepney and Shoreditch in March 1937. In Bethnal Green, where the BUF defeated the Liberals and won 23·1 per cent of the vote, Mosley subsequently claimed that 'we would certainly have won at that time on a Parliamentary Register which gave the young people the vote'. Police reports indeed confirm that Mosley's East End support came mainly from younger people.

Although the BUF's performance in subsequent elections was to prove lamentable – its 22 candidates around the country in the 1938 local elections achieved a paltry average of 112 votes each – Mosley's movement was vigorous enough in July 1939 to fill Earls Court with over 20,000 people in what was at the time the largest indoor political rally ever held in Europe.

It meant very little. The Fascist marches which much of the East End rallied to oppose in 1936 were themselves symbols of a spent force, outnumbered by the very police who guarded their right to speak. Each new direction which Mosley tried after he abandoned conventional politics ended in failure. The experiment with the New Party failed. The attempt to build an extra-parliamentary mass movement failed in 1934. The campaign to win the working class of the depression-hit cotton towns in 1935 collapsed as soon as the intensive initial drive ended, and the East End campaign created the antagonisms which led the state to ban his Blackshirts and forbid his and his opponents' marches. And even the state's reaction was caused less by Mosley than by the opposition he had aroused. His efforts in the East End municipal elections did little more than show that Cable Street had not quite put an end to Fascism in East London.

The root cause of Mosley's failure, irrespective of the national mood, was his abominable sense of timing. He miscalculated the progress of the Depression in Britain. He mistimed his launch of Fascism and lent it the reflected brutalities of the Nazis, rather than the earlier 'glories' of Mussolini. Mosley had abandoned the Labour Government, resigning a Cabinet post, in 1930, believing that his proposals to fight the Depression were too radical and too premature for a minority Government unaccustomed to power. But had he stayed inside the Government, he may possibly have convinced his colleagues that his ideas deserved implementation by the time unemployment reached its peak in 1933. In trying at various times to build a mass movement of Blackshirts to bid for power in the style of Mussolini, or a parliamentary party which could confront the long-established parties, Mosley hoped that passion and individuals could do the work of organization and numbers. Time and again, his experiments failed.

Mosley had once vowed to his followers 'We shall win, or we shall return upon our shields.' But the ancient Spartan symbol of death with honour was not for Mosley. He lingered on in politics, dependent on that very state he had promised to overthrow for police protection of his meetings. He was interned by a vengeful Government during the war, although any threat he had ever presented was long passed. He was released from internment on the grounds of ill-health; the complaint was phlebitis, but Mosley survived longer than any member of the Cabinet which had interned him. He returned to British politics within thirty months of the war's end, to spread a modified message and wait for the new slump which he believed would summon him to lead the nation at last.

The intensity of his conviction, his faith in his own and the nation's destiny, suggest the passion of Fascism – that element of the irrational and the primeval which enthralls it. The taste for torchlit marches, for massed ranks of disciplined men, for devotion to nation and duty, for sacrifice and challenge, for purity in race and life – it was not the real world of British politics and British people that Mosley saw as summoning him to power. It was an idealized world of noble men and dauntless virtue, a world of good and evil that knew no moderation or weakness. It was a fantasy of perfect causes and perfect companions, an idealized Britain whose ideal leader was himself. He hinted at his vision of the ideal world when he returned from seeing Mussolini in 1932 – 'It has produced not only a new system of Government but also a new type of man, who differs from politicians of the old world as men from another planet.'

The Fascist tradition in Britain has not been a happy or even remotely successful one. It is, however, persistent. Mosley was to revive it shortly after a world war had been fought to extirpate the creed. Younger men were to learn some lessons from him and make some of his mistakes. They were to create, by the 1970s, a political movement more soundly based than Mosley ever knew. They were to draw upon him and his old supporters for an ideology, but they were to lack the one real asset the BUF ever had – Mosley himself, a charismatic leader with recognized political gifts, a potential British dictator.

TWO

The Lunatic Fringe – 1945-1963

By 1945, the Fascist tradition had become synonymous with evil. The confirmation of Allied propaganda about the Nazi concentration camps, and the grim litany of genocide which emerged from the Nuremburg trials, made Fascism and all its adherents into political outcasts. Fascism ceased even to be a political option, and had become an obscenity.

Nevertheless the speed with which Sir Oswald Mosley and his former associates regrouped after 1945 and returned to the British political scene was remarkable. As early as 1944, Jeffrey Hamm, a former BUF member who had been interned (and had also fought with the Royal Armoured Corps) founded the British League of Ex-Servicemen, which was to become the nucleus for Mosley's Union Movement in 1948.

Throughout 1947, there were weekly meetings at Ridley Road in the East End, where Jeffrey Hamm learned his trade as a soapbox speaker. Hamm's League and a series of Book Clubs which specialized in nationalist and pro-Mosley literature, were preparing the ground for the return of Mosley to active politics in the winter of 1947–8. On 28 November 1947 Mosley called a press conference in Pimlico, outlining his plans for the establishment of the Union Movement. Mosley had already toured the forty-seven Book Clubs which Raven Thomson had organized, and in January 1948, these Clubs and four other political groups were summoned to the Memorial Hall in Farringdon Street.

Mosley was given a tumultuous reception. He said that he assumed those present had absorbed the policies outlined in his book *The Alternative*, which advocated a European nationalism, a new supra-national state of Europe, organized as a corporate state, using the continent of Africa as a granary and source of raw materials. He outlined a policy of apartheid, or separate development for different races, strikingly similar to that of the South African Government of Dr Verwoerd.

He told the meeting that a new great economic slump was imminent, and a new political movement must prepare to meet it. This movement, Mosley added, to ecstatic cheers, would be led by himself. On 7 February 1948, the British League of Ex-Servicemen was disbanded and the Union Movement was formed.

The austerity policies of the Labour Government, the housing shortages, the coal shortages, the general grimness of life in the years after the war, created a groundswell of dissatisfaction and discontent upon which the Union Movement could capitalize. Mosley did not even have to say that the war had been a mistake. He had simply to ask his audience if austerity Britain was what they had fought for.

By mid-April 1948, a Special Branch investigation of Fascist and Communist organizations, led by Deputy Commander L. Burt, had reported that there was serious danger of violence in London. On 29 April 1948, Sir Harold Scott, Metropolitan Police Commissioner, told the Home Office that his powers under the Public Order Act were inadequate 'to prevent serious public disorder'. Chuter Ede, the Home Secretary, used his own powers under the Act to prohibit public processions of a political nature in Bethnal Green, Stepney, Poplar, Shoreditch and Hackney, and through parts of Finsbury, Islington, Stoke Newington and Tottenham. On May Day 1948, 1500 members of the Union Movement marched through Camden, and there were 31 arrests.

The ban on political marches was then extended to cover the whole Metropolitan Police District, and was twice extended beyond its three month time limit. Although the marches were banned, the public meetings and the street-corner speeches continued. Mosley's opponents, in particular the Jewish 43 Group, mobilized to stop them. In March 1949, 5000 people gathered to oppose 150 Union Movement members at Ridley Road. There were 34 arrests. In the January of that year, tear gas bombs were dropped into a Mosley rally at Kensington Town Hall, which was attended by 700 people. The Mosley supporters who could not squeeze into the hall traded insults and slogans on the street outside with their opponents. The two groups were kept apart by a cordon of 100 policemen.

In the 1949 municipal elections, the Union Movement fielded 15 candidates who came bottom of the poll everywhere except Bethnal Green. The best percentage vote was 15 per cent in Shoreditch on a very low poll, and the 15 candidates together received only 1993 votes. At this time, there was an average audience of about 250 at the bigger London meetings, and the Movement secretary, Alfred Flockhart, was almost certainly exaggerating when he told the *Daily Herald* in October 1949 that the Movement had 38 London and 70 provincial branches, with minimum branch membership of 12 people. Mosley was even less of a nuisance than he had been in 1938–9.

The Movement limped on until February 1951, when Mosley

gave a last address at Kensington Town Hall. He denounced Britain as 'an island prison' and went off to a self-imposed exile and three year silence in Eire. Once again, as in the 1930s his rationalization for failure was that the expected slump had failed to come, that the economic and political crisis which he needed to succeed had unaccountably failed to happen. He later explained in his autobiography, 'A new party can never become effective as a mass movement before crisis comes. Until then, a new movement can only be a power house for new ideas.'

Apart from Mosley, other neo-fascist activity was barely perceptible. Arnold Leese, who had founded the Imperial Fascist League in 1929, celebrated the end of World War Two with a book which asserted that the Jews and Freemasons may have won a battle, but they had not yet won the war. He had been detained under 18B, and was imprisoned in 1947 for giving aid to escaped members of the Waffen SS. Leese was a veterinary surgeon whose anti-semitism was founded upon his horror of the ritual Jewish method of cattle slaughter. He edited a magazine, *Gothic Ripples*, until his death, which recorded the appointment of Jewish people to positions of public influence and attacked the fluoridation of water.

Something of a curiosity, this magazine commented on public events and personalities, and advocated the perusal of 'The Protocols of the Learned Elders of Zion' with obsessional fervour. From 5 November 1955 edition, comes this gem:

Richard M. Nixon, Vice-President of the USA, once showed great promise when he risked his career by insisting on the trial of traitor Alger Hiss. But he has sagged right back into the Jewish bag, and the Israelite M. M. Chotiner was his campaign manager during the last election. We have a portrait of Nixon's mother, who was born Hannah Milhous; she looked Jewish but of course we do not know what race she belonged to. Mr Nixon himself gives the appearance of race-chaos.

In 1946, Leese had received a letter from a recently demobilized soldier called Colin Jordan, who had volunteered for the Fleet Air Arm in 1942 and failed the flying training course, volunteered for the RAF and been rejected and ended in the Army Education Corps. Having been awarded an Exhibition in History to Sidney Sussex College, Cambridge, before joining the war effort, Jordan was making a survey of the British nationalist and neo-Fascist groups and intended to promote the cause at Cambridge.

At the university, he founded the Cambridge Nationalist Club, and after inviting John Beckett, general secretary of the British Peoples' Party, to address his Club, Jordan was invited to join the BPP national council.

He then moved to Birmingham, where he founded another Nationalist Club, stayed with the BPP and kept on very good terms with Arnold Leese. This relationship with Leese was later to become Jordan's major advantage during the schismatic and disorderly days of the National Socialist Movements of the early 1960s. Leese's widow (who had trained her cat to give the Hitler salute) gave Jordan the personal right to use a house in Notting Hill as his political HQ. Jordan's sole control of 74 Princedale Road, was to become a key issue in the later internal rows inside the National Socialist Movement.

After Mosley, the most prominent nationalist anti-semite in British politics was a Norfolk landowner, Andrew Fountaine. He had fought for Franco in the Spanish Civil War, and fought in the Royal Navy in the Second World War, rising from the rank of Ordinary Seaman to Lt Commander. A member of the Conservative Party, he was adopted for the Chorley (Lancs.) constituency as a parliamentary candidate in 1949, but attacked the Conservative Party at its annual conference for permitting Jewish people to achieve positions of public importance. Embarrassed and angered by his outburst, the Conservative Party withdrew its adoption of his candidacy and he stood as an independent Conservative in 1951, split the Conservative vote, and lost the election by only 341 votes. He then (as he was to do again) retired to his large family estate and occupied himself with farming, standing again as an independent Nationalist candidate in 1959 and losing his deposit.

In the ten years after the war, apart from Mosley whose personal charisma and record lent significance to even the abortive campaign of 1948–51, there was little Nationalist or anti-semitic activity on the British fringe. In 1954, a former leading member of Mosley's BUF formed the League of Empire Loyalists. This was A. K. Chesterton, who had won a Military Cross in the First World War for leading a day-long series of grenade attacks upon German machine-guns. He was a Shakespearian scholar, a man of intelligence and culture, who had left Mosley's movement when Hitler occupied the Sudetenland in 1938, and joined the Officers' Emergency Reserve. He fought against the Italians in Ethiopia during the Second World War, and fought fourteen successful libel actions against newspapers and individuals unwise enough to suggest that he had ever been a traitor, or anti-British. Before joining Mosley, he had been a Socialist, with a fervent (if contradictory) belief in the unique capacity of the British race for leadership and civilization. By 1954, little of his Socialism was left and politically he was on the extreme right wing of the Conservative party.

The foundation of the League of Empire Loyalists was essentially a response to the consensus politics of the 1950s in Britain. The acceptance of the Welfare State and the loss of India by the Conservative Party, the liberal Toryism of R. A. Butler and the gathering speed with which liberal Tories were accepting a diminished British role in world affairs and a renunciation of the Empire, created something of a vacuum on the right wing of British politics.

A. K. Chesterton was probably not the best man to fill it. His ideas of British racial superiority, of the need for the white man to continue to rule in Africa, and his abiding horror of Communism, were orthodox enough for the British Right. But Chesterton was a logical man. He was anti-Communist, and he shared the distress of many on the British Right at the expansion of American wealth and power. For the bulk of the British Right, anti-Americanism was something that had to be forgotten while the Atlantic Alliance was the mainstay against Russian Communism. Such pragmatic decisions were not for Chesterton. He had never forgotten the anti-semitism of his days with Mosley, when as editor of *The Blackshirt* he had written in August 1936: 'In every branch of capitalist brigandage which we have exposed, the hand of the Jew has been revealed. When we come to power we shall certainly deal with this lawless capitalist menace in its entirety.'

Chesterton combined his anti-semitism, his anti-Communism, his anti-Americanism and his fervent patriotism and concluded that Jewish Wall Street capitalism was the same thing as Russian Communism. Jewish capital had funded the Bolshevik Revolution of 1917, he believed, and Jewish capital had funded the development and technological base of Soviet Russia. The Moscow-Wall Street axis had as its major objective the ruin of the British Empire, the mongrelization of the British race, and eventual world government. The United Nations, NATO and Jewish people were all to be regarded with the deepest suspicion as agents of 'the money power'. Curiously, Chesterton never found any difficulty in agreeing with many writers of the American Right who also discerned a Wall Street-Moscow axis, even though they idealized American democracy and rugged individualism, rather than the British Empire.

It was perhaps the all-embracing nature of this conspiracy theory which made the League of Empire Loyalists such a key training ground for the next generation of British neo-fascists. Colin Jordan, John Bean, John Tyndall and Martin Webster were all active members. But the real impact of the League had little to do with disciples. It had little to do with the old BUF members, like W. E. A. Chambers-Hunter and Admiral Sir Barry Domville, or old right-wing patriots like Major General Sir Richard Hilton, keen supporters though they were. The impact and the success of the League rested on the fact that they represented a rallying point on the extreme (but still respectable) right wing of British politics in an age of political Butskellism, and upon the flair and imagination of their political demonstrations. The League of Empire Loyalists were ahead of their cultural time; they invented the political happening.

The technique was devised by Chesterton, and carried out by a handful of keen young supporters. The stunts relied upon daring and imagination and getting the opportunity to shout 'League of Empire Loyalists say . . .' adding whatever slogan was current at the time. 'Macmillan is a traitor' was always popular, and 'the UN is an anti-British plot' was another. It was not the sentiment, but the places and circumstances in which they were shouted that made the idea work. Conservative Party Conferences were most favoured. Leaguers hid under the platform overnight and leaped out at the feet of the Cabinet to make their point. They rang alarm bells, blew bugles, wore disguises and infiltrated almost any meeting they chose. A bearded member, Austen Brooks, once successfully impersonated Archbishop Makarios of Cyprus, and at a private lunch held for U Thant, secretary-general of the UN, on 5 July 1962, the organizer had barely finished bragging that he had checked under the tables for League members when from all over the hall, League members rose one after another, made their point and left.

The newspapers and television loved it, and a number of Conservative MPs and Conservative Party members supported the League enough to ensure a regular supply of tickets to such events until 1963, when the supply suddenly dried up. The League reached its peak in 1958, when it so effectively disrupted the Conservative Party Conference, and was receiving so much publicity, that the Conservative leadership let it be known that the stewards should make a determined effort to control them. The result was press and television pictures of League members bleeding and unconscious in the corridors, after being ejected from the meeting. One woman, Miss Rosine de Bounevialle was thrown over a balcony after setting off a very noisy alarm bell. The League made heckling into a political art form. They even ran illegal transmitters to break into TV programmes with League slogans. Less amusing was the bag of sheep entrails hurled at Jomo Kenyatta of Kenya by Wing Commander Leonard Young in November 1961, with the slogan 'Take that from the League of Empire Loyalists'.

Perhaps the joke went on too long. Perhaps the right wing of the Conservative Party was finally reconciled to the humiliation of Suez in 1956 and accepted Harold Macmillan as a politician who could at least give them victory in the 1959 general election, even if he could not restore the imperial glories for which the League mourned.

In 1961, according to the last activist to join, Rodney Legg: 'We were running out of money and the League had ceased to be credible. Chesterton was financing the League himself, paying our travel and subsistence allowances from his own pocket. The name itself was a joke, and membership was falling. So many supporters were old that our membership declined with every post and every obituary column.'

In 1958, the League had numbered about 3000 members and many more supporters. By 1961, according to Legg, who tabulated the subscriptions, it was down to about 300. The League also suffered from schisms. General Hilton left to form a Patriotic Party. R. C. Gleaves left to form a Greater Britain campaign which foundered after one tiny meeting in Trafalgar Square. Colin Jordan, having been Midlands organizer, had left in 1957 because the League rejected his proposal to ban Jews and non-Whites from League membership, and John Bean left in the same year to found the National Labour Party. He was discovered copying the League's membership and subscription lists before his departure. Both Bean and Jordan felt that the League's major weakness was its refusal under Chesterton to consider becoming a mass movement. It insisted on remaining an elite, seeking influence rather than power.

By that time, another issue had emerged which made the prospect of a mass movement in Britain very much more enticing than it had been when the thrust of Chesterton's ideas was aimed at reversing British policies of decolonization. The new issue was coloured immigration. A total of 132,000 coloured immigrants from the Commonwealth arrived in Britain in the three years 1955–7, of whom 80,000 were from the West Indies. In the House of Commons, the Conservative MP Cyril Osborne had begun a lone campaign for control of immigration as early

31

as 1952. Some ten years later, after the first Act to control immigration had been passed, Osborne received a knighthood. But for the first half of his decade of anti-immigration campaigning, Osborne's was a lonely battle, and one which led to regular snubs from the Tory leadership.

In 1958, there were race riots in Nottingham and in the London suburb of Notting Hill. By the standards of the 1960s in America, they were not severe, but they came as a savage shock to a Britain which preserved a myth about its own standards of tolerance, and provided Cyril Osborne and the ambitious dissidents who had split away from the League of Empire Loyalists with a new and explosive focus.

The riots of 1958 also heralded the brief return to Britain of Sir Oswald Mosley, who returned from Ireland early in October to launch what he described as 'the biggest post-war campaign'. He was to be disappointed. Kensington, Hornsey, Leicester, Derby, Liverpool and Leeds all cancelled bookings that had been made for Mosley to speak at civic halls. His campaign was reduced to a meeting in Birmingham on 12 October, where the presence of forty policemen in the hall was insufficient to prevent outbreaks of fighting, which seemed to confirm other local authorities in the wisdom of their decision to cancel Mosley's bookings.

In the election of October 1959, Mosley poured all of his resources into Notting Hill. At weekends, the Union Movement had up to 200 canvassers. They all preached Mosley's message of sending the coloured immigrants back. Mosley stressed that this was to be done humanely, the process sweetened by gifts of money, and justified by the argument that immigrants who had learned about industrial life and methods in Britain could make an enormous contribution to the development of their homelands. Some of Mosley's aides were less high-minded in their elaboration of the repatriation policy, and the leaflets issued by the Union Movement were acknowledged by Mosley to be 'strong stuff'. One example read 'People of Kensington – Act Now. Your country is worth fighting for – fight with Union Movement' – hardly the most helpful kind of message to feed into a community where gangs of whites had roamed the streets looking for black people to beat and kick into unconsciousness. Mosley, in spite or because of the intensity of his campaign, was decisively beaten, losing his deposit for the first time in his electoral career. He received 2821 votes, in an election where Labour and Tory candidates each received over 14,000 votes.

Mosley was astonished by the result. In his autobiography, he argued that the affluent society had been his downfall, and that the economic boom of 1959 had made the electorate too complacent to see the coming economic crash which only Mosley perceived, and from which only Mosley could save the nation. It was the same excuse as the one he used for his failure in the 1930s, and his failure in the 1948–51 campaign. 'An electorate never moves decisively except under severe economic pressure which is nearly always unemployment,' he wrote in *My Life*.

For the dissident graduates of the League of Empire Loyalists who were simultaneously active in Notting Hill, race was the only important issue. The National Labour Party had been founded by John Bean when he and John Tyndall left the LEL; Bean became policy director of the NLP and its titular leader was the Norfolk landowner Andrew Fountaine. From June 1958 the NLP was active in Notting Hill, with leaflets and broadsheets and street corner meetings. By the end of the summer of 1958, Bean told the *Times* (10 September 1958) that the NLP had gathered 250 members. The leaflets constantly referred to 'Britain steadily being taken over by the triumphant alien', and they were used again in the Notting Hill campaign of 1959, when Bean and the NLP first began to work closely with Colin Jordan, whose White Defence League had also been active in the area. On 24 May 1959, Bean's NLP and Jordan's Defence League held a joint meeting in Trafalgar Square, and some of Jordan's supporters helped the NLP candidate in the 1959 general election, when William Webster stood for the NLP in St Pancras North, a traditional Communist bastion in London, and received 4·1 per cent of the vote, against the Communist's 3 per cent.

Jordan had come to Notting Hill through his connection with the Britons' Publishing Society, which had been founded in 1919 to publish *The Protocols of the Learned Elders of Zion*.

In 1958, the Society was based in Arnold Leese House, in Princedale Road, Notting Hill, and acted as an informal co-ordinating centre for most of the Nationalist groups in Britain. In 1958, Jordan used the House as a base for his White Defence League and began to publish a local newspaper called *Black and White News*, which sold between 700 and 800 copies throughout the tense summer of 1958. Jordan also issued a flood of pamphlets to exploit and exacerbate the racial issue. The most widely distributed one read:

The National Assistance Board pays the children's allowances to the blacks for the coffee coloured monstrosities they father, regardless of whether they are legitimate or illegitimate. Material rewards are given to enable semi-savages to mate with the women of one of the leading civilized nations of the world.

The leaflet is a classic, of its pernicious kind, embracing the key themes of racial nationalism which are used by the National Front today: sex, spongers on the Welfare State, racial inter breeding, Government encouragement, stress on British civiliza tion – all the bases are covered in fifty words.

In June 1959, Jordan became the white extremist spokesman to whom the national press turned for an instant quote on racial problems in Notting Hill. His publicity-conscious imagination was never at a loss. 'I loathe the blacks – we are fighting a war to clear them out of Britain,' he told *Reynolds News* on 4 June. 'If a Fascist is a person who wants to keep Britain white, then I am a Fascist and proud of it,' he told the *Daily Herald* on 1 June.

For Jordan, the great advantage of the immigration issue was that it made people think in terms of race and thus be more sympathetic to his anti-semitic propaganda. By 1959, he was also publishing a four-page magazine called *The Nationalist*, to promote the cause of Nordic racial unity. 'Twenty years ago the Jews set us at each other's throats to make Europe and the world safer for Jewish control. The Jews won. We lost. Throughout the North European homeland, our Northland, the rule of the Jew and his lackeys now prevails, while the Mongol soldiery of Jewish Communism treads the soil of that homeland itself.'

The advantage of this kind of literature was that it revealed just how closely Jordan was in touch with other racist groups in Northern Europe. For John Bean and Andrew Fountaine, this conveyed an international perspective which increased their respect for Jordan. For Mrs Leese, it confirmed her judgement that Jordan was the right man to follow where her husband had led. By February 1960, Jordan's White Defence League and Bean's NLP had come together as the new British National Party, based in Arnold Leese House, with Mrs Leese as vice president. Fountaine was the President, Jordan was national organizer, and John Tyndall was a founder member. The move ment's motto was 'For Race and Nation'. Its first policy docu ment committed the BNP to freeing Britain from 'the domination of the international Jewish-controlled money-lending system and preservation of our Northern European folk'.

34

The December 1960 issue of *Combat* contained two further policies:

1) Send those coloured immigrants already here back to their homelands.
2) Impeach the Tory Cabinet and the 1945–50 Labour Cabinet for their complicity in the black invasion and hold a trial of all those journalists who have aided and abetted them.

BNP activities were limited by their lack of funds and lack of members. Demonstrations at railway stations when trains arrived carrying immigrants from the ports, two public meetings in Trafalgar Square in 1960, demonstrations against the parade of a Jewish Lord Mayor of London or a counter-demonstration against the activities of the Anti-Apartheid Movement – these were the campaigns of which the BNP publications were so proud. To expand beyond the London base, a special organization was established within the party. This was called Spearhead, intended particularly for younger members, was supplied with a Land-Rover and was led by John Tyndall, later chairman of the NF.

According to Colin Jordan, there had initially been a controversy within the groups who brought the BNP together over the question of permitting Tyndall to join. He was well-known and unpopular within Nationalist circles because of his arrogance, his overbearing personal manner and the way he brought the authoritarianism of his politics into his personal life.

'There was hardly ever a meeting of the BNP Council without Tyndall's name on the agenda. People always complained about him,' Jordan remembers. 'People talked about his "Prussianism". He was always wearing jackboots and would travel across London to BNP HQ wearing jackboots under his trousers. Terry Savage and Carl Harley were particularly opposed to him. On one visit we made to Germany for a Nationalist meeting, Tyndall, Harley, Denis Pirie and I drove across, and as soon as we got across the frontier into Germany Tyndall made us look for a shoe shop. Then he kept us waiting for an hour while he tramped up and down the shop in his first pair of genuine German jackboots. He was something of a figure of fun, but he upset people. He was always trying to persuade me to do away with the national council. He wanted a much more authoritarian structure. At least Spearhead got him out of the way at weekends.'

Tyndall led a small mobile group up to Leeds and Liverpool to recruit new members and boost the puny activities which were

all the provincial bodies could manage. The BNP active membership never rose above 350 during its first two years, of whom over
200 were in London. Lukewarm supporters boosted their numbers at the Trafalgar Square rallies, where the collections were
a vital source of funds. There is no reliable evidence to suggest
that the BNP was other than self-financed, in spite of contem-
porary rumours about funds from neo-Nazis in Germany. The
only supporter of real wealth was Fountaine, but his wealth lies
in land controlled by a family trust structure which prevents him
from realizing the land's value, even if he wished to do so.

But Fountaine's land did serve another purpose. It provided
the scene for the BNP summer camp, which Jordan tried to make
into a rally of European Nationalist groups. In 1961, twenty
European delegates attended, including Robert Lyons of the
American States Rights Party (whose membership forms pledged
recruits to fight 'to save our Race, Nation and Faith from Communism and Mongrelization') and Hans Rehnvaal of the
Nordiske Rikspartiet. The BNP's annual report for 1960 concluded:

> The most enjoyable part of the camp was the opportunity to
> get away from the cosmopolitanism of the cities and to live
> in the manner of our forefolk amidst the beauties of our own
> Northland, England. None will forget the comradeship round
> the campfire, with songs of our race and nation upon our lips
> and tankards of English ale in our hands.

There were also exercises – 'the most popular was storming the
Red platform', according to *Combat*. The songs came from the
official BNP songbook, which included a rousing English tune
called 'Comrades – the voices' which was sung to the tune of the
Horst Wessel.

The favourite BNP song was 'Britain Awake', which ran:

> We are the front fighters of the BNP,
> True to our soil and people we will be.
> Red Front and Jewry will finally fall;
> Our race and nation will smash them all.

The comradeship of the campfire did not last very long. The
internal rivalry between Jordan and Bean had started at the very
beginning of the party. At the 1961 party elections, Jordan had
only held on to his post as national organizer by the casting vote
of Andrew Fountaine. At the national council meeting on 11

February 1962, Bean presented this resolution: 'Mr Jordan's wrongful direction of tactics is placing increasing emphasis on directly associating ourselves with the pre-war era of National Socialist Germany to the neglect of Britain, Europe and the White World struggle of today and the future.'

Jordan was beaten by seven votes to five (a shift of one vote from the earlier election), but the BNP Constitution stated that he could only be replaced if he acquiesced, which he refused to do. Jordan also pointed out to the meeting that he controlled the house which formed the HQ. Personalities aside, the issue, in terms of policy, was whether to make the BNP a frankly and openly Nazi party. Bean was less concerned with specific items of policy than with the wisdom of presenting the policy package as a new Nazi movement.

The BNP split, with Bean and Fountaine taking the name BNP and the magazine *Combat* and over 80 per cent of the membership. Jordan was left with the house in Princedale Road, Tyndall, Denis Pirie and most of the Spearhead group, a bare majority of the Birmingham and West Essex branches of the BNP and the Land-Rover. On 20 April, Hitler's birthday, Jordan threw the inaugural party of the National Socialist Movement, complete with a swastika-covered birthday cake; the highlight of the evening was a transatlantic telephone call to Lincoln Rockwell, leader of the American Nazi party, to exchange congratulations and *Sieg Heils*. Finally, Jordan made a speech, on Britain's 'loss and shame' for its part in defeating Hitler, and concluded: 'In Britain – in Britain of all places – the light which Hitler lit is burning, burning brighter, shining out across the waters, across the mountains, across the frontiers. National Socialism is coming back.'

The important thing about the lunatic fringe up to this point was the lessons it had learned and the developing British society in which those lessons were to be put to use. By this time, the far Right had seen how the agitation over the Notting Hill race riots had brought two of the ideologically diffused factions together. Second, they had learned the importance of a secure and permanent national HQ. Third, they had learned the potency of the coloured immigration issue. The Government had already yielded to pressure and introduced legislative controls, after protesting for some years that it would contemplate no such thing. Above all, in the rise of the Campaign for Nuclear Disarmament, the Nationalists had seen how effective a new form of extra-parliamentary protest could be. The prospect of a genuine mass movement, in which only Mosley had really believed through the 1950s, became thrilling and insistent as the Nationalists watched the despised marchers from Aldermaston. It could be done.

The same process of Butskellism, of liberal Toryism and right wing Socialism, which had left a vacuum on the right of British politics had also left a vacuum on the left. The CND was one of the groups which had begun in response to that vacuum, and indeed, concentrated its purpose into changing the mind of the Labour Party Conference on the single issue of nuclear disarmament. But other more militant groups on the left were springing up in and beyond CND. The trauma of the British Communist Party after the Russian invasion of Hungary in 1956 led to a period of intense ideological creativity in the British Left. It took some time to consolidate, it took the lessons of the early American peace movement in Berkeley and it took the Vietnam War to give the New Left in Britain real shape and substance. (Some would argue that the key midwife for the British New Left was the performance of Harold Wilson's Labour Government after 1964.)

But the style of extra-parliamentary activity had evidently changed. Publicity had become a matter as much of attracting TV cameras as of informing newspapers. The role of the League of Empire Loyalists, by virtue of their imaginative example, has already been described. In 1962 to the League's chagrin, the Cuban missile crisis pointed to the fact that Britain was but one more of America's European allies. The mass youth hysteria of Beatlemania was but a year away, and so was the odd, but potent phenomenon of the generation gap. The satire wave was cresting and a Minister was about to lie to the House of Commons about his relations with a whore. When the Nazis came to Britain in 1962, it was a new kind of Britain, with new social and political forces at work.

In the eighteen months before the new Immigration Act became law in July 1962, 212,000 coloured immigrants had come to Britain. So the Nationalists and the racialists had their issue. The CND had shown how to build a mass movement, and Britain was becoming in its culture and in its extra-parliamentary politics a volatile nation. Were the Nationalists capable of responding to the challenge?

The National Socialists claimed that it was their Trafalgar Square rally of 1 July 1962 which began the racialist troubles of that year. Jordan was sentenced to two months in prison (later reduced to one month) for 'insulting words likely to cause a breach of the peace'.

What he in fact said was: 'More and more people every day are opening their eyes and coming to see Hitler was right. They are coming to see that our real enemies, the people we should have fought, were not Hitler and National Socialists of Germany but world Jewry and its associates in this country.' John Tyndall, sentenced to six weeks in prison on the same charge, said at Trafalgar Square: 'In our democratic society, the Jew is like a poisonous maggot feeding off a body in an advanced state of decay.' (At his appeal hearing later in the year, Tyndall argued that the use of the word maggot in this context was no worse than Aneurin Bevan's use of the word 'vermin' when he applied it to Tories.)

The meeting ended in a riot. A crowd of Jewish people, some members of the Communist Party, some CND members – none of them acting on behalf of their movements – charged the platform and the meeting ended in uproar. There had been racialist meetings, and anti-semitic meetings held in the same place by the BNP, and Mosley's Union Movement had met in the Square annually with little trouble. Part of the reason why a large crowd was ready and waiting for Jordan was that if the mass media had ignored the foundation of the NSM, the Jewish community and the Left were accustomed to keeping abreast of events on the far Right. And Jordan was known, after being fined in 1960 and 1961 (for insulting behaviour likely to cause a breach of peace), as a rabid and aggressive speaker. The anti-fascists were waiting for the Nazis before they even began as an organization.

And so were the police. During 1961, the Special Branch had been aware that the Spearhead group had been formed within the BNP. In July 1961, Sergeant David Pemble and Detective Constable David Corder went to investigate slogans scrawled on the wall of an old stables in Culverstone, Kent. 'Race War Now', and 'Free Eichmann Now' excited their curiosity, and on 4 August, the two policemen returned, disguised as electricians, and took photographs of John Tyndall and Roland Kerr-Ritchie drilling a squad of eighteen men, all dressed in full Spearhead regalia of armbands, grey shirts, boots and belts. In April and May of the following year, Detective Alex Hilling of the Special Branch spent his weekends hiding in a bush near Dorking, observing the Spearhead squad, led by Colin Jordan, engaged in what he reported as 'military manoeuvres'. They were in fact, mock attacks upon an old tower on top of Broadmoor Hill.

A week after the 1 July rally, the *Sunday People* published photographs and a story on the Spearhead group. The NSM had already announced that it was to hold a summer camp, incorporating an international Nazi conference, and had booked Trafalgar Square for another mass meeting on 19 August. Press and public opinion, including pressure from Jewish MPs and the Jewish community upon the Home Office, were against the idea of granting the Nazi delegates visas to attend the Conference, and on 2 August the Home Secretary announced that the delegates would not be permitted to land in Britain.

But unknown to the Home Office, when the NSM first announced that Lincoln Rockwell might be coming for the Camp-Conference, he had already been smuggled into the country. He had come in via Southern Ireland; Jordan and Tyndall had smuggled him over the border, and thus to England. When Rockwell arrived in London, Jordan publicly announced that the American was hoping to attend the Camp-Conference, and security arrangements were thus set in motion at all the sea and air ports some days after his arrival. Rockwell was then driven to Cheltenham to await the opening of the camp. However, attacks by indignant local villagers and the intensive interest of the press and the Special Branch eventually proved too much. Rockwell, after hiding out in Jordan's Coventry home, decided to go to Fleet Street and give his story to the *Daily Mail* before giving himself up to the police. The Home Office got him on an early flight out, thwarting Jordan's plans for applying for a writ of *habeas corpus*.

Jordan's Coventry home and the Notting Hill HQ of the NSM were raided by the police early in August, and records, knives, pistols, black helmets, uniforms, Nazi flags, jackboots, swastika armbands, tapes of Hitler's speeches, portraits of Nazi leaders and walkie-talkie radio sets had been seized. They were all to appear on the exhibits bench at the Old Bailey (including those genuine German jackboots which Tyndall had purchased) where they were joined by five cans of weedkiller which the police had found in the basement. On one label, the word 'weedkiller' had been scratched out and 'Jewkiller' written in its place.

On 16 August, summonses were issued at Bow Street court and Jordan, Tyndall, Kerr-Ritchie and Denis Pirie were charged with organizing and equipping a para-military force. This delighted Jordan. 'We were well aware that the Establishment would get us one way or another. We had to ensure that we would get massive publicity for our cause, and that we would fight a show trial in which we could present our case and our ideas. It was clearly going to be a political trial and we wanted the opportunity to present a political case.'

The main purpose of the summer camp had been the formation of an international Nazi body, the World Union of National Socialists. Jordan was elected world Führer, and Rockwell was named his heir. Its major objectives, set out in a long and pompous statement called 'The Cotswold Agreement', were:

1) To form a monolithic, combat-efficient, international political apparatus to combat and utterly destroy the international Jew-Communist and Zionist apparatus of treason and subversion.

2) To protect and promote the Aryan race and its Western Civilization wherever its members may be on the globe, and whatever their nationality may be.

3) To protect private property and free enterprise from Communist class warfare.

Thus far, and in the long-term objectives of 'unity of all white people in a (National Socialist) world order with complete racial apartheid', the Agreement was acceptable to many right-wing theorists. It would, for example, have been acceptable to A. K. Chesterton. But paragraph 7 of the 25-paragraph codicil was implacable: 'No organization or individual failing to acknowledge the spiritual leadership of Adolf Hitler and the fact that we are National Socialists shall be admitted to membership.' The long-term objective 'To find and accomplish on a world-wide scale a just and final settlement of the Jewish problem', also served, as was the intention, to mark a clear distinction between WUNS and the rest of the Nationalist Right.

The NSM was always tiny. A police search of Jordan's card index in 1966 discovered that there had been a total of only 187 full members in the Movement's history, of whom 35 were still fully paid-up and active in 1966. There were also 271 active supporters (who paid a lower subscription and did not have full voting rights) of whom only 77 were still subscribing. There were 105 Book Club members and 114 subscribers to the National Socialist magazine.

But they had won publicity and recognition out of all proportion to their size. They had also served to embarrass their former allies on the Right. The BNP summer camp of August 1962, again held on Fountaine's estate, was surrounded by press photographers looking for the same sensational pictures. In vain, Fountaine pleaded 'This is just a holiday camp for guests who have come along to relax and amuse themselves', but the presence of the Spanish Falangist, Jose Martinas, a French member of the OAS and the Italian representing the Pan-Europa neo-fascist group all served to confirm the press in its suspicion that here was another group as news-worthy and as sinister as the Nazis.

It was the Union Movement which was most embarrassed by the NSM's activity. Three weeks after the NSM meeting in Trafalgar Square of 1 July 1962, Mosley was scheduled to hold his ninth public meeting in the Square since 1959. These events had normally passed off with little incident (there had been one arrest in 1959) and with little attention from the Left. But on 22 July, there were 7000 people in the Square, most of them determined to stop Mosley. The rally was stopped after fifteen minutes. There were 56 arrests.

Mosley later accounted for the troubles, and for the full-scale campaign that developed around his speaking tour of that summer, by arguing that it was his own party's successes which had alarmed the Left. 'Violent disorders at our meetings all over Britain followed the conference in Venice on 1 March and the local elections of May – this was clearly something more than a coincidence.' (In fact, a handful of Union Movement candidates had won an average 5·5 per cent vote in municipal elections.)

What had alarmed the Left (and the authorities) was the clear sign, from both the Venice conference and the Cotswold Agreement, that the Right was hoping to become an international force. The factional dog-days of the 1950s were over, and the Right was clearly trying to re-group. The goals and strength of this new Right were unclear, but it was a threatening new departure.

A week after the disruption of the Trafalgar Square rally of 22 July, Mosley, with 30 supporters, tried to march through Manchester to Belle Vue. Mosley was knocked down three times, there were 47 arrests, and the meeting was called off after seven minutes before a hostile crowd of 5000 people. On 31 July, in Ridley Road, Dalston, the meeting lasted four minutes. There were 300 police, 54 arrests (including Oswald's son Max) and Mosley was knocked down and punched. The *Daily Telegraph* reported a crowd of 'several thousands'.

On 25 August in Leeds, a Union Movement meeting was broken up by a crowd of 200. The speaker was Robert Taylor, an old associate of Jordan. On 30 August, the police banned all political marches in London for a 48-hour period. On 2 September there were 40 arrests in Bethnal Green, and Mosley was kicked and punched. And on the same day, in Balls Pond Road in London, 40 BNP members were beaten up by the now militant

Yellow Star Movement. No Nationalist meeting could now take place without opposition.

On 9 September, Mosley was allowed to finish his speech in Bethnal Green, well-guarded by ranks of police. But on the same evening, a Union Movement meeting addressed by Barry Ayres in Croydon was brusquely broken up with three arrests. On 29 September, in Manchester, 250 policemen kept Mosley and the Northern Council against Fascism apart, but Mosley had had enough.

He announced that he would stop holding open-air rallies as part of his campaign in the provinces. His provincial activity would be limited to private, unadvertised meetings, door to door canvassing and the publication of journals. The campaign had yet to sputter out in London. On 7 October, there were 30 arrests at a turbulent meeting in Bethnal Green, which was followed by a Union Movement lorry tour, with members in the back of the lorry yelling slogans. In court, where two of them were fined and thirteen others bound over to keep the peace for twelve months, it was said that they had yelled 'Get out you black bastards' and 'Down with the fucking Jews'. A last meeting in Tunbridge Wells was broken up in disorder on 20 October, but the campaign had been hammered into the ground.

After voicing his concern for some months, the Home Secretary Henry Brooke finally acknowledged in November, after the campaigns and the trouble had ceased, that the present penalties under the law were inadequate to deal with demonstrations of this kind. By then, it did not matter. Very much more effectively than in the 1930s, the anti-fascist groups had organized a nation-wide campaign and had stopped Mosley. But it was no great achievement. The Mosley campaign of 1962 was limited to these rallies and meetings. He had no political organization which could capitalize upon them, and his membership numbered perhaps 1000 in 1962. The anti-fascists had shown that they could defeat a man of straw, and mobilize more effectively than they had in the 1930s. This too was a lesson for the Right.

Tyndall and Jordan in particular realized that it was no longer possible for the right-wing movement to grow and to maintain a secure base if it limited its activities to the kind of public marches and meetings which the Left was able to disrupt. They also realized that the new kind of publicity which TV could give, could rebound upon the anti-fascist demonstrators, making them appear the aggressors, making them attack the police and thus jeopardize the support of moderate opinion which an anti-fascist group could have been entitled to expect. In later years,

Tyndall was to write of each of these elements separately in *Spearhead*, but according to Jordan, it was in the post-mortem of the events of 1962 that the strategy of a modern right-wing mass movement was explored by the two men. John Bean was also talking of the prospect of a 'National Front' of like-minded bodies, with the numbers to protect themselves, and a political organization which meant that the rallies and public demonstrations would be just one tactic of a strategy which included standing in carefully chosen by-elections, and building up a local group in each place. They all agreed it would mean a long haul. The catalyst in this long process of re-assessment had been Sir Oswald Mosley himself, not only because his supporters were the fall-guys for the summer of 1962, but because of the seeds he had planted in the minds of Bean and Jordan at the beginning of the year. He had approached the two men through Mary Taviner, and had offered to make them his national organizers, on a par with his veteran supporter Jeffrey Hamm. He had outlined the advantages of unity, pointed out that he still had a name to conjure with, and stressed the experience of the Union Movement in fighting elections. Bean and Jordan were too close to their own leadership struggle in the BNP, and too mistrustful of Mosley's politics, for the negotiations to advance to the stage of a meeting with Mosley. But his arguments bore fruit in the minds of both men. Jordan discussed the matter with Tyndall, who again argued in favour of an authoritarian structure within the party, and pointed to the dangers of diluting structure and policies. But the re-assessment had begun.

To round off the turbulent year, there was the Spearhead trial at the Old Bailey. Jordan was able to quote the whole of the National Socialist Manifesto, and large sections of his vaunted Cotswold Agreement. In the literature of the Right in the US and in Europe Jordan, Tyndall, Pirie and Kerr-Ritchie were portrayed as heroic victims of a Jewish-controlled establishment. It was all very uplifting.

There were two main charges. The first, on which they were found guilty, was of 'organizing, training and equipping Spearhead in such a manner as to arouse reasonable apprehension that they were organized and trained to be employed for the use or display of force in promoting political objectives, contrary to the Public Order Act, 1936'. The key phrase was 'to arouse reasonable apprehension', which Jordan argued was to punish them for a crime which need only exist in the minds of their opponents. They were found not guilty of 'organizing, training and equipping Spearhead for the purposes of using or displaying

44

force to promote political objects'.

Jordan was sentenced to nine months in prison. Tyndall (who had successfully appealed against the presence of a black man on the jury) got six months. Kerr-Ritchie and Pirie were sentenced to three months each. As they were led down to the cells, Pirie gave a Hitler salute. 'The Spearhead man,' one of the documents produced at the trial had read, 'steps forward and marches on as the Stormtroopers of the National Socialist revolution in Germany in 1930.' Henceforth, Spearhead was only to be the title of Tyndall's future magazine.

It was at this time that Martin Webster wrote in the National Socialist magazine an article entitled 'Why I am a Nazi'. He was leader of the London A section of the NSM and was the proud winner of the shield for top team sales of the National Socialist.

'It became obvious to me that if I really wanted Britain to win through I and young men like me would have to join a movement which could ideologically, and in the future physically, smash the Red Front and Jewry,' he wrote. He dismissed the Union Movement as 'a waste of time' and the BNP – 'most of the membership were little more than a bunch of down and outs who, if it were not for the presence of blacks in the country, would find refuge in the left wing of the Labour party.' He continued, 'After visiting the HQ of the National Socialist Movement I became convinced of the correctness of the Nazi ideology . . . Not a day goes past without some act of stupidity by the Jews and their allies coming to light – acts of foolishness brought on by the chill North wind flaunting the swastika banner in the sky . . . In every White land in the world Nazi movements have been formed, and we join with them in the historic Nazi battle cry. Victory Hail! Sieg Heil!'

Before becoming a Nazi, Webster had briefly been a member of the Young Conservatives. He claims that they expelled him after he wrote an article for the newsletter asking 'Why aren't the Conservatives conserving any more?' He went on to spend eighteen months very loosely connected to the League of Empire Loyalists, where he had a reputation for cowardice. Assigned to reconnoitre Marlborough House in preparation for painting the front door with slogans before a Commonwealth Conference, he had gone there with Rosine de Bounevialle, who remembers 'He was very timid about it, and did not want to go round the front. He was never very much use to us and always seemed to be rather frightened.'

The major problem of the NSM, which was to cause the split

in 1964, was the attractive French heiress, Françoise Dior. She had been married to Count Robert-Henri de Caumont-la-Force and had been a fervent monarchist. She had first appeared at the Princedale Road HQ in the summer of 1962, and Jordan courted her. While Jordan was still in prison, she became engaged to Tyndall, and on Jordan's release the two men vied for her hand. Her marriage to Jordan took place on 5 October 1963, and a curious ceremony it was.

For the occasion, she wore a black and gold swastika necklace, encrusted with diamonds. They supped mead, toasted the British Nazi movement to the strains of the *Horst Wessel Lied*, and over a swastika-draped table, swore that they were of untainted Aryan blood, cut their fingers and let the mingled drop of blood fall on to an open page of a virgin copy of Hitler's *Mein Kampf*. Within three months they were separated; they were briefly reconciled, but Jordan was granted a divorce in October 1967. In 1965, Françoise was the French representative of the World Union of National Socialists, and in January 1968, was sentenced to eighteen months in prison at the Old Bailey for conspiring to commit arson on synagogues. On the eve of her trial, she told the *Daily Telegraph*: 'I would like to make an Act of Parliament to burn down all synagogues by law.'

Tyndall never forgave Jordan for the broken engagement, and inevitably began to find ideological differences with his leader to justify his increasing criticism and opposition. In December 1963, he was suspended by Jordan for a week for insubordination. But Tyndall was based in London. Jordan lived in Coventry and more and more of the daily administration of the Movement passed under Tyndall's control. When the split came in May 1964, the staff of national HQ unanimously followed Tyndall, leaving Jordan once more with the Princedale Road premises and the rump of the movement. Tyndall's ideological criticisms took the same general line as Bean's had done two years earlier. Jordan was too obsessed with Hitler, too unwilling to set National Socialism in the context of Britain in the 1960s. And Tyndall has always been a passionate British nationalist. 'An extreme Tory imperialist, a John Bull,' is how Jordan describes him, 'unwilling to recognize the call of race beyond British frontiers.' By the time of the Movement's annual conference in April 1964, Tyndall had virtually established his own organization as a separate entity, and had taken office equipment and files to his own rooms in Battersea. He insisted that Jordan surrender the leadership. Jordan refused. On 11 May, Jordan announced that he had expelled Tyndall 'for maladministration and disloyalty'.

On the following day, Tyndall countered with the claim that he had expelled Jordan after a 'unanimous decision of an emergency council comprising the entire administrative staff of NSM HQ' because of 'woeful neglect of his duty as leader of the movement and undignified conduct in public detrimental to the good image of National Socialism'. Tyndall claimed to have 90 per cent of the membership with him, including Webster. If there had been any possibility of reconciling the break, it was ended by Mrs Jordan, who insisted that her husband expel Tyndall. As she told the *Daily Mirror* of 13 May: 'I warned Colin that Tyndall was plotting to overthrow him. I once thought Colin was weak. Now, by firing Tyndall, he has proved his strength and I love him for it.'

Since Jordan still had the house, and the bookshop and magazine were registered in his name, Tyndall's new group had to find another title. In August of 1964 he launched the Greater Britain Movement, with its own magazine, *Spearhead*. It never had more than 138 members, and lasted for three years until it was finally absorbed into the National Front in 1967. The official programme of the GBM asserted that:

For the protection of British blood, racial laws will be enacted forbidding marriage between Britons and non-Aryans. Medical measures will be taken to prevent procreation on the part of all those who have hereditary defects, either racial, mental or physical. A pure, strong, healthy British race will be regarded as the principal guarantee of Britain's future.

Meanwhile in the League of Empire Loyalists, morale and membership had fallen disastrously. The old imperial policies seemed to have little relevance in the 1960s. Rodney Legg remembers: 'Not only were we running out of money but the name was ceasing to be credible. People did know of the League's existence but that was no longer enough. The title was anachronistic. Political realities had made the name a joke.'

Chesterton confided his own fears for the future of the League after his death to the young Legg, saying that Brooks did not have the calibre to maintain the League, and that for the League to live on, it would need the injection of new blood and perhaps association with some other organization.

There were still the imaginative demonstrations at the party political conferences, but the once innovative happenings were becoming the commonplace of the commercial theatre. There were CND meetings to heckle, but the spice of the League had gone. In 1964, Chesterton was persuaded to put up three Independent Loyalists as parliamentary candidates for the general election of 1964. They did very badly, getting a total of only 1046 votes, but Chesterton discovered to his delight and surprise how easy it was to raise money for elections. This seemed to offer him a new way forward, and served to lift him from the political depression under which he had laboured since South Africa had left the Commonwealth and was fast becoming the pariah of the world. It was not until the spring of 1966 that Chesterton actively began to sound out other Nationalist groups with the view to a merger, but throughout the early sixties, he was an unofficial political advisor to most of them, and Jordan, Tyndall, Bean and Webster were frequent visitors to his Croydon apartment.

Two matters obsessed Chesterton at this time. The first was the will of his long-standing benefactor Robert K. Jeffrey, who had never met Chesterton but entrusted sums totalling £70,000 to him over many years, to be used for whatever political purpose Chesterton saw fit. In 1959, this eccentric millionaire, who lived on a diet of porridge and walnuts (keeping a bathtub full of walnuts in case of a world shortage) made a will which left Chesterton as his sole heir. Jeffrey died in 1961, and twenty-eight hours before he died he is alleged to have agreed to a new will, and sealed it with his thumbprint, leaving his entire estate to a woman called Elba Smith de Zencovic, whom he thus recognized as his natural daughter. The legal disputes over this will dragged on unsuccessfully for a decade, and still exasperate Chesterton's friends. Appeal after expensive appeal went through the various courts in Chile, where Jeffrey was inconsiderate enough to die. This legal battle preoccupied Chesterton throughout the 1960s.

But he was also keenly interested in that astonishing, and almost forgotten, phenomenon, the rise of Mr Edward Martell and his Freedom Group. Martell, a former Liberal candidate and a committed, crusading believer in free enterprise, built up a national reputation and a kind of national movement largely through his genius as a fund-raiser and his determination to take on the trade unions in the printing industry. In 1954, he brilliantly organized the Winston Churchill birthday fund, and during the printing strikes of 1955, '56 and '59, he brought out his own daily newspaper, printed other magazines on contract, paid his non-unionized employees more than the union rate and began to appear to the same kind of Conservatives as those who had joined the LEL, as the kind of man who could save them all from the perils of Socialism and the trade unions. His political philosophy, staunchly for free enterprise, his stress that 'Britain's right to world leadership has not yet been superseded', and his occasional crankishness (he wanted the stripes on zebra crossings to be painted sideways) matched a declining, but still important, element of the conservative mood.

Martell prepared a card index of supporters who had particular skills and who were prepared to put them at the Government's service in the event of a general strike. It was an early version of General Sir Walter Walker's Unison Movement, and in so far as Martell collated specialist skills to maintain public services and special equipment (such as transport or radio transmitters) of key supporters, he was also foreshadowing Colonel David Stirling and his GB 75. In February 1965, Martell was acknowledged to have some 190,000 supporters, with membership rising by 1000 a week. The figures appear to be incredible, the more so when the whole organization was to vanish in the spring of 1965, with little trace, under the strains of bankruptcy. But it appeared to be just the kind of movement which Chesterton and the Nationalist Right wanted. Chesterton was deeply suspicious of Martell's economic theories, but he recognized something of a kindred spirit.

The split of 1962, and the subsequent publicity for Jordan, Tyndall and the Mosley campaign had left the BNP in a sad state. It had not moderated its policies. In the January 1963 issue of *Combat*, John Bean spelled out the racialist heart of his party's programme.

At the age 18, the half-caste would be given free passage to the country of its choice or he or she would be allowed to remain in Britain, enjoying all rights and privileges, including marriage, except for the fact that he or she would be legally enforced to undertake sterilization, under correct medical supervision.

But the May 1963 issue of *Combat* made it clear that the BNP was in trouble. 'A crisis is imminent,' Bean wrote. 'Unless substantial funds are forthcoming in the near future, the activities of the BNP will be restricted to local units and could even lead to the death of the party.'

There had been little real activity since Jordan's departure. The words 'Jewish-controlled' were removed from the BNP pledge to free Britain from 'the domination of the Jewish-controlled money-lending system', and the BNP's one major foray into the campaigning, violent summer of 1962 had led to a severe mauling for forty of their members in Dalston.

For the groups and parties of the far Right, 1963 was the lowest ebb. The previous year's bonanza of demonstrations and publicity had been little more than a sensational panic in the media and a series of humiliating defeats. Martell's movement collapsed, the legal battle for the funds in Chile continued, and the LEL was drawing peacefully towards its close. Most bitter of all was the frustration of so many partial successes leading to overall failure. The history of the LEL and of Martell showed the Conservative Party's weak right flank; the failure of Mosley indicated that any new movement on the Right no longer need fear having to grow in his shadow; even the pathetic posturings of Jordan and Tyndall suggested that publicity was easy to come by. But success, or even new directions seemed to elude them.

THREE

Smethwick, Southall and the Birth of the National Front

Both John Tyndall and Colin Jordan were in prison when the first signs came that the race issue was beginning to rear its head again, three years after the bloody street fights of Notting Hill. It was a cloud little bigger than a man's hand – a local issue, not a national one. It was based upon the simple social phenomenon – which could have been easily predicted – that immigrants from specific regional areas, speaking the same language and deeply committed to family bonds, tended to settle as near to each other as they could. New arrivals were welcomed and given hospitality by family members who had already found homes and jobs. Certain kinds of light industry and service jobs, requiring little training, tended to be grouped in certain towns. In Southall, near London, in Smethwick, Birmingham, and the Moss Side, Manchester, the communities began to form. Some of the immigrants' wives opened small shops, others began restaurants. The ghettoes acquired a certain permanence, until finally the local cinemas began to screen Asian films.

And one cannot simply blame the local white population for objecting to this process. It was, as subsequent propaganda was to maintain, their localities which were being transformed, without their consent. The sudden growth of the local anti-immigration groups was to surprise national politicians, but local councillors and officials were in many cases so involved in the protest groups that they forfeited their party loyalty to support their neighbours. And finally, in Smethwick, the local Conservative party was to merge itself fully with some of the more strident spokesmen of this community discontent.

If we can give this confused movement a starting point, let it be early September 1963, in Palgrave Avenue, Southall. A house for sale was visited by eight separate Indian families in one afternoon. That very day, a Palgrave Residents' Association was formed by observant neighbours which successfully petitioned the Labour council to purchase the house – and thus keep it in white hands. The publicity which followed this venture, which had been promoted by a leading local Conservative, Mrs Penn, led to the formation of the Southall Residents' Association, under the chairmanship of a Mr Arthur Cooney, later in the month. In class terms, we can define these early groups precisely. They were secure and prosperous enough to be purchasing, in most cases, their own homes and to fear a decline in the value of their houses. But the neighbourhoods tended to be cheap enough to attract the less than affluent early immigrants. The Residents Associations were almost wholly lower-middle class and respectable working class, tasting post-war prosperity for the first time and now finding it threatened.

The Southall Association started as one more community pressure group, writing to the Council on a number of local problems. Margaret Penn and three other members of the committee wanted the SRA to continue along these general lines, and to work for a successful integration of the immigrants into the town. Mrs Penn visited the local Indian Workers' Association and told them she hoped they could work together. For this initiative, she was censured by her committee. In February 1964, Mrs Penn and her three friends resigned, in protest against what they saw as the SRA's policy of racial discrimination. Arthur Cooney told the *Guardian*: 'They seemed to favour working for integration, but I can't see integration being achieved here.'

In the local elections of 1963, Arthur Cooney, SRA chairman and Doris Hart, treasurer, had nominated two BNP candidates. The candidates stood in Hambrough and Glebe wards, where they had won 27·5 per cent and 13·5 of the vote respectively. In Hambrough, a safe Labour ward, the BNP had come second in the poll, ahead of the Conservatives.

It was very much a local issue, and yet insistent enough for the Labour MP George Pargiter to brave the wrath of many in his party and call for 'a complete ban on immigration to Southall', in January 1964. In the same month, Cooney called for segregated education in the borough. Political parties were re-grouping around the single issue of immigration. By 1966, the Tory group on the council were calling for a fifteen-year qualification period before immigrant families could go on to the council's housing list, and two Labour councillors – one a former mayor of the borough – were expelled for voting with the Tories. The two expelled Labour men then stood as SRA candidates. The issue of immigration created political chaos in Southall, and the able and energetic Southall organizer, Ron Cuddon, exploited it and built a keen BNP branch in the process.

In Birmingham too, the same issue was creating local anti-immigration groups as vocal as the SRA, and with better links to the Conservative Party. The BNP's direct exploitation of this kind of community concern was effectively limited to Southall by the party's lack of funds and lack of organization. But there is little doubt that John Bean and his party realized that this wholly new kind of political concern – self-generated and self-sustaining within a community – could not only provide the boost the BNP sorely needed, but could also be the base for the kind of mass movement which Bean now had in mind. He decided to stand in the 1964 general election for the Southall constituency.

His platform was a ban on all further coloured immigration, and no National Assistance for unemployed immigrants unless they applied for repatriation. He warned, 'It is only a question of time, and certainly in our children's time – before this land of ours ceases to exist as a centre of Northern European civilization.'

He won 9 per cent of the vote, the highest percentage yet won by a blatantly racialist candidate in a British parliamentary election.

Only one individual result stood out more starkly than Bean's vote in a bitterly contested election. Although Labour had won a narrow victory by four seats over the Conservatives, there was one constituency where the national swing to Labour had been sharply reversed. That was in Smethwick, Birmingham where a nationally unknown local Tory called Peter Griffiths beat the man who would have been Labour's Foreign Secretary, Patrick Gordon-Walker. Such was the shock to Labour, especially when it became known that the election issue in Smethwick had been overwhelmingly the immigration problem, that Harold Wilson, the new Prime Minister, made the mistake of prophesying in Parliament that Griffiths would be treated as a 'parliamentary leper'. The attack provoked sympathy for Griffiths, particularly when he ably – if speciously – defended his campaign and denied all responsibility for the most famous of the racialist slogans which had graced Smethwick's politics – 'If you want a nigger for a neighbour, vote Labour'.

Griffiths's polling day leaflet read simply: 'The only Smethwick candidate who has always called for the strictest control of immigration is Peter Griffiths. Remember this when you cast your vote.' This, Griffiths successfully argued before the House of Commons, was fair and defensible. The Conservative Party warmed to him from their defeated unfamiliar and bleak position on the Opposition benches.

For a time, Griffiths was even lionized, speaking in London, Liverpool, and even being invited to address the Cambridge Union. When he spoke to Conservatives, the message was clear. 'At least twenty seats in London, the West Midlands and else-where can be won if the Conservatives take a firm line on immigration,' he told the London Young Conservatives. Gaining twenty Labour seats would put the Tories back in power. It was a

53

potent message.

There was nothing spectacular about immigration to Smethwick. The town suffered a net population loss during the 1950s and early 1960s, and proportions of immigrant schoolchildren were markedly lower than in neighbouring constituencies. But somehow the issue had taken hold. Local Conservatives, accustomed to being the minority party, could barely believe the electoral inroads they made in 1960, on the strength of a promise to evict immigrants in overcrowded houses without any obligation to rehouse them. After the Conservative Government's Immigration Act of 1962, though the municipal elections showed a nationwide swing to Labour, in Smethwick the Tories gained three seats. By this time, one of their candidates was Don Finney. He had joined the Conservative Party in the month before the election, although from his post as local chairman of the British Immigration Control Association, he had supported them for the past year.

Finney's letters to the local newspaper, and those of a retired bank official called Lawrence Rieper (whose letters tended to stress 'our racial future is at stake'), had attracted the attention of the Tory Councillor Charles Collett. Collett, a long opponent of immigration, had joined with four other men in October 1960 to establish the Birmingham Immigration Control Association. In 1961, the BICA had a violent internal disagreement over whether or not to support the Conservatives in the local elections. Neither Collett nor Peter Griffiths had yet been able to make it widely and publicly clear that many Birmingham Conservatives were more than ready to control immigration. Harry Jones left the Birmingham Association to found the British Immigration Control Association. Tom Jones left to found his own Vigilante ICA in Handsworth. He was later to be chairman of the Argus British Rights Association, which was to blend into the Racial Preservation Society.

Harry Jones and Councillor Collett persuaded Finney and Rieper, the letter-writers, to form a Smethwick branch of the BICA in March 1961. Anti-immigration was a schismatic business in Birmingham, partly because local Conservatives who joined the various groups were determined that no single body should evolve which might jeopardize the Tory opportunity to garner the bulk of the new anti-immigrant vote. But as in Southall, the anti-immigrant groups confused the old political boundaries. Labour Councillor Ken Bunch helped to run the Sandwell Youth Club, which kept a colour bar and was one of the centres of the BNP's National Youth Movement. Ron Badham, later secretary

54

of the local Labour party, fought one local by-election on a policy of a total ban on immigration. Even Patrick Gordon-Walker was moved to announce, in his vain campaign to cling to his once safe seat, 'This is a British country, with British standards of behaviour. The British must come first.'

By the time of the 1964 election, it was clear to anyone with local knowledge that the growth and activities of the anti-immigration groups, the memories of the brief racial skirmish of 1960, and the unremitting propaganda of the local Conservatives were going to combine to produce an electoral upset in Smeth-wick. Attention had even been drawn to the possibility (and to the nature of the Conservative campaign) by the Midlands cor-respondent of *The Times*. The campaign had attracted the interest of the BNP and of Colin Jordan. Bean and Jordan each sent helpers to assist – as private individuals – in Griffiths's campaign. Both Bean and Jordan were aware that by helping Griffiths, they were helping the Conservatives to take up an anti-immigration stand. In doing this, they were jeopardizing their traditional monopoly of the one policy which gave them any prospect of widespread public support.

'I was certainly aware of this danger, but equally aware that once people started to think racially, their own logic would take them well beyond any position the Conservatives could ever adopt. We may have helped Griffiths, but we knew how much the Conservatives were to blame for immigration in the first place. The Smethwick result proved what we had been saying – that immigration was the election issue. And this was a victory for us,' Jordan says.

In short, Jordan and Bean saw the 1964 campaign as an investment, an investment which would have succeeded if it brought the question of race (not simply that of immigration) into the forefront of British politics. Part of the work was already done. In the debate on the re-enactment of the Immigration Act in November 1963, Harold Wilson told the House of Commons: 'We do not contest the need for control of immigration into this country . . . there are loopholes in the Act and we would favour a strengthening of the legal powers . . . We believe that health checks should become more effective.'

The new Labour Government was just as firm. In re-enacting the Immigration Act in 1964, Labour's new Home Secretary, Sir Frank Soskice, told the House 'the Government are firmly convinced that an effective control is indispensable'. Ray Gunter, Minister of Labour, confirmed the policy at the end of the debate with an almost total ban on further C vouchers, which had permitted unskilled immigrants to enter. Within three months, Soskice promised that he would secure the repatriation of immigrants who had entered the country illegally. It had taken three years of mounting agitation in a handful of urban centres to transform the Parliamentary Labour Party's policy from staunch and principled opposition, to full-hearted enforcement of the Immigration laws.

The Labour Party's own justification for its conversion was perhaps best expressed by Roy Hattersley, the MP for Birmingham Sparkbrook, in a speech to the House of Commons on 23 March 1965. Confessing that, on reflection, he and the Labour Party should have supported the 1961 Immigration Acts (although the economic arguments suggested that British industry required more immigration), he added, 'I now believe that there are social as well as economic arguments and I believe that unrestricted immigration can only produce additional problems.' The intractable problem, as he saw it, was the pace of the desirable economic process of immigration, compared to the pace of the desirable social process of integration. Government could dictate the pace of immigration, but nobody could dictate the pace of integration. As Hattersley put it, 'We must impose a test which tries to analyse which immigrants . . . are most likely to be assimilated to our national life.' Accordingly, during a period when the Labour Government was introducing progressively tougher Immigration laws, it was also enacting the Incitement to Race Hatred and Race Relations Acts to improve and facilitate the process of integration. Toothless and barely effective as the anti-racialist laws were, they at least served to salve the Labour Party's nagging conscience.

They also served to inflame yet further the passions of those anti-immigrant groups who were now given an opportunity to defend their rights to make racialist remarks and racialist decisions when selling their houses, employing workers, accepting boarders or serving customers. They argued that traditional British rights to freedom of speech and freedom to discriminate in personal or social life were too valuable to be sacrificed in the attempt to promote integration. Anti-immigration groups like the Racial Preservation Society gladly seized the opportunity to appear the underdog, defending traditional British freedoms against an authoritarian Government or dictatorial 'Race Relations Industry'.

In a sense, the Labour Government (and the Conservative leadership) had played into the racialists' hands. By introducing and strengthening the laws to stop coloured immigration they had acknowledged that the racialists had a case, and had moreover shown how susceptible Governments and MPs were to racialist agitation. And by introducing the well-intentioned, but badly-phrased, Race Relations Act to promote integration, they had given the racialists an on-going grievance to exploit.

Belated and inadequate as the Race Relations Act proved to be, the parliamentary mood in which it was passed was sweetened by a convergence of Labour and Tory opinion which led many liberals to see the period 1965–8 as a golden age of British racial tolerance. Liberal Tories like Norman St John Stevas, Humphrey Berkeley and John Hunt began to exert effective pressure upon the Conservative Party. The 1965 Conservative Party Conference addressed itself to a motion on immigration which made no mention of further controls and which called for 'positive and wide ranging measures for the integration of existing immigrants'. The Shadow Home Secretary, Peter Thorneycroft, supported the motion and stressed that it reflected Conservative policy. The only anti-immigration speech which was made was greeted by hisses and scattered booing.

The general election of March 1966 seemed to suggest that the Liberals had won the racial argument in Britain. In Smethwick, Peter Griffiths lost his seat after a swing to Labour of over 7 per cent. Brian Walden, successful Labour candidate in the nearby Birmingham seat of All Saints, announced 'We have buried the race issue.' Enoch Powell had referred to immigration in the course of his campaign, and the need for further controls. Suggesting that Britain could have a coloured population of 2,500,000 by the year 2000, he told his electorate 'an addition of that magnitude is an appalling prospect which would render the social and human problem we already have well-nigh insoluble'. Powell's majority was cut by 3271 votes.

For the Nationalist parties, for the community groups which had coalesced around the issue of anti-immigration and for all those who had seen the prospect of a mass movement stemming from the populist appeal of racialism, this golden age of racial liberalism was a bitter disappointment. John Bean's BNP had made a major effort to stand in three constituencies in 1966. In Southall, his own percentage vote fell from 9·1 per cent in 1964 to 7·4 per cent, in spite of assiduous canvassing and organization in the previous eighteen months. In Deptford, where the BNP had been working since 1962, the candidate secured 7 per cent, and in Smethwick, where the BNP had some hopes of taking votes from the increasingly soft-spoken Peter Griffiths, the BNP candidate won a puny 1·5 per cent of the vote.

For A. K. Chesterton, the renewed success of Labour in the 1966 election was made the more bitter because of Rhodesia' decision to declare unilateral independence in November 1965. The call of race, of skin colour and of kith and kin should have swept Labour from office on a tide of white solidarity, believed Chesterton. He played his part, being the first to organize petrol convoys to beat the oil blockade through his Candour Leagues. The 1966 election convinced him that all of the groups on the Right must now unite; the situation was desperate. John Tyndall, leader of the tiny Greater Britain Movement and frequent visitor to Chesterton's London home throughout the summer of 1966, was quick to agree. In *Spearhead* of July 1966 he wrote that the 1966 election had been the turning point. 'The humiliating defeat of Conservatism has served only to underline our repeated contention that there is now in Britain no longer any great political force representative of patriotic right-wing principles.' Far from mourning this development, he welcomed it. 'The demise of Conservatism is a boon to the Right,' he declared, and concluded that the overriding need was now for 'a political party which will embrace and employ *all* the combined resources and talents the Right has to offer, which, though small enough, at least offers a springboard for success in the future'.

The real catalysts of that coalition of the Right which brought the National Front to birth in February 1967 were the general election of 1966 and the convergence of Labour and Tory policies on immigration, each party agreeing to the need for controls and the need for integration. The Nationalists had seen their agitation succeed in bringing about immigration controls, but this was a frustrating and questionable victory. Certainly their electoral activities in a few key constituencies had contributed to the passing of the Immigration Acts, but there was a vast gulf between being part of the pressure which had led the established parties to pass those Acts and getting any of the credit once the Acts were passed. John Bean, John Tyndall, Chesterton, Mosley and Jordan had all seen immigration as their issue – the great shoe-horn which could lever them into political credibility if not to power. And they had been right. There was an issue there, there were votes in anti-immigration and there was possibly the potential for that elusive mass movement which obsessed them. But the issue had been taken away from them. They had not been able to build an organization upon the inchoate agitation they had stirred.

The problem lay in the fact that a large proportion of voters who supported the Nationalists on the issue of immigration were concerned solely with immigration. They were not prepared to go on from a belief in the need to stop immigration and start repatriation to a belief in a racially-conscious political party, allied to the white governments of southern Africa, and in the idiosyncratic world view of a Moscow-Wall Street axis which Chesterton and the Nationalists upheld. Between the Nationalist groupings and the mainstream political parties lay a twilight zone of people who could move in either direction at elections. In so far as this twilight zone had a political organization it lay with the community groups like the Southall Residents' Association and the Birmingham Immigration Control Association.

We have seen the schismatic tendencies of these groups in the Birmingham area, and how their political focus was dissipated by the allegiance of individual Conservatives and Labour members who were prepared to support an immigration campaign. There were several attempts to establish new bodies which could spread beyond the local appeal of the community groups and which could agree on a wide and vague enough political platform apart from immigration which would permit Labour and Tory supporters to join the new bodies. There was the English Rights Association, founded by Tom Finney who had been brought into the Birmingham Conservative Party by Peter Griffiths. By June 1965, Finney had arranged an affiliation procedure by which the Southall Residents' Association (with Grace Woods and Arthur Cooney), the London and Home Counties Housing Association (run by Mrs Joy Page) and the Cardington Federation of Housing Associations were all linked to his ERA. Then Tom Jones of the BICA established his Argus British Rights Association, which brought in the Labour councillor Ken Bunch and Ernest Shelly, who had been on the BICA committee. None of these *ad hoc* groupings worked very well, until the Racial Preservation Society.

The RPS brought together the two regions where these community groups had become established – the Midlands and the South. (When a similar local group developed around Bradford in June 1970, called the Yorkshire Campaign to Stop Immigration, it too merged with the rump of the RPS in early 1972.) The Midlands branch of the RPS was Tom Jones's Argus British Rights Association writ large. The Southern group was begun by a Sussex antique dealer called James J. Doyle in June 1965. (Within eighteen months, Doyle disappeared from the political scene to serve a three-year prison sentence for receiving stolen goods.) But the bodies were closely linked. Vice-chairman of each was Ray Bamford, a wealthy writer of tracts on that elusive concept 'the race soul', which appeared in *Combat*, the *Northlander* and even the German Nationalist-Nordic publication *Nordische Zeitung*. Bamford was also the chaplain to the BNP's National Youth Movement (of which General Hilton, an ex-Leaguer, was sponsor) and owner of an Edinburgh bookshop and publishing company which specialized in what its catalogue described as 'good conservative literature', including the works of the South African propagandist Ivor Benson. Bamford had been President of ABRA and president of the Sandwell Youth Club, and formed the Scottish Rhodesia Society in 1966. Bamford's importance lay not only in this width of involvement and contacts, but also in his political respectability. He was close to Scottish Conservatives and to that significant sector of the Conservative Party which supported the Rhodesian rebel government, while being revered by the Nationalist groups as a racialist intellectual.

He was also a man of private wealth, and the major single advantage of the RPS lay in its access to adequate funds to fuel its campaign of printing and distributing broadsheets. The *Sussex News*, the *Midland News*, the *British Independent*, *New Nation* and *RPS News* – over two million copies of the various publications were printed from 1965–9 and the bulk were distributed free. They carried shock headlines like 'Five Million Coloured Asians now in Britain?' (*RPS News*), and stories about leprosy and the dilution of the British gene pool.

The RPS never attempted to swallow the various groups with which it affiliated, but acted as a co-ordinating body, to concentrate on publications and provide a forum within which the various community groups, pro-Rhodesian societies and Nationalist parties could keep in contact. The RPS never tried to develop the kind of central organization which could have administered all of the separate groups. The idea was to encourage each body to administer itself, but for the group leaders to keep in touch through the central RPS committees. The policy was broadly effective. The RPS central committee, as listed in the 'London Times' (a RPS broadsheet) for January 1966 included R. F. Beauclair as chairman, Ray Bamford as vice-chairman, and Arthur Conney and Grace Woods (of the Southall Residents' Association) as Treasurer and Secretary. Beauclair, the chairman, brought many of his own supporters in the RPS into the National Front in the winter of 1966–7 and has continued to play a vital role as contact man between the NF and the non-affiliated racialist and Right groups until the present day.

The RPS occupied the centre ground of British racialist

politics during the summer of disappointment and re-assessment which followed the 1966 general election. Chesterton, ageing and concerned about the LEL's future, had a further cause for concern in the growth of the Monday Club. This body, on the Right, but still respectable, wing of the Conservative Party, shared his concern for Rhodesia and for the white cause in Africa. It tended towards his view on immigration, matched his patriotism and was an obvious refuge for the nostalgic imperialists who were Chesterton's natural supporters. Chesterton's greatest asset had always been his respectability. He may have supported Mosley in the 1930s, and he may have been anti-semitic, but nobody could ever dispute his war record or his patriotism. But the economic conspiracy theories which Chesterton upheld always meant that his support from the right wing of the Conservative Party was less than secure. The growth of the Monday Club added to that insecurity.

So Chesterton returned from his regular winter holiday in South Africa with the resolve to unite the Right. Throughout the summer of 1966, his Croydon apartment became a forum within which the various leaders of the right came with their ideas and their credentials to explore the idea of a coalition. In principle, everybody was in favour, but in practice, personal rivalries and the varying degrees of credibility which people attached to Chesterton's conspiracy theories made the process a difficult one. Chesterton's widow recalls that among the visitors to their home that summer were John Tyndall, Martin Webster and Gordon Brown of the Great Britain Movement, whose *Spearhead* magazine had been advocating such a coalition since Tyndall had first split away from Jordan in 1964. In fact, Tyndall was one of the first to realize the opportunity which the Right had been granted by the ascendancy of Tory Liberalism.

'Into the vast vacuum created by the Tory eclipse a new force of the Right is now emerging,' he argued in December 1964, 'a force not delineated by class and vested interest but a force inspired by only one thought and one loyalty – the Nation.' Tyndall's mind was made up in January 1965 when Lincoln Rockwell informed him that Colin Jordan was still recognized as the proper British representative of the World Union of National Socialists. It was a decision Tyndall received with deep regret. (He and Webster had prepared a long and savage dossier on Jordan, and sent it to Rockwell in the hope of winning the support of the American Nazi Party. Rockwell forwarded the dossier to Colin Jordan.) Nonetheless, it closed down, probably permanently, the Nazi option which had always attracted

Tyndall. His visits to Chesterton also helped to convince Tyndall that there was little future for a Nazi-orientated group in British politics, or at least little prospect of its ever emerging from the lunatic fringe of politics. In January 1965, Tyndall made a plea for co-operation, if not unity: 'Union is not only desirable, it is essential to our success. But at the moment the Right cannot see its way to unite . . . What the groups can do is to at least negotiate methods of co-operation,' he wrote in that month's *Spearhead*.

He went on to argue that 'while they agree to differ in identity – at least for the time being – they can work together under cover and they can join to promote certain objects they have in common.' Unilaterally therefore, in March 1965, Tyndall authorized his Greater Britain Movement members to give active help to the League of Empire Loyalists, the BNP, the Patriotic Party and the National Student Front. Tyndall's new direction was set. He even steeled himself to the prospect of promoting a unified group from which he could be excluded. By March 1966, he asserted 'we must do all we can to bring together the tragically splintered forces of the National Right. It may mean snubs. It may mean continual frustration. It may mean total failure. But somewhere, some time, an example *has* to be made.'

Tyndall's campaign temporarily collapsed in the spring of 1966 when he and seven other GBM members were arrested and charged with possession of weapons including staves and blades after one of their lorry campaigns. He and his followers were fined and, later in the year, Tyndall was sentenced to a total of six months in prison for possessing a gun and ammunition without a permit. (The sentence was doubled from three months because it had occurred within five years of a previous prison sentence.) This made Tyndall an embarrassment to the rest of the Right. Offensive weapons and firearms all smacked too much of Colin Jordan and the Nazism which Chesterton wanted desperately to avoid. And some of Tyndall's own members had yet to be convinced of the need for unity. Tyndall and Webster had long told them that the quality of the tiny GBM contingent was of greater importance than any quantity of members.

In July 1966 Tyndall returned to the attack. *Spearhead* increased its size from eight to twelve pages and carried an article by Tyndall which had been well publicized among Rightist groups during the previous month. GBM members told acquaintances in other groups that a major statement was forthcoming. The article was called 'Where is the Right?' and was a bitter attack on the particularism of the individual groups and their leaders: 'the little men who talk about uniting Britain, the white

62

race, Europe or whatever you prefer, cannot even unite themselves. Any talk of a common fight against a common enemy is treated by them as a sinister plot to undermine their own precious private identities.' He listed the opportunities which were now open, with the immigration issue and the liberalism of the Conservative Party – 'the demise of Conservatism is a boon to the Right' – and returned to his chastisement of the Right as an 'incohesive mass of jealously squabbling tin-pot Caesars, more concerned with the pursuance of private vendettas than with the aim of ultimate national salvation.'

Tyndall did not explain the bitterness of this attack in *Spearhead*. But its motivation lay in abortive negotiations he had undertaken with the RPS and the BNP early in 1966. The RPS had turned him down out of hand, and the BNP Council discussed the matter before it replied that it did not choose to merge its identity. (John Bean had spoken of the idea of a loose coalition with interest, but Ron Cuddon, Southall branch organizer who controlled liaison with the SRA, issued a flat veto.) After Tyndall's 'Where is the Right?' article, John Bean telephoned Tyndall and suggested a meeting. The two men agreed that the best course would be a joint BNP-GBM conference to thrash the issue out, but once again Ron Cuddon was opposed. Indeed, as soon as Cuddon heard that Bean and another BNP executive member, Bernard Simmons, had met Tyndall, he resigned. In September 1966, the BNP leadership met Dr David Brown of the RPS and they reached temporary agreement on unification as the National Democratic Party, stipulating that there should be no links with Tyndall and his GBM.

Within a week, this idea foundered, partly because of Brown's insistence on being the sole and undisputed leader and partly because Bean warned that banning the GBM out of hand meant banning several other people with Nazi backgrounds (including himself and many BNP members) and an inevitable dilution of the future party programme. These chaotic negotiations were closely observed by Chesterton, whose discussion evenings with the various leaders of the Right continued. His widow remembers that Colin Jordan came at least once, although Chesterton told her after Jordan had left that it would be suicide to include him. Dr David Brown also came to Chesterton's home, and although the two men got along very well, Chesterton later confided to his League supporters that Brown was playing too clever a game, too convinced that with the RPS he had the vital piece of the jigsaw puzzle and determined to sit the game out until he was finally brought in on his own terms. Chesterton told the LEL annual meeting of 1966 that 'there had been talks with the RPS – with the Society wanting everything handed over lock, stock and barrel to a National Democratic Party headed by Dr David Brown.'

Chesterton pinned his hopes on the BNP, and in particular on Andrew Fountaine and Philip Maxwell, whom he saw as moderate BNP types, who would not besmirch the name of his League. This was precisely how the BNP had planned that Chesterton see it. Bean resigned from the BNP Council in September, and Maxwell was elected in his place. Once he was accepted within the National Front, Bean confessed in *Combat* of March 1967, 'quite frankly, it is doubtful whether the merger with the LEL would have come off if I had remained a prominent figure in the BNP.' As a result, he added, 'I was not a member of the negotiating committee.' In the same article, Bean explained the difficulties with the RPS negotiations. 'Due to the desire to dictate terms to the BNP, a much stronger political body, by the chairman of the RPS, negotiations were broken off, but not without building up a very friendly relationship with other RPS officials.'

This was to understate the case. Chesterton's doubts about the respectability of the BNP were removed when Maxwell and Fountaine pointed out that the BNP could bring a dowry to the union – a substantial proportion of the RPS, led by Robin Beauclair. So Beauclair too came to the Croydon apartment and the coalition began to come together. There were other groups to see, including Mary Howarth (RPS) who was already discussing the prospect of a blanket-group Immigration Control Association with Mrs Joy Page. Joyce Mew, a former member of the LEL who now ran a body called the Housewives League, also called on Chesterton, and promised support, but not participation for the moment.

Throughout the summer, the BNP had been forcing the pace in the talks because it was running out of money. The publication of *Combat* was suspended for six months because the printer could not be paid. It was proposed that *Combat* should merge with the RPS publication *British Independent*, but as long as David Brown was RPS chairman such a merger remained only a proposal. Finally, the *British Independent* itself (largely subsidized by Beauclair) paid *Combat*'s printing debts. The question of finance was to embitter the merger as soon as it began. Chesterton had to disabuse the BNP negotiators that in joining with the LEL, they were marrying money. He held out the prospect of winning the legal battle in Chile and eventual riches, but for the moment, e stressed, *Candour* and the LEL were largely supported by his own limited funds. The BNP men asked what kind of support could be expected from the various wealthy-sounding Generals, Admirals and gentry who graced the LEL's notepaper and Chesterton had to confess that their support was nominal. In fact, Chesterton had long 'padded' the LEL's executive council to give it an appearance of respectability and numbers. Lesley Green, for example, was listed as organizing secretary, but she was inactive. 'We would post her some press cuttings so she could write her annual report,' Rodney Legg remembers. 'This was always A.K.'s way. It was just padding.'

In October 1966, Philip Maxwell of the BNP was invited by Chesterton to address the LEL annual conference on the possibility of a merger. The only warning to the bulk of the League members (forty of whom came to this conference) had been a small item in *Candour*: 'The policy directorate of the LEL is in touch with some leaders of high calibre, and a working party is at present busily engaged in seeking the basis for a merger of like-minded groups.' Chesterton told the meeting that the working title for the new body was the National Independence Party, which was agreed to be unsatisfactory. British Front was considered and rejected for its unfortunate initials, but 'it is not worth busting the merger over one word,' Chesterton insisted.

Chesterton also told the meeting, in strong terms, that there could be no question of bringing in those 'who wanted to relive the Nazi daydream', and that Colin Jordan and John Tyndall would be beyond the political pale for many years to come.

The BNP had given the same assurances about excluding Tyndall and Jordan in its round of negotiations. Bean had even tried to reassure the sceptical Ron Cuddon in the BNP Council that his meetings with Tyndall meant nothing. Bean later wrote that the Council had been 'assured that Mr Tyndall's group would not be coming into the new movement and that their past utterances on anti-semitism and pro-Nazism would most certainly not be part of NF policy'.

At the LEL Conference, it was agreed to set up a working committee to investigate the policies and structure which the two organizations could agree. The chairman of the working party was Austen Brooks, the League Secretary; Rosine de Bounevialle, Avril Walters and Nettie Bonner, business manager of *Candour*, were the League representatives. For the BNP, Maxwell, Bernard Simmons and Gerald Kemp were nominated. They met twice a month from November 1966 until February

1967, but there was, in fact, little to negotiate. The League members were particularly concerned to keep something of their old name in the new party's title, but since Chesterton had already said the merger must not be broken for the sake of a word, their position was not strong. Nor was the working party. Avril Walters and Maxwell rarely attended the meetings, and Bernard Simmons (a former Colonial judge) was too concerned with presenting long and worthy discussion papers on such topics as 'Britain in the Year 2000' to take any active part in the discussions. Voting aside (which the Leaguers could have dominated anyway) the League members negotiated mainly with Gerald Kemp, a moderate BNP member who did not really represent the bulk of the BNP members' thinking. He was to resign from the NF within two years, in part because of his distress at the participation of Tyndall and the GBM. Had Simmons paid more attention to the discussions, and less to his discussion papers, he could have informed the group of his arrangement to write a column for Tyndall's magazine and his meetings with GBM members. He did not do so, and the League members never really knew how determined were many BNP members to bring Tyndall into the new group.

John Bean later wrote: 'During the early stages of the negotiations, Mr Bernard Simmons, myself and one or two other BNP Council members were of the opinion that if we were to abandon the BNP then we should try to find a place for as many groups and individuals in the new movement as possible.' Nor, according to League members who took part in those discussions, were they concerned to stress the limits of the coalition.

'We wanted to ensure that we were not just going to have another political party. A.K. always told us that a party ends up like all the other political parties – a tool of the money power. We wanted something rather more like an organization to back independent candidates for Parliament. Lesley Green and Austen Brooks and I had stood as independents in 1964 and money just poured in,' remembers Rosine de Bounevialle. 'We had dash and style in the LEL – we were an elite and we wanted to amalgamate this with numbers, but not to coarsen it. All we finally got out of the working committee was to keep the word "party" out of the title – but we had to lose the word "Loyalist".' By December, the working title 'National Front' had been agreed.

There was little else to argue about. The BNP council had already decided it was not going to be difficult about policy – confident that policy could be changed once the new body was established, in which the BNP members could easily outvote the

League. 'With the possible exception of the point on the Commonwealth and, in my view, the unfortunate dropping of the BNP proposal for a European confederation, NF policy is basically the same as that of the BNP,' Bean commented in *Combat* in the spring of 1967. Not that individual subtleties of policy mattered very much. The key points were to stop immigration, promote repatriation, support Rhodesia and the white dominions, fight Communism and oppose the old gangs of British politicians. BNP members were not informed of policy changes, which led the Kent organizer of the NF, Gerald Rowe, to tell the *Kentish Gazette*, 'The policy of the NF is the same as the old BNP . . . a membership requirement is that applicants are of natural British or European descent through both parents.' This was not the case, and Chesterton and the LEL members were furious at the statement.

Rowe was hardly to be blamed. The BNP members knew little of the negotiations until they were called to a meeting on 15 December 1966 in Caxton Hall. There was an audience of 250, including several LEL members, and riots outside the Hall. Andrew Fountaine, in the chair, read a message from General Hilton, saying that the merger was 'the best thing that has happened in the history of both organizations'. Maxwell had only one line to stress: 'There is a rumour that the NF is thinking about including in its ranks a neo-Nazi movement. This is not true. No neo-Nazi movement will be included in the NF.'

The difficulty about Rowe's comment to the *Kentish Gazette* was soon smoothed over, and on 7 February 1967, the National Front came into being. It claimed 2500 members from the LEL, the BNP and Beauclair's group from the RPS. There were in fact some 1500 members in anything more than name, 300 from the LEL, almost 1000 from the BNP and rather more than 100 of the RPS. And many of those members, whose subscriptions were automatically transferred to the NF, did not stay very long. For the great union of the Right, the National Front was a feeble beginning, and Dr David Brown could be forgiven for thinking complacently that his waiting game would yet prove to be successful.

FOUR

John Tyndall and the Early Years of the National Front

In June 1967, John Tyndall told his 138 followers in the Greater Britain Movement that the organization was being 'discontinued' and that they should individually join the National Front. For the previous year, the issue of John Tyndall and his handful of members had come to dominate the young National Front. The bulk of the BNP had long expected and desired that any coalition of the Right would have to include Tyndall. This was partly because he had now been active, and permanently active, in Nationalist politics for ten years. He knew the people and the organizations. He had also flirted with Nazism without being tainted with it to quite the same degree as Colin Jordan. Although he was in his late twenties when he was a keen member of the Nazi movement, Tyndall always subsequently dismissed his involvement as a youthful folly. Men do change their minds. But in the January issue of *Spearhead* for 1972, he pointed out that he was not ashamed of his Nazism, but simply regretted it. 'Though some of my former beliefs were mistaken,' he wrote, 'I will never acknowledge that there was anything dishonourable about holding them.'

Tyndall had not been a clever boy at school, but had concentrated on sports. He was given trials for Kent county teams at cricket and at soccer, and his passion for fitness and early morning runs has long been a joke in Nationalist circles. After National Service in the Army, where he became a lance bombardier, he began to explore politics, flirting with Socialism and even visiting the USSR in 1957 for a world youth festival. But the 'anti-British attitudes' of the Left appalled him, and he joined the League of Empire Loyalists. He left the League with John Bean and helped in the formation of the National Labour Party and later of the BNP before leaving with Colin Jordan for the heady delights of uncompromising Nazism.

At the Trafalgar Square rally, he spoke with Jordan, and at the Spearhead trial he told the court 'I am convinced that a peaceful social revolution as set out in *Mein Kampf* is what Britain requires to carry her back to the place in the world I believe to be hers.' At the Princedale Road HQ of the NSM he was even more outspoken. A reporter for the *Guardian* attended one public meeting there in June 1962, before the Trafalgar Square riots which first made Tyndall's name widely known.

Tyndall told that meeting:

Hitler roped in the riff-raff and put them in camps. Some of them may have died from starvation, but there was a food shortage . . . We want to see the whole democratic regime come crashing down . . . we shall get power with whatever means are favourable . . . the Conservatives are degenerate, the greatest betrayers of our nation, utterly decadent.

The anti-semitism of Nazism, and the racialist pattern of thought which accompanied it had been a part of Tyndall's ideology long before he joined Jordan. His earliest known published work was an article called 'The Jew in Art' which he wrote for a NLP journal. Referring to the Jews he wrote:

If the European soul is to be recovered in our country and throughout Europe it can only be done by the elimination of this cancerous microbe in our midst. Let us remember this eternal truth – that Culture is Race, Race is Culture and only by the purification of its culture can our race and nation arise to its highest ennoblement.

Although his supporters and detractors still dispute whether or not he remains a convinced National Socialist, nobody has ever questioned Tyndall's drive and dedication. Until the National Front was able to give him a small salary (£6 a week after 1969), Tyndall had supported himself by working as a salesman, and almost every evening and every weekend for a solid decade was given to political work. He is unmarried, very close to his mother and, apart from the courtship of Françoise Dior, is not known to have had lovers of either sex. He gives an impression of absolute, if brittle, self-control.

Perhaps the best single key to Tyndall's early thinking is in a pamphlet he wrote in 1961, called 'The Authoritarian State'. (This pamphlet is no longer in print, and the NF bookshop denies all knowledge of it.) It is an odd mixture, including classic economic Fascism, calling for a corporate state, with private enterprise operating under state guidelines, and the electorate voting not for a parliamentary representative but for a representative of his trade or industry:

What we oppose is the method whereby the man in the street is called upon to pass judgements on aspects of affairs of which he has no understanding.

It is based on a racial concept of limited freedom:

> What we intend to build is a national community in which that
> natural Nordic birthright of freedom is not something to be
> taken for granted by the dregs of society, but something earned
> by labour, loyalty and service.

It is passionately anti-democratic:

> Parliament daily resembles a market place in some far Eastern
> city, where the cackle of hysterical voices resounds back and
> forth as each little trader tries to sell his wares and at the same
> time deride those of his competitors;

and anti-semitic and anti-black:

> As Democracy allows droves of dark-skinned sub-racials into
> our country, the Jew cleverly takes advantage of their presence
> to propagate the lie of racial equality, thus gradually encourag-
> ing their acceptance into European society, with the ultimate
> results of inter-marriage and race-degeneration that he knows
> will follow . . . Liberalism or Bolshevism: whichever the people
> follow – there is only one master – Judah, the all-powerful!

Tyndall includes an intriguing reversal of the blame for the death
toll of the Second World War:

> Such a toll matters little to the Jew engaged ruthlessly in his
> conspiracy for world mastery.

Tyndall uses quotations from the *Protocols of the Learned
Elders of Zion*, without mentioning that the book is usually
considered to be a forgery. He argues:

> The Jew knows that only within a state governed according to
> his self-proclaimed theories of Liberalism and 'Freedom' will
> he be permitted to continue, unhampered, the activities by
> which he has corrupted every nation that had opened his doors
> to him.

Tyndall's answer is uncompromising:

> In place of the modern Jew-inspired illusion of 'freedom' we
> substitute the honest reality of freedom, i.e. Freedom for those

fit to use it and a curb on those who are not. Such a principle forms the basis of the authoritarian state, which we seek to build in Britain.

The pamphlet concludes with a brief nod to Plato:

Under such a system we will be able to make certain that no parasite or self-seeker can gatecrash into the political world. In time we will have available a political elite from which our future national leaders can be chosen ... Authority proceeding downwards and responsibility proceeding upwards – that is the simple formula upon which administration must be based ... Then it will be that nature's purpose is fulfilled. The best will rule.

It was a policy Tyndall was quick to try as soon as he left Jordan and established his own Greater Britain Movement. Acting on the principle that if the best should rule then they should have the means to do so, Jordan and Tyndall began a squalid process of stealing or 're-possessing' office equipment backwards and forwards from each other. This led to Jordan bringing a private prosecution against Tyndall, and the court very wisely dismissed the whole case. The first act of the new movement was an assault by Webster upon the Kenyan head of state, Jomo Kenyatta, as he left a London hotel. Webster was sentenced to two months in prison, and was fined £2 for an incidental assault on a policeman. Tyndall, who shouted slogans from across the street through a megaphone, was fined £25 for insulting words.

The official programme of the GBM forbade marriage between the races, and called for state powers to sterilize:

For the protection of British blood, racial laws will be enacted forbidding marriage between Britons and non-Aryans. Medical measures will be taken to prevent procreation on the part of all those who have hereditary defects, either racial, mental or physical. A pure strong and healthy British race will be regarded as the principle guarantee of Britain's future.

The GBM was determined to assert itself as the most active of the right-wing groups – even though it had neither the resources nor the inclination to fight the general election of 1964. So, in election month, Tyndall decided to restore the tradition of provocative outdoor meetings in the East End and Dalston. Such events had not been seen for two years, which gave the

GBM the advantage of surprise, if nothing else. The first meeting was on 4 October, the GBM claimed 100 in the audience and the *Spearhead* report laconically said it had been attacked 'by Jews'. Then there was the 'World Sticker Blitz', with sticky-backed labels printed with Hitler's portrait and the phrase 'He was right' in the language of your choice, English, German, French, Spanish, Italian and Dutch, at two shillings per hundred. In August 1965, five shots were fired at Tyndall in the Norwood office. Curiously, this incident was not reported in the November *Spearhead* bulletin, and it was not published by the GBM until the March 1966 *Spearhead*. But Tyndall had long stressed the courage and dedication of his supporters – 'If the timid rabbits find our campaign too hot for comfort so much the better. We are best rid of them for our place is not with the weak.' In October, the GBM held a meeting in Dalston, which was attacked by opponents and the battle continued all the way across London to the Norwood HQ. Four GBM members and twenty of their opponents were arrested.

'The public had to be shown that we were masters of the streets. The mission of the Jewish gang had failed. We had not been broken up,' reported *Spearhead*. But the issue in which it appeared reflected the curious fortunes of the movement. It was the first magazine since July, was published on two sheets of duplicated paper (the previous issues had been expensively printed) and they reported a deficit of £60. Tyndall blamed the irregular appearance of the magazine on the effort involved in establishing the Viking bookshop. (Martin Webster, although a keen GBM member, was speedily dissipating a legacy left to him by an aunt in another unsuccessful bookshop venture in St Albans.) Yet this same crude issue of *Spearhead* boasted of the newly expanded transport fleet of the GBM – three trucks and a Morris van. Transport and yet no publication – it was a curious contradiction for a small Nationalist group, where the tradition had always been to have a magazine as a showcase of the group's activity.

The GBM's main benefactor was a man called Gordon Brown, a general dealer who could also be described as an antique merchant or seller of second-hand furniture. A member of the NF Directorate at the time of the 1974 split, Brown had the curious talent of emerging on the winning side in every internal putsch the NF had known. He also subsidized the GBM's acquisition of a small shop and house which became the National-ist Centre in Tulse Hill in late 1966. (Tyndall saw this as his greatest single asset in his campaign to get into the NF – this tactic of controlling the premises and maintaining a secure base he had learned from Colin Jordan.) Brown also financed the NF's move into its headquarters in Croydon, and regularly subsidized *Spearhead* and the NF's office equipment needs.

By late 1966, when Tyndall was hammering at the door of the NF negotiations, he did not have a distinguished record. The GBM was a small body, with a magazine that was influential on the Right but which needed subsidies in order to appear even irregularly. He had premises and three trucks and his own boundless energy and dedication. It was little enough to offer.

It is important to appreciate that for much of the Right, and in particular for the BNP, Tyndall was a symbol. He symbolized (at the most extreme) the National Socialism with which the BNP and John Bean had been associated. Tyndall was still throwing parties on Hitler's birthday as late as 1966. Both Tyndall and Webster had been assiduous in maintaining their personal contacts with the rest of the Right. BNP members were always welcome at the Nationalist Centre, and Rodney Legg remembers that lurid tales came back to the appalled League veterans of loaded revolvers and Nazi salutes and Germanic uniforms. Legg has written a private memoir of this period, which points out 'whether these stories were true or not did not matter much – they were accepted as being the sort of thing you would expect the man to do and no one disbelieved them. Some admired him for it, and that was dangerous.'

Webster was the key man in maintaining the links between the GBM and the new NF. Quoting Legg again:

> Martin Webster frequented the League's office in the basement of Palace Chambers at Westminster. It had now become the National Front's first office. Webster was discouraged on several occasions and then found it more convivial to meet the NF leaders in the dive bar of the Red Lion pub next to Cannon Row police station. 'Tubs', as he was known to the League, was a large young man who had come into money and opened a second-hand bookshop specializing in military and firearm titles. He was a first-class comedian.

(A sample joke of Webster's referred to the sodium chlorate weedkiller found at Arnold Leese's House in the police raid before the Spearhead trial in 1962. 'How could we explain that away?' was Webster's quip. 'We hadn't even got a window box.') As a result of this humorous bent, Webster became accepted. Legg records: 'NF Directorate meetings were always held in a public house (booked in the name of the Anglo-Asian Friendship Society) and Martin would frequently happen to be there downstairs in the bar.'

The final and decisive reason for the incorporation of the GBM into the Front lay in the division between the BNP and the old Leaguers in the new body. John Bean had deliberately resigned from the BNP council lest he jeopardize the negotiations (and Legg remembers that an original LEL condition of the merger had been that it did not include Bean), but by April 1967, Chesterton had been forced to appoint Bean to the NF Directorate. He acknowledged in *Candour* that Bean was a case where 'the dissensions of the past should give way to the logic of the present and the needs of the future'.

With Bean restored to the fold, the question of the GBM, in spite of the staunch assurances of the merger negotiations about excluding neo-Nazis, became the BNP faction's own symbol of whether or not it had yet begun to dominate the Front.

The inclusion of Tyndall would serve as testament and as confirmation to the militants of the BNP that they were in control. The BNP's leading moderate, Ron Cuddon, had resigned in mid-1966 and Gerald Kemp, another moderate, walked out with Rodney Legg within the year.

Rosine de Bounevialle confirms Legg's account of the NF's first year as a power struggle between the BNP and the old Leaguers:

We had tremendous difficulties in the Directorate meetings – they, the BNP types, saw everything as a mass movement and eventually they began to see that they couldn't get their kind of mass movement while A.K. remained in charge. We Leaguers only numbered about a third at Directorate meetings and I was always struggling to keep the whole thing going. They wanted to fight elections all the time. A.K. thought we had too few suitable candidates of calibre.

Early in the year, Austen Brooks, the LEL secretary and a joint secretary of the Front, collapsed with a nervous breakdown after the strain of the Front's first months. Rosine de Bounevialle gradually attended fewer and fewer meetings and with Chesterton wintering each year in South Africa, Legg was often the only LEL representative at the Directorate meetings. Brooks's job was taken over by a retiring man called Ken Foster, who was known only for always carrying a large holdall. Once it was opened in a pub and a guinea pig climbed out.

74

It was not simply a matter of numbers, with the BNP out-numbering the League on the Directorate, nor was it a question of policies. It was a vast gulf of styles. Or as Rosine de Bounevialle puts it: 'I did try to keep the League traditions up but it was practically impossible – they would chant.' Chanting was the chorused shouting of slogans, a method of total heckling at which the BNP was very good. The LEL abhorred chanting, believing it to be mindless, not amusing and – at its bluntest – lower class. Chanting at demonstrations was something which upset the Leaguers; it made their own 'creative' form of protest appear cheap, as though it were just another political manoeuvre.

It was not just the chanting. It was a BNP member being drunk when demonstrating against a play and clambering on stage to give a garbled harangue; it was the mulishness of some of the BNP attitudes; it was the echo of violence which rang in their politics, violence rather than wit. Chesterton tried to put it with delicacy in *Candour* of June 1967:

> If the NF does not become an elite movement it will fail. Ideally we should seek to recruit only the dedicated elite, but we do not live in an ideal world and must make the best use of the material at our disposal. Even so, we have so to conduct our movement that it is considered an honour to belong to the NF.

The BNP members saw this as a rebuke, and began to sneer at Chesterton as 'the Schoolmaster'. They were not even mollified by his attempt to weld their passion to what he saw as his own grace.

Tyndall, who cultivated Chesterton in private, made public overtures and gestures of self-abnegation. In June of 1967, *Spearhead* slackened the links which bound it to the GBM and declared:

> Up to now this journal has worked closely in conjunction with one of these (nationalist) groups, the GBM. Henceforth, while still co-ordinating its work with this organization, it will become a more general organ of patriotic opinion in Britain and will aim above all to foster the movement towards unity which we believe essential if a new political party is to be built.

It was a convincing – and perhaps sincere – declaration, weakened a little by an appeal for £750 to keep the magazine going. *Spear-*

head had just acquired some expensive new typesetting equipment. Tyndall was already convinced that a wider audience awaited him.

The GBM called a meeting to pass the resolution that: 'In overall principles and objectives we believe that there is no essential difference between the NF and ourselves', and GBM members were advised 'to join and give their wholehearted support to the NF.'

A cynic would have pointed to Tyndall's assets, or as the GBM resolution put it: 'Whilst the council of the GBM will no longer function as such, certain enterprises that have been run in conjunction with it have, we feel, a definite use and will be continued.' These included *Spearhead* magazine, Albion Press (of both of which Tyndall was the proprietor), Viking Books and the Nationalist Centre, thanks to the generosity of Gordon Brown. The terms of the dowry are hinted at it in the GBM's promise that these institutions 'will be kept going and will be, as planned, developed as a meeting place and social centre for patriots generally'.

Spearhead of September 1967 announced on its cover: 'Unity one step nearer – we line up behind NF.' In his editorial comments, Tyndall combined a proper humility with a sense of the inevitable having been finally accomplished:

As the NF is a considerably more substantially founded organization than the GBM, being the combination of two groups each larger than our own to begin with, we believe that the most appropriate way of linking forces with it is the very simple one of discontinuing the GBM and calling on all those who have been members of, or have in some way supported that organization to join and put their whole efforts behind the NF. This we have done and already most of our leading members have taken the step advised . . . that we should give our wholehearted support to such an organization has been clear to me from the time when it was first conceived. It has merely been a case of when and by what manner of agreement this support should take form. This has required a little negotiation and some spirit of tolerance over the matter of past disagreements.

It also required the flagrant contradiction of those solemn promises which Chesterton had given the League and which Maxwell had given to the BNP, that no neo-Nazi groups would be permitted to join the NF. And it required the domination of the

NF's councils by the militant wing of the BNP. It had not taken very long.

There was a price to be paid, and patience had to be shown. But as Chesterton told Tyndall one night, he had been in prison only the previous year. In the August 1967 *Candour*, Chesterton welcomed Tyndall back into Nationalist respectability:

> Mr Tyndall, leader of the GBM, has shown the utmost selflessness in refraining from any attempt to negotiate for himself a position within the NF. He intends to occupy himself with matters which, although in a sense residual, are nevertheless potentially very important.

Encouraged by this general amnesty of the Right, Colin Jordan, who was in prison at the time for distributing a strongly-worded pamphlet entitled 'The Coloured Invasion', smuggled out his own proposals for unity on the Right. They were sent to Tyndall, Chesterton and Fountaine, but were not taken up. At least, they were not taken up immediately.

On his release in 1968, Jordan received a discreet message from Tyndall, suggesting they could meet secretly at Denis Pirie's home. Jordan remembers:

> It was a very friendly meeting. We all knew each other and Tyndall had written something friendly about me when I was sent to prison. I think he was attacking the Race law, but it was friendly. Tyndall finally appeared to have got over the past. He seemed much more relaxed – he said he noticed that my divorce had come through from Françoise. That was the only time the matter was referred to.
>
> We talked politics. Tyndall explained that he had had to humble himself to get into the NF and that at present he was functioning merely as editor of *Spearhead*. But he was fully confident – and I can remember the phrase he used – he was confident that eventually 'we will obtain our rightful elevation'. I remember he looked at Pirie and Webster when he said that.
>
> Then he turned back to me and said, 'Don't start a new movement.' By then, of course, the whole NSM had been wound up. I didn't reply and Pirie added that if I did start a new movement 'it would be stamped on'.

Tyndall then suggested that I could start writing for *Spearhead* under a pseudonym – and maybe eventually, as he had done, come into the movement. In fact I started the British

77

Movement that summer and put out another circular on the possibility of unity. Chesterton told me that it was premature. I would have to wait awhile to become acceptable.

From the way the conversation developed that evening there was no doubt in my mind that Tyndall was planning to take over the Front and that he was quite confident he knew how to do it. He kept advising patience. All we needed was patience, and him as leader. That was his line.

Clearly Tyndall was confident that his past was behind him and that he could now work his way to prominence in the NF – and indeed, through perseverance and hard work on the NF's behalf, he won his redemption, at least in Chesterton's eyes.

Tyndall believed that the single most important factor in his welcome by Chesterton was the pamphlet he had published in 1966, presenting a fundamentally revised political theory, called 'Six principles of British Nationalism'. Now into its second edition, the book is described by the NF's catalogue as 'required reading for all nationalists, particularly NF members'.

It compares the authoritarian benefits of his earlier pamphlet 'The Authoritarian State' to the more difficult, but more acceptable path (to a British audience) of nationalist government by consent. Since the pamphlet still forms the basis of overall NF policy, it is worth examining at some length.

The fundamental difference between the Tyndall of 1961 and the Tyndall of 1966 (and 1970 – all quotations are from the 1970 edition, which was slightly updated) is in his acceptance of the idea that the Government must be acceptable to the people. This is a far cry from the uncompromising authoritarianism of 1961 even though – and this is important – Tyndall does not specifically reject the idea of dictatorship:

> Nationalists seek a type of government with a firmness and a strength that we have not seen in this country for at least half a century, but at the same time a Government that acts within the democratic terms on which it has been elected. Firmness and strength can more easily be exercised within a dictatorship; within a democracy of the British character they call for leadership of a very high order. Persuasion rather than suppression must be the usual practice.

If we are not to have dictatorship, what we certainly do need is a governing party that can gain ascendancy in British politics of sufficient dimensions, and for a sufficient period of time to attend to the vital tasks uninterrupted until they have become part of the permanent pattern of British life.

With an ineradicable faith in British greatness, Tyndall must explain the nation's retreat from power and prosperity:

> For the past half-century British genius and British strength have been paralysed by a poverty of leadership, by archaic political institutions and by naïve and flabby political philosophies . . . the weakness of Britain today is the product of an intelligentsia which during living memory has been hypnotized by the madness of liberalism and internationalism.

The argument proceeds: 'There is no fundamental weakness in our nation that cannot be cured through the emergence of new leadership . . . We believe it is right for Britain to be great and remain free.' National unity must be restored and the established political parties, Labour and Tory, are too committed to their class identities to permit the unity which transcends class differences: 'Only a community of people with a truly national sense will be immune to the insidious disease of class warfare.'

Tyndall's first principle was that faith. His second principle is the need to see Britain as a world power through a new white Commonwealth. (This argument is taken much further and supported with a degree of evidence in the NF Policy pamphlet 'Britain: world power or pauper state?'.)

> In the boundless lands of Empire and Commonwealth lie all the ingredients of modern power, waiting only for a determined national policy aiming at their full co-ordination and development in the service of the British future . . . We must not only recognize the Commonwealth as the singular source of our future existence; we must urgently begin to remake the Commonwealth into a genuine instrument of national power.

This, he acknowledges, will demand a considerable shifting of the trade and defence links which the white Commonwealth nations have developed with other countries, and a considerable reconciliation with South Africa and Rhodesia. Tyndall recognizes – with a certain glee – that this 'Will only be possible on the basis of our acceptance of those countries' internal policies. We should do more than acknowledge acceptance; we should give complete support.'

Such a reconciliation (which could be joined by some of the

black Commonwealth countries if they are prepared to enter on the terms laid down by the white countries) would involve the mass resettlement of Britain's own overcrowded population in 'the great spaces of the Dominions'. The results would be 'the makings of a civilization that could surpass in its splendour anything yet achieved in the history of man'.

The third principle is that of economic nationalism, which accords with Chesterton's conspiracy theory of international finance:

> Many people are coming to believe that international finance has a vested interest in the creeping internationalism of the world, and that behind all the slogans about 'peace' and 'brotherhood' lurk sinister designs which are likely to place total world control in the hands of a few ruthless financial operators.

Tyndall's answer is to give Britain the large market of the white Commonwealth and to use the Commonwealth as the only source of raw materials – creating a self-sufficient and enclosed economic system. Specifically, Tyndall rejects the alternative of a European common market, and he does so in terms which justify Colin Jordan's suspicion that Tyndall was very much more of a British than a Nordic nationalist. For Jordan, the ties of the Nordic race are supreme – for Tyndall, they appear no longer to exist. Tyndall had adopted the Chesterton line on Europe. Of Europe he writes: 'Its peoples are not united by kinship and cannot be kept together by any bond other than mutual economic interest – which is the very last bond that they in fact have.'

The fourth principle is that of preserving the British race:

> If ever the basic character of the British people were to alter and their inherent qualities be lost, then no amount of improvement in their institutions would avail against the certainty of a dark future . . . We therefore oppose racial integration and stand for racial separateness . . . To make a scheme of repatriation (of coloured immigrants) really work in the long-term interest of white and coloured races we must have the courage to make it obligatory.

Simply, Tyndall recommends the adoption of the apartheid policy of South Africa, and stresses moreover that the African white regimes deserve total British support:

The white settlers fighting to retain their position are fighting for our cause and our future, the future of British civilization the world over . . . White Rhodesians and South Africans should be under no illusions; they should recognize that their only true friends in this country are those who are prepared to speak out openly in defence of their right to stay in power *for all time* and not just for the few more years of grace that our modern Tories would condescend to give them.

On this issue, Tyndall makes no compromise:

It is based on the simple principle of white leadership . . . while every race may have its particular skills and qualities, the capacity to govern and lead and sustain civilization as we understand it lies essentially with the European.

Tyndall presents his own proposal for improving the black condition:

Provide them with work suited to their own capacities and with progressively better rates of pay, decent houses in their own township where they may mingle harmoniously with their own kind . . . but to give him power and responsibility which he is ill-fitted to use wisely is something entirely different and in fact ends by defeating his quest for a better life.

The fifth principle deals with the duties of government, and goes on to present the final vision of the supra-class, supra-party national government, or national will, which had begun to obsess the British Nationalist mind since the early 1960s. Tyndall begins by arguing that the traditional political parties are unable to implement the changes he suggests. More to the point, he argues that even new political parties (on the old models) would not suffice. It is not a party that Tyndall wants to create, but a mass movement, an organic product of the national will, with the Government as its expression:

Such changes call not merely for a new type of political party but entirely new types of men to take over the nation's destinies . . . Given the character, image and psychology of Conservative and Labour Parties, such a prospect seems remote. Long standing class divisions, however irrational, do not appear as if they can be reconciled by the traditional followers of one attaching themselves to the other. Such a reconciliation could only be achieved by a synthesis of both elements in a new political movement which by tradition was identified neither with one class nor the other . . . This then is the object of Nationalists in Britain: a new party of the character that can capture a majority following from both sides of the present political spectrum so as to be able to obtain a long and assured term of power necessary to its tasks.

It is important here to re-emphasize that Tyndall prefers to achieve this through the democratic political process of consent. (Whether the British electoral system is flexible enough to permit such a new movement to win political power is another matter – although Tyndall could reasonably argue that the system should be so adaptable.) His argument against the mainstream political parties is that they have lost the legitimacy of consent:

> In recent years the issues of the Common Market, Immigration and several spheres of permissive law-making, notably capital punishment and abortion, have provided glaring examples of government by consensus of a liberal minority and without the remotest mandate from the population as a whole. It is a complete mockery of the term 'democratic' to permit government to be carried on in this way.

Not only has Tyndall moved away from the authoritarian position of 1961, he has shifted the authoritarian label to the mainstream parties and portrays Nationalism as the truly representative voice of the citizens. In short, the lessons of the sixties, the agitation for immigration controls and the agitation for law and order and the opposition to the Common Market have transformed Tyndall's estimation of the political intelligence of the British people. They have become a body to be trusted, whose instincts are true and Tyndall, the former authoritarian, is transformed into the legitimate representative of democracy. Tyndall has become a populist because the people now appear to be espousing his views against the policies of their elected governments. So what has changed is not Tyndall's politics, but his interpretation of the people's beliefs. He is now convinced that the people agree with him, and as a result he is prepared to call for the fulfilment of the people's wishes. The ominous use of the word 'usual' in his statement 'persuasion rather than suppression must be the usual practice' suggests that if the people's opinion diverges from Tyndall's, then the authoritarian

Tyndall of 1961 is prepared to reappear.

The final principle of Tyndall's nationalism calls for 'a complete moral regeneration of the national life'. A start must be made on the organs of public opinion: 'Press and television, as well as the schools and universities, have become the breeding grounds of all those ideas that are systematically rotting the nation from within . . . There is almost no attempt to instil into youth the basic principles of patriotism.' He suggested first 'a clear programme of legislation which will render liable to prosecution all persons or agencies responsible for the promotion of art, literature or entertainment by which public moral standards might be endangered', to be reinforced by 'the back-straightening influence of service life, with its emphasis on smartness and discipline and the virtues of manhood, which made me fitter altogether not only for the emergencies of war, but also for the everyday tasks of peace.'

This involves a radical reform of the Welfare State, which 'thwarts every effort to get Britain moving into the twentieth century . . . Let social security be commensurate with the useful effort that the worker contributes to the prosperity of the nation . . . Let those who prefer the life of slothful ease suffer for it by hardship, shortage and insecurity until they decide to mend their ways.'

Tyndall has presented two separate arguments. The first is a generalized vision of a Nationalist Britain with which the bulk of the Nationalist Right (and a large section of the Conservative Party) would be able to agree. This was also his appeal for political rehabilitation on the Right, accepting the democratic traditions of British politics, and rejecting the overt Nazism (and the Nordic racial link with Europeans) of his 1961 pamphlet. But of very much greater importance than this was the vision and justification of a new kind of political movement which 'Six Principles' contains. This alone entitles Tyndall to be seen as a theorist of the Right. Britain is a country with a feeble populist tradition. Tyndall had seen and explained how such a populist movement could now be built.

This involved nothing less than the destruction of the two-party system in British politics, and the weakening of the class loyalties and institutions which underpinned those two parties. This carried the vital tactical implication that any attempt to infiltrate political institutions was not to be done solely in order to take over the institution, but (a less ambitious and easier task) to disrupt it to the point where its traditional role of reinforcing the class or party system was destroyed. For example, NF policy

83

in the trade union movement, as expressed by Tyndall in 1974, is 'to do what the Tories have not done and cannot do, to fight the Left on its own ground in the Unions and wrest the control of the Unions from it.'

Even an unsuccessful attempt at this 'wresting of control' would have the effect of weakening the Labour Party and Labour Movement without giving an advantage to the Conservatives. Similarly, the formation of the NF Students Association did not have to envisage NF control of the student unions; its very presence (tiny and feeble as it was) was disruptive. If left-wing and right-wing students joined together against the NF, then that very process had served to undermine the traditional two-party or left-right structure. By making the initial target for NF activity the two-party system, and the class and political alliances which maintained that system, the NF was given the opportunity to make any kind of short-term political alliances (as it was to do with the Conservative Party's Monday Club over the Ugandan Asian issue, and as it tried to do with the trade union movement by supporting the miners' wage claim in 1974).

It is significant that Tyndall's argument did not adopt the Mosleyite position of expecting an economic slump to disrupt the traditional political structure and thus lead to the summons to power. In Tyndall's system, an economic slump is a bonus which could accelerate an inevitable process. The rise of the Liberal Party to five million votes, the growth of Welsh, Scots and Ulster nationalist parties all serve in Tyndall's eyes to disrupt the two-party system and sweeten the NF's supra-class, supra-party appeal.

At the very least, such an analysis of political change, which can interpret almost any development as a positive advantage, is calculated to work wonders for the morale of its adherents.

As a political statement, and as a political programme, 'Six Principles' had a fair claim to be seen as the most considerable theoretical production from the Nationalist Right since Mosley had left the stage. Chesterton was deeply impressed by it and so was Fountaine. For them, much of its attraction lay in its straddling of the concept of government by consent and the idea of administration by authority. It held out the best of both worlds, it echoed Chesterton's fears of 'international Finance' and it eased his doubts about the wisdom of including Tyndall in the NF.

On 7 October 1967, the NF held its first annual conference, and the LEL veterans were reminded of just how different this new movement was by the instructions from the stage about leaving the hall in groups, to which guards would be assigned to protect members against the left-wing demonstrators who were waiting outside. This had never happened at LEL conferences, and those Leaguers who laughed at these precautions were chastened when they did face a running skirmish as they left the Hall. One BNP member had his arm broken at a nearby tube station.

In his speech, Chesterton had to deal with several issues that threatened the NF's fragile new unity. First, he had to appease his own League supporters who were disturbed at the increasing influence of the BNP in the Directorate, and at the inclusion of John Bean and Tyndall. So he warned the BNP members: 'What we have had to guard against has been the attempts at the game of one-upmanship by zealots endeavouring to make the NF a mere enlargement of one or other of the pre-existing organizations.' He went on to warn of the perils of racialist extremism, while wholeheartedly agreeing with the racialists' arguments about the 'deadly peril of mongrelization'.

'We have to oppose these evils with all our might,' he agreed. But if in the act of doing so we label ourselves "Jew-haters" or "nigger-haters" we shall lose the battle for survival in which we are engaged . . . If scapegoats have to be found, do not look for them among the Jews or the coloured people, look for them among the 600-odd traitors or dripping wets in the House of Commons, look for them among the champions of Sodom in the House of Lords and in Lambeth Palace.'

But Chesterton had done little more than paper over the cracks when he departed after his speech to spend his customary winter in Cape Town. *Spearhead*'s report on the conference hailed it as a great success (although only 200 delegates attended) and boasted from the cover 'NF – A Movement is born'. But that same issue of *Spearhead* contained a subtle reminder that unity on the Right had not yet been achieved. It carried an article by Dr David Brown, who had kept the bulk of the RPD out of the NF and who was still convinced that his own NDP provided a more suitable vehicle for the coalition of the Right than the NF. The NF activists, and in particular the GBM and BNP militants who now tended to act more and more as a single group, worked assiduously to prove Brown wrong. It was largely their efforts which secured the recruitment of the Liverpool organization, British Aid for Repatriation of Immigrants, in January of 1968. Its leader, W. R. Williams, had written for *Spearhead* when it was still the voice of the GBM, and he brought into the NF not only a provincial organization, but also David Jones and

J. B. Dodd, whose contacts in north-west England encouraged further recruitment. In the spring of 1968, *Candour* acknowledged that 'Merseyside still boasts the biggest and most active group outside London'. In the same year, the Liverpool-based People's Progressive Party joined the NF, and a trickle of support began to come from the English National Party. The pace of recruitment to the NF was encouraging, if not speedy.

The NF leadership itself, however, had its problems. Chesterton and Fountaine, the two senior officers, realized early that their similarly dominant personalities could lead to a clash. Accordingly, wrote Chesterton in *Candour* for June 1967, 'while retaining the rights of all men to differ on occasion, in all that concerns the integrity of our movement and the vital need for unity at the top, Andrew and I have given each other the pledge of absolute mutual loyalty and that pledge we will uphold if need be in the very maws of doom.'

Tyndall hastened to exploit this implicit rivalry between the two leaders. After Fountaine had left the NF in the following year, Tyndall boasted in *Spearhead* of his quiet comments to Chesterton – 'I remember saying at the time to A.K.C. "this man is poison and the next person his poison will be directed at will be you".'

In May 1968, after the student riots in Berlin, Warsaw and Paris, Fountaine was not the only English Rightist to foresee an imminent continental revolution. Accordingly, he issued circulars to NF branch organizers round the country, warning them that civil war was imminent and they should report with their local activists to the nearest police station, to put themselves at the disposal of the forces of order.

Chesterton was horrified and arranged Fountaine's dismissal. Fountaine sought and won a High Court action which said that he had been unconstitutionally dismissed and at the annual conference later in the year he stood against Chesterton for the leadership, receiving a derisory 20 votes against Chesterton's 316. The result came as no surprise. The High Court action and the savage anti-Fountaine propaganda in the NF publications had done him a great deal of harm, and the issue of *Spearhead* which was ready for the Conference charged:

A small band of discontents, masquerading under the holiest of pretexts, has striven night and day for months to foment internal dissatisfaction and disharmony, conducting malicious campaigns against fellow members and supporters, planting suspicion and occupying time at key conferences with endless arguing, quarrelling and obstruction . . . they have only had eyes to see foes within . . . a ludicrous attempt at a civil action against members of the NF Directorate.

It was a golden opportunity for Tyndall to be merciless to an important opponent, Fountaine, and to underline his loyalty to Chesterton. Even more to the point, Tyndall was able to attack those who had aligned themselves with Fountaine, not on the nonsensical issue of the circulars about action groups reporting to police stations, but because they saw Fountaine as the only bulwark against Tyndall and the militant members of the BNP. The two key targets were Gerald Kemp of the BNP and Rodney Legg of the old LEL. Legg was unlikely to get any support from other Leaguers, because in supporting Fountaine he was opposing Chesterton. As an intrigue, it was masterly. Tyndall had forced each of his opponents into one weakly-linked and uncomfortable coalition which had no broad support in the movement.

Rodney Legg describes the final confrontation:

Chesterton was newly returned from South Africa and had decided to admit John Tyndall to respectability. It was the one thing I was prepared to make a stand on. A.K. came into the room at the end of the meeting. He had given an ultimatum and wanted our reaction. We had either to submit or get out. There was no compromise offered. His leadership was in question and a personality clash had developed between A.K. and Fountaine. Andrew refused to back down and A.K. was equally stubborn in his determination to have a confrontation. He stood at the door, wearing a dirty raincoat, and demanded we approved his actions. Andrew walked out and Gerald Kemp and I went with him.

The importance of the Fountaine split for the future of the NF had been underlined shortly before the divisions surfaced by one of the key events of post-war British politics, Enoch Powell's speech at Birmingham on 20 April 1968. It was given to the annual general meeting of the West Midlands area Conservative political centre and it marked a major departure from the political conventions for two reasons. First, the tone of its language was far more urgent and more desperate than any previous statement by one of Ministerial rank, or by a leading spokesman of his party.

Those whom the gods wish to destroy, they first make mad. We must be mad, literally mad, as a nation to be permitting the annual inflow of some 50,000 dependants, who are for the most part the material of the future growth of the immigrant-descended population. It is like watching a nation busily engaged in heaping up its own funeral pyre . . . As I look ahead, I am filled with foreboding. Like the Roman, I seem to see 'the River Tiber foaming with much blood'.

Second, by repeating unsubstantiated tales of old ladies being victimized by immigrants it gave credence to the kind of anti-immigrant gossip which until Powell, had been the currency of the pub rather than the material of serious political discussion. Powell argued that politicians 'simply do not have the right to shrug their shoulders' when constituents tell them 'in this country in fifteen or twenty years the black man will have the whip hand over the white man'. Powell's speech, which adhered to the Conservative Party policy in supporting immigration controls and encouraging repatriation, created a political sensation and Edward Heath, the Tory leader, expelled him from the shadow cabinet.

The resignations of Fountaine, Legg and Kemp from the NF Directorate had given the old militants of the BNP and the GBM the opportunity to develop the NF in their own image, restrained only by the increasingly isolated Chesterton. Recalling these years, Webster explained in 1972 (in an article titled 'NF: a movement of action'):

Because of the unwillingness of the national press to give fair coverage to the policies of the movement, the party soon realized that it was necessary, in its early formative stage, to 'hit the headlines' as often as possible by all manner of demonstrations, marches and stunts.

In principle, Chesterton was in favour; his own League had achieved prominence through well-planned and intelligent 'stunts'. But as early as October 1967, Chesterton was criticizing in private the daubing of Karl Marx's grave at Highgate cemetery and a demonstration outside an anti-war film that got out of control. In December 1968, while Chesterton was in South Africa, the NF invaded a London Weekend TV show, gaining publicity but also a reputation for rowdiness that appalled Chesterton when he heard of it. His return to London in the spring of 1969 came shortly after the most militant of all the NF demos, when two Labour Ministers, Denis Healey and Arthur Bottomley, were assaulted in a general brawl at a public meeting. It had begun with flour bags being thrown (an old LEL tactic), continued with chants of 'NF . . . NF . . . NF' (and Chesterton abhorred chanting) and ended with Bottomley being kneed in the groin and Healey clambering to his rescue. Among the participants were Ron Tear and Steven Wade – Webster was later to expel Wade from the NF, accusing him of disloyalty.

The row within the party was more deeply rooted than the immediate issue of demonstration tactics. It was over the very nature of the movement. The BNP and GBM faction wanted the NF to hurl itself into electoral politics, to catch and exploit the rising wave of anti-immigrant feeling which Powell had unleashed. Chesterton had given way to their demands for the Acton by-election, where the BNP could exploit their traditional strength in Southall. Fountaine was the candidate – it was almost his last act before leaving the NF – and the party put a great deal of effort into the campaign, for minimal results. He won 1400 votes and only 5·6 per cent of the vote. *Spearhead* acknowledged this was 'a disappointment' and Chesterton smugly claimed that this confirmed his view that the NF was not yet equipped to fight elections, even if that was the kind of party it wanted to be.

The lines of ideological strain between the two constituent groups within the NF were becoming more marked when the issue of a new HQ arose to add personal rancour to the arguments. The lease on the NF HQ in the old LEL offices in Palace Chambers, Westminster was running out, and new premises had to be found. Gordon Brown, who had been waiting for this opportunity, said that the old GBM HQ, re-named the Nationalist Centre, would be ideal. It was already under NF control and most members knew it. It was, however, in Tulse Hill, some distance from the centre of London. Brown was supported by Martin Vaux and the bulk of the BNP and GBM men on the Directorate. The old Leaguers who still occasionally came to Directorate meetings, Rosine de Bounevialle, Aidan Mackey and Avril Walters, joined Chesterton in insisting that new offices be found in Central London, in keeping with the Front's ambition to be seen as a serious national body. Brown's argument that the Tulse Hill HQ would save a great deal of money which could then be spent on elections infuriated the Leaguers.

Rosine de Bounevialle remembers it as the Sycophants row:

That was what they called us when we supported A.K. on this, Sycophants. A very sharp division emerged between us over the matter and the row went on for weeks. The BNP people were quite unreasonable about it, and were most offended when A.K. said that fighting elections was one thing but having candidates of the right kind of calibre was another. It all became rather bitter, particularly when Frank Clifford, who was an old Leaguer who had always supported A.K. decided that fighting elections was a good idea.

Chesterton once again argued that his personal authority was being called into question and insisted that the HQ stay in Central London. He was successful and an expensive lease was taken out on a small office in Fleet Street. The immediate need to organize demonstrations in favour of the South African rugby team, which was being bitterly opposed by the Left and the Young Liberals, got the NF working together as a team once more. George Parsons, a former leader of the Liberal group on Cardiff council and one of the NF's major converts, organized a pro-Springbok march in Cardiff to which NF members from London and the Midlands were driven in hired coaches. The beating up of Martin Webster and Pat Addis in October by 'Zionist' counter-demonstrators at least proved the NF was being noticed, and the gaining of recruits from the Anti-Communist League and the Anglo-Rhodesian society later in 1969 helped to restore morale. *Spearhead* claimed that 180 membership enquiries a week were being received at HQ (which was an exaggeration – there is no evidence of the NF ever growing at a rate of 10,000 members a year) but the NF was confident enough to demand in April 1970, when the prospect of wider coalition of the Right was raised, that any other groups submerge themselves into the NF.

'It should be the pride of all NF members to be called extremists and not only that – it should be a matter of guilt to any person opposed to the Left that he is not labelled as extreme,' wrote Tyndall. But much of this internal effort at morale-boosting was whistling in the dark. The NF was deeply concerned that it had missed the Powellite boat, and that it was not expanding as it should.

The overall impression of gloom was reinforced by the 1970 general election results. In the May 1969 municipal elections, the NF had put up 45 candidates around the country who had polled an average of 8 per cent. In some strongholds the figures had been even more encouraging: nine candidates in Huddersfield won an average 12·5 per cent of the vote, polling as high as 18·7 per cent in one ward. In Cardiff, George Parsons had polled 10 per cent of the vote, and in Sheffield six candidates in three wards had won an average 9 per cent. Municipal by-elections later in the year saw an 11·5 per cent vote for NF candidates in the London boroughs of Wandsworth and West Ham.

The 1970 municipal elections, held shortly before the general election, were not fought nearly as hard by the NF, who wanted to husband their strength for the national poll; but, once again, the results from their strongholds seemed to indicate a general level of support of over 10 per cent of votes. In Huddersfield, where the NF fought 13 out of 15 wards, they won 10·5 per cent of the vote. In Wolverhampton, in a straight fight with the Conservative candidate, Ron Davison won 753 votes, against the Conservative's 1204. The Indian Workers' Association had advised its members to vote for the Conservative, and *Spearhead*, estimating over 500 Asian electors, sneered that 'the NF gained slightly more British votes than the Tories'. Even in Bristol, with a small and inexperienced NF branch, two candidates won 6·5 per cent of the vote.

The proportion of electors who bother to vote in local elections is traditionally between a third and a half of those who vote in national polls. This gives a clear advantage to small parties with dedicated support. Even so, the NF had reason for quiet confidence. This confidence was badly shaken by the general election results. Ten candidates had been nominated, all in areas of NF strength. The percentage votes were appalling: in Leicester 2·3 per cent, in Cardiff 1·9 per cent, in Huddersfield 3·5 per cent, in Wolverhampton 4·7 per cent. Nor were the figures in London, where the membership was not only larger, but more able to move into specific electoral areas, any improvement. In Southall the NF polled 4·4 per cent, in Enfield 3·1 per cent, in Battersea 3·3 per cent, in Ilford 1·8 per cent. The only remotely encouraging results were 5·6 per cent in Islington (where the Reverend Brian Green, a close friend of the Reverend Ian Paisley, had a significant personal following) and 5·5 per cent in Deptford, where Martin Vaux received some discreet Conservative support.

This was a marked reduction of the percentage NF candidates had achieved previously in local elections, and although some drop had been expected, the decline was bitterly disappointing for Brown and the pro-election faction.

The growing confidence of the NF (up to the general election) had been confirmed in its own eyes by the increasing attention it was getting from its militant opponents on the Left. In May 1969, the office of its Croydon organizer was raided, documents were stolen and the Union Jack was burnt. The following month, a stolen lorry was reversed into the Nationalist Centre at Tulse Hill, doing little damage but rudely awakening John Tyndall who was asleep upstairs. (Chesterton was always rather unhappy about the way the old GBM members lived in the Centre and particularly criticized Webster for his habit of working late at night and sleeping until noon.) The NF's annual conference of 1969 had to be switched to another hall when two men sneaked into the Caxton Hall's switch room and smashed the electrical gear with axes.

In response to this, the NF evolved its own counter-infiltration system. In July 1969, a young man in North London going under the name of Peter Johnson began producing anti-fascist leaflets so virulent that he was interviewed by the police. He got in touch with local Community Relations officers and left-wing groups and successfully applied to join the Young Liberals. He was asked to work with Paul Hodges, who was then establishing the Party's Anti-Racialist Commission. 'Johnson' then established the South London Anti-Racialist Group, in an effort to get the various left-wing and trade union organizations to work together against the NF south of the Thames. During this time, Johnson compiled a list of the names and addresses of all the anti-NF activists in the region. The defection of Mrs O'Connell from the Wandsworth Tories to the NF late in the year boosted SLARG activity and a Wandsworth Anti-Fascist Group was founded, which 'Johnson' joined as the Putney Young Liberal delegate. The experienced members of this group, which included Communist Party members who were watching for NF infiltration, began to suspect 'Johnson' and the copious notes he took at each meeting.

'Johnson' was aware of the problem. His second secret report to NF HQ read:

There should be no great difficulty in getting a 'plant' into the meeting, providing that whoever is chosen is (a) reliable (b) not known to the South London reds (c) had a convincing cover, always remembering that as there will be IS, Anarchists, YL and Community Relations persons present plus other assorted odd groups and thus it may be better to get him in as an ex-member of SHARC or some vague multi-racialist group based outside South London. Credibility is essential and someone who may get hot under the collar when the NF is ridiculed or abused or who may show dislike of the overtly pro-black sentiments that will be expressed at the meeting will be of no use at all.

'Johnson' himself had already been blown, and he suspected that this was the case. When he turned up for a committee meeting on 5 January, he took two car-loads of tough supporters with him in case of trouble. In the event, he was simply refused access to the meeting. In the course of his infiltration, 'Johnson', who was in fact a North London NF branch organizer, was beaten up by two NF members after shouting insults at the NF march through Southall. At least one of his reports on the South London anti-fascist militants was forwarded to the Special Branch as part of the NF's deliberate policy to cultivate good relations with the police.

But although the NF was exciting alarm on the Left, it was deeply concerned about its own performance. In the wake of the 1970 election, Chesterton launched 'Operation Shake-Up' in an attempt to stop the sense of drift which he felt had taken over the movement. It involved a minor restructuring of organization, but it was mainly an attempt to boost morale and improve communications between the branches and national HQ.

At the Directorate meeting at which Chesterton broached his scheme, John O'Brien, whom Chesterton had just hired to be office manager, was surprised to hear Pat Addis mutter to Gordon Brown 'That's not the *real* Operation Shake-Up.' At the time, O'Brien dismissed it, but this was the first signal that a putsch against Chesterton was being prepared.

The putsch was planned and prepared by Gordon Brown, the paymaster of the GBM, who had been so offended at Chesterton's blunt refusal to allow the NF to move into the house which Brown had provided at Tulse Hill. Throughout the summer of 1970, he mobilized his support, and persuaded Mike Lobb, Peter Williams, Ron Tear and John Cook to join him in an Action Committee. Pat Addis was also recruited, but was kept out of the real preparations. Some of the news leaked out, enough to raise tiny stories in the press about a split in the movement between Powellites and the rest. *Spearhead* for September 1970 firmly denied the rumours, and the annual conference of 1970 re-elected Chesterton as leader with a unanimous vote.

But that conference confirmed the arguments Brown had been muttering into the ears of all who would listen. Chesterton was old and past his best, out of touch with the needs of a thrusting young movement. The distinguished and elderly friends Chesterton brought to sit with him on the platform – who were never seen throughout the rest of the year – underlined Chesterton's own age. Two of them fell asleep during the course of the day. This was the folly of Chesterton's traditional practice of padding the organization with names that few but he thought lent lustre to the movement.

As a result, Brown was able to recruit the NF Treasurer, Clare Macdonald, Peter McMenemie the NF's literature designer (he also worked on *Spearhead*, and had been convicted of stealing a gun when in the GBM in 1966), Albert Mitchell the bookshop manager, Ken Taylor the parliamentary candidate for Enfield and Martin Vaux. All of them, with the exception of Mike Lobb, signed a letter to Chesterton which was sent to him in South Africa, asking for his resignation. This came as no real surprise to Chesterton. He had already received a telegram from a loyal member, Jock Shaw, which read 'There is a revolt against your leadership. Please send instructions.' Chesterton cabled back 'Who and how many are involved? Essential to safeguard membership list.'

The press reports of a split (which included speculations about police raids on HQ, and suspension of NF activities for a year while a 'clear division of trends' was resolved) had unsettled the party membership. 'I had barely joined, but something was definitely in the air,' recalls O'Brien. 'A feeling that people were waiting for something to happen.'

When the letter from the Action Committee reached Chesterton, copies were already on their way to the NF branches round the country, with requests for further signatures to be added. The letter accused Chesterton of 'sorry lack of judgement concerning appointments and dismissals in the movement' and complained of his 'dictatorial methods and pettiness in the leadership'. It demanded that 'voluntary workers must not be denied admission to the movement' – which was widely interpreted as opening the way to Colin Jordan to join the NF with his British Movement, which Chesterton had expressly forbidden. The letter also showed how desperate the militants were to capitalize on support for Enoch Powell – a course of action which Chesterton had resolutely opposed because of Powell's economic views. Referring to Powell, the letter said: 'Rightly or wrongly he is respected by a huge majority of the British people and to attack him incurs the hostility of that majority. Let us direct our energies to attacking those who are unpopular with the people and who we know are on the other side.'

Chesterton had expected that his supporters would immediately suspend the rebels and maintain his authority until he returned in the spring. This was the immediate reaction of Rosine de Bouneviale, who knew nothing of the putsch until a Portsmouth member happened to pass her home with a copy of the letter while on his way to London. She and Chesterton's other close supporters had deliberately not been sent the letter.

She got in touch with Aidan Mackey and Avril Walters, who initially agreed that the rebels should be suspended, but they quickly realized that support could not be mustered for this within the rest of the leadership. John Bean, John O'Brien, John Tyndall, Malcolm Skeggs and William Palmer were all prepared to agree that they were loyal to Chesterton, but stressed that the priority was to avoid a split in the party – particularly since exploratory and informal talks were in progress with Dr David Brown's NDP again to see if a merger could be arranged. All Chesterton's supporters could arrange was a second letter to Cape Town. He later wrote that it was 'so very half-hearted in its wording . . . bent so far backwards to appease the dissidents and so avoid a split', that he determined to resign.

But the dissidents had already been so encouraged by the muted reaction of Chesterton's supporters that they met in Newham ten days after sending the initial letter to discuss the next step. There was some hope at this stage that Beauclair of the RPS and Andrew Fountaine (who later denied it) had agreed to raise £16,000 to finance a new broadsheet and so reduce the NF's dependence on Chesterton's own *Candour* and *Spearhead*, since Tyndall had lined up with the loyalists. Tyndall had been secretly approached by Brown and asked to take over the leadership of the NF. Tyndall refused point-blank, on the grounds that Chesterton was the leader until the members voted him out. (Brown and Tyndall had had their differences before, but it was Tyndall's loyalty to Chesterton which began the antipathy between the two men which culminated in Brown's support for the anti-Tyndall group in 1974.)

At this point, the Action Committee had opened its own lines of communication to the NDP and to Colin Jordan. The story leaked to *The Times* of 19 October, which ran a statement from Ron Tear that 'I do not want to talk about it; it is just a growing pain'.

Three days later, Tear told the *Ilford Recorder* 'there is no question of a split in the party. All we have done is asked him to resign as leader. We hope he will stay in the party.' Once Chesterton's supporters had decided that the priority was to

95

keep the party united, the success of the rebels was assured. But Chesterton's warning about safeguarding the membership lists had been justified. During his absence, the party had been entrusted to a six-man inner council. It included Mike Lobb, Martin Vaux, Malcolm Skeggs, Ron Scott, Tyndall and Webster. Brown also endeavoured to attend the bulk of its meetings. On the Saturday morning after the dispatch of the first letter to Chesterton, O'Brien had decided to go into the office to finish some work. He was surprised when Lobb and Addis used their own key to come into the office – and they were taken aback to see him. Lobb said he had come for the membership lists, and as one of Chesterton's appointed deputies, O'Brien could hardly object.

The second raid was a greater surprise. Shortly after opening the office on 22 October, O'Brien was knocked to the floor by three unidentified men who took with them the subscription files on 6000 members and other documents. The culprits were never identified nor found, although both factions within the NF accused the other, and there were some who suggested that O'Brien had faked the whole story. (Since that time, it has been an open secret in Left and anti-fascist circles that a copy of the NF membership lists was available through discreet channels to those in need. Access to these files has saved more than one newspaper from a libel writ when someone denied ever having been a member of the NF.) Within ten days, every NF member had received a letter of expulsion, purporting to come from HQ. Whether the anti-fascist group had used their own files to circularize the members, or whether one of the NF factions had its own motives for clouding the issue, has never been established.

Webster cabled to Chesterton in Cape Town that he need not worry. Referring to the rebels, Webster advised that all was under control – 'let them sweat it out'. Chesterton later commented: 'Instead of sweating it out, the fixer and the more scruffy minded of his colleagues went the round of the branches whispering their falsehoods.' He sent off his resignation not only from the leadership but also from the movement.

The rebels had won, but they did not know what to do with their victory. Brown had originally planned to replace Chesterton with Tyndall, but Tyndall had refused. Quite simply, the rebels had no-one to replace Chesterton. Brown cast around for available ideas. He thought of Fountaine, but Fountaine had made too many enemies before his walk-out in 1968. He thought of Beauclair, who was unwilling and was too unknown within the

Front. As a woman, Clare Macdonald would not have been acceptable to the Directorate. The NF was left leaderless. Tyndall commented bitterly in the January *Spearhead*: 'The campaign to oust A. K. Chesterton from the leadership of the NF was conducted seemingly without a moment's thought for what was to follow him, or if there was thought it was based on the most naïve and shallow speculation.' Tyndall still hoped that he could act as a bridge between Chesterton and the Front, and bring him back not as leader but as President.

It was not to be. At a special meeting called by John Bean, at the North Eastern Hotel in London in November, Bean suggested they should ask Chesterton to withdraw his resignation. A furious Rosine de Bounevialle retorted that he would never return until the Action Committee were expelled. Nor was Brown ready to compromise – he and Tom Lamb even opposed a proposal to send a vote of thanks to Chesterton for his long work for the movement. Chesterton's comment, in the December issue of *Candour*, gave his terms: 'If the right leader comes along and if the twilight creatures are relegated to the sewers, the NF will have no stauncher friend than me.'

He later wrote a veiled account of the putsch against himself in *Candour* for April 1971. It clarified little more than his extreme bitterness:

After four strenuous years and the expenditure of much money from my own and *Candour* resources, stamping out nonsense such as plots to use stink bombs or set fire to synagogues among the feebler-minded and the development of 'counter-revolutions' among the more idiosyncratic, I had had more than enough.

He went on to describe the NF as he saw it:

Eighty per cent of the movement's members are first class, honest to God British patriots. Ten per cent are drifters who will go with the tide. Five per cent place personal ambition above all else. Three per cent are totally unable to distinguish between good faith and bad faith and the remaining two per cent are really evil men – so evil that I placed intelligence agents to work exploring their background with results so appalling that I have felt obliged to entrust the documents to the vaults of a bank – some of these men are at present placed close to the centre of things.

(Chesterton's widow authorized me to see whatever papers Chesterton had entrusted to his bank, but there were none. Chesterton did discover that Gordon Brown's real name was Marshall, and received at least one 'intelligence report' on the meetings which took place before the putsch. It read: 'It was mentioned that A.K. could be very ruthless in a crisis whereupon "B" said that he suffered from a weak heart and would be likely so far from home to fall down dead when he hears of our ultimatum. That would be admirable, as it would avoid a split. Chesterton informed his friends that he did not have a weak heart, and that the mysterious 'B' was in fact Brown.)

Spearhead maintained a discreet silence about the coup, apart from Tyndall's acid comments on the lack of foresight of the plotters, and a brief note that McMenemie had resigned from the magazine's staff because Tyndall had signed a motion of confidence in Chesterton. He concentrated his efforts on binding up the wounds: 'We face a struggle ahead that is going to occupy all of us for the major part of our remaining lives . . . Ours is a duty which is endless and timeless when viewed in historical perspective – much as the duties of the Christian and other churches.'

It was a pompous and rather silly statement, but it was precisely the kind of message the bewildered NF members needed. Many of them still see this as Tyndall's finest hour, working tirelessly to reconcile the still bitter factions and to win Chesterton back to the NF. He wrote a moving tribute to A.K. in *Spearhead*, referring to his friendship with the man which had begun soon after Tyndall left the Army, 'a friendship which has survived numerous clashes', and acknowledged 'as a contributor to nationalist thought in Britain in the post-war period he stands supreme'. Chesterton was touched and mollified – even though his 'friendship' for Tyndall had not extended to inviting him to the Chesterton parties.

For Webster, who had been privately suggesting to his friends that he was Chesterton's spiritual heir, A.K. had even less time, writing of 'The Fat (and fatuous) Boy of Peckham, waving his arms about wildly, accused me of being "out of touch" with the movement'.

The only antidote to the NF's malaise after Chesterton's resignation was action, and Tyndall and Webster hurled themselves into Front activities, planning to open a regional HQ in Huddersfield and organizing a major march in Wolverhampton late in November 1970, for which 100 of the London members went up by coach to swell the ranks of the marchers. At the rally which followed, John O'Brien made a fighting speech, in the middle of which he was stopped by a standing acclamation of the meeting. He had said:

> The territory and soil of Britain, defended by the blood of our ancestors – and our contemporaries – and moistened by the sweat from the brows of countless thousands of our people who have laboured to improve it, is by that blood and by that sweat made sacred, and is not for sale or barter to immigrants.

Observers reported that Webster and Tyndall looked very thoughtful at O'Brien's reception. It was then that they decided he could be the man to take over the leadership – in part because he appeared to be pliant enough to act as a respectable figurehead while the real power was still exercised by their own administrative control of party activities and branches.

O'Brien had begun his venture in Nationalist politics with Enoch Powell's speech in April 1968. Until then a member of his local Shropshire Conservative Association, he founded the British Defence League and then joined with Dr David Brown's National Democratic Party and was appointed to its national council.

In the course of the next year, O'Brien got to know every Nationalist group on the British Right. He became a personal friend of several of the key people outside the NF, including Mrs Joy Page of the Immigrant Control Association, and Mary Howarth who was now working with Page. He delved through the tangled skein of anti-immigrant groups, meeting Jim Merrick of the Yorkshire Campaign to Stop Immigration (a former Tory councillor) and Roy Bramwell of the Monday Club and ICA. He visited the Hancocks at the Heidelberg guest house in Brighton; saw Tom Jones and Ernest Shelly, old stalwarts of the Birmingham anti-immigration groups of the early 1960s and later of the Racial Preservation Society. He met Dan Harmston of the Union Movement and George Knuppfer, a white Russian émigré who ran a small but intellectually influential body called the Integralists, much concerned with the conspiracy theory of international finance. He visited Anthony Baron, whose East Anglia Forum worked closely with the NDP, and the tiny National Party of St George in Reading.

On one of these tours he met Martin Webster. They were both in Birmingham to scoop up a small group called the Association of British People, run by a Mr Broomhall. It had fewer than 200 members, most of them on paper, but O'Brien representing the

NDP and Webster for the NF were both trying to recruit them According to O'Brien, his personal antipathy for Webster begar at this moment. He took an instant dislike to Webster (a not uncommon phenomenon) and was particularly pleased that the group joined the NDP and worked with the NDP in the 1970 election campaign in Roy Jenkins's seat.

The two men O'Brien respected most after his tour were Chesterton of the NF, and John Davis, a former associate of Andrew Fountaine, who now ran his own National Independence Party on policy lines broadly similar to those of the NF. He continued to correspond with Chesterton, who asked him to come and work for *Candour* in London, and also to be office manager for the NF. There was a possibility at this time – September 1970 – of a merger between the NDP and the NF. Chesterton saw Brown's NDP as containing less of 'the loutish element' which so distressed him in the NF, and hoped that by joining with the NDP, the militants within the NF could be controlled. In *Spearhead*, Tyndall was less sure, making it clear that if any more unification was to take place then other groups could join on the NF's own terms. But Chesterton certainly saw O'Brien's appointment as bringing the NDP merger appreciably closer.

O'Brien walked into an office that was already bristling with hostility. There was the Directorate row between Brown and Chesterton and then the putsch, but O'Brien threw himself into his first task – trying to work out an electoral pact between the various right-wing groups for the Marylebone by-election in November 1970.

The NDP had intended to stand at Marylebone, but O'Brien and Davis of the NIP persuaded them to stand down and let Malcolm Skeggs, the NF candidate, collect whatever Nationalist support there was. It made little difference. Skeggs won a disastrous 401 votes, and even Ken Taylor's 1176 (4·4 per cent) at the Enfield by-election did little to raise NF spirits. 'We are still no more than a speck on the British political horizon,' brooded Tyndall. The prospect of a merger with the NDP was still very much alive, since NDP morale had not recovered from the 1970 election. Ironically, they could claim the best vote of any Nationalist candidate in Southampton, where their candidate had won 9581 votes, 21·8 per cent of the vote. But this was in the constituency of the Speaker of the House of Commons, and by tradition, the major parties did not oppose the Speaker. The NDP had simply won the protest vote. In Leicester, it had won only 2·5 per cent of the vote, and 3·5 per cent in Birmingham

Stechford. Dr Brown claimed a moderate success in Ipswich, where his vote had risen from 400 in 1964 to 800 in 1966 to 2322 (3·7 per cent) in 1970. But the NDP, like the NF, had hoped to do very much better.

Although O'Brien was not able to secure a merger – indeed the NF Directorate refused to give him a mandate to seek one – he was able to arrange a working relationship, of which the Marylebone election pact was the first fruit. In 1971, Eddie Bray, the NDP candidate in Southampton, brought a coachload of supporters to a NF march in Bristol. O'Brien was able to secure further working relationships with the Immigration Control Association, and through them with the Monday Club and the Powellite support groups. And in December 1971, the NF persuaded the Newcastle Democratic Movement to join, and form the focus of a Tyneside branch.

The NF was recovering better than it had dared hope, but a chairman was needed. Aidan Mackey had chaired two Directorate meetings after Chesterton's resignation, but he refused to do more. He was afraid that too close an identification with the NF could hurt the private school he ran, and his personal loyalty was committed to Chesterton. Webster and Tyndall had been impressed by O'Brien's performance at Wolverhampton, and broached the idea to the other Directorate members. Brown was unconvinced, but in the absence of alternatives, accepted O'Brien. Brown would probably have agreed with Chesterton's ambiguous comment: 'John O'Brien is far and away the best man for the job as far as he was the only one willing to accept it.'

He was voted in by the Directorate, pending confirmation at an emergency general meeting, which was held in February 1971. The NF also took the opportunity to reform its constitutional procedures, which had been designed by Chesterton to facilitate his own autocratic methods of control. Henceforth, one third of the Directorate was to be elected each year (Chesterton had simply appointed Directorate members before this), and the Directorate was divided into sub-committees to control different aspects of the movement. They included administration (which Gordon Brown took over), branch development (with which O'Brien concerned himself), activities (Webster), finance (Clare Macdonald, the NF treasurer, took this field), policy (Tyndall) and publicity (Webster again).

Having confirmed O'Brien as chairman, the NF turned to the Government's new Immigration Bill, which fulfilled the early NF (and Powell's) demand of making immigrants enter on the same terms as aliens. Undismayed, the NF now charged that the

101

legislation on aliens was too lax. The NF also attacked the idea of paying immigrants who chose repatriation.

'Entry into the UK for Commonwealth citizens can only properly be decided on the basis of race,' it added. Having hardened up its line on immigration, the NF – under O'Brien's influence backed by Tyndall – decided to try and widen its appeal by stressing other items of its policy. In particular, it decided to conduct an anti-Common Market campaign and to launch a drive in support of the Unionists in Ulster. A whole issue of *Spearhead* was devoted to opposing the EEC in August, with Tyndall declaring 'we are at war', and reporting on its anti-Europe campaign rallies in London, Bristol, Leicester, Wolverhampton, Manchester, Liverpool and Huddersfield. *Spearhead* warned: 'The average British family will be reduced to a wartime diet – beef a luxury, margarine instead of butter and potatoes eking out bread.' Predictably, it charged that the real pro-Europeans were the 'Dollar Imperialists behind EEC' and repeated its attacks on the 'money power'.

As a list of activities, it sounded impressive, but the NF's new drive was not borne out by the 1971 local election results. Although it put up a record number of 84 candidates, they could only muster an average vote of 5·2 per cent. In Huddersfield, the bright spot of the previous year's local elections, only 7 candidates stood (as against 13 the previous year) and the percentage poll fell from 10·5 per cent to 8·3 per cent. Eleven candidates stood in Bristol, but only managed to win between 3 and 5 per cent of the vote. Nor was there much comfort to be got from the occasional success like Tunbridge Wells (9 per cent), West Bromwich (8·5 per cent) or Deptford (7 per cent). As Gordon Brown reported to the Directorate 'when you only have one candidate, it really doesn't mean very much'. To add to the disappointment, NF candidates' homes in Bristol had been attacked with bricks and daubed with swastikas on the eve of the poll. It was a depressing election.

The one cause for celebration was O'Brien's recruiting tour in the north of England in May. (This had included speaking in Huddersfield before the local election date, reinforcing the effort of Martin Webster, who had been in the town for two weeks in an attempt to win the electoral breakthrough that once again eluded them.) O'Brien spoke to the Manchester branch of the National Democratic Party, run by Walter Barton. O'Brien had long been a friend of Barton, and much of the pressure for coalition within the NDP had come from the Manchester branch. O'Brien made a rousing speech to the branch, after which Barton announced that he was going to join the NF and he rest of his branch followed him.

Even this success did little to alleviate the gloom at national HQ. O'Brien described the mood:

> A frightful atmosphere of mutual distrust and intrigue. Clique against clique. There was the Brown clique, there was the Tyndall clique. I had to keep this witches' brew from boiling over and putting out the fire. The anti-Chesterton coup had left a universal feeling of mutual suspicion, everyone was watching his neighbour and few trusted others sufficiently either to give or seek counsel.

The mood in the Directorate continued to be bitter. In retrospect, O'Brien describes the meetings as 'monthly bear gardens'. Webster was particularly curt. When Alex Marshall claimed that he had contacts with Ian Paisley, and if the NF was to try to establish itself in Ulster, it should send him, Webster retorted that he and Tyndall would go, adding 'we're sending the organ grinder, not the monkey'.

Through a mixture of personal rancour and real alarm for the NF, O'Brien had decided that he must get Webster and Tyndall out:

> It had been brought to my notice by a member of the NF that Tyndall and Webster had connections in Germany with ex-supporters of the Hitler regime, and that reciprocal visits had been paid by parties of Germans who heard a speech by Tyndall at a meeting at a London hotel. I taxed Tyndall with this, and his reply had been 'Are my friends being called to account?'

O'Brien had also been shown a copy of the German neo-Nazi magazine *Das Reich* for October 1971. It referred to successful liaison with Tyndall, and described him as 'Führer' of the National Front. O'Brien had also been told of NF members attending a Northern League rally in Brighton in November of 1971, with Colin Jordan. The meeting was invaded by fourteen demonstrators, who attacked the assembled Germans and NF members (the Monday Club later denied any of its members had attended), yelling 'Nazis, SS, Nazis'. One of the Germans who attended, Horst Bongers, a German Naval veteran, told reporters he did not know why they had been attacked. (The next week Molly Brandt Bowen, a reporter for the *Jewish Chronicle* who covered the attack, was herself beaten up and left unconscious in the street outside her home. While she was being beaten, one of the gang told her 'this is from our German friends. This is for your Jewish thugs and our compliments to the *Jewish Chronicle*.')

It was little use Tyndall denying any connection with the Northern League – not when his journal *Spearhead* was still running an advertisement for the *Northlander*, the League's magazine, as late as November 1972. It read: 'The *Northlander* – an informative cultural journal devoted to the international friendship and solidarity of all Northern European Nations and the preservation of their common heritage. Official organ of the Northern League.'

Appalled by this evidence of continued neo-Nazi links, O'Brien gathered his support. On the Directorate, he was sure of Clare Macdonald, Alex Marshall, Ken Taylor, Peter Applin and Frank Stockham of the Bristol group. Alex Marshall and George Wilson of the HQ staff were also determined that Tyndall and Webster should go. At the annual conference in September, O'Brien studied the votes for the National Directorate with care. He had led the poll, followed by Tyndall and Clare Macdonald. Five of his trusted supporters had come in the first ten in the poll, and Walter Barton, Alex Marshall and Frank Stockham had also been voted on to the Directorate. But Tyndall had Webster, Brown, McMenemie, Peter Williams, Colin Cody, Vaux and almost certainly Frank Clifford on his side. Four neutral members held the balance; O'Brien still had to hold his fire. The nearest O'Brien's friends came to testing the water was with a proposal to change the NF's name to the 'National Party'. Clare Macdonald proposed it, and made the point that a name change might persuade other groups to join who were jealous of the NF's particularism. Her proposal was defeated.

O'Brien finally believed he had found an opportunity to get rid of Webster when he, Tyndall and Webster made a second northern tour in February 1972. In Manchester, at a meeting of the branch organizers of the region, the Liverpool organizer proudly related how his branch had arranged coach outings and trips for old age pensioners. Webster interrupted angrily – 'The National Front is a political party – not a burial society.'

The Northern members, particularly one pensioner in the Manchester branch, were furious. Walter Barton too was indignant and, canvassing opinion in the north and in London, O'Brien reckoned the time was right to get rid of Webster. He informed Tyndall that a motion to sack Webster from all his functions would be on the next Directorate agenda.

O'Brien was briefly optimistic of Tyndall's support. Tyndall had telephoned him late one night, just before the northern tour, and said there was a dispute between him and Webster over an article Webster wanted to write for *Spearhead*. Tyndall read out the two versions over the phone and asked O'Brien to adjudicate. 'While this was going on,' O'Brien recalls, 'I could distinctly hear Webster screaming abuse in the background and behaving as one demented. I gave my opinion and on meeting Tyndall later, remarked on the unbalanced behaviour of his colleague, and suggested that surely such a man ought to be considered expendable. Tyndall said he knew what I meant and that Webster was at times very tiresome, but he was useful and "I can get rid of him any time it suits me". I made the rejoinder "A man is known by the company he keeps." The shot went home – I could see Tyndall wince.'

After Webster's outburst at Manchester, Tyndall hinted that Webster might have to go, but shortly before the Directorate meeting Tyndall asked if he and Webster could see O'Brien informally to talk things over O'Brien agreed, and was shaken to hear Tyndall supporting Webster's statement in his own defence. It was impossible, O'Brien realized, to separate the political Siamese twins. At the Directorate meeting, Webster staunchly defended his position, and threatened that he would leave the NF altogether if he was fired from his positions. O'Brien had made a canvass of the Directorate and knew he would have to use his casting vote as chairman to vote Webster out. The factions were evenly divided – but Terry Savage had failed to turn up. O'Brien was one vote short, and Webster survived.

The next week, Tyndall told O'Brien he had lost confidence in him and wished to resign as vice-chairman. To Tyndall's surprise, O'Brien agreed gratefully, saying that he had lost confidence in Tyndall, and would Tyndall please write a note of resignation to reassure the members – pleading heavy duties as editor of *Spearhead*.

Tyndall had expected O'Brien to ask him to reconsider, and left the office a shaken man. The next week, O'Brien wrote to Tyndall asking for his resignation in writing, and Tyndall replied that it had all been a mistake, that he had merely discussed the question of resignation. The matter had to be patched up – but not before the Directorate had been informed that O'Brien had replacements lined up for vice-chairman and activities organizer. This increased Tyndall's and Webster's alarm. Once again, luck came to their aid.

O'Brien got married, and disappeared on honeymoon. Tyndall and Webster correctly deduced that Frank Stockham had been O'Brien's choice to replace Tyndall as vice-chairman, and prepared to expel him in O'Brien's absence in a Directorate order which Tyndall signed. O'Brien returned a day earlier than expected, and was able to stop the notices of expulsion being sent to the whole Bristol branch just as Webster was preparing them for the post.

O'Brien and his allies now decided that they had to leave the NF, and take as many supporters with them as they could. Their preparations took four months, as they secretly copied membership lists and key documents, yet not a word of their preparations leaked out. They planned to resign as a body, and join John Davis's NIP. They also planned to circularize each member of the NF with their account of the reasons for leaving, and issue an appeal to the whole membership to join the NIP, leaving Tyndall and Webster with the rump of the party. During this long crisis of the spring and early summer of 1972, the NF could only organize one major activity – in support of the Ulster Vanguard march in London, for which the NF provided loudspeakers and transport facilities, and a large contingent of marchers. In June, they organized their own pro-Unionist rally in London.

In the meantime, Webster and Tyndall counter-attacked. They won the vote of Walter Barton on the Directorate, whom O'Brien had once thought would join him in the walk-out. But Barton showed his new allegiance when Webster and Tyndall proposed that the NF stop paying O'Brien a salary, since it was the salary of the office manager, a job which O'Brien had ceased to perform as soon as he was made chairman. O'Brien vainly argued that the Directorate had agreed from the beginning that he be paid as Chairman, since he could not afford to live in London without a salary, but twice the matter went to a vote in the Directorate and twice O'Brien was defeated by the one vital vote. He accepted the defeat, knowing that by the time the salary had stopped he would have left the Front.

In July, O'Brien left the office ostensibly for his summer holiday, in fact to make the final preparations for the split. He secretly returned to London, and by the same post sent off his letter of resignation and the bulletins to the members informing them that eight members of the Directorate had left and set up a new organization. A new office phone number was given and all members invited to call and speak to the group which had resigned. After two days, during which over 200 calls were received, the phone went out of order. The Telephone Exchange explained that someone claiming to be the subscriber had asked for the service to be discontinued. It took over a week to restore the line – by which time Tyndall had visited the key branches and issued his own version of the split.

FIVE

The Respectability of Racialism –
the National Front and the Conservative Party

In the early 1960s, Enoch Powell had the reputation of a moderate on the immigration issue. He had refused Cyril Osborne's plea to join his campaign for immigration controls in 1959, even though the Conservative Party Conference of 1958 had defied the party leadership and voted for controls. As Minister of Health, he had presided over, and indeed encouraged, a process of transfusion of coloured staff into the understaffed National Health Service. In the 1964 election, Powell said simply that he was in favour of the 1962 Immigration Act. By the next year, his attitude had hardened, almost certainly in response to the electoral success of Peter Griffiths at Smethwick. Powell wrote in the *Sunday Times* three days after the election 'I do not agree with people who say that the result (at Smethwick) is a disgrace.' In March 1965, Powell joined Sir Alec Douglas Home and Edward Heath in voting for Sir Cyril Osborne's Bill for 'periodic and precise limits' on immigration. In May, Powell made a major speech at Wolverhampton which called for the same controls to be exercised over immigrants from the Commonwealth as were in force against aliens. The major implication of this approach was to remove the automatic right of Commonwealth immigrants to bring their dependants into the country after them. The *Daily Mail* headlined its account of the speech 'Powell's send them home plan'. In November 1965, he talked of 'the desirability of achieving a steady flow of voluntary repatriation'.

Some of Powell's critics have interpreted his hardening line in terms of his humiliating defeat at the election for the Tory party leadership, after the resignation of Sir Alec in July 1965. Heath won the election, with 150 votes, Reginald Maudling got 133 and Powell mustered a bare 15. If this interpretation is correct, it does not explain why Powell's election campaign in March 1966 stressed the other political issues which faced the nation. He did make one speech on immigration, saying that 'the rate is still far too high', but after the Conservative defeat, his diversions from official Tory policy focused on Defence and Rhodesia. Although something of a rebel in the Shadow Cabinet, he held his fire on immigration until 1967.

On 9 July he published an article in the *Sunday Express* entitled 'Can We Afford to Let Our Race Problem Explode?', which argued that families of immigrants should not be allowed to follow them into Britain. Once again, an anti-immigration mood was building inside the Conservative Party and Powell was prepared to exploit it. In September 1967, the Monday Club called a meeting at Caxton Hall which was addressed by Sir Cyril Osborne. He called for 'stringent limitation of immigration into the United Kingdom for the next five years', and was overwhelmingly supported. The issue which Powell chose to take up was that of the Kenyan Asians, who were British passport holders even though Kenya had been granted independence.

In the early months of 1968 Powell returned again and again to the question of the Kenyan Asians. He and Duncan Sandys and the Monday Club kept up the pressure until the Government introduced a panic Bill to the House of Commons, which was passed in the course of twenty-four hours, introducing a voucher system for the Kenyan Asians. The British passports with which they had been issued were no longer operative. Powell was surprised at the speed and success of his own campaign, and was astonished (and encouraged to pursue the profitable issue) by the size of his post-bag. His Walsall speech and his stand on the Kenyan Asians had got him the largest public response of his career. Meanwhile, the Race Relations Bill was proceeding on its stately way through Parliament, Duncan Sandys was calling for an end to immigration for an unspecified number of years, and the agitation of the Monday Club and Tory MPs like Osborne, Ronald Bell and Harold Gurden continued. It was Powell's 20 April speech which transformed immigration from just another political issue to *the* issue which dominated politics and the media, and he took a stance which permitted him to justify his course as the defender of the native English people and culture who 'found themselves made strangers in their own country. They found their wives unable to find hospital beds in childbirth, their children unable to obtain school places, their homes and neighbourhoods changed beyond recognition, their plans and prospects for the future defeated.'

Nor was Powell unaware of the political thrust of his speech. By setting himself forward as the champion of the ignored Englishman – 'strangers in their own country' – he was echoing a speech he had made in Gloucester the year before, a speech in which he showed that his antennae were tuned to the same wavelength as those thinkers on the Nationalist Right who believed that Britain was ripe for a populist appeal.

'Night and day,' mused Powell, 'through the months and years, a babel of voices dins unintelligible moral denunciations into the heads of ordinary English men and women, for whom they bear not the slightest relationship to any of the facts of their daily existence . . . Some time there has to be an end to this. Some time – and why not now? – the citizen will put his faith again in the great simplicities and will confound the merchants of mumbo jumbo.'

The response to his April speech must have suggested that the time was indeed now. The London dockers and the Smithfield meat porters combined to march on the House of Commons under the slogan 'Enoch is Right'. It was a spontaneous outburst. According to Harry Pennington, one of the dockers' committee of four who organized the march, 'It just happened. When Powell made his speech he seemed to me to be talking a lot of sense. I told some of my mates and before you could blink everybody was agreeing with everybody else.' Not all the dockers felt strongly enough to join the demonstration. There were 4400 strikers (leaving 25 ships idle) but only 800 on the march. It is also significant that the organized union movement was not at its strongest in the docks at this time since they had just reluctantly accepted the heavy redundancies which the Devlin Report had advised. The dockers had an industrial grievance and their morale was low, even before Powell spoke. By contrast, the dockers refused to march against the Ugandan Asians in 1972, when they were united and confident in the wake of their success in securing the release of the dockers who had been imprisoned in Pentonville. At both times, morale and faith in the trade union were clearly vital factors.

At Smithfield meat market, the response for Powell was equally spontaneous. It was exploited, but not initiated, by one of the porters, Big Dan Harmston, a member of the Union Movement and fervant supporter of Mosley. Harmston has never tried to organize the market politically. 'I've got too much respect for the blokes there. The whole thing just happened. When the lads were all together and blokes were getting up and having their say they got me up there as well,' Harmston recalls. 'There was a mood about the place – if that day I'd said "Pick up your cleavers and knives and decapitate Heath and Harold Wilson" they'd have done it. They really would – but they wouldn't have done it the next week. It was just that mood of the moment – like storming the Bastille, I suppose.'

There is no reason to doubt Harmston's account. As a Mosley-ite, he opposes Powell and much of what Powell stands for. Mosley's own description of Powell is 'a middle-class Alf Garnett', and Harmston was later to horrify Monday Club activists at a TRU-AIM (Trade Unionists Against Immigration) meeting by attacking Powell. Quite apart from fundamental political differences between a Conservative like Powell and a Mosleyite, Harmston felt, and so did the NF, that Powell had trespassed upon their own ground, and that he had taken up the immigration issue too recently for his approach to be anything other than political opportunism. *Spearhead*'s cover featured the working people who had responded to Powell's speech with acclamation, rather than Powell himself. Its editorial section was cool. 'That Mr Powell has now spoken is to be welcomed. But let us not forget those who uttered the warning long, long ago.' Tyndall went on to analyse, in terms of his own theories of disrupting the two-party system, why the agitation could do the NF good and why it was unlikely to switch much support to the Conservatives: 'The leaders of the Left have not the slightest thing in common with the mass of the British workers . . . *and* . . . the workers as a whole will never go Tory, despite their respect for Enoch Powell.'

Powell's speech, although officially condemned by his party leadership, did serve to underline just how powerful was the anti-immigration feeling in the Tory Party. In December 1968, the Conservative Political Centre's analysts were staring in disbelief at the results of a confidential survey they had designed to establish the views of 412 constituency groups. 327 wanted all immigration stopped indefinitely. A further 55 wanted 'strictly limited' input of dependants of people already in Britain, combined with a five-year halt on immigration. Some suggested special housing areas on an apartheid system, and one even talked of permanent camps in which immigrants could be placed. This was grim and barely credible news for the Tory leadership.

Powell's influence clearly ran far beyond the Conservatives. One academic analysis of two Gallup polls showed that for being the public choice to succeed Edward Heath he went from 1 per cent just before the speech to 24 per cent immediately after it. Perhaps more significantly, an analysis of the Opinion Research Centre's study of 1029 voters immediately after the 1970 election shows how Powell's support was maintained. Asked if they agreed that Powell was the only British politician they really admired, 25 per cent agreed.

Powell's support was clearly concentrated in the West Midlands. The regional sample showed that 42 per cent of people in the West Midlands supported him (compared to 25 per cent nationally) and this reflects the general election result of 1970, where a nation-wide swing to the Conservatives of 4·7 per cent became 6·1 per cent (the highest of any region) in the West Midlands and rose to over 9 per cent in Powell's town of Wolverhampton. (The swing to the Conservatives was concentrated in those constituencies with the lower – less than 1·5 per cent – proportions of immigrants. The All Saints constituency, which had a swing to Labour, contained 13·8 per cent immigrants, and it seems clear that Powell swung the immigrant vote to Labour.)

An analysis of a Marplan study of three West Midland marginal seats in the February 1974 election showed that Powell's support had survived the passing time – even though Powell himself was not a candidate in the election, and had advised his supporters to vote Labour, in order to take Britain out of the Common Market. The survey, of 1500 voters, showed that Powell was the most popular candidate after Heath and Wilson, and his was the only support to cross party lines, drawing 19 per cent from Tory, 16 per cent from Labour and 30 per cent from Liberal voters.

It was Heath's realization of the width of Powell's support – long before any of these academic studies were published – that led the Conservative Party to stiffen its own position on immigration. In September 1968, Heath announced in a speech in York that Commonwealth immigrants should only enter Britain under the same conditions as aliens (for which Powell first called in May 1965) and that dependants should also be subject to controls. It was a major departure from the Labour Government's position, and put a racialist nail into the coffin of a bi-partisan, non-political stand on immigration which had appeared a brief possibility in the mid-sixties.

In spite of this concession Powell returned again to the attack. At the Tory Conference (which had received 80 resolutions on immigration – four times the number of the previous year), he went beyond immigration controls to the question of the immigrants who were already in Britain: 'We deceive ourselves if we imagine, whatever steps are taken to limit further immigration, that this country will still not be facing a prospect which is unacceptable.'

In a speech at Eastbourne in November he came back to this theme, and pointed to the 'key significance of repatriation or re-emigration'. He then went further than he – or perhaps any senior and reputable politician – had in suggesting that integration could never work: 'The West Indian or Asian does not, by being born in England, become an Englishman. In law he becomes a United Kingdom citizen by birth, in fact he is a

West Indian or an Asian still.' Once again he was attacked by Mr Heath and the Conservative leadership and once again Mr Heath let a decent interval pass before stiffening his party's policy once again. In January of 1969, Heath spoke at Walsall for the toughest policy yet adopted by a major political party. He demanded legislation from the Government within the next nine months to stop any further settlement in Britain by immigrants. They should only be admitted 'for a specific job in a specific place – for a specific time'. A new permit would have to be applied for each year, and for each change of job, and they would not have the right to bring their dependants or families 'however close' with them. Enoch Powell was in the audience.

Three weeks later, 126 Conservatives voted for a Bill introduced to Parliament by Duncan Sandys which presented these demands. Powell, Sir Alec Douglas Home, William Whitelaw, the Tory chief whip and more than twenty former junior Ministers all voted for the Bill, while Heath abstained. Less than a year had passed since Powell's speech.

Powell's campaign on immigration continued into the 1970s. In *Still to Decide*, a collection of his speeches published in 1972, a whole section was devoted to the issue:

> a subject which for the future of this country dwarfs every other . . . In your town, in m c, in Wolverhampton, in Smethwick, in Birmingham, people see with their own eyes what they dread, the transformation during their own lifetime, or if they are already old, during their children's, of towns, cities and areas that they know into alien territory . . . cries of anguish from those of their own people who already saw their towns being changed, their native places being turned into foreign lands, and themselves displaced as if by a systematic colonization . . . in all our history our nation has never known greater danger . . . when he looks into the eyes of Asia the Englishman comes face to face with those who will dispute with him the possession of his native land.

This was the language, and it came within an ace of being the policy, of the National Front. Powell had but one reservation – he would not propose compulsory repatriation. He did, however, call for a Ministry of Repatriation to assist and encourage a 'massive, albeit voluntary, repatriation'. When the Conservative Government passed the 1971 Immigration Act, which provided for the assistance of immigrants who wished to return home, Powell claimed that this was inadequate. 'The Government

113

took their own policy and systematically emasculated it . . . as nice a little job of sabotage as you could wish to find.'

A. K. Chesterton was exaggerating when he told *The Times* of 24 April 1968 'What Mr Powell has said does not vary in any way from our view'. There were, however, items of policy which were identical, in spite of the vast gulf which separated a free marketeer and Conservatives like Powell from the corporate state thinkers of the NF. Fundamentally, there was Ulster, where Powell and the NF agreed that the loyal Britons of the Orange state were fighting a traitorous rebellion.

Powell and the National Front also agreed on staunch opposition to the Common Market, predominantly because they agreed that it involved an unjustifiable diminution of British national and parliamentary sovereignty. The closest agreement on policy, reinforced by an identical economic rationale, was in the feasibility of massive repatriation of coloured immigrants. The issue of *Spearhead* for May 1969 boasted from its cover – 'Repatriation – how it can be done'. Inside, the article gave thanks to Mrs Joy Page and her Immigration Control Association for the following figures of the 'cost' of immigration. It listed £25 million in direct aid to selected local government authorities, £10 million in 'illegal currency rackets' of immigrants sending money to their homelands, £3 million for special aid to primary schools in 34 immigrant areas and so on. The largest single cost item was £227 million in aid to the Afro-Asian Commonwealth. (In fact, Britain – like most donor countries – ensured that the bulk of this aid was spent on British goods and services, and acted as a reinforcement to the British economy as well as aid to the recipient country.) The total 'cost' was listed as £266,783,000.

Spearhead went on to suggest that allowing £100 for transport costs for each repatriate, and a further £100 as a resettlement grant:

It would be possible in the space of two years to repatriate 2 million immigrants from Britain for much less than the sum given above . . . in fact, repatriation would not work as quickly as this, since it would be necessary to replace immigrant labour in those industries and services which have become heavily dependent on it. This would certainly take more than two years.

The month after this *Spearhead* appeared, Powell made a speech using arguments and figures which were also similar to those produced by Joy Page and the ICA, although he reckoned many

114

fewer immigrants would choose repatriation. Speaking in his own town of Wolverhampton, he spoke of the need for repatriation and then came this passage:

> Financially if one estimates that 600,000 to 700,000 would be involved and that the average size of family is five, then to give each family £2000 for passage and resettlement would cost £260 million. Raise this to £300 million to include all the costs of administration etc. and it would still only represent the cost of eighteen months' aid to underdeveloped countries, at the present rate, and it is hard to imagine a more effective or realistic form of 'aid' than this transfusion not only of finance but also of skill, experience and education.

The immediate boost which Powell's speech gave to the NF was described by Robert Taylor, then the NF organizer for Huddersfield:

> We held a march in Huddersfield in support of what Powell had said, and we signed eight people up as members of the branch that afternoon. Powell's speeches gave our membership and morale a tremendous boost. Before Powell spoke, we were getting only cranks and perverts. After his speeches we started to attract, in a secret sort of way, the right-wing members of the Tory organizations.

Taylor was speaking of men like John Briggs, a local solicitor and member of the Conservative Association who witnessed and completed eight of the thirteen nomination forms of NF candidates in the 1970 local elections. In 1968, Briggs published a bitterly critical guide to the Race Relations Act called *Inroads to ruin: race legislation in perspective* which was published by Chesterton's firm, the Candour Publishing Company. Briggs, a gun collector and assiduous writer of letters to the local newspaper, had been at Stowe school with another local Conservative, Colin Campion, who was a councillor and chairman of the local Conservative Association. Immediately after Powell's speech he established a 'British People's Union', a body which organized meetings for Conservative and NF members until the local Tory leadership exerted pressure to stop them.

The NF was quick to respond to the organizational opportunity they had been granted. In the autumn of 1968, it was announced that a training scheme for branch officers and group organizers had been established at Tyndall's Nationalist Centre.

The course covered topics such as public speaking, branch organization, the case for Nationalism, the art of propaganda, know the enemy and arguing the NF case. The training course was repeated the following year, and was attended by forty local organizers.

The NF's problem was that the confirmation of their long belief that there was a great deal of submerged racialism in British society did not automatically mean that there was a corresponding potential for natural NF recruits. In January 1969, Tyndall summed up the problem: 'Nothing is more depressing than meeting, as one often does these days, people whose political outlook starts and finishes with an embittered sourness towards immigrants. No serious movement in politics can ever function on a sentiment such as this.'

The NF also had to guard against erosion of its own members to the Powellite wing of the Conservatives, and it was keen to point out to NF members that Powell's policies did diverge widely from their own. In particular, the NF attacked his statement in Parliament of 16 October 1969, that 'I did not vote for any legislation which would legalize a constitution for Southern Rhodesia under which there would not be evident and relatively early advance to majority rule'. In 1971, after an exchange of letters between Powell and Tyndall, in which Tyndall asked Powell how he responded to the NF's policy of a re-united white Commonwealth based on the links of British race, Powell replied 'my judgement is that especially in Canada, but also in Australia and New Zealand, these are bound to diminish with the passage of time and that no political structure can be based on them'.

The Powellite organizations which had sprung up after his April speech were not all as amenable to NF pressure as Campion's group in Huddersfield. In areas of traditional BNP and later NF support like Southall, the NF had to re-assert its presence and its links with the Southall Residents' Association. The SRA secretary, Grace Woods, was keen to help, speaking at the NF rally on the day of its 1969 annual conference and welcoming a special march through Southall which the NF organized, summoning 250 of its supporters from throughout the Home Counties. *Spearhead* commented that they were 'greeted like a Liberation army' and Grace Woods's letter of thanks congratulated them that 'the party's efforts seemed to have had an effect which this town needed'. The NF and the SRA organized the local elections so that their candidates did not stand against each other. When Grace Woods's political attacks ed the Labour MP Sid Bidwell to sue her for libel, the NF organized a defence fund for her among its members to help raise the legal fees. In defending its own strongholds, and in improving its structure to respond to Powell's challenge, the NF worked harder than ever before.

The NF's overwhelming rival for the political benefits which sprang from Powell's new prominence was the Monday Club. The Club accepts (as does John Tyndall) the name 'Radical Right', is firmly patriotic, committed to Christianity and free enterprise, supports white rule in Africa and is passionately anti-communist. It was founded in January 1961 by four young Conservatives, Ian Greig, Cedric Gunnery, Anthony McClaren and Paul Bristol, in horrified response to Macmillan's 'Winds of Change' speech in Africa. Its first meeting, on the subject of Kenya, was held later that year and was ignored by the press, with the exception of Edward Martell's publication, the *New Daily*. In January 1962, the Club secured the patronage of Lord Salisbury, the embodiment of the patrician tradition in the Conservative Party, and by the end of 1963, when the Club had taken a leading role in Conservative opposition to Harold Macmillan's leadership, it had grown to some 250 members, eleven of whom were MPs. Through an early member, Harold Soref, the Club was addressed at major meetings by Ian Smith, the Rhodesian Prime Minister and Moïse Tshombe, who had led Katangese secession in the Congo.

Having lost the rearguard action against granting independence to black Africa, the Club concentrated on support for Rhodesia and a growing hostility to coloured immigration. Ronald Bell MP, a Club member, led the opposition to the Race Relations Bill in Parliament. Its influence within the Conservative Party rank and file grew quickly, and the Club deserves a great deal of the credit for the Party's swing to the Right at its 1967 annual Conference. This had followed a long internal debate on whether the Club should remain a small and elite pressure group, or whether it should go for mass influence and a mass membership. It decided on the latter, in part because of the vigorous campaign of George K. Young, a merchant banker and former senior official in MI6 (his official title was Deputy Under-Secretary at the Ministry of Defence). He was brought into the Club by John Biggs-Davison MP.

Young's two principal concerns were expansion of the Club and immigration. He wrote the Club's pamphlet advocating repatriation, 'Who Goes Home?', which was published early in 1969, and he was chairman of the Club's Action Fund,

117

launched in June 1967 with a target of £100,000 'not for fanc
overheads or an overblown London set-up but for action throughl
out the country'. By April 1969, membership had grown t
1500 and the Club's activities, with protest meetings on Defenc
cuts and on 'The grip of the Left on the BBC' attracted nationa
publicity. The 1970 election brought a large proportion of ne
and right-wing Tory MPs to Parliament. Sixteen Club MPs ha
retained their seats, eleven Club members won seats and fiv
Tory MPs joined the Club after the election. Six Club member
including Geoffrey Rippon, Julian Amery and John Peytor
took office in the new Government.

Although Enoch Powell never joined the Club, his links wit
it were very close. As guest of honour at its 1968 annual dinner
Powell told the Club that it brought many people into th
Conservative Party who would otherwise be estranged from it
This was accepted as an endorsement of the Club's policy o
immigration. Shortly before Mr Powell was again guest o
honour at a Monday Club fund-raising luncheon, the Clul
issued a major policy statement on immigration: 'The Govern
ment must now accept Mr Powell's remedies as well as hi
diagnosis . . . The social fabric in our great cities is alread
breaking up under the strains of communalism and caste.'

Although bitterly divided on the Common Market, the Clul
had become, by 1971, the stronghold of the Tory Right. B
deciding in 1967 to attempt to achieve a mass base it had adopte
the same interpretation of British politics as the Nationalist
outside the Conservative Party. Chesterton had been right t
deduce that the growth of the Club meant the end of his Leagu
of Empire Loyalists. The great question was whether the Monda
Club had permanently pre-empted the position of the respectabl
Right to the exclusion of the NF.

The Club's growth was rapidly reaching a peak in October 197.
of 2000 members of the national organization, 55 groups ir
universities, 34 MPs and a claimed regional membership o
6000. (According to the current Club leadership, this provincia
membership was 'highly inflated' and their 'official' record
show barely more than 1000 provincial members). It was thi
expansion G. K. Young had sought through his control of th
Action Fund. He spent heavily on press advertisements fo
membership, publications and pamphlets and newsletters and o
hiring young right-wing staff for the Club's headquarters. Som
Club members like Harold Soref claim to have opposed thi
development in private from the very beginning, and to hav
issued direct warnings to the new chairman, Jonathan Guinness

118

when he was elected in June 1972. Soref himself warned of the dangers of take-over by extremists and Guinness was aware, when he took office, that a former member of the Union Movement called Lesley Wooler had been brought into the Club HQ to examine membership lists in an attempt to purge the Club of known NF members. 'I deliberately set my face against making any enquiries into that,' Guinness recalls. 'We had enough troubles on our minds.'

The growth of the Club, and its strong line on immigration, at first attracted some grudging praise from the NF. *Spearhead* commented in February 1970: 'At least the gentlemen of the Monday Club are learning. And for those who are prepared to learn there is always hope.' But the NF's hope was that the Club would not only rally more and more members of the Conservative Right, but would at the same time lose a similar proportion of members to the NF. The Club was to be a halfway house between the Tories and the NF – and this approach was made clear in a major article in the March 1970 *Spearhead*: 'The Monday Club has a useful purpose as a rallying point and recruiting ground for people of patriotic inclinations. It does *not* serve as a reliable source of guidance for Britain's future.'

The Club's limitations were spelled out in detail. It had: 'No comprehensive doctrine and no scientific understanding of the machinations of international politics', and although 'it prefers the Union Jack to the Red Flag, basically it is internationalist . . . (with its) . . . thinking in world affairs dominated by East-West relations, it . . . does not recognize the part played in the promotion of world revolution by Western finance.' In particular it pointed to Lord Salisbury's acceptance of the principle of eventual majority rule in Rhodesia, to Biggs-Davison's support for the EEC and to Patrick Wall's support of NATO.

The Club's May Day rally in Trafalgar Square in support of law and order was heavily supported by the National Front, who brought supporters by coach from all over England to ensure that their members and their banners swamped the rally and TV cameras and the press photographs. 'Half the crowd and 90 per cent of the banners came from the NF,' boasted *Spearhead* and the claim was justified. After the rally, the NF march was joined by the Nottingham branch of the Club, and by many individual Club members.

Martin Webster, the NF activities organizer, was delighted at this response to his special appeal. Ten days before the rally, in a special activities bulletin, he had circularized all branches with this message:

Last year the NF won a considerable amount of excellent publicity by turning up in force with a profusion of banners to a Conservative Party Rally in Trafalgar Square, London. After the rally, many Young Conservatives, despite a warning from Duncan Sandys, supported a NF march through London. This year the Monday Club wing of the Conservative Party is organizing a similar rally with the theme 'Law and Liberty'. It is most important that as many NF members as possible attend the rally . . . This is a *most important* activity and members from London and the provinces are urged to make every effort to attend.

At this time, the NF was preparing to field ten candidates in the 1970 general election. But Webster made his priorities clear to the *Sunday Times* on 5 April – 'We don't expect to win any seats – we are fighting a guerilla war'. It took some time off to cheer the friendliest of its enemies in June. 'Bravo Enoch', said its cover, acknowledging that his 'enemies within' speech had gone some way towards the NF position on left-wing subversion in the media, the universities and Ireland.

Powell's speech, five days before polling day in Birmingham, caused almost as much of a sensation as his speech on immigration of April 1968. 'Britain at this moment is under attack,' he began, and went on to point to

the forces which aim at the actual destruction of our nation and society . . . We have seen the institutes of learning systematically threatened, browbeaten and held up to ridicule by the organizers of disorder . . . civil government itself has been made to tremble by the mob . . . (our troops) are in Northern Ireland because disorder, deliberately fomented for its own sake as an instrument of power has come within an ace of destroying the authority of the civil government and because the prospect of that authority being easily recovered is not foreseen . . . The exploitation of what is called 'race' is a common factor which links the enemy on several different fronts . . . 'Race' is billed to play a major, perhaps a decisive part in the battle of Britain, whose enemies must have been unable to believe their good fortune as they watched the numbers of West Indians, Africans and Asians concentrated in her major cities mount towards the two million mark.

In the growth of the Monday Club, in Powell's support and in Powell's message, the men on the Nationalist Right who had

120

built the NF coalition could see their analysis of British society being confirmed. But the political fruits of that analysis came no nearer.

In his days in the BNP, John Bean had always reminded his colleagues that the full title of Hitler's party was the 'National Socialist German Workers' Party' and he was convinced that the NF had to win votes in the working class and not spend too many of its resources in the Monday Club and the Powellite groupings. In *Spearhead*'s election issue, he tried for a new approach with an article entitled 'NF must win Labour votes', in which he argued 'a minimum wage must be established, and this should be pegged to the cost of living index and adjusted accordingly each year'. In an earlier issue, he had appealed for the NF to accept 'a radical wing, with a more flexible view towards Europe than its present orthodox line of complete rejection'.

The summer of 1970 was a time of re-assessment for the NF. It was the time when a small group calling itself the Action Committee organized its putsch against Chesterton's leadership which succeeded later in the year. The NF's main grievance was that the Monday Club (and in some areas, even Dr Brown's NDP) was doing a better job of scooping up Powell's support. Morale was very low, and it declined even further after the disappointing election results, in which the highest NF vote was 5·6 per cent and its overall average vote a humble 3·6 per cent.

Tyndall, however, looked on the bright side. 'There will not be a successful Powellite revolution in the Tory Party in the forseeable future,' he forecast, and went on to note the 'natural downward evolution of old guard politics'. He pointed to the doubled Liberal vote, to the increasing divisions inside the two major parties, Wilson's Government having alienated much of its left-wing and trade union support, and the Conservatives struggling with the problem of Powell, who on the one hand had clearly brought the Conservatives a lot of votes, but who was also clearly opposed to the party leadership. Tyndall's faith in the collapse of the two-party system remained firm.

The problem of the Monday Club continued. One of the NF's answers to this, although its leaders have frequently denied it, has been infiltration. This had begun in the NF's first year, in 1967, when Ron Tear, the NF West Essex organizer and a former member of the National Socialist Movement, John Cook, joined the Conservative Party in Ilford. Tear, who kept a Nazi shrine in his home complete with swastika flags and who entertained German neo-Nazi leaders like Wolfgang Kerstein of the Viking Youth at his home, was a former military police-man and member of the BNP. (Standing as BNP candidate in a local election in Ilford in 1962 he had informed the electorate that Hitler was a genius, and had received seventeen votes.) By sheer perseverance he had developed several useful contacts within the local Conservative parties. They included Councillor George Owen and Monday Clubber Kay Tomlin. But Tear and Cook played their hand too soon. In the summer of 1967 the local Conservative MP, Tom Iremonger, wrote to the *Daily Telegraph* that his constituency party was being deliberately and insidiously infiltrated. His view has never changed. Seven years later he recalled how close they had come to winning office in the party: 'There was a serious threat that these people would get the majority of serious offices. I just didn't like the smell of the thing. They talk about repatriation of immigrants. Physi-cally what they want to do is put them all in cattle trucks and shoot them off the end of Southend Pier.'

The two men resigned, and Chesterton denied that any attempt at infiltration had taken place. Shortly afterwards, Chesterton publicly congratulated the two of them for 'sterling organiza-tional work'. It was in Essex again that the NF made its greatest breakthrough into the Monday Club, where the local branch defied its national leadership (and was expelled as a result) to invite John Tyndall to address them early in 1973. The branch Chairman, Len Lambert, was one of the key Monday Clubbers in the plot to get rid of Jonathan Guinness as national chairman and replace him with G. K. Young.

The NF leadership was in favour of infiltration so long as it was not made public. In October 1969, two Wandsworth Tory Councillors, Mrs Athlene O'Connell and Peter Mitchell, resigned the Conservative whip and announced that they would hence-forth support the National Front. In December, they said they would re-apply for the Tory whip. Martin Webster told the *Evening News*: 'We said they would be able to help our cause more if they did not make public the fact that they were joining us but they both insisted.' Three months later, the chairwoman of a group which had sprung up after a policeman was tragically killed while on duty, a Mrs Jennifer O'Connor, announced that she was resigning because 'everything has gone wrong and the National Front seem to be poking their noses in'. The President of this group, the Police Wives' Action Committee, was the very Mrs Athlene O'Connell who had so mysteriously joined and then left the NF.

The frankest single account of NF infiltration came from its

Worthing organizer, Oliver Gilbert, who had been a member of Leese's Imperial Fascist League before the Second World War and had been an 18B detainee during the war. He wrote to *Spearhead* to protest against an attack by Martin Webster on 'a group of reactionaries on the fringe of the Worthing Branch of the NF who think they can save the soul of the Conservative Party'. Gilbert retorted: 'I believe that the Conservative Party can be made far more right-wing by the infiltration tactics now operated by men like myself who for years have been members of the Conservative Party and who put over the policy of the NF at ward committee meetings and general meetings of their local Conservative associations.'

But Gilbert had missed the point. The object was not to make the Conservative Party right-wing, the object was to destroy it. In August 1970, Tyndall returned to the attack on the internationalism and the financial policies of the Conservatives with an article called 'No – we are not Tories'.

For Tyndall, the vital object was to destroy the two-party system:

The only permanent hope of getting Britain on her feet lies in the emergence of a political party that can gain a sufficient majority following among both main classes to achieve a long and secure supremacy on the political scene – a position similar to that of the National Party in South Africa, the Socialist Party in Sweden or, nearer home, the Unionist Party in Northern Ireland. This is necessary to give the ruling party the long-term freedom of action that it needs as well as to sink the Left.

In February 1971, he returned to the theme – 'The Right will always be weak so long as it is based predominantly on white collar support.' This argument did not go far to appeal to those NF members who had noted the Tory Party's move to the Right before the 1970 election, and had applauded Heath's election promises to control the trade unions, sell arms to South Africa, sell off the profitable parts of the nationalized industries and limit the amount of state aid to ailing private enterprise. But as the Heath Government grappled with the realities of power, these election promises were steadily retracted. This led to dissent within the Conservative Party, and more particularly, within the Monday Club, which Tyndall felt able to exploit.

By April of 1971 he was asking 'Are the Clubbers waking up?' He began by denying that the NF was the organization behind the 'extremists' who were accused of taking over the Club and piously pointed to the praise the NF had been given by the Club's national chairman, George Pole, who had declared 'the National Front must not be turned aside as if of no account; they have people who are motivated by the highest motives'. Thus buttressed, Tyndall declared grandly: 'If the Club were to purge itself of its dead wood and evolve into a genuine right-wing popular movement the possibility would then exist for the Club and the NF to work as allies and as friends.'

Tyndall went on to offer an open alliance: 'There seems a distinct possibility now that the genuine Rightists in the Club may start to weed out the fakes and jettison their policies. If so, *Spearhead*, for whatever modest influence it may wield among Club followers, will support them to the hilt.' Tyndall's stress on the support of his magazine *Spearhead*, rather than NF support, is important. The magazine was his personal property under his own control. He could still describe it, as in those days between the ending of the GBM and his acceptance by the NF, as 'a patriotic organ of the Right'. This status not only gave him a freedom of manoeuvre within the party, but also freedom to conduct his own campaigns outside it. (Only once was there a conflict. In 1970, Chesterton demanded that an issue of *Spearhead* which he thought 'boosted Enoch Powell and broke one of the movement's most important rules' should be withdrawn. There was a bitter fight on the Directorate which Chesterton finally won. Tyndall argued that to boost Powell in the wake of Powell's influence on the general election would help to exacerbate divisions within the Conservatives, but Chesterton was adamant, and said that his personal authority was in question. Tyndall backed down, and loyally implemented the withdrawal of the issue. From then on, he could do no wrong in Chesterton's eyes.)

The wisdom of Tyndall's course in offering this alliance to the Club was underlined by the Club's decision to establish an immigration committee in 1971. Again, this was an idea of G. K. Young, whose personal influence in the Club made him something of an unofficial chairman. Young sat on this new committee, which was run by a young ally of his called Geoffrey Baber, who had been director of the Action Fund which Young controlled. Bee Carthew, a prominent Powellite later to join the NF, was the committee secretary and Gerald Howerth, a son of Mary Howerth of the Immigrant Control Association, joined Ronald Bell MP, Harold Soref MP and John Stokes MP on the committee.

On its own authority, and without reference to the Club executive, the committee wrote to all Club branch chairmen:

> While the Committee is and will remain a purely Conservative organization, it is felt that opposition to coloured immigration and lack of proper repatriation arrangements also exercise many of other political views who should be encouraged to lend their support in a campaign, which, when it succeeds, will be of benefit to all.

This gave the local Clubs (which were the strongholds of Young's support) a free hand to work with the National Front or anyone they chose. Some of them needed little prompting. In March 1971 a series of articles in the *Daily Mirror* led to the resignation of John Ormowe, the chairman of the Sussex Monday Club. He had told the *Mirror*: 'I accept I am a racialist. If you read *Mein Kampf* you will see it has been wrongly derided. I personally am an admirer of Hitler . . . I doubt whether he knew about all those people who were cremated.' Ormowe had attended a Pan-Nordic conference in Brighton in 1970 which had been organized in conjunction with the Northern League. Its symbol was a swastika. Ormowe had originally joined the Monday Club with the son of Alan Hancock, of the Heidelberg guest house. Young Hancock was also asked to leave the Club.

John O'Brien, chairman of the NF from early 1971 to July 1972, confirms that the question of infiltration 'arose three or four times a year at Directorate meetings. It was always unanimously supported. There was a general idea that any sort of liaison between ourselves and the Club would be good and we could gain. It was understood that our best links were with the West Middlesex Club, but our sympathizers were fairly widespread. And some members of the Directorate occupied themselves with little else.'

The key men were Michael Lobb and Martin Vaux. Vaux was the link man with West Middlesex, where the Club secretary was Mrs Gillian Goold. At the Uxbridge by-election of December 1972, Mrs Goold told a meeting of some 30 of her members (out of a branch total of 65) that 'Heath has betrayed us' and that they should join her in working for the National Front candidate during the campaign. They agreed, and worked for the campaign of John Clifton, the NF candidate and South-west London organizer. Clifton himself, working in the same area, developed an acquaintance with a property developer called Roy Bramwell, chairman of the South-west London Monday

125

Club and a leading member of the Immigration Control Association. Bramwell had long worked inside the Monday Club to oppose immigration, writing in the Club newsletter for January 1971: 'The sooner immigration is stopped and large scale repatriation commenced, the sooner will our people regain the will and purpose to work together for our country's future. In order to serve a nation, it is first necessary to have one.' He spoke on the same theme at a NF rally in London's Conway Hall on 22 July 1972, and when the NF provided the stewards for the September 1972 Monday Club rally in Central Hall, Bramwell appeared to be in charge of them. His wife Anna was Young Members secretary at Club HQ.

Harvey Procter, Conservative Party candidate or Hackney and Shoreditch, was a member of Bramwell's branch, and a keen member of the Society for Individual Freedom (G. K. Young was its chairman for four years). A kind of electoral pact seems to have kept NF candidates from standing against Procter until October 1974, although it was clearly a fertile constituency for the NF. In October 1974, the NF candidate won 9·4 per cent of the vote, the highest percentage it has achieved at a general election. Procter and Mrs Bramwell both worked at Club HQ with a young unemployed actor called Tony Van der Elst, whom Young had brought in to work on repatriation proposals and the Halt Immigration Now Campaign.

Van der Elst, who was adopted as a Council candidate by Hampstead Conservatives, attended the Italian neo-fascist MSI party's 1972 Conference with Neil Hamilton, a past vice-chairman of the Federation of Conservative Students. Their air fares and expenses were paid by the MSI. The FCS was later to be hailed as a bastion of liberal thinking by rejecting and exposing a discreet Monday Club request that Conservative students assemble and furnish lists of left-wing student activists and agitators.

The links and flirtations of Club members with the NF were legion. There was Ray Shenton, expelled from Chelsea Conservative Association for canvassing on behalf of the NF in Battersea, who then joined Bramwell's branch of the Club. There was Young's agent in his constituency of East Brent, David Lazarus, whose membership of the League of Empire Loyalists had run on into the NF. Gillian Goold of West Middlesex joined the NF after being expelled from the Club, and after moving to Norfolk, stood as NF candidate in Norwich in February 1974.

Lengthy though the list is, it was not the key factor in the crisis the Club faced in 1973. The Club was going through the kind of strains which were bedevilling the parliamentary Conservative party, after the Tory Government insisted on entering the Common Market, and facilitating the entry of the Ugandan Asians. The ghost of Powellism in the parliamentary party is still not laid and it was the Powellites, rather than the NF sympathizers, who were in the kind of strength and position to make an attempt to take over the Club. Powellism, Young's own ambition to lead the Club, and the bitter debates on the EEC in 1971 were in themselves enough to account for the crisis.

The Club's crisis began in May 1972, over the election of a new chairman. Jonathan Guinness was the favourite to win the election against the anti-EEC MP Richard Body. Young supported the campaign of a third, last-minute candidate called Tim Stroud who was little known in the Club. Young financed him to the tune of organizing a press reception at a London hotel, in the hope that Stroud would take the pro-EEC votes away from Guinness, and ensure Body's election. Not only would this stop Guinness, but since Body knew little of the Club's workings and membership, it would give Young a very much freer hand inside the Club administration. In the event, Guinness was elected with 676 votes, Body won 228 and Stroud managed a bare 48 votes.

Almost at once Guinness was pitched into the controversy over the Ugandan Asians. It split the Conservative Party in the House and in the country and although the Monday Club was united in the belief that they should not be permitted to enter Britain, there was a deep division over the kind of campaign to be fought. Harold Soref, for example, still maintains that the HINC group (Halt Immigration Now Campaign) was deliberately set up by Young to by-pass Soref's opposition on the Immigration committee. Nor were many of the older members happy with the tone of the HINC campaign. Calling for 'a new Battle of Britain' it organized a massive rally at Central Hall.

Ronald Bell MP claimed the campaign had 'tremendous and widespread public support'. It certainly had great support from the NF. Out of the 2000 people at the rally, at least 400 were NF members. The Club leadership tried to cancel the march on Downing Street to deliver a petition which followed the meeting, but in a question from the floor of the hall, Martin Vaux, well known to many of the Clubbers in the hall, demanded that the march take place. The NF formed up outside the hall and many of the Clubbers followed, including Ronald Bell MP. Harold Soref and Biggs-Davison ostentatiously refused to join.

The division within the Club became more bitter. In a blatant attack upon Soref and the old leadership of the Club (whose authority had been sharply diminished with the death of Lord Salisbury in February 1972) Bee Carthew wrote of a 'small, China-tea drinking Chelsea set' and in the provincial clubs, men like Peter Dawson of Birmingham (who was shortly to join the NF) were demanding within the provincial council that the national executive either take a firmer line on immigration or resign. Increasingly, the militants called for compulsory repatriation of immigrants, which was the NF policy. The gulf between executive and provincial clubs was deepened when the Special Branch called upon the Club's director Michael Woolrych in the course of enquiries about gun-running to the Ulster Defence Association. Woolrych said he knew nothing about it and the members of the executive began openly to question the kind of membership the Club had attracted with Young's press advertising campaigns and policy of expansion. Later in the year came the Uxbridge by-election, with Club members openly helping the NF candidate against the Conservative, and members of the North Kent Club helping the anti-EEC candidate, Christopher Frere-Smith at the Sutton and Cheam by-election against the Conservative. When this Tory seat was lost to the Liberals, the anger at the North Kent Clubbers' 'disloyalty' was redoubled.

The NF candidate at Uxbridge, John Clifton, then admitted that Clubbers had also helped in his local election campaign at Wandsworth. Len Lambert, chairman of the Essex Club, announced on 2 December:

> There is a strong possibility that this branch would support the NF candidate or any other right-wing candidate if, in an Essex election, the Conservative candidate was not following what we believe to be Conservative policy. This feeling is general throughout the Monday Club branches – especially in the Midlands. The Ugandan Asian business is probably foremost in everybody's minds.

Lambert's statement came as a shock to Guinness, since Lambert had supported his campaign for the leadership against Richard Body. And Lambert was probably correct in saying that feeling was running high in the Club branches. But in the odd structure of the Monday Club, the branch membership mattered little so long as the national members, who tended to be influenced by the national executive, remained loyal. This was to be Guinness's major asset in the struggle that was to come.

Young had decided to stand against Guinness for the leadership in 1973, and he had some formidable advantages. He was running the HINC campaign, which launched a petition in March 1973 seeking a million signatures against immigration. On 8 April, the Club's Provincial Council resolved that Guinness had to go. One of the supporters of this move was Len Lambert, whom Guinness had determined to expel when Lambert rejected Guinness's request to revoke an invitation to John Tyndall to address the Essex Club in February. Young's supporters also argued that in the eighteen months to March of 1973, over 35 per cent of the Club's press publicity came from its stand on immigration (compared to 14 per cent on the EEC and 9 per cent on Ulster). Moreover, press coverage in the last five months of 1973 was 400 per cent higher than it had been the previous year – thanks mainly to the Ugandan Asian campaign.

Bitter as the election was, it was made worse by a prolonged 'dirty-tricks' campaign. A forged letter was sent out to Club branches in Guinness's name; 20,000 copies of an anonymous document entitled 'The Monday Club – a danger to democracy' were distributed to Club members, journalists and Labour and Conservative MPs. There was some unsubstantiated speculation in the *Sunday Telegraph* that Israeli Intelligence agents had helped to compile it. The 30-page pamphlet contained a series of highly scurrilous allegations of homosexuality, Fascist links, gun-running and financial fraud against Monday Club and anti-immigration movement members. Some Clubbers began a private competition to see how many of the allegations within the booklet they could confirm. The winner claimed that he had verified over 70 per cent of them. And to counter the charge made by Guinness's supporters that Young was an extremist came the allegation that Monday Club HQ was infiltrated by Mosleyites. Len Lambert pursued this theme in May 1973, when he refused to hand over a membership list of his branch to HQ, claiming that 'in the past some twenty members of the Essex branch whose names were on file in Monday Club offices were circulated with Mosleyite propaganda and we have strong reason to believe Mosleyite elements in the national Club were responsible'.

Whether Lambert was referring to the occasion when Lesley Wooler was permitted access to Club files to spot NF members (he found twelve, according to Guinness) or to Guinness's own family connection to Sir Oswald Mosley was never explained. But the charges and counter-charges flew. The Young supporters made great play with Guinness's defeat at the Lincoln by-election in February 1972, pointing out that Guinness's widely publicized suggestion during the campaign that murderers should have razors left in their cells so that they could decently commit suicide had held up the Club to ridicule and led to its leader being known as 'Old Razor-Blades'. Few people used this nickname as frequently as the Young supporters. The election, which Young lost by 625 votes to 455, was something of an anti-climax.

The NF protested its innocence throughout the campaign. The May issue of *Spearhead*, written just before the Club elections, blandly asked 'who is trying to kill the Monday Club?', and Webster was quick to deny any NF role: 'There is not and never has been any intention on the part of the NF to take over the Club,' he affirmed, adding the now traditional NF statement about the differences between Club economic principles and the NF's view: 'The NF has no interest in promoting the ideas of either candidate, for both hold reactionary economic ideas and both are directors of City of London international banking houses and both are pro-Common Market.'

Webster was keen to dispute one of the dirtier tricks of the campaign. He had been telephoned by a *Sunday Telegraph* reporter, Peter Gladstone-Smith, who said that he had heard of a meeting between G. K. Young and Tyndall in a Shoreditch pub on 13 March, just after an anti-immigration march. Could Webster confirm this? Webster checked, and replied that Tyndall had had another engagement that evening. He could not have been in Shoreditch. Nonetheless, the *Sunday Telegraph* did publish the proposals which Young and Tyndall were supposed to have agreed at the mythical meeting. They included a 'promise' by Young to reduce the cost of the subscription for national membership (thus making it much cheaper and easier for NF members to join), to abandon the traditional insistence that Club members support the Tory Party, to permit the induction of 3000 NF members to form a majority of an expanded Club, and ultimately to break away from the Conservatives and found a new populist political party.

But why, asked Webster, should the NF have bothered to negotiate? 'So far as the NF is concerned the Monday Club is like a tree laden with over-ripe fruit which does not need to be picked. The defection of rank and file members of the Club into the NF is as inevitable as windfalls from an apple tree in autumn.'

After the election, Young's supporters continued their campaign to oust Guinness, even though Young himself resigned. In the course of his campaign he had called for the resignation of Geoffrey Rippon, the Club's last member of major Ministerial rank, for his part in the negotiations which led to the arrival of the Ugandan Asians. He had thus made himself anathema to the

Tory leadership, and by advocating compulsory repatriation of immigrants he had flouted the executive of the Club. Ian Greig, a founder member of the Club, privately warned Young that compulsory repatriation could never become part of Club policy, but Young persisted. It also emerged that a crude anti-immigration film, called *England, whose England?* had been made with Young's backing.

Realizing that the battle was still not over, Guinness promised 'fairly drastic action' within the Club as soon as he had won the election. His first action was to dismiss Len Lambert, which he followed by disbanding the Essex Club in June. This was countered on 21 May by the Provincial Council, which included Lambert, demanding an enquiry into Club leadership. But in July and August, by a combination of expulsions (Bee Carthew) and consequent resignations (including Ronald Bell MP, Geoffrey Baber, Hugh Simmons, James Harkness and Anna Bramwell) and one key conversion to the National Front (Roy Painter, former Tory candidate for Tottenham), the Guinness purges succeeded. There was still some sound and fury to come. A hundred Club members signed a motion demanding that Guinness should resign and that the Club be suspended for one year. A further 50 members were expelled. Even when a stormy special general meeting at Caxton Hall voted by 236 to 54 to ask Guinness to resign, he was able to refuse. The executive council supported him, and the provincial membership of the Club simply did not have the constitutional weight to overcome that support. But the Club itself was in grievous shape. Only ten MPs were still members and its national membership had dropped below 1800. Moreover, Guinness's critics went off vowing to form a 'Tuesday Club'.

Little more was ever heard of that idea. Some more expulsions followed. In February 1974, the council asked Geoffrey Hunt to resign, since he was contesting a parliamentary seat as an independent Powellite against a Conservative, and H. B. de la Perriere was also asked to leave for standing against a Tory in Bath. But the crisis was over, leaving the Monday Club almost wrecked in its wake.

'The real question,' Guinness said in retrospect, 'was the personal position of Powell. He didn't lift a finger to support his followers in the Club. I think this was because Powell thinks that political middle management is unimportant – he relies upon his mystic relationship with his followers. I think this has always been his weakness.' Guinness also points out that the Club leadership received no support from the senior ranks of the Tory Party – 'I think the Conservative Party leadership would have happily watched us go under – it would have freed them from another source of grass roots pressure.' There was one acknowledgement. When all was over, Guinness bumped into Lord Carrington, the party chairman. 'Well done that,' said Carrington 'Getting it under control.'

But then Carrington had never forgiven the Monday Club for the temerity of one of its early officers, Paul Bristol, in courting Carrington's daughter. This was made easier by her employment in Club HQ. At one crisis of his ardent wooing, Bristol stuck his foot in the door of the noble Lord's home in his insistence on seeing the daughter. For Lord Carrington, *that* was the end of the Monday Club.

SIX

Tyndall Takes Over;
Growth and the Populist Challenge

With the departure of O'Brien, Tyndall assumed control of the NF and stepped into the most hectic and successful six months the party had ever known. The decision by the Ugandan Government of Idi Amin to expel all the Asians in that country, and the early estimates of up to 70,000 immigrants arriving destitute in Britain, led to the greatest surge of popular discontent and protest since Enoch Powell's speech of 1968.

Throughout the summer and autumn of 1972, the NF had little time to dwell upon its latest schism, little time to ponder the implications of the resignations of its chairman and half the Directorate. The campaign against the Ugandan Asians mobilized even those members who had sympathized with O'Brien. The momentum of the NF continued throughout the following year, partly because NF branches in the regions were able to exploit the Ugandan issue as the refugee families were gradually moved into new homes and jobs, and partly because the Ugandan Asians had served to demoralize the anti-immigration wing of the Conservative Party. Throughout 1973, the NF took advantage of the bitter fights for control inside the Monday Club, and continued to welcome the disillusioned converts from a Conservative Party which had promptly and decently agreed to help these refugees with their British passports.

Tyndall was lucky in the timing of the Asians' arrival. In the few weeks between the departure of O'Brien and the first news from Uganda, the NF were faced with disappointing results in the local elections, and the need to replace the Directorate members who had resigned with O'Brien.

The disappointing local election results of Spring 1972 had encouraged O'Brien and those who resigned from the Directorate with him in the belief that they were leaving a demoralized and declining movement. But this recognition had only a slight impact on the general membership of the NF, since Tyndall and Webster were able to make their case heard first, and because the NIP (which O'Brien and his friends joined) was barely known and little regarded. Tyndall's own response to the split came in the August *Spearhead*, where he grandly attributed it to: 'The great limitations of certain individuals, their weakness, gullibility, personal frustrations, jealousies and vendettas.' Behind those problems, Tyndall claimed, was another 'of much mor serious import. It is the determination of the enemy establishmer to foment division in our ranks by playing upon these huma frailties and exploiting them to the utmost.'

Tyndall could not have been more mistaken. O'Brien ha tried desperately to enlist the aid of that establishment and ha failed. While the split was being prepared, O'Brien used th opportunity of one of the regular visits the Special Branch pai to HQ to pass a note to the detective. It read: 'We may b bugged – where can I meet you?' The Special Branch man's eye widened, but he scribbled a telephone number on the paper an handed it back. When they met later, and drove around Londo in a car for an hour, O'Brien explained that Gordon Brow was always tape-recording meetings and telephone conversations and he was convinced the office was bugged. What he wante from the Special Branch was any kind of information he coul use against Tyndall and Webster. He pleaded that for the good o British political life, the Special Branch should help him t destroy the men he called 'the neo-Nazis'. The Special Branc refused.

Tyndall knew nothing of this, but he had sought ammunitio against O'Brien through his own channels. In the summer o 1972, driving up to Leicester for a meeting, Tyndall stopped o by arrangement in Coventry where he met Colin Jordan in th lounge of the Leofric hotel. 'He was very amiable,' Jordan recalls 'and sounded me out about the possibility of my joining th NF. He told me that he needed someone to take charge of th Midlands, and hinted that a coup was about to take place insid the movement. He made it clear that I could run the Midland for the NF if I would join him and we parted on good terms although I was non-committal.' On his return to Londor Tyndall wrote to Jordan, asking if he had any informatio damaging to O'Brien which could be used in the coup. Tynda knew of O'Brien's brief association with Jordan, but Jorda was unable to provide anything of importance. Later in th year, when both Jordan and the NF were making politica capital out of the arrival of the Ugandan Asians, Webste warned Jordan that he might have to face 'elements I canno control' unless Jordan kept away from the NF patch.

The single issue which allowed the NF to climb out of thos troubles was a revival of the anti-immigration passions in a their raw fury. General Idi Amin became the saviour of the N when he expelled the Ugandan Asians. He was the best recruitin officer the NF ever had.

The NF leaders are still proud of the speed with which they reacted to the opportunity Amin had given them. Their propaganda was able to focus on three issues at once. By attacking Amin as representative of black nationalism, arrogance and cruelty, the NF was able to claim that its warnings of black 'unfitness' for independent government in Africa were justified. Secondly, they could return to their favourite ground of opposing coloured immigration to Britain – and the early vague estimates of the numbers of Ugandan Asians who were to be expelled ranged up to 75,000. The Heath Government's 1971 Immigration Act had outflanked a considerable proportion of the anti-immigrant feeling in the Conservative Party and in the country. By taking the honourable decision to grant the refugees free entry and assistance in resettlement, the Government made itself vulnerable to anti-immigration sentiment. So the third issue the NF was able to exploit was the 'feebleness' of the Heath Government – an argument which was to prove particularly effective within the Monday Club.

Within 24 hours of the first alarming headlines from Uganda, the NF had organized a 100-strong picket of Downing St in the afternoon of 14 August, followed by the delivery of a petition of protest by John Tyndall to Number Ten that evening. Tyndall and 200 followers then joined a protest march to Uganda House, where Mrs Joy Page of the ICA delivered a letter of protest. And, as after Powell's speech in 1968, the meat porters in Smithfield were rumbling with discontent. This time, the NF deliberately nurtured their anger. Tom Lamb brought the loudspeaker van to NF HQ, and Gordon Brown delivered it and leaflets to Ron Taylor who began a series of speeches and rallies in the Market. On 24 August, after being addressed by Martin Webster, the meat porters marched through London to the Home Office.

In Smithfield, the NF redoubled their efforts and on 7 September, there was a second protest march to Smith Square, which housed the HQs of both Conservative and Labour Parties. The NF paid for an advertisement for the march in the *Evening News*. NF marchers joined the porters, carrying their anti-immigration placards with the NF insignia carefully covered with brown paper. At the rally before the meeting, Martin Webster and Ron Taylor and Mrs Joy Page all spoke. They were followed by Dan Harmston of the Union Movement and Air Vice-Marshal Donald Bennett, whose capricious political loyalties were at this time focused on the NIP. Colin Jordan was in the crowd, but Webster managed to ensure that Jordan was not permitted to speak. For Webster, the Ugandan Asian problem was the NF's greatest opportunity for effective agitation and recruitment. He was therefore willing to work closely with Joy Page and the other community protest groups, whose organizations would never be in a position to rival the NF. He was also prepared to work with the Monday Club, confident that Heath's decision to welcome the Asians would strain the Clubbers' Tory loyalties. But Jordan was a threat to be stopped.

While the London NF were demonstrating against the arrivals at Heathrow, Walter Barton and the Manchester NF were picketing Manchester airport every Sunday, and distributing a total of 20,000 leaflets. The Hounslow, Kingston and Richmond NF branches combined to occupy the public gallery of Hounslow Town Hall and read a statement of protest during a council meeting. (The organizer, Bill Brown, was given a merit award at the next annual conference.) The same branches organized another demonstration at Ealing Town Hall, and at Leicester on 9 September, Jim Merrick of the BCSI came down to speak at an open air protest rally, for which *Spearhead* claimed an audience of 2300 with more than 1000 on the subsequent march. The audience were promised 16 NF candidates at the next local elections in Leicester – a pledge which the NF was to fulfil. On 16 September came the great Monday Club rally at Central Hall, with 400 NF members attending and virtually taking over the rally to lead a march on Downing St. On 30 September, the NF took 100 London members and 100 Midlands members to Blackburn by coach to swell a local march of protest. Some 600 people heard speeches from the Dowager Lady Birdwood of the Anti-Immigration Co-ordinating Committee, Merrick Tyndall, Webster and a leading local Conservative called John Kingsley Read who was to join the NF before the year was out.

For once there was no need for *Spearhead* to exaggerate its figures of new membership and growth. The October issue proudly informed the members: 'During the last month or so, the NF has experienced the most rapid growth in its five year history. It has become commonplace to receive 100 enquiries in a day at Head Office . . . By 20 September, 250 new members had been enrolled during that month alone.' The magazine was confident enough to admit that its earlier development had been less than inspiring – 'After quiet but unspectacular progress for some time, the NF has suddenly started to shoot ahead at a tremendous pace.' Two years later, Martin Webster told the *Birmingham Mail*: 'The Ugandan Asian invasion sparked our real growth.'

Nor was it simply a matter of numbers; the calibre of the new NF recruits was markedly higher than in the past. Monday Clubbers with experience of political organization were beginning to join. Peter Dawson, soon to become Birmingham NF organizer, came from the Monday Club; Mrs Gillian Goold, West Middlesex Monday Club secretary; the Conservative Kingsley Read of Blackburn. Moreover, there were other Monday Clubbers whose loyalties had been so loosened that the final defeat of G. K. Young in the Club election of 1973 pushed them into the NF – one such was the Tory candidate for Tottenham, Roy Painter. The rise of such recruits in the NF was rapid. By October 1974, Kingsley Read was NF chairman and Painter had been elected on to the NF Directorate and to its Executive Council. In 1972, the NF leadership was delighted at this sign of growth – they had not yet realized that by attracting new members with political expertise they had introduced an alternative leadership, a new elite into the NF which would within two years challenge Tyndall and Webster for control.

The NF's leaflets on the Ugandan Asians were designed to raise other political issues:

If the British people have to worry about fighting for a job in the face of a tide of cheap immigrant labour, and are occupied in trying to get decent housing in competition with teeming millions of immigrants, then they will not have time to think about how the International Big Business Establishment is robbing them with such gigantic swindles as the Common Market.

By the traditional standards of the British Right, such a leaflet was propaganda of high quality, delivering six separate messages for the price of one, and moreover introducing the NF's traditional economic conspiracy theory in a new and more credible guise.

But in these last six months of 1972, the NF had almost more issues than the party needed. The campaign in support of the Ulster Unionists, begun early in the summer and continued throughout the crisis of O'Brien's resignation, was maintained. And as the year went on, the NF's anti-EEC campaign gathered momentum, designed to peak with Britain's accession to the Treaty of Rome in January 1973. The November issue of *Spearhead*, which now carried the additional authority of Tyndall's chairmanship of the movement outlined the NF policy in an article entitled 'Fight the EEC'.

It encouraged NF members to break and frustrate the laws relating to the Common Market and to act as some weird kind of clerical guerillas against the EEC bureaucracy – 'Obstruct, disorganize and sabotage the working of the Bureaucracy as much as you possibly can,' it advised. 'Defy the law – be prepared to go to prison too as a gesture of defiance against the imposition of foreign laws on Britain.'

Even for the NF, this was a bizarre policy. Ever concerned to uphold law and order, to bring back the death penalty and demand that courts be tougher with criminals, the NF was now telling its members to behave criminally. This was no aberration. At the largest indoor rally the NF had then held, at Church House, Westminster, in November 1972, Tyndall told the meeting 'the man who signs the Treaty of Rome on January 1 will put himself in the same bracket of history as those who at the end of war were hung as collaborators.'

For Tyndall, who had spent five years of his life in parties which asserted that Hitler had been right, this was a curious way of making the point that Heath was some kind of anti-British traitor. Clearly, with the pressure of the Ugandan Asian affair, O'Brien's resignation and the anti-EEC campaign, the strains upon Tyndall were beginning to tell. The passion of his anti-EEC campaign was out of all proportion to the mood of opposition in the country as a whole. The growth of the NF had come when Tyndall's political antennae were finely tuned – he caught and timed the opposition to the Ugandan Asians with energy and skill, and won many recruits to the NF in the process. But within two months, he had clearly misjudged the intensity of anti-EEC feeling. Part of the reason for this lay in his over-confidence over the NF's prospects in the wake of the Asian arrival. At the time of the anti-EEC speech, Tyndall knew of an increasing number of Monday Club defections to NF ranks. He knew that Clubbers were actively helping a NF by-election candidate, and he knew that one Monday Club in Essex was planning to invite him to address them. For Tyndall, this appeared to be the breakthrough.

The Remembrance Day parade had seen 1500 marchers turning out under the NF banners – twice as many as in 1971. The collection at the meeting afterwards raised £564. Within a month, the NF was to achieve its first dramatic by-election result, with John Clifton gaining 8·2 per cent of the poll, and 2960 votes at Uxbridge. Moreover, he had trounced the other rivals for the Nationalist vote, including Dan Harmston of the Union Movement, Clare Macdonald (who had resigned with O'Brien only six months earlier) of the NIP and Reg Simmerson, an independent anti-Marketeer. The NF had worked harder for this result than ever before, bringing in up to 100 (and never less than 40) volunteers to canvass throughout the campaign.

The pace of events and campaigning in 1972 had upset more than Tyndall's balance. It had also forced the shelving of one of the NF's key strategies. Just before the Ugandan Asian affair began, the NF Directorate had decided that they needed a base in the trade unions. They had many union members in their ranks, and were particularly proud of Tom Lamb, a former member of the NF Directorate who had also risen in the ranks of his union, the ETU. When he was elected to a relatively minor committee post with the Union's superannuation scheme, *Spearhead* devoted an article to his success. The support of the dockers and meat porters for Powell in 1968 had convinced the NF leaders that there was a reserve of nationalism and racialism within the unions, ready to be tapped and the NF had long pondered how this was to be done. They had kept a close eye on the abortive experiment of TRU–AIM (Trade Unionists Against Immigration), and the Directorate meeting of July 1972 decided to hold a NF Trade Unionists' conference to discuss what should be done. Announced, with Tom Lamb as chairman, in the September issue of *Spearhead*, the plan had to be shelved when priority was given to the Ugandan Asian demonstrations.

At the annual conference, the issue was raised again, the Leicester branch proposing that a separate union should be established for NF members. This proposal was defeated, after wiser union members pointed out that if the NF did want to have the implacable opposition of the organized trade union movement, there was no better way than to set up an organization in direct rivalry. Far wiser, they suggested, to build up NF support groups within existing trade unions, and this the conference agreed to support. For the rest of the year, this support group was an informal idea. It took the Mansfield Hosiery strike, and, in 1974, the Imperial Typewriters strike at Leicester to convince the NF that they could exploit the racial problem inside trade unions. And it took the Ulster Workers' Council strike of May 1974 to convince the NF that trade unionists could be organized in a nationalist, even racialist, cause. The NF Trade Unionists Association was finally established in July 1974.

The immediate need for 1973 was to improve the organization of the party to cope with the new recruits from the Ugandan Asian campaign. During the last four months of 1972, the NF gained over 800 new recruits. A new branch was established in Jim Merrick's stronghold of Bradford, and the new chairman was Merrick's deputy, G. Lupton. In January, Kingsley Read was named as the new chairman of the Blackburn branch, and in March and April Tyndall outlined in *Spearhead* the future development of the NF. He wanted five new departments to be administered from national HQ – research, social activities, fund raising, a film-unit and a mobile recruiting group to pioneer new areas. An appeal was launched for a £20,000 development fund to hire more full-time staff – in particular Tyndall wanted full-time regional organizers. It was now plain that Webster as national activities organizer was being overloaded. There were simply too many provincial groups for one man to co-ordinate their various plans and ensure good turnouts at each demo by bringing coachloads of members from nearby branches. Some of the burden was taken from Webster by Walter Barton's role as northern organizer, where he began to develop a network of NF groups around his Manchester base. By October 1973, there were groups established at Oldham, Stockport, Rochdale and Accrington, and much larger, more autonomous branches at Bolton, Blackburn and Liverpool.

Tyndall spelled out the organizational problems: 'We need full-time organizers for the South, the Midlands and the North of England. We need also a full-time co-ordinator of election campaigns and not less than two full-time secretaries at HQ. We need to place the services of the national activities organizer on a proper basis of regular paid employment.'

A permanent staff of this size involved a minimum annual expenditure of £10,000 on salaries alone, without counting the costs of three regional offices. Since Tyndall and Webster were already receiving a small income from *Spearhead* (which still depended on annual appeals for its solvency), the £20,000 for which Tyndall appealed was clearly going to have to be an annual subsidy. And in May 1973, the Directorate decided to fight a minimum of 50 seats at the next general election, which meant a further expenditure of £7500 in election deposits. This sum was seen as an investment to ensure better organization in the future by training each branch in campaign tactics, and also as a guarantee of cheap nation-wide publicity. A party which fielded 50 candidates was entitled to make a free party political broadcast on radio and televison. The Directorate made the motive clear in announcing its decision to fight the 50 seats – 'use the elections as a massive publicity exercise to impress the presence of the NF upon the country as a political alternative of potential force.'

Their confidence had been raised by the result in the West

Bromwich by-election which was held in the same month. In the NF's own mythology, the West Bromwich result has become as significant a victory as the shock victory of the Orpington by-election had been for the Liberal Party ten years earlier. It was the first time an NF candidate had saved his deposit, and *Spearhead* proudly printed a picture of the cheque for £150 which was repaid to the candidate, Martin Webster.

Even before the West Bromwich by-election, the NF had been given some indication of the impact of their Ugandan Asian campaign by the local election results of April 1973. The greatest success was in Leicester, where sixteen wards were fought, and over 10,000 votes were won.

Most significant of all was an analysis of the local vote in terms of parliamentary constituencies. Adding together the NF votes in the Leicester South seat (where the NF candidate in 1970 had mustered 738 votes or 2·3 per cent) brought a total of 2358 NF supporters, which suggested at least a 7 per cent poll in a general election. In Leicester East the NF votes totalled almost 5000 – which suggested that an NF candidate could at least save his deposit – and four of the five wards which make up Leicester West had delivered 2317 votes.

The six NF candidates in the Greater London Council elections won an average vote of 6·8 per cent, with peaks of 11·3 per cent in Feltham and Heston and 8·5 per cent in Hayes and Harlington. These were West London areas near Southall, which had been a BNP stronghold ten years earlier. But in Bermondsey (5·8 per cent). Battersea South (4·8 per cent) and Enfield (4 per cent) the results were disappointing. The fourteen candidates who stood in Wolverhampton, Leeds, Bristol, Bath and Norwich did badly, averaging barely 4 per cent of the poll. Huddersfield had barely stopped its rot, with only three candidates getting 5·6 per cent, 5·8 per cent and 7·5 per cent.

Two wards in Blackburn brought some consolation, with votes of 23 per cent and 16·8 per cent, but the poll had been low and the major parties had not fought energetic campaigns. So in spite of *Spearhead*'s brave assertions of the success of the Ugandan Asian campaigns, and in spite of the new membership, the first submission of the revitalized NF to the electorate had not been a rousing success.

For the NF leaders this was puzzling. They ought to have been doing much better, and they came to the conclusion that they needed some real symbol of success before their new support was reflected in increased votes. They had to convince electors that it was not a waste of time to vote for a minority party, and they had to find some kind of dazzling single image which would make the NF appear both credible and glamorous. They were convinced that there was a great deal of latent support for the NF, but it had to be given a focus. The hope was that the West Bromwich by-election would provide it. NF supporters were brought into West Bromwich from all over the Midlands. At weekends, supporters drove up from London to participate in the campaign. For the NF, West Bromwich was a saturation attack.

Webster's own skills as a publicist were vital. No sooner had Pakistan declared its intention of leaving the Commonwealth than he demanded that all Pakistanis be removed from the electoral rolls as aliens. He made a virtue of his own tubbiness, and campaigned as 'Big Mart'. There were parades with pretty girls, parades with flags and Union Jacks and endless NF activities. It was the NF's most professional campaign.

There were two NF mass rallies, and one – suitably strengthened by supporters from all over the country – attracted some 3000 people. This activity took place in a general atmosphere of political apathy, with the Tory candidate suffering from the traditional unpopularity of a Government in mid-term (which had moreover introduced the unpopular Value Added Tax the previous month). Most damaging of all for the Conservative, Enoch Powell refused to come and speak on his behalf.

On polling day, only 43·6 per cent of the electors bothered to vote. The Tory vote had collapsed from almost 19,000 in 1970 to 7532. The Labour vote too was down from over 23,000 in 1970 to 15,907. But the NF candidate, with 16 per cent of the poll, received 4789 votes. It was a notable achievement, and the press and TV greeted it with surprise, distress and the kind of wide publicity of which the NF had hitherto but dreamed. *The Times* ran a major article entitled 'The National Front's growing challenge to Mr Heath', which concluded that the NF's opposition to the EEC had won it as many votes as its opposition to immigration. The Conservatives were particularly disturbed that even the campaigning efforts of two senior Cabinet Ministers, Sir Keith Joseph and Mr Peter Walker, had failed to stop the disastrous decline in the Tory vote. 'This is what I warned Mr Bell [the Conservative candidate] would happen,' Enoch Powell commented.

It was precisely the breakthrough the NF had needed; the publicity they received, and the aura of success and growth which now surrounded them, paid off handsomely in the local elections of 7 June. The vote rose dramatically – but so intense was the attention of the media in the wake of West Bromwich that the NF grew alarmed. 'We were depicted as having election targets which we knew we could never reach,' *Spearhead* complained, 'just so it could be publicized as a failure and a defeat.'

Whatever targets the NF may have had, and whatever the press may have attributed to them, their results in the June elections were by far the best they had ever achieved. In Leicester, the NF grew from 10,000 votes at the April elections to 18,000. Only in one ward did the NF vote fall below 10 per cent and in three out of the ten wards fought they won over 20 per cent of the vote. On average, they won over 15 per cent of the city's vote. In Nottingham a new NF branch, fighting its first election in two wards, won 22 per cent and 14 per cent. In Bournemouth, another new branch won 15 per cent. In Blackburn, fighting five wards, every candidate won over 20 per cent of the vote for an average of 23·7 per cent. In Bristol, where the NF had traditionally polled between 2 and 5 per cent, the NF fought four wards, and won 17·7, 17·2, 10·2 and 7·8 per cent. In Brighton the vote more than doubled, in Staines it went from 7 per cent in the April to 24·9 per cent in the June election. A new branch in Dartford won an average 13·5 per cent with three candidates and a new candidate in Norwich won 9 per cent. These were the figures the NF leaders had hoped to see. They were not yet winning power, but it was a triumphant justification of the decision to take the electoral road.

This soaring of morale alarmed Tyndall, who had seen sudden electoral successes before, and watched them decline. After the lessons of Smethwick and the Conservatives, and having seen the NF collapse in Huddersfield, he tried to sound a note of caution. He wrote an article, 'Common sense about by-elections', in which he stressed that before the NF presented itself to the electorate, that electorate had to be prepared. Inside the Directorate, Gordon Brown was proposing that the NF should leave no by-election uncontested, that its name and policies should constantly be before the voters. Tyndall insisted that before a seat was fought there must be local NF strength and that it must be the right kind of constituency. He refused to permit the NF to stand in the by-elections at Manchester Exchange, Berwick, Ely and Ripon.

On one by-election, Tyndall allowed himself to be overruled. Against his better judgement, the NF stood at the Hove by-election in November, where Brown insisted there was a great deal of NF support. He pointed to the tradition of the RPS in Sussex, and to the healthy local branch. Tyndall replied that the Liberals and Conservatives would be fighting very hard and he was proved right. The NF candidate, Squadron-Leader Harrison-Broadley, won a disappointing 1409 votes, 3 per cent of the poll.

Tyndall salvaged what he could. In *Spearhead*, he wrote 'I hope we have learned a most important lesson, which is that we should at all times pick our ground carefully and not be rushed into fighting by-elections again just because some of us feel that it is "about time".'

In September of 1971, he had made a similar point in a somewhat sinister way: 'If British Nationalism is to survive then Nationalists must learn patience; must learn the techniques so successfully employed by their enemies; must learn from the mistakes of other countries at other times who "went Nationalist" and who thought they could cut corners and take on the whole world all at once.' This was the closest Tyndall has come to comparing the NF to the German Nazi party since he first joined the NF, and the implications of his comparison are frankly alarming. But it does indicate that in the long years from 1957 when he first entered Nationalist politics, he had developed the political experience and perspective which was needed to bring the NF back to reality in that euphoric summer of 1973.

Not that Tyndall wanted to dampen enthusiasm; he simply wanted to ensure that enthusiasm was not wasted by inadequate organization. Indeed, Tyndall is a subtle political psychologist, well aware that if the NF is to grow it will have to appeal to loyalties and passions which are fundamentally irrational. On 15 July 1973, Tyndall spoke to 43 of the more active members, people who had been picked out as future regional and branch organizers, at a leadership training seminar. The speech he made provides a significant and useful insight into Tyndall's concept of politics and mass psychology. It is worth examining at some length.

He began by suggesting that the NF was fundamentally different from all other political parties, because the motive forces of its members were based on loyalties which transcended reason and rational conviction. 'There is a unique quality of enthusiasm in the NF that an appeal to reason alone could not possibly create,' he said. 'We are not ashamed to appeal to people's feelings and to utilize those feelings in spurring them on to ever greater efforts.' He went beyond this to suggest that the emotions of people who had already joined the NF should be exploited for as long as they were members, that the original emotive appeal which had won them to the NF must be continued, almost as though the NF were a faith rather than a political force.

But the NF had to win a special kind of recruit. It wanted very much more than the vote of its supporters: 'Our job is not just to win sympathizers but to win activists; not just to get people to agree with us but to get them to work and if necessary, to *fight* for us.' This was not to be achieved by rational argument or intellectual persuasion – 'Reason may play its part in deciding people as to what is the right course, but the forces that spur them into action . . . to go into the night working for a cause with no prospect of personal reward, are entirely forces of feelings of emotion.'

For Tyndall, emotion was the source of loyalty and the source of conviction. Rationality, and the process of the intellect, were subordinate factors – 'In the last analysis, reason simply builds on a foundation that feeling supplies in the first place.' Therefore in Tyndall's politics 'Colour and pageantry are as important as speeches and articles'.

This was the essence of Tyndall's argument, his definition of the kind of people he wanted to recruit to the NF and his vision of the manner in which they should be recruited:

What is it that touches off a chord in the instincts of the people to whom we seek to appeal? It can often be the most simple and primitive thing. Rather than a speech or printed article it may just be a flag; it may be a marching column; it may be the sound of a drum; it may be a banner or it may just be the impression of a crowd. None of these things contain in themselves one single argument, one single piece of logic . . . They are recognized as being among the things that appeal to the hidden forces of the human soul.

Tyndall went on to draw the obvious practical lessons from this analysis:

It is always a necessary part of political psychology to seek to show strength. This is why at certain intervals of the year we concentrate our forces together by transporting members hundreds of miles by coach. We have got to show strength to the public and to our own people . . . The British may sympathize with the underdog on the playing field, but they certainly don't sympathize with the underdog in politics – they tend to fall in step with the big battalions.

Tyndall was speaking not simply to the converted, but to hand picked representatives of the NF who were being groomed for high office. He could be frank. Whether he would have talked so easily of the source of the NF's support being 'the hidden forces of the human soul' to another gathering is uncertain. But clearly the force which Tyndall is building is not a political party in the accepted sense of the term. It is more even than a movement it is an act of collective will, based upon feeling rather than reason and finding the well-springs of its loyalties and the sources of its passions in some deep and atavistic zone that lurks below the conscious mind. It is a faith, a crusade, more than it is a political party. And it is a crusade shaped by Tyndall's conscious design, by his will to exploit 'those hidden forces of the human soul'.

But Tyndall combined this insight into the psychology of the NF with a keen political mind. Hence his concern for organization, for the meticulous planning of where the NF should present itself to the electorate and where it should not. And if Tyndall's major concern in the summer of 1973 was to restrain the over enthusiasm of many of his members, he at least acknowledged that the NF had reached a take-off point from which its appeal and its message could be broadened. *Spearhead* almost erupted in those months with fresh and new ideas, new policies of nationalization, of opposition to multi-national corporations, of support for trade unions and strikes and proposals for the reform of industrial relations. The final defeat of the Powellites in the Monday Club came in the August of 1973, and as if this were a signal that the Club and the Tory Party had been milked of all the support they could deliver, the NF began to present Labour-oriented policies and to stress its friendship for the working man. The thrust of the NF's policies moved sharply to the left.

In August of 1973, Webster launched a furious attack upon 'Tory Corruption', alleging that Enoch Powell's seat at the previous Conservative conference had been deliberately bugged and the Conference itself had been packed by Liberals who had no right to vote, but had been brought into the hall to swell the ranks of those who voted against Powell. In the same issue, Mike Lobb attacked Labour's nationalization proposals on the curious grounds that they did not go far enough. Why not nationalize the foreign-owned industries, he suggested, and specifically why not nationalize the American-owned car companies? Why had the Government not sought powers to nationalize the major banks, he asked, so that the banks' influence on the country's economic life could be exercised in the national interest and not in the interests of private shareholders?

The next month, *Spearhead*'s cover carried the picture of an oil rig with the caption 'Hands off Britain's oil'. It attacked the American companies who were exploring the North Sea, and demanded that the oil be brought under British control for British benefit. The NF election manifesto of the following year repeated this demand – 'We must go flat out to get North Sea Oil flowing out at the same time we must ensure that it is under British ownership and control.' One of *Spearhead*'s reasons for control of the oil was – intriguingly – as a protection against foreign sanctions if and when the NF achieved power: 'It is precisely in the 1980s or shortly afterwards that we hope to see a Nationalist government instituted in Britain. Such a government would immediately encounter economic trading difficulties in the form of world trading sanctions instigated by international finance.' For the first time, the NF's own time scale for achieving power was published.

In December 1973, the NF announced its support for workers on strike at London sugar refineries. Two thousand leaflets were distributed in the factories and at the trade union mass meetings. Headed 'Sweet talk – but nothing else', the leaflets argued that the workers should join the NF and combine their industrial action with political action. Lobb's branch at Newham joined the strikers on picket lines and launched a recruiting drive at the factory gates. 'British workers will only defend their national-class interests by joint industrial and political action,' ran the argument. Lobb was calling on the vocabulary of his political past in the Communist Party and combining it with the Nationalist arguments of the NF.

That same issue of *Spearhead* announced that the NF supported the miners' pay claim, against which the Conservative Government was preparing the 'confrontation' election of February 1974. When the miners' strike and the Government's refusal to countenance their pay claim led to the state of national emergency and the three-day week, the NF had its own answer to solve the problem of industrial relations, and called for workers' participation and partnership in industry, and for a profit-sharing scheme to be established throughout British industry. They attacked the Conservative Government's Industrial Relations Act (without pointing out that when that legislation had been introduced, the NF had said of its provisions: 'They seem to be an attempt to do the right thing but with a machinery that is likely to prove too weak'). By the time of the February

147

election, the NF was demanding free heating services for old age pensioners, and pensions to be two-thirds of the average industrial wage. In the six months after the defeat of their allies in the Monday Club, the NF had moved not only to the Left, but towards a coherent populist programme. It was a key change.

Tyndall himself had agreed with the bulk of these shifts in policy, and was happy to see the NF adopt an increasingly populist platform on which to campaign for the general election which was widely recognized to be imminent. What was to disconcert him was the way other elements within the NF were winning the credit for the change. Inside the NF, Tyndall lost the credit for this new thrust of the party's policies. Partly through their skill in public relations and exploiting the media, partly through their wider political experience in the major political parties, people like Roy Painter and John Kingsley-Read, recent converts from the Conservative Party, and Mike Lobb with his espousal of workers' nationalism, became identified with the populist image inside the party.

Equally damaging to Tyndall was the growing electoral impact of the NF. The more successful it became in local elections, the more left-wing and liberal bodies throughout the country recognized the threat and began to mobilize against it. The obvious weapon for them to use, in leaflets and in speeches, was the political histories of Tyndall and Webster. From the West Bromwich by-election onwards, the NF was not able to field a candidate or fight a campaign without facing the problem of leaflets which publicized Tyndall's participation in Nazi parties in the early 1960s. Photographs of Tyndall in *Spearhead* uniform at the 1962 camp, and photographs of Martin Webster posing in front of a portrait of Arnold Leese (who wore a prominent swastika armband) were widely distributed. In Leicester, for example, during the June local elections, 20,000 such leaflets were handed out through the town by local trade unions. They may not have done much damage to the NF's final vote, and Webster may have bragged in *Spearhead* that they did the NF more good than harm, but an increasing number of NF members, their faith in the NF unshaken, began to wonder whether Tyndall and Webster were not a liability.

New recruits – whom Tyndall had been so delighted to welcome into the NF – knew little and cared less about the sacrifices he had made in the last seven years for the NF. The kind of loyalty that he inspired among the older members, their conviction that in a very real way Webster and Tyndall were the National Front, was not shared by the newcomers. When in February,

he NF was able to field 54 candidates at the general election
nd so claim its free time to present its policies on national TV
nd radio, Tyndall had assumed that the programme would be
entred on him sitting before the cameras to address the nation.
Ie was taken aback (but finally agreed) when the Directorate
nd the more influential new members suggested that the pro-
ramme should focus on other members of the party as well in
n attempt to show the breadth of its appeal. The leaflets, the
ccasional TV programme and the press stories had undermined
he NF's faith in John Tyndall and Martin Webster.

The full scale of this challenge was not to emerge until later
a 1974, with the elections for a new Directorate and that Direc-
orate's own elections for the party chairmanship. But as early as
'ebruary, just before the general election, press speculation
bout this new division in the NF was beginning. In particular,
he *Guardian*, which was covering the election campaign of Roy
'ainter, began to talk of the emergence of a populist wing of the
NF, and began to talk of Painter as its leader. The division that
he *Guardian* (and subsequently the rest of the press) was able to
raw was between the populists and the neo-Nazis. This distinc-
ion was echoed by John O'Brien, the NF's previous chairman,
/ho in two TV programmes in December 1972 and September
974 repeated his attacks on Tyndall and Webster and repeated
is charge that they were still in close and regular contact with
Jerman neo-Nazi movements. The first programme was shown
ate in the evening and had little impact. The September 1974
rogramme was shown in prime time on independent television,
ad an audience of over eight million, and had a shattering effect
pon the morale of NF members. It was a hostile programme,
nterviewing Tyndall closely about the precise implications of
is racialist policy, making it clear that the NF opposed mixed
aarriages, and that coloured people would go to the bottom of
very queue for housing and social services before they were
epatriated. Within a month of its being shown, Tyndall was
oted out of the chairmanship of the NF, the former Tory
Kingsley Read had replaced him, and Roy Painter was sitting
n the NF Directorate and on its controlling executive council.

n January 1974, the NF had 30 branches and 54 groups around
he country. The bulk of their support lay in South-east England,
vith eleven branches and eight groups in Greater London, and
ive branches and 22 groups in the rest of the South-east. The
Vidlands had five branches and three groups, the North had
even branches and eleven groups. Scotland and Northern

Ireland were each represented by a group (Belfast was to become a branch within the year) and the West of England had one branch at Bristol and seven groups, including the Welsh group of Cardiff and Barry.

But in early January 1974, the Directorate gloomily surveyed the prospects for an early election. The reports from more than half the branches were depressing, pleading that they had been unable to raise money for a candidate's deposit, or had too little money to get leaflets printed. Some even said they could not afford to buy the envelopes and take advantage of the free delivery of an election message which the Post Office traditionally offers each candidate. Gordon Brown and Peter Holland were given specific election responsibilities, and Webster and Tyndall joined them when their other nation-wide speaking commitments (and Webster's own campaign in West Bromwich) permitted. It was little enough on which to organize a national campaign. But it was somehow done, and branch officials were persuaded that they could afford the deposit money. At the Croydon HQ, the Directorate decided to allow local branches credit on election printing costs even though this meant gambling with the movement's bare solvency.

Nineteen of the candidates were to receive fewer than 100 votes. One received fewer than 500 votes, a category normally reserved for joke candidates. This was Mr Budden of Hove where the party had done so badly at the November by-election of 1973. These made up the bulk of the branches which had not originally wanted to fight the election. But larger branches in Leicester and Wolverhampton and North and West London were persuaded to fight three, rather than two, local seats. It was a notable achievement, and the fact that every candidate lost his deposit was not seen as a cause for despair. The new strength of the Liberal Party meant that in more than 40 of the contested seats, the NF and the Liberals were each fighting for these voters who would break the national tradition and not vote for one of the two major parties. Only one of the five candidates who won more than 6 per cent of the vote had Liberal opposition – Mike Lobb in Newham. The NF also claimed that the Post Office attempted to sabotage their campaign by refusing to distribute NF election literature on the grounds that it contained 'advertising'.

But when allowance is made for the intervention of the Liberals in so many seats, and for the effect of the Post Office decision, the fact remains that the NF was bitterly disappointed with the election results. Martin Webster's share of the vote in West

Bromwich dropped from 16 per cent to 7 per cent, from 4789 votes to only 2907. In North London, the NF were even beaten by the despised NIP, where Roy Painter, a former Tory candidate, who was well known locally and who had a considerable amount of coverage in the national press and London radio, received 100 votes fewer than his NIP opponent. In Wolverhampton, where the NF had worked tirelessly to reap the advantage of fighting on the anti-immigration ticket in Enoch Powell's town, they won only 5·3, 3·8 and 3 per cent of the vote in the three seats they fought. In Leicester, where they had won over 18,000 votes in the local elections six months earlier, they could muster a total of only 7880 votes – a dramatic fall of support. In Islington North they won 3·4 per cent, compared to 5·6 per cent in the 1970 general election. And in Battersea South, the NF vote had fallen from 3·3 per cent in 1970 to 2·3 per cent in 1974. Even the feat of fielding 54 candidates was not quite proof against disappointments such as these.

There were many who pointed to the smear campaigns against Tyndall and Webster. In the first *Spearhead* after the election, Webster was alarmed enough by the criticism to issue a 3000 word warning against 'Populism': 'Don't let the press fool you . . . Populism is not Nationalism.' It alleged that newspapers which had discerned signs of a Populist wing within the NF were engaged in subtle and vicious attempts to split the NF. Webster was driven to attack the very concept of populism: 'The election of just one policy-trimming "Populist" would be a blow from which the NF might never recover . . . the mass of the people can only identify with the Nationalist cause if we maintain for our cause a separate identity far removed from the blurred images of the corrupt Old Gang parties.'

The internal debate had barely begun. In the next issue of *Spearhead* Roy Painter wrote an article which demanded 'Let's make Nationalism Popular'. Tyndall grumpily wrote an introduction which said he was publishing it because 'we do not wish it to be thought that *Spearhead* operates a censorship on all views that do not meet with the Editor's endorsement', and followed Painter's article with a 1200 word rebuttal which said that 'with the greatest respect to him this is claptrap, sheer unadulterated claptrap'.

The Populists found fertile ground when they suggested that the NF was a growing party, with a new and enthusiastic membership that was not fully reflected in the party's leadership. There was room in the party leadership for more than Tyndall and Webster and their old associates of the BNP and the GBM.

In June 1974, when Frank Clifford (an old BUF member) died and Mike Lobb, after a bitter personal row with Webster, resigned, an attempt was made to broaden the leadership by co-opting a young lawyer from Leicester, Tony Reed-Herbert, on to the Directorate. But the Populists were infuriated at the appointment to the second vacancy of Peter Holland, who had left the National Socialist Movement with Tyndall and Webster to join the GBM. It was also sourly noted within the Populist group that two other former neo-Nazis on the Directorate, Denis Pirie and Colin Cody, had only been dismissed the previous year because even Martin Webster refused to stand for their attendance at a celebration of Hitler's birthday. They could also point to the presence on the Directorate of another BUF member, Peter Williams, or to another old associate from the early 1960s, Andrew Brons, or even to Gordon Brown, who had been in the GBM with Tyndall. All of these men, the Populists could argue, were liabilities, and more important, they did not represent the membership of the expanding NF of 1974.

Tyndall found himself having to face other challenges on policy in the columns of *Spearhead*. In the June 1974 issue David McCalden, secretary of the NF Students Association, suggested that the NF's opposition to a measure of regional autonomy could be amended, and Tyndall took a full page to rebut him. At another NF leadership training course in August 1974, a weekend-long event held at a country hotel in Wiltshire, Tony Webber, one of the NF's keen younger members (who had first written for *Spearhead* as a youth in 1968) challenged Tyndall's proposal to abolish the Stock Exchange, and won the support of the other NF candidates at the conference. When drafting the NF manifesto, published for the October election of 1974, the Populists forced Tyndall to amend his language in the policies for the social benefits of agriculture. References to 'sound peasant stock' were not what they wanted to see in a 1974 manifesto. On issue after issue, on decision after decision, Tyndall found his authority challenged. It was a new and bitter development.

He faced criticism because he had never stood in an election for the NF – his enemies whispered it was because he feared the smear campaigns. In vain, Tyndall tried to re-assert not only his authority but also those policies which had identified him as a hard-liner throughout his career in Nationalist politics. In the September 1974 *Spearhead*, he threw down a challenge to the Populists, questioning even the principle of democratic government.

152

This journal is not a doctrinaire supporter of parliamentary government as an end in itself; it is a supporter of good government that operates in the national interest . . . The survival and the national recovery of Britain stands as top priority over all. We will support whatever political methods are necessary to attain that end, although we admit to a marked preference to democratic methods so long as such methods are found which will work.

The Populists were appalled, and concluded that Tyndall had never changed his views since his days with Colin Jordan.

The growth of the NF simply emphasized that the NF was now bigger than Tyndall and his old supporters. In fact it was large enough to need a regional reorganization of the party structure, to which the Directorate agreed in April. The country was to be divided into regions, with the long-term objective of establishing a NF regional council in each county. But for the present the regional council was to consist of the area covered by three contiguous branches. Each branch in the area would send two representatives to the regional council, and each group would send one. Regions with less than three branches would be designated as areas, but would select their councils on the same basis.

The Populists were further cheered when one of their number, Mike Lobb, won more votes than the Conservative candidate at a by-election in Newham on 23 May. This safe Labour seat was easily won by Labour on a low poll, followed by a Liberal with 1862 votes, Lobb with 1713 votes and the Conservative with 1651 votes. It was hailed as another NF electoral success by the media, and the 11·5 per cent of the vote which Lobb secured was the best performance the NF had ever achieved in a seat where they also faced a Liberal candidate. But within six weeks, Lobb had resigned from the party, over an essentially personal difference with Webster. Once again the Populists could claim that the Tyndall-Webster clique were doing the party positive harm.

The Populists' belief in their own importance in the party was reinforced by the development and change, not so much in the content, as in the presentation of the NF's policies. In the course of 1974, the NF successfully moved away from its traditional image as a one-issue movement.

The 'new' policy fields were focused on four central issues: Ulster, Europe, trade unions and post-immigration. Having become a national party, fielded 54 candidates and won 76,429 votes in February, the NF Directorate resolved that it should identify itself in the public mind with each of these four issues, rather than with immigration alone. Recognizing moreover that the nature of immigration as a political issue had been fundamentally changed by the Conservative Immigration Act of 1971, which applied all the controls for which the NF had originally campaigned, and which differed from their policy mainly on whether repatriation should be made voluntary or compulsory, the NF shifted its focus to the question of black people already in Britain.

Applying the new racialism to the black people in Britain meant not only reasserting the NF policy of compulsory repatriation of immigrants, but also direct attacks on the children of racially mixed marriages, allegations that race riots were being regularly hushed up and that black people and black youths were a major cause of mugging and violence in the streets. It was a potent, if savage, method of spreading the racialist doctrine. In the April 1974 *Spearhead*, all of these elements were brought together in a vicious portrait of Liverpool, which had been a model city for race relations in the 1960s. It read:

> The inhabitants of Liverpool became painfully aware of a new menace to their society, that of the embittered half-caste offspring. Uneasy with the West Indians and alien to the existing population, their resentment exploded in an orgy of violent crime. Usually their victims were chosen for racial reasons, i.e. they were white . . . The simmering discontent of the white population . . . erupted in a fortnight of bitter race riots which have continued sporadically ever since . . . Pray God the British wake up.

It is a far cry from Tyndall's blunt attacks on 'racial subhumans' of 1962, but the objective of the propaganda was unchanged. To ram the point home, came Webster in July 1974, writing on what he saw as 'the global struggle for survival between various species of humanity. The British people are in the front line of this struggle and must be made to realize it . . . in multiracial Britain, every 1000 Asian women of childbearing age produce 200 babies per year – three times the birthrate of the native British population . . . White man, are you ready to fight?'

The same message could be profitably inserted into the NF's second major sphere of policy in 1974, its attempt to create its own group within the trade unions. Commenting on the outcome

154

of the strike at the Imperial Typewriters factory in Leicester, a strike of the Asian workers against racism in the factory and race prejudice in the trade union (in all of which the local NF was heavily involved), Tony Reed-Herbert, the young Populist whom Tyndall had co-opted on to the NF Directorate, argued 'the industrial action by Britons at Imperial is a racial struggle . . . the struggle of a united British people fighting to preserve their freedom and identity against the forces of communism and international capitalism which seek to destroy the British nation and which use as their tool the immigrant minorities placed by them in our midst'.

This is not empty phrasing. The NF was active inside the factory – and the Imperial management itself announced that they were 'amazed and disturbed at the amount of confidential company information known to the NF'. NF members inside the plant fed information to NF branch HQ, which in turn made its announcements in the local press and radio, and distributed the company's plans for the strike to white workers at the factory gates. Almost a week before the company's compromise was ready, the NF was informing the work force – accurately – that the company planned to end the strike by re-employing those Asian workers who had been dismissed.

The NF had learned from the failure of TRU-AIM, which had been an unsuccessful attempt to unite various right-wing groups, including the Monday Club, the Union Movement, the NF and the Immigration Control Association, to mobilize anti-immigrant feeling in the trade unions. The NF concluded that TRU-AIM's failure lay in the attempt to bring together widely differing political forces who could only exploit trade union support for essentially non-political events such as marches and mass meetings. They were non-political in the sense that they were merely protests, from which no political base could be founded, and from which no agreed political action could be taken. The NF saw little point in bringing union members out on marches unless the NF could dominate the organization of the march and use it as a recruiting ground, as they were to do with Ugandan Asian marches from Smithfield. Henceforth, NF strategy in the unions was to build up joint NF-TU membership, and work within the unions against the Left, exploiting racial issues wherever they could.

Tyndall spelled out the NF options: 'To be ready to embark on a campaign of repression of the Left in the unions, which could in the process involve the repression of much that is legitimate union activity, or to win the battle in advance by winning control of the TU movement by the normal democratic process.' The NF believed it had the numbers to at least make a start in the process of challenging the left. E. E. Evans, of the NFTU group in the West Midlands, told the *Birmingham Mail* in August 1974 'approximately half the NF members in the (Black Country) region, namely several hundreds, are in fact trade unionists', and Tyndall had made the object plain: 'The intention of the NF is to fight the Left on its own ground in the unions and wrest control of the unions from it by the democratic process.'

The first real opportunity for the new NF approach came with the strike of Mansfield Hosiery Workers in 1973, where the Asian members of the work force struck against what they saw as discrimination against them in wages, promotions and hours worked.

A prominent member of the Hosiery Workers Union in the district was Ken Sanders, who had established the NF Leicester branch with Brandan Willmer in 1969, and who stood as NF parliamentary candidate in February 1974, when he won the NF's highest percentage vote. He immediately mobilized NF supporters in the area in support of the white workers, and was effective enough for a later Race Relations Board enquiry to suggest that both white trade unionists and white management had collaborated in discriminatory practices. An Enoch Powell Support Group was founded inside the factory, a barely-veiled NF group which acted as the co-ordinating force for white opposition to coloured workers' new militancy.

The new trade union policy did not focus solely on the exploitation of racialism on the shop floor. The objective of the NFTUA, established in May 1974, was to offer an alternative leadership within the unions. As Philip Gannaway, ETU shop steward and NF candidate in Bristol put it in *Spearhead*: 'It is imperative that as nationalist trade union members we prove to our fellow workers that we really care about every aspect of their welfare, that our policies embrace what is best in the interests of Britain's future, regardless of class and social status.' The two key weapons were to be firm opposition to the Left and the Communist Party in the unions, and exploitation of racial problems.

The NF proposals for the emergency of the winter of 1973–4 suggested that their vision of legitimate union activity was very different from union orthodoxy. It demanded a system of compulsory arbitration for all industrial disputes for a specific period, and secret ballots for all strike decisions thereafter. (At one point, the Directorate even proposed that workers' wives should have the opportunity to vote on the secret ballot, or at least that the vote should be by post, so that the wife could exert influence when the worker filled in his ballot in the home.)

The NF went on to propose that any trade union official who held or who had ever held a membership card of the Communist Party should be instantly dismissed. (This would have affected their own Directorate member, Michael Lobb.) Furthermore, the NF suggested powers to detain without trial any union leader who sought to sabotage the effort to get industry moving again. It was a vague demand, which could be fiercely interpreted, and seemed to be an attempt to appeal to the feeling of urgency at the time of the three-day week, rather than as a specific point of policy.

But the long-term objective of the NFTUA, as described in the NF Manifesto, is to abolish the present trade union structure in its entirety and replace the present unions of craft with single large unions for each industry. This is a classic facet of the corporate state, as designed by Mussolini. The NF is firmly opposed to the policy of the closed shop, and would forbid workers to take industrial action against attempts by management to de-unionize the work force. The NF also wishes to introduce that key clause of the controversial Tory Industrial Relations Act, and make all agreements between employers and unions legally binding and therefore enforceable in law. It would also introduce a compulsory 'cooling-off' period before a strike could be called.

Feeble as the NF effort was inside the unions, it has been undermined by the growing opposition of the official trade union movement. The general executive council of the TGWU resolved early in 1974 to call on the TUC and the Labour Party 'to mount a campaign to expose the NF as a Fascist organization, pointing out the disastrous effects of Fascism and racialism in the 1930s in Europe which could be repeated in this country now'. In Coventry, Manchester and Kent, local trades councils became the nucleus of anti-fascist committees in 1974, alarmed by the NF's electoral performance and by its new policy of penetrating the unions.

But in one vital sense, the trade union leadership – vehemently opposed to permitting the NF to exploit racialism on the shop floor – have missed the point. The NF activists at the Imperial Typewriters strike directed their propaganda not only at the Asians, but also at the idea of multi-national corporations. Imperial Typewriters is owned by the American-based Litton Industries, and it was an American executive who flew to secret talks with the TGWU union negotiators at Llandudno, where the deal to re-employ the sacked Asian workers and recommence full production was made. And it was American control, as much as Asian workers, which the NF made its target. As Reed-Herbert said in his report: 'The NF has made British workers see just how much their real bosses, the plutocrats of international capitalism snug in their office penthouse suites 3000 miles across the Atlantic, care for British interests and the concerns of British workpeople.'

The once-embarrassing conspiracy theory of international finance was beginning to pay off, as the NF subtly shifted its target of attack to the multi-national corporations, about whose influence the Labour Movement and Labour Party were already concerned. It was a strategy for which the trade union leadership had no answer, and on which the NF trade unionists determined to concentrate.

The trade union action which did most to influence NF thinking in 1974 was, however, the strike of the Ulster Workers' Council against the Sunningdale agreement, and the power-sharing executive of Protestants and Catholics. That strike, massively supported by Ulster workers, reinforced not only the hostility of Ulster Protestants to any compromise with the Catholics, but also underlined the increasing confidence of the trade union movement as a whole in its capacity to overthrow governments and government decisions with which it did not agree. The release of the dockers imprisoned under the Industrial Relations Act's provisions in 1962, the success of the miners' strikes in 1972 and 1974, the defeat of the Heath Government at the 'confrontation' election of February 1974, all pointed to a new militancy, a new confidence and a new sense of power in the trade union movement. The lesson was not lost on Ulster, where Protestant workers like Glen Barr, once known as a militant shop steward at the Du Pont factory in Londonderry, and a supporter of the local Labour Party, decided that their Protestant loyalties demanded an end to power-sharing through industrial action.

It would be unwise to minimize the impact of the support the NF had consistently given the Loyalist movement in Northern Ireland. Not only did *Spearhead* and the NF join in the chorus of attack and fierce opposition to the IRA and their militant campaign for Republicanism. The NF went further. It gave wholehearted support to the principle of a Loyalist state, wholehearted support to the Orange dominance of Stormont, and even acquiesced in the Loyalists' own violent response to the IRA. Tyndall told the 1973 annual conference of the NF: 'The duty of Britain is to fight republicanism and destroy republicanism, not just violent republicanism – as represented by the IRA – but republicanism in every shape and form.' Of the Vanguard movement, which had been widely accused of involvement in acts of counter-terror against the IRA, he waved criticism aside: '[Vanguard] at its most extreme has consisted of a few injudicious political statements and – possibly – physical action against selected opponents.'

In the summer of 1972, the NF helped to organize the London demonstration of the Vanguard movement, at which Tyndall spoke and told the Loyalists 'You have acted in the finest traditions of the British race.' For the rally, he had produced a special issue of *Spearhead* containing an Ulster supplement, which gave the traditional message of the international finance conspiracy a specific Irish dimension.

'The international pressures and the network of conspiracy and violence with which they are linked represent the New Papacy – which is not the same thing as the old Papacy,' he wrote. As an exercise in public relations, this phrase was masterly, embracing what Tyndall wanted to propose in the vocabulary they wanted to hear. He went on:

Ulster protestants and indeed loyal Ulstermen of all creeds would do well to come to grips with the meaning of the New Papacy. Its capital is not Rome and its purposes are not Christian, but it is today the most potent contender for a world monopoly of power. Its financial centre is New York; its forum is the United Nations; it is strangely friendly to the Soviet bloc; its enemy is the survival of national sovereignty, and most of all of British national sovereignty. That is why it is attacking Ulster.

This enthusiasm had to be tempered early in 1974, with members' bulletins stressing that any involvement with para-military bodies would meet with instant expulsion from the NF. But by then, the contacts between Loyalists and the NF were at a very much higher level than simple joint membership among the ordinary ranks. At the 1973 annual conference, the Directorate sought and obtained a mandate from the members to negotiate 'official working alliances with Loyalist movements in Northern Ireland'.

UDA leaders, concerned about these new allies, appealed to London contacts for information about the NF. Through three separate channels, notes on the previous activities and allegiances

159

of the NF leaders were sent to Andy Tyrie, the UDA leader, who studied them and warned his supporters to end any links they might have with NF members. On 5 September, the UDA formally proscribed the NF and Tyrie issued a confidential memorandum which read 'we regard the NF as a neo-Nazi movement', and forbade UDA members to participate in a major rally which the NF had scheduled in London for 7 September.

The NF was very much out of its depth in Ulster, knowing little of the roots of Loyalism, simplistically seeing it as the same kind of nationalism as the NF's own. The NF leaders had little idea of the communal roots and complex social traditions which held Ulster Loyalists together, and misjudged the growing mistrust of all things British which began to affect the Loyalists just at the time when the NF began its Ulster initiative. (At one time during the summer, just after Tyndall's visit, it was being rumoured in the UDA that Tyndall was collecting intelligence for the British Army's SAS unit.) The Loyalists themselves, with the exception of the suspicious UDA, were prepared to use the NF as propagandists for their own cause and opponents of the IRA in Britain, but little more. The Loyalists had their own political wing at Westminster, which was more than the NF could boast. They had the most charismatic of English politicians in Enoch Powell and the security of their Ulster base. The NF needed the Loyalists more than the Loyalists needed the NF.

The NF remained convinced that it had a role to play, and as the war in Ulster began increasingly to send its bombs and its violence over to England, the NF seized its opportunity. The week that twenty people were killed by bombs in Birmingham pubs in November 1974, Roy Painter commented to one reporter 'they couldn't have done more to help us if we paid them'. The day after the explosions, individual NF members were active in the pubs and factories in Birmingham, playing a key role in the sudden strikes and stoppages with which the Birmingham workers marked their own horror at the deaths, and fomenting anti-Irish propaganda in the pubs. In so far as public opinion in Birmingham against the IRA caused what the Home Secretary described as the 'Draconian measures' against the IRA and against travel between Britain and Ireland, the NF more than played its part in mobilizing that opinion.

By the end of 1974, the decision to play the Orange card did not seem to have greatly helped the NF. The fourth of their major policies, their opposition to the EEC, seemed to offer a greater chance of success. The NF had opposed the EEC from the beginning. Before British entry, Tyndall called for NF members to 'Defy the law – be prepared to go to prison too as a gesture of defiance against the imposition of foreign laws on Britain.' He had launched an abortive 'British Resistance' to sabotage the workings of the EEC once Britain formally joined in January 1973. In that month, and in January 1974 the NF organized torchlight marches in opposition. Cynics claimed they also sought the £1,000,000 which Air Vice-Marshal Donald Bennett had promised to put at the disposal of anti-EEC groups, but there can be no doubt of the NF's sincerity. Their espousal of the cause of the white Commonwealth, their staunch British Nationalism and their agricultural policies would alone have ensured their hatred of the Common Market.

During 1973, their opposition seemed almost weary, as though the deed had been done and there could be no reversal. But during 1974, as the NF's conviction grew that Labour too was determined to keep Britain in the EEC (provided, as the Prime Minister Harold Wilson always insisted, that he re-negotiated the right terms), its interest in the EEC revived. As soon as the Wilson Government came to power in March 1974, the NF began to argue that Wilson had no intention of leaving the EEC, and that those electors (including Enoch Powell) who had voted Labour on the grounds that Labour was better than Europe, were being duped: 'The Government's current renegotiations are just a sham,' Tyndall insisted in *Spearhead* in June. 'The last Labour Government ratted on a previous pledge to oppose the Market . . . the public has been the victim once again of a gigantic confidence trick.'

These four issues, the post-immigration attack on black people born in Britain, opposition to the EEC, Ulster and the trade unions, set the ideological pattern of the new NF. But the familiar old cause of anti-immigration still had a little life to be exploited. In passing its Immigration Act, the Heath Government had made retrospective the duty to deport illegal immigrants, a measure which had caused deep distress in the coloured community and had given the police the distasteful task of ascertaining the landed status of immigrants with whom they came into contact. The Labour Government repealed this measure when it came to power, and on 15 June the NF held a protest march against what it called 'the amnesty sell-out'. But the march itself was to gain the NF more publicity and more public recognition than any of the causes it had hitherto espoused.

The NF's growth had alarmed the Left. The various factions

of the extreme Left, the International Marxist Group, the International Socialists, the Communist Parties, Marxist-Leninist and Maoist, and trade union representatives and Labour MPs combined under the banner of the Liberation group to stage a counter-demonstration. Liberation was the new name of the Movement for Colonial Freedom. It had no history of violence and no reputation for militancy. Its intention was to march to Red Lion Square, and demonstrate outside the venue for the NF meeting in the Conway Hall. The result was bloody and confused. One young student named Kevin Gately was killed, whether by the chaos that resulted from a police charge to clear the square, whether from trampling or crushing or from a violent fall we do not know. People who were in Moscow at the time and saw a TASS news film of the violence have reported that they saw Gately struck by a police truncheon. But his death gave Red Lion Square a permanent place in the mythology of the British Left.

The NF had not been involved. They had marched in orderly ranks, to the step of their drums, with their massed files of Union Jacks waving in the summer afternoon. They had obeyed police instructions, had amended their route when requested, and were able to file into their hall and hold their meeting. But to clear the streets for the NF, the police had had to withstand one deliberate charge upon their cordon by the International Marxist Group contingent. The Police had then charged with Special Patrol Group reinforcements and mounted policemen into the ranks of the militant Left to force them from the Square. And finally, having ordered the NF to march in another direction, the police charged another cordon of the Left, clearing a path which the NF did not need. This final charge caused chaos and fear in the crowd. It led to individual acts of police violence against demonstrators and it gave the far Left permanent ammunition in its long arguments against the police as the physical weapon of the Establishment.

The tragic events of that afternoon gave the NF further ammunition for its own attacks upon the violence of the Left. But both sides had distributed the kind of literature and propaganda in the weeks before the march which made some kind of clash almost inevitable. For the Left, the message was 'Smash the Nazi Front'. The IMG's paper *Red Weekly* reminded its readers of 'the policy that the ultra-right must be stopped by any means necessary'. The Communist *Morning Star* asked its supporters to 'Show your hatred of NF propaganda'. For its part, the cover of the NF's *Spearhead* asked 'Left-wing extremists – has tolerance

gone far enough?' An inside article demanded 'Red violence –
will we have to meet force with force?' The same issue carried
a long obituary by Tyndall on Frank Clifford, the veteran of
Mosley's BUF who had just died as NF vice-chairman.

Tyndall recounted pleasant afternoons spent taking tea with
Clifford, when 'he would recall with a glint and a chuckle some
particularly lively political encounters of the 1930s in which
Communists who had come to smash up patriotic meetings
were repaid in their own coin by being hurled from a balcony or
dispatched from the scene on the end of a well-aimed British
fist or boot.'

Violence hung above both marches on that afternoon, but it
was the NF which emerged as the innocent victims of political
violence, the Left who emerged as the instigators, and it was a
21-year-old student who died. The police, as ever, were in the
middle, praised by some for a restraint which they did not show,
bitterly attacked as the brutal thugs they were not by others.

For the rest of the summer, the NF had to march with police
escorts and a concentrated band of left-wing counter-
demonstrators. In August, the NF organized a march in Leicester,
the scene of the Imperial Typewriters dispute, and 1200 police
protected 1500 NF marchers from 6000 left-wing student and
Asian counter-marchers. On 7 September in London, marching
with almost 2000 people in support of the Ulster Loyalists,
the NF was forced to turn aside from its planned route to Hyde
Park, which was occupied by 7000 opponents, and move to the
other side of London. Heavily outnumbered, and with many
middle-aged people and women in its ranks, the NF column
would almost certainly have been roughly handled without police
protection. NF members had no such fears. Or as Walter Barton
told the meeting which followed in Red Lion Square – 'It's time
to turn our young men loose on the Reds.'

It was a tragic and vicious new element to intrude in the traditionally staid British political life. And it served to unsettle yet
further those observers who saw in rising inflation, a minority
government, trade union militancy and the growth of the extreme
Right, currents of violence and the irrational which echoed the
sinister times of Europe in the 1930s. It also served to take the
NF into the October general election more widely known than
ever before. The elections and the demonstrations of 1974 had
made the NF into a household name. Its canvassers reported
that voters no longer looked blank when asked if they would vote
for the NF. The movement was nationally recognized.

*

When Tyndall took over the party chairmanship from O'Brien in July 1972, and centred all of the NF's activities in the new Croydon HQ, his personal control over the NF was assured. *Spearhead*, membership, publicity, administration, recruiting and policy all came under his sway. His lieutenant, Martin Webster, maintained a firm grip on the functions of all the branches through his role as national activities organizer. It was he who organized the coaches for rallies, he who controlled the budget for provincial activities, and, as disciplinary officer, he had power of expulsion. As paymaster of the NF, provider of its HQ and of its office equipment, and major subsidizer of *Spearhead*, Gordon Brown was a vital ally. His own home and the centre of his business were in Croydon, minutes away from HQ, and in spite of Tyndall's distress at Brown's coup against Chesterton, Brown's association with Tyndall from their days in the GBM seemed guarantee enough of his fidelity.

Tyndall's control over the provincial groups was extended during his period of chairmanship. Branch activity was monitored monthly by the Directorate. and assessed annually. Specific targets were set for each branch, and the minimum obligation included buying and distributing 3000 leaflets per week, selling 100 copies of *Spearhead* each month, 300 copies of the irregularly appearing NF newssheet *Britain First* and fighting at least one council election each year. With *Spearhead* costing 10p, *Britain First* costing 5p and leaflets at an average sale cost of £1.25 per thousand, this meant a minimum branch expenditure of £480 a year, which went directly to HQ. In addition to these minimum obligations, branch targets were expected to be set progressively higher, with parliamentary election goals being set in 1974, and minimum attendance ratios imposed upon branches for 'major national activities'. Individual groups, by mid-1974, were expected to fulfil what had once been the branch obligation of fighting one local election a year. These regular expenditures on HQ materials had to be paid in advance to stimulate local fund-raising.

The available evidence for the NF's sources of money overwhelmingly suggest that it is a self-financed body, permanently short of funds, and constantly urging its branches to be self-supporting. Several branches, such as Leicester, Birmingham, Blackburn, Enfield, Camden, Haringey and Hounslow are able to finance their own election activities and all branches cover at least a proportion of their costs. NF subscriptions are £2 a year for each member, and all of this money is forwarded to National HQ – any idea of giving branches a guaranteed income from a proportion of subscriptions is actively discouraged. It was proposed at one annual conference and defeated, with the argument that branches raised funds more effectively if they were totally responsible for their own finances. The best estimates of dues-paying members approach 20,000, which suggests a £40,000 income for HQ in 1974. The financial obligations of each branch to purchase £500 of publications from HQ each year meant an income of at least £15,000 from branches and £10,000 from groups in 1974, although much of this has to be spent on purchase of materials.

The NF takes a great deal of money at the collections which are a regular feature of its rallies. These 'Dutch auctions' are invariably orchestrated by Webster, whose talent it is. The sums have grown with the membership. In July 1972, the summer rally raised £300, in 1973 it raised £645 and in 1974, the collection just topped £1000. Remembrance Day rallies have always been a reliable source, collecting £320 in 1971, £564 in 1972, £1240 in 1973 and just over £1000 in 1974, when the rally had to be held in the open air, and many members drifted away from the cold. Regional marches also hold collections, taking £230 in Huddersfield in March 1973, and £400 in Leicester in August 1974, swiftly followed by £600 at the pro-Ulster march in London in September.

Election meetings too are milked of their loose change. One at Watford in February 1974 raised £132 from a meeting of perhaps 100 people. Branch bulletins regularly report the money the events raise, from Camden's £82 profit from a jumble sale, to £72 from a sponsored swim by a young member in Manchester, and £133 from a dance in Haringey.

For the 1974 elections, HQ went into debt to provide election materials and leaflets for branches without ready cash. By November of 1974, this had become an acute problem, and the members' bulletin appealed: 'It is essential that central NF funds be refurbished immediately. This need is very urgent.'

Allowing for subscriptions, collections, profits from publications and ties and special appeals, the NF Central fund received at least £50,000 in 1974. The heaviest expenses were salaries of five paid staff, which totalled about £11,000, and election subsidies to poor branches. Candidates were expected, where possible, to furnish their own deposits, but HQ had to contribute in October when many candidates argued that they could not afford to lose £150 twice in one year. Of the total sum of £21,600 which the NF paid in lost deposits in 1974, over £7000 came from central funds. The NF's total expenditure in 1974, with two elections, five major rallies to organize, election printing costs and running expenses must have approached £100,000 (at the AGM in January 1975, the NF treasurer announced that turnover for 1974 had been £100,000), and it seems a reasonable assumption that rather more than half came from central funds, with branches and groups providing the rest. The largest individual donation – which was anonymous – to which the NF has admitted in public was £400 – although its 1973 election fund was launched with an anonymous donation of £1000.

If members cannot give money, they are expected to give time, and every effort is made to promote activities which involve them. Leafleting, for example, has always been a vital branch function; through letter boxes, in shopping centres, pubs, outside schools, the leaflets are a year-round duty. As early as 1968, Denis Pirie reported to the annual conference that a million leaflets had been distributed that year. By August 1971, over three million anti-EEC leaflets had been sent out to branches, and four million were delivered in 1972–3, the bulk of them attacking the Ugandan Asian arrival. Members were advised in November 1974 that 'hundreds of thousands' of various leaflets were now ready for distribution. Each branch's obligation to purchase 3000 leaflets a week means a minimum distribution of five million in 1974.

Different leaflets are aimed at different markets. There is one for schoolchildren which reads 'Are you tired of younger students being bullied or subjected to the alien cult of mugging? . . . Are you tired of lessons where the teacher has to go at a snail's pace to allow immigrant kids who don't speak English a chance to keep up . . . Are you tired of having to endure social studies or history lessons where the teacher continually tries to run down Britain, while at the same time Black kids have "Black Studies" to give them more self-respect and Black pride?'

Older students have two leaflets, 'Don't be bullied by the crackpots and gangsters of the extreme Left' and one which demands 'Does your student union represent you?'. There is one message to the troops in Ulster: 'We ask all serving soldiers in Ulster to recognize the Loyalist community in Ulster as their friends and as their allies', and one for the factory gates which asks: 'Does your trade union represent you?' Other leaflets attack immigration, drug traffickers, appeal for law and order, for a moral 'clean-up' of Britain, against the EEC, against inflation and against two-party politics, and there is an all-purpose recruiting leaflet: 'Do you care about your country?' They all contain the NF HQ address for further information, and the

166

bulk of them contain membership application forms. There is a special message for 'all those who value personal independence and private enterprise'. It is entitled: 'Can the independent businessman survive?', and is addressed to that class of shop-keepers, traders and owners of small firms which have made up the bulk of populist nationalist groups from Germany in the 1930s to Poujade's movement in France in the 1950s. The leaflet attacks the monopolies, the 'big business' chain stores and viciously attacks the immigrant traders – 'alien-owned businesses are able to survive – even prosper – because the authorities turn a blind eye to practices which would not be tolerated on the part of British traders: sub-standard, dangerous or unhygienic premises, very low staff wages or no wages at all to "members of the family", employment of minors, etc.'

Members are also encouraged to write frequently to their local press and to their Councils and MPs, conveying a permanent impression of grass-roots opinion behind the NF. *Spearhead* even runs a competition each month, awarding a prize for the best letter printed in a local newspaper. The NF has claimed that its Melton Mowbray group was formed when a flood of enquiries followed a letter on the need to support British troops in Ulster which appeared in the *Leicester Mercury*. 'By diligent attention to this activity,' *Spearhead* encourages, 'many people have got the name of the NF widely known in their areas.' One letter to the *Birmingham Mail* in September 1974, purporting to come from a black American stationed in Britain, warned of the horrors of racial violence in his own country and advised immigrants to apply for repatriation and British people to vote for the NF. Subsequent checking established that his avowed unit, the 22nd Air Strike Unit, was not based at the airfield he claimed, that the USAF had no records of the Lee J. Dickson who signed the letter, and that the purported rank of Leading Airman did not exist in the USAF.

NF members are encouraged to take part in local community affairs and use them as recruiting grounds. In Accrington, the NF has organized a local protest against the establishment of a prisoners' hostel in a residential area. In Blackburn, Kingsley Read was elected chairman of the Residents' Liaison Committee to oppose a council plan to demolish 4000 houses. The committee included Tory and Labour councillors, and when the local council said they would accept a delegation if Read was not included, Read maintained the support of the group and led them in a protest march. George Bowen, NF election candidate in West Bromwich, led a delegation of old-age pensioners to the town hall in protest against their noisy (immigrant) neighbours. In Newham, the NF ran a housing advisory service for local people; 'We upstaged the Liberals in community politics,' commented Lobb after his by-election success in the constituency.

The Waltham Forest Residents' Association was founded by Michael Burrows, the local NF organizer. Its aims were published in a leaflet 'to fight for the rights of the indigenous people of this borough, which is of course mainly English . . . more is done for unwanted aliens, while many of our own continue to be homeless and jobless and our old folk and infirm are almost totally ignored.' Eleven of the fifteen committee members finally resigned in disgust at the direction the Association was taking. One of them, Ron Bateman, told the local press of his alarm at Burrows and his secretary Cyril Brewer: 'I would hate this thing to get that big, where you would have these two calling the tune – it could be nasty.'

The NF's strategy of infiltration is not confined to the Monday Club and the Conservative Party. Ratepayers' and Residents' Associations are prime targets. After questions in Birmingham Council, the NF organizer Peter Dawson admitted to the *Birmingham Mail*: 'We have decided to make some sort of approach to ratepayers' associations.' When the Hunt Saboteurs' Association launched a magazine called *Howl*, which contained strident attacks upon Jewish and Moslem ritual methods of slaughter, investigation found that its editor was NF student secretary David McCalden.

Nor did the NF confine its efforts to active organizations. A local report from the Leicester branch referred to its 'systematic cultivation of hundreds of local people who several years ago joined the Leicester anti-immigration movement, which had a life of about two or three years. Having divided NF membership into ward units, each was allocated a section of the lapsed AIM membership. Each month, the AIM members were given a personal visit, at which time they received a selection of free NF literature. Many have now agreed to join a voluntary subscription scheme whereby they agree to donate 25p to branch funds each month and receive copies of *Spearhead* and *Britain First*. A hundred AIM members, so far, have been drawn into the NF orbit by these means.'

The NF likes to maintain the morale of its members, and attract new recruits by regularly launching immigration scare stories. *Spearhead* and *Britain First* gleefully co-operate in providing these phased boosts to anti-immigrant feeling. From April 1971, with a 'Blacks hired – Whites fired' cover on *Spear-*

ead, to 'Labour plans new coloured invasion' in April 1972, o 'Kenyan Asian invasion menace' in September 1973 and Thousands of Kenyan Asians on the way – target Britain' as *Britain First*'s headline in October 1974, the thrust was maintained.

It was accompanied by the same kind of phased alarms over mmigrant health. Leprosy and TB were the key issues, with a *Spearhead* cover in 1969 screaming 'Leprosy in Britain – the idden facts'. It was a topic to which NF publications returned hroughout 1973, to continue the momentum of support which hey had won from the arrival of the Ugandan Asians. Immigraion scares, health scares, attacks on what it calls the 'Race Relations Industry', are the standard forms of NF propaganda, nd clearly represent the favourite field of operation. The NF eized gratefully upon the controversial conclusions of scientists ike Jensen and Eysenck who suggested that there may be ongenital differences between the races in such barely-measurble aspects of human capacity as innate intelligence. As Webster vrote in April 1973: 'The most important factor in the build-up f self-confidence among "racists" and the collapse of morale mong multi-racialists was the publication in 1969 by Professor Arthur Jensen in the *Harvard Educational Review*.'

The NF deliberately sought opportunities to challenge the Race Relations Act, arguing that British people had the right to iscriminate. The NF was convinced that such opposition would ring them not only publicity, but widespread public support.

The NF took comfort in the fact that its campaigns and s policies were having a measurable impact upon the two ajor parties. It collected a special file of acknowledgements om other politicians of the impression the NF made, and used ie quotations in the constituencies to stress their own importnce. And some parliamentary candidates were clearly frightened f the NF threat. In Huddersfield West, the Conservative John tansfield was driven to appeal in February 1974: 'There are ertain things in me which I think those who voted NF will find ttractive. I have, for example, strong views on crime and unishment.' Another hopeful Tory candidate in Birmingham alled upon the local NF with his deputy chairman to appeal to ie NF to stand down from the election – and he offered to lefray their expenses'. In Leicester in October, the Labour MP om Bradley ruefully admitted to the *Guardian*: 'Some of my ormer supporters will be voting for the NF this time. The ousewives in the streets, the men in the clubs, everybody wants o talk about immigrants. They're obsessed.'

169

By the October election, the Labour Party had acknowledged the NF to the point of forbidding Labour candidates to appear with NF candidates on public platforms or on radio and television. In effect, if there was to be a public debate between the candidates, the Labour representative had to walk out rather than appear with the NF. Under the broadcasting rules of fair access for all candidates, this meant that the broadcast simply did not take place. This hurt the NF, but the real threat to their opportunity to present their arguments to the public came from the far Left. Its several groups had declared a policy of mobilizing against the NF wherever possible, of demonstrating outside the halls where the NF met, and asking landlords to ban the NF, of physical occupation of places where the NF was scheduled to meet, and of vocal and even violent opposition to all NF speakers. The National Union of Students declared a policy of no platform for racialists, on college territory, at its 1974 annual conference.

The NF could also plead that it was not a neo-fascist movement, but that it was a wholly legal, wholly respectable political party with a sound and well-established national organization and a coherent national policy. Accordingly, it could insist upon a right to present its case to the electorate, it could demand police protection for its meetings and could accuse its violent opponents of 'Red Fascism'. Its opponents retorted that the NF would not permit free speech if it came to power. They pointed to the NF's insistence that Nationalism be taught in schools, that Communist Party members be expelled from union posts, and they pointed to the venom with which Tyndall regarded the media. He had written to the BBC after its programme on the NF in 1972, to attack it as 'a politically prejudiced organization, riddled with extreme Leftists prepared to use totalitarian techniques to demolish their opponents . . . there will come a time when these termites will have cause to bitterly regret their behaviour.'

The NF and the far Left had been on a collision course long before the Red Lion Square demonstration. There had been attacks on NF speakers, demonstrations at their meetings and their conferences since 1967. Webster had been beaten up three times, and NF offices had been raided, homes of NF officials had been visited by people masquerading as police officers who sought to remove documents. A state of ideological guerrilla war had been in intermittent progress for years.

The NF itself was frankly alarmed at the growth of opposition and initially unsure of its physical capacity to meet it. In November 1972, Webster complained that the use of violence against the

NF was an Establishment plot, designed to stop the NF before grew to be a threat:

If the name of the NF can be associated in the public mind more with violent incidents than with legitimate political expression, then a potentially serious threat to the Government could be neutralized. In giving the wink to the Red terrorists, the Government is deliberately encouraging a post-war tradition of violent conflict along the lines of that which existed in the 1930s, in the hope that the emergent Nationalist movement will dissipate, discredit and neutralize itself after the manner of the Mosleyites . . . it is vital that Nationalists observe a strict discipline and refrain from any precipitate action.

o the NF claimed that the left-wing militants were the tool of a ostile Government, and the left-wing claimed that the Government's tool was the NF. But as the NF grew in strength from 972, it also grew more confident, and more determined to sist the Left from its own resources.

By the Red Lion Square demonstration, the NF was still ware of its dependence on police protection against massed pposition, but had evolved its own rudimentary defence structure for the march. The row of men lined up around the drum and had been instructed to gather as 'defence groups' in case f attempts at disruption, and fleet-footed young members were nt ahead to ensure that side streets did not contain anti-NF emonstrators. At the front and rear of the march, two groups f 150 men had been stationed with instructions to link arms to lock any attacks. It was a defensive arrangement, and one that ad been heralded by the warning in that month's *Spearhead*: 'Red violence – will we have to meet force with force?'

These 'defence groups' had become, by the 1974 Remembrance Day parade, an organized body of tough young militants who ore the name of the 'Honour Guard'. Webster made his promise at the time had come 'to turn and smash our enemies into a ulp'. (Ironically, the immediate effect of this speech at the eeting was to confirm the Populists in their determination to ject Tyndall and Webster from what they believed was otherise a legitimate political party.)

1974 saw the development of a kind of verbal arms race etween the NF and the Left. Both sides could have quoted Dr Goebbels – 'Whoever controls the streets controls the masses nd whoever controls the masses controls the state' – but the

171

militant Left saw its strategy in terms of Hitler's admission i 1933 – 'Only one thing could have stopped our movement – our adversaries had understood its principle and from the fir day had smashed with the utmost brutality the nucleus of ot new movement.'

The Left and the NF have discreetly infiltrated each other organizations since 1967, following a tradition which stretche back to the militant Jewish 43 Group, founded to oppose Mosle and the League of Ex-Servicemen in the immediate post-wa period. To meet the threat of Colin Jordan in the early 1960 veterans of the 43 Group founded a 62 Group, under the loos control of Harry Bidney, manager of the Limbo Club in Soh and a man with close contacts throughout the British under world. Bidney paid at least one spy inside the NSM £7 a wee for copying letters and repeating phone messages. The spy, young man called Peter Compton, lived in the NSM HQ a Arnold Leese House, and was ejected from the NSM when h was overheard telephoning Bidney.

The infiltration game is now very much more organized depending less on the planting of individual infiltrators than upo the sophisticated build-up of card index and photo files c opponents. The flavour is caught best by this extract from th NF members' bulletin of November 1974:

> As the NF grows, attacks on it in the form of direct violence printed smear attacks, infiltration, subversion and the lik will be stepped up. This being so, it is necessary for us t further expand our facilities for keeping 'tabs' on thos enemies of our party who seek to oppose it by other tha lawful, constitutional and democratic means. This means th left wing in general and also some organizations and person who have a seemingly respectable Establishment image. A members – but particularly organizers – are asked to send t our research department at head office the following material all copies of all leaflets, booklets, magazines or newspaper which attack the NF . . . Letters attacking the NF publishe in any local paper or any other publication should also b sent in, appropriately marked.

Thus far, a mundane intelligence job. But the bulletin continues

> Trade Unionists should send in the minutes of any Branch c Regional Committee meetings where action against the N is discussed. The names and addresses of known left-win

extremists active in promoting anti-NF activity within trade unions should be supplied. Organizers should keep their own cross-reference filing system on hostile organizations and hostile individuals operational in their districts, and should arrange for such activists – including street sellers of extreme left wing publications – to be photographed and the photographs filed. The development of our party's self-defence arrangements becomes absolutely crucial as our party grows.

is important to note, however, that the escalation of the ar of words was the work of the extremists within the NF and xtremists within the Left. In neither body was there any sign of verall determination to take their opposition to the extreme of reet warfare. The real cause of their hostility was that they both w themselves as revolutionaries against the liberal capitalism ' the British state. They each desired passionately to win the legiance of the working class, and to destroy their opponents. s Tyndall told the Essex Monday Club, the NF's aim was ne complete and final political eclipse of the Left . . . to accom-ish this means winning over millions of working class voters a patriotic and non-leftist movement.'

The passionate vocabulary of the Left, and the equally pas-onate speeches of Tyndall and Webster suggested that they ere unsuccessful rivals for the support of the same social groups neither Tyndall nor the Trotskyists had made any real headway ithin the mass of the British Labour Movement, and until they d the violence of which they spoke was unlikely to materialize.

he NF entered the October 1974 election with a new Directorate, ected for the first time by postal ballot. The organization was isty enough for some members to receive no ballot papers, and r the closing date to be quickly revised when it became plain at the organization could not cope. Widespread criticism, d hints that the HQ staff might have their own ulterior motives r losing ballot papers, led to demands that future elections be vigilated by the independent Electoral Reform group. NF embers in the Midlands were most distressed – their only presentative on the new Directorate was Reed-Herbert. He as joined by the Populist Roy Painter. The rumblings in the Iidlands had been made the more ominous by a number of efections from the Leicester branch, led by its former chairman ohn Kynaston. They joined the local Enoch Powell support roup, led by Stan Wright, to establish an English National arty. On 7 August, the ENP attended a meeting at Derby with

173

the new and tiny United party, with whom they were to unit
for the October election. It was a minor loss for the NF, but
troublesome reminder that all was not well with the Midlands

Equally worrying for Tyndall and Webster was the increasin
amount of comment in the better informed of the informatio
journals circulating in anti-fascist groups about Painter's plan
for a Populist coup against them. One such, which was bein
widely circulated in Jewish circles in July 1974, read: 'Tyndal
and Webster have been manoeuvring to prevent the coup whic
Painter has said he can achieve at the next AGM by bringin
back such old hard-liners as Andrew Brons, Peter Williams an
Andrew Fountaine, the old leader of the BNP.' (This pamphle
might have been better-informed – it described Williams as a
18B detainee during the Second World War, when in fact h
fought with the British Army in 1940, having left Mosley befor
war began.)

Nonetheless, the NF went into the October elections stronge
and larger and better organized than ever before. Its membershi
had tripled in the last two years, and during 1974 had grow
dramatically in certain areas thanks to the publicity of the Feb
ruary elections and the demonstrations. In Birmingham, fo
example, membership leapt from rather more than 50 at the star
of the year to almost 200 in October. Moreover, the branch wa
self-financing, through an ingenious system of tote cards and o
collecting waste paper and selling it for an income of £100
week. Enfield branch was making £1000 a year from its wine an
cheese parties. Birmingham's growth was to continue after th
election with the division of the branch into four constituenc
groups. Whether all the new members were active is anothe
matter. The Birmingham branch newsletter for October com
plained of the election campaign that 'despite nearly a three
fold increase in branch membership we had practically the sam
number of helpers as at the last election'.

The NF were able to field 90 candidates, once again winnin
the TV broadcasting time which they valued so highly. The
even had a candidate in Scotland – hoping to attract the Orang
vote, he secured a miserable 86 votes. Once again there was n
NF breakthrough, and every candidate lost his deposit. Th
national poll was 6 per cent lower than in February, with 72·
per cent of the electorate voting, compared to 78·7 per cent i
February. The NF increased its average vote by 0·3 per cent
which is rather more impressive when we recall that 44 new seat
were being fought. Leicester, in the wake of Kynaston's defection
suffered a slight fall in its votes. One NF candidate had won ove

174

per cent of the vote in February – the feat was not to be repeated in October. In the West Midlands, two out of eight NF candidates had won more than 7 per cent in February – in October, not one of the ten candidates could attain that figure.

The post-election members' bulletin pleaded that every NF candidate faced Liberal opposition in October, that NF funds had been exhausted after the February effort and that branches were making superhuman efforts to fight as many seats as possible. In eighteen of the seats which the NF had also fought in February, its vote fell – although in seven of these cases there was a Liberal candidate in October, and six of the branches concerned were fighting more seats than in February. In all, the NF received 113,625 votes – although Tyndall had privately hoped for 200,000. Without one key region, the vote would have been at that tantalizing stage where it was respectable enough to be mildly encouraging, but too static to give that vital promise of success. The key region was Greater London, where the NF vote had risen sharply and spread thoroughly across the north and west of the city.

In February, 22 seats had been fought in Greater London – in October the NF fought 36. In February, only one candidate had got more than 7 per cent, and one other had won over 5 per cent. But in October, six candidates won over 7 per cent, and three more won over 5 per cent. In February, seven candidates had won less than 2·5 per cent of the vote – but only four did so badly in October, although thirteen seats were being contested for the first time.

One of the surprises of the London vote was the amount of NF support that had lain unexploited. Of the seats which gained more than 7 per cent of the poll, three had not been fought before by the NF. From Newham on the River to Tottenham in the north of London, there ran a swathe of NF support of at least 5 per cent of the poll. Moreover, the three London candidates who did particularly well, Robin May in Shoreditch with 9·4 per cent, Roy Painter in Tottenham with 8·3 per cent and Keith Squires in Wood Green with 8 per cent, were all identified with the party's Populist group.

A further rash of anti-NF leaflets during the February election had swung more waverers into the Populist camp during the campaign. The discontent in the Midlands branches, fuelled by disappointing election results, swung further against Tyndall. He and Webster had performed badly on a critical TV programme in September, and in the NF's election broadcast its candidate for Blackburn, the Tory convert Kingsley Read, had been

175

tremendously impressive. Bearing a close physical resemblance to the American politician George Wallace, he gave the same impression of being a plain-spoken, common man, speaking for the people against the intellectuals and the planners and the arrogant politicians who could be blamed for the nation's problems.

Painter, who feared that the widespread discussion of his Populist threat and of his ambitions within the NF had made his own candidacy too controversial at this early stage (he had been in the party for only sixteen months) was happy to support Kingsley Read's candidacy against Tyndall. Reed-Herbert, John Fairhurst and Tony Webber, who were Painter's closest allies on the new Directorate, agreed. And the Populists had won a new and vital recruit in Gordon Brown, who had organized the putsch against Chesterton four years earlier. The Populists were also convinced that they had the votes of Richard Lawson, Ted Arthurton and John Sandland. Even one of the old hardliners from the National Socialist Movement, Peter Holland, whom Tyndall had brought in to bolster his own position on the Directorate, decided to support Painter. The Populists also believed up till the vote itself that they could count on the vote of the Manchester organizer Walter Barton.

Tyndall suspected that a plot was afoot. He took Painter to lunch the week before the vote to ask if he could count on Painter's support. Painter said he would wait and see. The morning of the Directorate meeting at which the vote for the Chairmanship would take place, Tyndall realized that his support was dwindling. He spent much of the available time with Barton, and apparently persuaded him to switch his support back to Tyndall. At the vote, the two sides tied with ten votes each for Tyndall and Kingsley Read. But Tony Reed-Herbert was acting chairman for the vote, and his casting vote went against Tyndall. Kingsley Read then took the chair, and the vote for deputy chairman between Tyndall and Painter was again tied, ten votes to each man. This time the casting vote went in Tyndall's favour. The Populists had made their point. Tyndall was not supreme in the party, and by giving him the deputy-chairmanship they hoped to minimize the chances of his organizing an immediate counter-coup. They had under-estimated the man. He began immediately to plan re-election to the chairmanship at the next annual conference.

His hope in this was those 'young men' Barton had wanted to turn on the Reds after Red Lion Square. At the Remembrance Day parade in November, Tyndall followed Roy Painter to the platform. As soon as he stepped forward, the 40 young men of the 'Honour Guard', those who carried the Union Jacks and had marched as a disciplined squad from the Cenotaph to the meeting, surged forward like some Praetorian Guard. The flags waved with their cheers and the stamping of their feet. It looked like some ancient *comitatus* welcoming the warrior chief. Tyndall made a brilliant rousing speech, overshadowing Painter and the other speakers. As Tyndall ended his speech, the Honour Guard surged forward and roared their approval again. Webster spoke in the same vein, and spoke directly to the flag-waving young men to promise them 'the time is now for us to turn and smash our enemies into a pulp'.

For Tyndall and Webster, the thought of losing this movement they had so carefully built and nurtured for the past seven years, of not profiting from the ten and fifteen years they had spent in Nationalist politics, was simply intolerable. They were determined to win it back.

SEVEN

The Populist Split
and the National Front Revival

The mild success of the October 1974 election created a sense of euphoria among the less cool-headed members of the NF Directorate. Gordon Brown's proposal that the next general election – probably four or five years hence – should see 318 NF candidates was greeted by acclamation in the party. The objective was to wring more broadcasting time from the authorities, and to maintain the momentum of morale for the mass of the party. Simultaneously, Roy Painter launched a plan, of which little more was to be heard, for the NF to purchase a large house in central London as a permanent HQ. It was to be equipped with a bar, social club, dormitories, offices and large meeting rooms. He had counted on securing a large loan from a brewing company, but the brewers cautiously refused to commit themselves.

Behind these offerings of bread and circuses for the membership, the Directorate embarked upon its civil war. Tyndall's supporters were first in the field with a communication from his supporters in Kent to all NF candidates, agents, branches and groups. It spoke of Tyndall's loss of the chairmanship as 'the first step in a well-planned attempt to get rid of a number of very long-standing senior officials of the movement . . . by a power-hungry faction . . . This faction has been attempting to solicit support for its action by lobbying other members of the Directorate and local officers of the Party, by telephone and other means, over a considerable period of time.' This document, which went on to claim that the 'Populist' faction was working in collusion with 'a left-wing columnist of the *Guardian* newspaper, who is known to be a vicious enemy of the NF', was signed by five senior members of the NF in Kent. They included David Smith the Regional Agent, John Moreland, the Thanet chairman and Kenneth McKilliam, the Ashford Secretary.

This was to be the first of a series (and finally a flood) of such open letters and broadsheets, from both sides of the impending split, as 1975 progressed. They became steadily more scurrilous, culminating in a bizarre and scrubby communication in October 1975 which talked of mass homosexuality among Tyndall's supporters. Nicknames like 'The Daisy Chain' and 'The Fairy Ring' became common, to the bewilderment of the vast bulk of the members who were not in the know. The impact of this campaign is hard to assess. The notes were circulated primarily among branch and regional officials, and not all the members had very much idea what was going on.

In *Spearhead* and *Britain First*, there were regular articles warning against internal troublemakers. John Bean, the old BNP activist, was brought back to *Spearhead* in January to write an article on the Left's smear campaigns, which he warned were not aimed at the average voter, but at causing disunity in the NF. Martin Webster, in the same issue, again warned of the enemy within in an article entitled 'How you could help kill the NF', which included a series of side-swipes against 'the trimmers, the popularity-seekers and moderates' – by which he meant the Populists.

The first public sign of the bitterness of the split came at the Annual General Meeting in January, when Tyndall was greeted with jeers and boos of 'Nazi, Nazi'. Tyndall in turn launched an attack on Richard Lawson, the young editor of *Britain First*. Tyndall listed his objections to the way Lawson presented the NF in the publication, including Lawson's rejection of the leader cult, his rejection of Mussolini, and his analysis of the structure of the NF Directorate. Even for the NF members, this was arcane stuff, and so Lawson widely distributed his own reply, accusing Tyndall of 'a totally dishonest attempt at character assassination'. Lawson went on to describe the opposition and cat-calls he received at the AGM as 'a public whipping-up of emotional hysteria and clearly definable public factionalism'.

As the cracks within the structure of the NF became more apparent, the external threats also began to appear more threatening. Chairman Kingsley Read, who had hoped to make a *cause célèbre* of his dispute with the Race Relations Board over his appeal to the home-owners of Bradford to sell only to British buyers, faced a large and hostile demonstration in Manchester when he led a 400-strong NF march against the RRB. By this time, the Left had organized its opposition to the point where NF public appearances invariably found themselves opposed.

The election of Mrs Margaret Thatcher to the leadership of the Conservative Party promised a tougher Tory stance on the kinds of issue, like immigration, terrorism, Ulster and law and order, which the NF had hoped to make their own. Almost as a reflex, *Spearhead* and *Britain First* began to attack the new Conservative Party, and the private armies formed by Colonel David Stirling and General Sir Walter Walker. But again this had to be seen in terms of the NF's internal row. In *Britain First*, the attack on

Walker and Stirling became a barely-disguised attack on the authoritarian tendencies of John Tyndall: 'People like Walker and Stirling claim to be anti-Communist but offer no ideological alternative other than vague ideas of authority, order and discipline. These are, of course, the hallmarks of any authoritarian state.'

By the spring of 1975, the misfortunes of the party had begun to assume the pace and scale of a Greek tragedy. Membership and new recruitment had begun to stagnate, and even decline, except in a few personal strongholds such as Blackburn and North London. An increasing proportion of the energies of the key regional and national organizers was being expended in the internal rows – so much so that only 60 candidates fought in the 1975 municipal elections, and only five of them won more than 10 per cent of the vote. The previous year, 73 candidates had stood in London alone.

The great effort of the NF during the year was to have been campaigning against the Common Market, a campaign to last through the spring and culminate in the national referendum on the EEC in June. The NF had also believed that by being part of the anti-EEC coalition, which included Conservatives, Labour, trade unionists and other respectable elements of British politics, it too would come into the acceptable mainstream of British politics. This was foreseen by a number of Labour and Conservative politicians, and in March 1975, the National Referendum Campaign, the umbrella organization for voting No in the referendum, took a private decision to bar the NF as well as extreme Left groups. Mr Neil Marten, the Conservative anti-Market MP, replied to the NF application for affiliation in curt terms: 'Your letter was discussed but your request for affiliation turned down.'

In April, the NF appealed to Mr Edward Short, Leader of the House of Commons and the referendum referee, claiming unfair treatment. They quoted a bulletin from the Hertfordshire branch of the Campaign which stated that 'members of most political parties are welcome to join the NRC, except members of the NF'. The NF response was to disrupt the next NRC meeting, held at the Conway Hall in London on 13 April. Some 200 NF supporters went to the Hall, on instructions from the party's HQ, to make a peaceful protest and walk out. But the demonstration got out of hand, there were scuffles, attempts by NF members to storm the platform, and the police had to be called to restore order. As a direct result, the NF were banned from using the Hall for three months by the owners, the South Place Ethical

Society. The decision by more than 120 Labour-controlled councils not to permit the NF to use municipal halls for meetings made it even more difficult for the NF to hold any kind of meeting. Indeed, when NF speakers managed to address an anti-EEC meeting in Hackney, where they had been banned by the council, as guests of the Shoreditch women's anti-EEC group, this was portrayed by the NF as a major victory.

The NF was on the defensive. Its very protests against exclusion from council halls smacked more of an underdog crying 'foul' than of a determined party fighting for its right to free speech. In Islington late in March, a major NF demo of more than 1000 supporters protesting against the council ban, depended on massive police protection (over 600 police had to be mobilized) as they marched past some 4000 counter-demonstrators who jeered and booed the NF's Union Jack-bedecked parade, almost hidden by the blue uniforms of the police.

On 12 May, in Oxford, an anti-EEC rally addressed by John Tyndall led to five arrests, and four policemen were injured, as more than 500 demonstrators tried to charge through the police cordon to break into the hall. The streets were blocked for 90 minutes by the fighting, and the NF's Honour Guard, mobilized for the occasion, also entered the fray. One of their leaders was identified as Gordon Callow, a veteran of the old National Socialist Movement.

Twelve days later in Glasgow, there was another riot as the mobilized Left tried to stop an anti-EEC meeting called by the NF. Among the 65 arrested were David Bolton, vice-president of the National Union of Mineworkers, Ian Mackay, secretary of the Scottish Communist Party and John Reidford, general secretary of the Glasgow Trades Council. The NF were reaping the whirlwind of organized opposition that had been sown at Red Lion Square. When the NF meeting finally took place, after Kingsley Read had given the demonstrators an ironic Nazi salute, twelve people attended. The NF later claimed to have been heartened by the way the Glasgow police gleefully went into action against the Left, provoking angry comments of 'Gestapo-tactics' from James Milne, secretary of the Scottish TUC, who was among the demonstrators. Other observers were more struck by the fact that as the police moved in, batons swinging, they were singing a mournful dirge called 'O Flower of Scotland'. It is the anthem of the Scottish National Party.

In short, the NF's anti-EEC campaign failed to get off the ground. The Left had stopped it, and the NF's own leaders were increasingly obsessed with their internal troubles. Sales of NF publications had begun to sag. *Spearhead* had begun 1975 with the cheerful boast that it was now self-supporting and would need no further special appeals. But by June, the appeals began again, with the failure of a special anti-EEC issue, which proved almost unsellable, and the decision of many branches, on the advice of the Directorate, not to distribute the May issue, which contained a lengthy and deeply divisive supplement by John Tyndall on proposed constitutional reforms.

This was but one part of a concerted ideological campaign by Tyndall and his followers against the Populists, re-asserting the old hard line of uncompromising racial nationalism. It had begun in February, with Tyndall writing in *Spearhead* on 'Democracy – What does it mean?' It meant, he concluded, leadership: 'We should believe in it as one of the central props of our political faith. We should recognize that lack of it is precisely what is wrong with our modern society and nation.'

His proposed constitutional reforms reflected his concern. He called for the election by the party of a four-man National Executive, for a term of three years. These four were then to appoint eight chairmen of policy sub-committees. These eight nominees were then to join the four on the National Directorate, which would also contain the regional chairmen, who were elected by the regional membership. The ruling four would each have two votes on the Directorate, the rest one vote each. This was leadership with a vengeance, particularly since the four-man Executive could meet whenever they wished, but the Directorate was to meet every three months, or when summoned by the Executive. These proposals proved offensive to the NF Directorate, the Populists decried them as authoritarian and Tyndall was called to account for having appealed, through *Spearhead*, to the mass membership over the heads of the Directorate.

The Populists on the Directorate, by now an identifiable group of ten, were furious over the circulation of another of the NF *samizdats* which did so much to pollute the atmosphere of NF life during the year. This one, titled 'John Tyndall's case for calling an emergency general meeting of the NF', contained a series of personal attacks upon the ten 'troublemakers'. Roy Painter, the key target, was dismissed as 'a vain, bumptious and insufferably conceited little man who has limitless ambitions . . . a political know-nothing'. John Fairhurst was 'not very different from Painter, but less capable'. Richard Lawson, the editor of *Britain First*, was acknowledged to be 'the most intelligent and literate of the faction. Arrogant and self-opinionated. Ideologically to the Left'. David McCalden, Lawson's close friend, was said to be 'like Lawson, ideologically to the Left, but much more so. Is thought to dominate Lawson and certainly has a lot of influence on him.'

The real poison was reserved for Gordon Brown: 'Real name not Brown but thought to be Marshall. The key figure in the Chesterton trouble and no doubt in the present trouble too. The orchestrator, instigator and co-ordinator of the whole thing. An absolutely evil and poisonous character. Motives: Power, jealousy and personal vindictiveness – particularly against John Tyndall.'

This document, and the charge of going over the Directorate's head, were brought against Tyndall at a Directorate meeting at the Coram Hotel on 14 May. The first 40 minutes were spent searching the room for bugs. None was found. Tyndall denied responsibility for the smear document, and defended his decision to present the constitutional reforms in *Spearhead*, as well as his own informal poll of the membership for their views of his proposals. The result was an unprecedented vote of no confidence in him which was not opposed, not even by Martin Webster. This was his weakest moment. The Directorate decided to consider the matter of his expulsion, and had this been done, Tyndall would have been isolated and left with too little time to mobilize his support.

Kingsley Read hesitated to take this decisive step. He was too unsure of his own position, and Tyndall and Painter each believed at this stage that he had the secret support of the chairman. In fact, it seems more likely that Kingsley Read was hoping to play the two men off against each other, and feared that his own control of the Party would not long survive the eclipse of either. Both had to go, or neither. From this point, Painter's own suspicions of Kingsley Read began. Painter and Brown had hoped for clean, surgical exclusion of an isolated Tyndall. Kingsley Read's hesitation condemned the NF to a continuing wrangle, and Tyndall used the time well, arguing to Webster, Robin May and Andrew Fountaine that it was not his own head that was at stake, but the purity of the NF ideology. With his customary energy, he threw himself into theroetical writing, using *Spearhead* as his platform, and driving home the message to party meetings. Force, will, power, indomitable drive – these were the themes he chose, reflecting his own determination to fight back in the face of the greatest challenge of his political career. 'We have got to dedicate ourselves to producing, as we used to do, young men who are tough and hard. Not only young men with the knowledge and crafts to survive in the modern world, but the physical stamina, the character and the will to survive,' he told a summer meeting in Tunbridge Wells. He returned to the theme in a major article in *Spearhead* in September. The strain upon him, and also the exhilaration, comes clearly through: 'The day that our followers lose their ability to hate will be the day that they lose their power and their will to achieve anything worthwhile at all.' The passion of his theme led him to throw down the gauntlet to his opponents, and the article continued as perhaps the most precise example of the emotive, spiritual creed which had sustained him through the years. It is pure Nazism in that it reflects exactly the mood and spirit of *Mein Kampf*.

First, the re-affirmation of faith in emotion:

I believe that most people have been won over to our movement in the most committed and active sense of the term by a deep personal compulsion to be involved in our work, which may be influenced by duty or self interest or both to a degree, but which is mainly stimulated by some mystical emotive power within us that compels allegiance, by an appeal to forces within the human character which defy rational analysis.

Then comes the description of the danger and the means of fighting it:

Nothing, absolutely nothing, can be accomplished if the political temperature remains at that level at which the nation has been lulled to sleep while its enemies within and without have plundered its wealth and destroyed its freedom. We have to raise the temperature several degrees if people are to awake and something is to be done. Enthusiasm has to be created and that can only be achieved by an appeal of dynamic force which arouses the feelings of the masses just as electric shock waves arouse life, feeling and movement in an inert body . . . I believe that our great marches, with drums and flags and banners, have a hypnotic effect on the public and an immense effect in solidifying the allegiance of our followers, so that their enthusiasm can be sustained.

The implications of this message for political opponents, or for that mass of the population which fundamentally wants a quiet and prosperous life, are dramatic. 'We have to raise the temperature several degrees if people are to awake' is an almost direct quotation from *Mein Kampf*, and moreover, Tyndall goes on to challenge the conventional view of the English people. He sees them as a volatile mass:

> The propaganda of our enemies constantly told us that the British as a race are congenital liberals in politics and will always be repelled by anything strident, forceful or militant in the way of a political appeal . . . most of the picture the British people have about themselves and their national character is a picture drawn for them by the alien and cosmopolitan clique who control most of the media of propaganda in this country.

Under threat from the Populists, Tyndall reverted to the old and still potent faith of his youth, in the full knowledge that the NF still contained a hard and influential core of comrades of the old Nazi days. In the vital East London and Essex region, John Cook and Ron Tear, the former an old member of the NSP and the latter a man who kept a shrine to Hitler in his home, took control of the NF organization in the summer. In the October *Spearhead*, in an article entitled 'Nationalism and Race Survival', Tyndall returned to the language and ideology of the Nazi days, talking of a renewed and powerful Germany, justified in seeking new *Lebensraum* in Eastern Europe 'if and when a reduction of Russian power in that area makes that feasible'. The article was a rallying call to the old comrades, extolling the virtues of the white race – 'Western civilization to us means that which is the biological source of all our values, standards and culture – the White Race.'

Webster, with accustomed cunning, played the game both ways. He too re-affirmed the hard line in a *Spearhead* article in July, 'Race is still the big issue'. It was safely militant, unlikely to sever the tentative relationships he had developed with Lawson and Painter, but staunch enough to reassure the hardliners that he was still with them: 'Racialism is the only scientific and logical basis for nationalism . . . our objections to immigration and multi-racialism spring not from the fact that "There are too many Blacks in Britain" . . . we seek to preserve the identity of the British nation . . . if the British people are destroyed by racial inter-breeding, then the British nation will cease to exist.' The fact that the British nation had been created by racial inter-breeding was tactfully ignored; Webster had re-affirmed the faith.

But as a kind of insurance, Webster chose this time to establish some stout anti-Nazi credentials, launching a bitter personal attack upon a tiny and insignificant sect known as The League of St George. He publicly condemned it as the backdoor 're-cruiting ground' for Column 88, the shadow para-military Nazi group in Britain.

Webster returned to the attack in the October *Spearhead*, replying to a plaintive complaint from the League's President, Mr H. Grestock, who claimed that the League was simply a cultural body, without links to Column 88. Webster, aping the style of investigative journalism, alleged joint Column 88-League membership and spoke darkly of Hitler birthday parties held in a farmhouse near Marlborough, marked by the presentation of biro pens to each attendant marked 'Column 88 Führerfest 19 Marlborough'. Webster named no names, but gave the impression that he knew a great deal more than he chose to write, and referred to a neo-Nazi conference held in Las Palmas on 23 May 1975, which delegates from the Southern African League Afrika, the Italian Ordine Nuovo, the Argentine Anti-Communist Alliance and the French, Brazilian and British chapters of Column 88 had attended. It was an attack designed to do no harm, say to the reputation of the League of St George, and to do Webster's credentials with the NF's Populists a great deal of good.

In private, the telephone calls and the lobbying intensified aimed at the September elections for the Directorate. Tyndall had to prove that he still enjoyed mass support in terms of personal votes, and this forced him increasingly to compete with Kingsley Read, the chairman. Throughout the summer relations between the two men deteriorated and Kingsley Read drifted further and further into the Populist camp. Both sides strained every nerve to mobilize their support and as a result private branch meetings took over from public parades and demonstrations as the NF's prime activity. Organization at National HQ suffered, and the membership levels – even on paper – began to fall. The only major activity to be organized was an anti-mugging march in Hackney in September, which was notable for a large banner claiming that 80 per cent of muggers were black and 85 per cent of their victims were white. The police ordered the black face of the mugger on the poster to be covered over. Only 1200 NF supporters joined the march against a counter-demonstration by Hackney Trades Council which attracted 5000 people. The march was held on the Jewish New Year, which local councillors attacked as a deliberate provocation, particularly in Mosley's old East End stamping ground.

When the Directorate votes were counted, Webster had com-top of the poll with 1201 votes, and Tyndall had scored a more than respectable 1028. Richard Edmonds, a teacher at Tulse Hill comprehensive school whose NF membership had led to calls for his dismissal and a great deal of publicity, won 501 votes, the least number of the nine who were elected from 40 candidates. But for a party which was claiming 22,000 members, it was a remarkably low poll. Two years earlier, when Webster had again topped the poll, he had received 850 votes, and those two years were supposed to have seen the NF's greatest ever period of growth.

Attention now focused on the Annual General Meeting in October, where Tyndall believed he had organized enough support to force through his controversial constitutional reforms, even though it would need a two-thirds majority. Discreet funds were established by both sides to pay the travel costs of their supporters down to London for the meeting in Chelsea Town Hall. The Populists also printed a new broadsheet, called *Beacon*, edited by Tyndall's old comrade in the National Socialist Party, Denis Pirie, who had been radicalized – at least in NF terms – by his time as a mature student at Sussex University and by his friendship with Lawson. *Beacon* was widely distributed by post and at the AGM itself.

Its main thrust was a series of personal attacks upon Tyndall by the Populist leaders and their converts. 'If the NF falls under the control of John Tyndall and his style of doing things, it will become totally discredited in the minds of all self-respecting Britons and will degenerate into some small insignificant group of sycophants around a tin-pot Führer,' wrote Roy Painter. Walter Barton was more succinct: 'The system John Tyndall wants is the short way to dictatorship.' Carl Lane, the Treasurer, claimed long service: 'I have not worked seven and a half years for the NF to see it turned into a one-man dictatorship.'

The result of the Directorate vote, and his own assessment of Tyndall's likely support, had convinced Webster to remain loyal. The key resolution for the AGM, which would allow constitutional changes to be voted by a simple and not by a two-thirds majority, was proposed by Webster and seconded by Tyndall. From this victory, they hoped, the other constitutional reforms would flow and Tyndall would be back in control. But in the event, with over 800 members present, Tyndall failed to receive even a simple majority on this key vote. He was defeated by 54–46 per cent. The second objective, proposed by the old stalwart Blaise Wyndham and seconded by the new ally Andrew Fountaine, was that the chairman and deputy chairman of the

187

party should be elected by the whole party, not by the Directorat
Tyndall's objective was to outflank the Directorate which h
could not dominate – even after the September elections. Kingsle
Read opposed the motion, and it was narrowly defeated.

The simple record of the votes glosses over what was in fa
a chaotic meeting. Outside the hall, there was the usual peacef
counter-demonstration by the local Trades Council and a viole
scuffle by the International Socialists. Inside the hall, matte
were little better, with harsh recriminations between the tw
wings of the NF and charges and counter-charges about accusa
tions of attempts by the other side to mount a coup on 4 Octobe
the date of the first meeting of the new Directorate. Tyndal
believing that if he was elected chairman he would find th
National HQ and its vital files lost to him, sent a group of su
porters to Croydon to occupy the building. The files had gon
removed on the direction of Painter, Brown and Kingsley Rea
in the belief that Tyndall was attempting a coup. The vote f
the chairmanship was narrowly won by Kingsley Read, wh
announced an enquiry into what he called the 'illegal occupatio
of HQ' by Tyndall's men. Thus began the first breach.

The final blow against Tyndall was planned for 8 Novembe
the next meeting of the Directorate, where a disciplinary tribun
against Tyndall, Webster, Fountaine and their supporters w
to be established. The plan was for Tyndall to be expelled, b
the others to be suspended and then re-admitted to the NF. O
23 October, Gordon Brown called a secret meeting at the pu
down the road from the Croydon HQ, the Cherry Orchar
Brown undertook to organize a series of members' protes
against the invasion of the HQ, and calls for Tyndall's dismissa
The ten Populists on the Directorate were primed and all w
ready. Andrew Brons, a Tyndallite, proposed that no furth
action should be taken over the occupation, and that the enqui
should be stopped. The vote was taken, and Walter Bartc
abstained. He had been counted as a firm Populist supporter, an
this came as a surprise. In fact, Barton was a sick man, and nev
known for his intelligence. He had simply misunderstood th
purpose of the vote and Brons's resolution was carried by 10–9
Kingsley Read had no opportunity to use his vital casting vo
as chairman. The meeting was adjourned, and the Populis
resolved to meet again the following evening, after the annu
Remembrance Day parade, to decide on further plans.

The meeting was again held at the Cherry Orchard, an
Kingsley Read, Richard Lawson and Carl Lane, all three mem
bers of the Executive Council, declared themselves in sessio

The plan, supported by Peter Holland and David McC·lden who were also present, was opposed by Painter on the gr·und that it was constitutionally weak, and that it would be wise· to wait until the next Directorate meeting and thoroughly rehearse Walter Barton. Kingsley Read swept aside the objection, and the Executive Council voted to suspend Tyndall and his nine supporters on the Directorate. Kingsley Read declared this carried by 4–3 on the Executive, the fourth vote being his own casting vote, and the three objections being the absent Andrew Fountaine, Webster and Andrew Brons. The next morning, Kingsley Read personally changed the locks at HQ, and refused to admit Webster when he arrived, informing him of his suspension.

Webster was told not to be too alarmed, that he would shortly be reinstated, but that Tyndall was to be expelled. Webster left, to call a meeting of the ten suspended members. Fountaine proposed to fight the matter through the courts, and offered to foot the bulk of the bill. On 16 November, the disciplinary tribunal was held for the ten, who had agreed not to appear. Anthony Reed-Herbert was chairman of the tribunal, and it formally expelled Tyndall, and suspended Webster and Fountaine.

The Tyndall supporters, reinforced by the surprising figure of Mrs Bee Carthew, the former Monday Club official and publicist for Enoch Powell, were reinstated in the NF by Mr Justice Goulding in the High Court on 20 December. He declared that 'Mr Read took the law into his own hands,' and awarded costs to the Tyndall faction. He made it clear that his ruling was based on the 10–9 Directorate vote to take no further action on the events of 4 October and the occupation of HQ. Walter Barton's misunderstanding had saved Tyndall.

Kingsley Read, Painter, Lawson and Brown immediately drew up contingency plans to form a new party, to be called the National Party, and Gordon Brown began the long process of evicting the NF from its HQ, which he owned. On the day after Boxing Day, Brown was informed he would face disciplinary charges for bugging the NF HQ. A bugging device and tape recorder were found in the attic. Two days later the National Party was officially formed, and Martin Webster informed the five full-time employees at HQ that they were fired. The NF could no longer afford to employ them. An immediate check on the finances showed an overdraft of £2500. Webster claimed that the accounts had been in the black at the time of his suspension. On the same day, Brown evicted Webster and the NF from Lawsons Road. Five days later, another court ruling reinstated the NF in the premises. Walter Barton, joining in at last, informed the *Guardian* that he was leaving the NF becaus Tyndall and Webster had threatened him with prison. 'They a a menace to the trade union movement,' he added. The gran coalition of the Right was over.

Once again it was a split which the national media, with th exception of the *Guardian* and the *Sunday Telegraph*, large chose to ignore. But its implications were momentous. There wa the opportunity for a new party of the Right to emerge, shor of the neo-Nazi taints that could so easily be hurled at Tynda and Webster. Certainly Dennis Pirie, as a former NSM membe and Gordon Brown as an old militant of Tyndall's GBM would have become propaganda targets, but as personalitie and as politicians they were too lacklustre and too unknow ever to achieve the hallowed place of Tyndall and Webster i the demonology of the Left. And a new party energetically led b Kingsley Read and Painter, backed by the unstinting finance c Gordon Brown and the wealth of Robin Beauclair, should hav been able to take over the reins of the NF's membership. Kingsle Read, during the legal battle in the High Court, had receive promises of support from two-thirds of the branch organization: Mistakenly, he felt this was enough.

The National Party leaders were simply overconfident. The believed they had maintained the national HQ and the vita membership files that went with them. They were wrong. Webster re-occupation of the premises on 29 December, backed with court order, meant that all the telephone queries coming in fror branches and bewildered members were given the Tynda explanation of events. Most important of all, on 6 January, th NF secured another court order prohibiting the NP fror using the NF membership lists in any way. Strenuous efforts wer made to copy them, but the lists had to be surrendered befor the task was completed. Almost at a stroke, the NP lost it essential means of communicating with the NF members it ha to convert. And in the meantime, Kingsley Read's over-confidenc since November had given Tyndall's supporters the time person ally to canvass each branch. Tyndall and Webster, as the NF' best-known personalities, most-attacked targets and mos charismatic figures were very much better known to the mas membership than were Kingsley Read and Painter, who counte on the support of branch leaders and the organization machine

In Blackburn, Kingsley Read's own town, one-third of th branch stayed with the NF after tireless efforts by David Riley the North Lancs regional organizer. In Crawley, which Painte had seen as a Populist stronghold, daily personal visits b

190

Brighton's chairman Charles Parker kept the majority in the NF. In Blackpool, Kingsley Read kept the branch chairman, but the members went to the NF. Webster himself spent almost a week on Merseyside, where the NP had won the regional council, and re-organized the area, forming a truncated Liverpool-Merseyside branch and a Merseyside-Greater Manchester region. In Feltham and Heston, Brentford and Isleworth, NP influence was strong but within a week the NF supporters had been re-grouped into a new Hounslow branch. And thanks to the court order, the branch records and files and finances stayed with the NF. They had a nucleus to work from. The NP was largely starting from scratch.

The key battlefield for NF loyalty was North and East London, where the highest NF vote had been won in the October '74 election. Again, the NP was over-confident. Painter reckoned his personal influence would hold Wood Green and Tottenham, since he was backed by Keith Squire, the Wood Green parliamentary candidate. But Squire was losing interest; after a disappointing vote in the first NP internal elections, he resigned. The important NP personnel found themselves too embroiled in their own branch struggles to spend enough time campaigning in East London. Mike Lobb and David McCalden had to fight hard in Greenwich, and Richard Lawson spent the bulk of his time in Lambeth. As a result, the majority of the members of Wood Green, Hackney, Tower Hamlets, Newham, Waltham Forest, Barking and Islington, were lost to the NF almost by default. Quite simply, the NF strongholds were real strongholds, from which the activists could sally forth to other uncertain branches. The NP had to fight every inch of the way even to retain its own areas of influence. By the end of February, the NP had largely gained some 29 branches and groups; the NF had clung to 101. In membership, the NF had kept perhaps two-thirds, some of them attracted by the promise of branch offices when the old officials defected to the NP.

Among the NF's advantages in this struggle for the membership was *Spearhead* and its subscription list. The November issue launched into an attack on *Beacon*, the anti-Tyndall broadsheet distributed at the AGM as consisting of 'hysterical abuse and libellous attacks'. Webster began a months-long campaign on the old, familiar issue of race, cannily reckoning that the 'populists' weakness was their vaunted moderation. 'Race war spreads,' he wrote in November. 'Huge cover-up on Immigration figures' was the February headline, and the magazine contained a long account of the Racial Preservation Society's new publication 'Racial kinship – the dominant factor in nationhood', *Spearhead*'s editorial comment went back to basics: 'The negro has a smaller brain and a much less complex cerebral structure.' In March, *Spearhead* returned full bore to the old anti-semitism in a major article entitled 'The Jewish Question'. 'So long as Jews are to the fore in promoting Communism and World Government, fuel is going to be given to those who maintain that there is a Jewish conspiracy for world power as outlined in the Protocols of the Elders of Zion.'

April was an even more poisonous month. Richard Verrall, whom Tyndall had appointed *Spearhead* editor to leave himself more time for the membership drive, wrote on 'The Reality of Race – scientific evidence which substantiates inequality'. Webster, as ever, was more dramatic, writing, 'There will be millions of potential Red shock-troops wandering about in our Black Ghetto-land within a decade . . . where are *our* shock troops coming from?' Webster went on 'It is only a matter of time before even the most stupid and cowardly of our white fellow citizens realize that they are at war . . . the uniforms in this war will be the colour of your skin.' The Jews were a target again, with John Tyndall attacking even the loyal Neil Farnell for his complaint over Tyndall's 'Jewish Question' article the previous month. And *Spearhead* reprinted an anti-semitic article 'Zionism is the issue' from the US neo-fascist magazine *Insaturation*. There was little pose now of the would-be national statesman. Tyndall was back in the fray, in the political and journalistic gutter where he had learned his trade.

The abuse of the NP was savage at first, moderating as the NF success became more apparent. In the December *Spearhead* came a bitter personal attack on Richard Lawson and his editorship of *Britain First*. 'Left-wing shift in the NF' was the headline, and Lawson was taken to task for having written that people were joining the NF 'because of their determination to make democracy work by actually involving themselves in its processes'. Tyndall himself, in February, launched another volley, characterizing the NP as 'Misfits, Inadequates, Failures Ltd'. He described a series of categories of rebels, of which the most revealing was 'people who can be seen to belong to a thoroughly unprepossessing racial type . . . there is a moronic set of the jaw and a sullen and shifty look in the eyes'.

But Tyndall remained aware that in the fringe politics to which the split had restored the shrunken NF and the NP, the essence of success is action. The new NF's first Directorate meeting, in December, quickly turned from accusing Gordon Brown of bugging the building to a programme of activities. Stunts, publicity and demonstrations – all would be needed to keep the NF name before the public and hearten the supporters. It was decided to fight the two forthcoming by-elections at Coventry and Carshalton and, as some recompense for his vital financial and legal support, Andrew Fountaine was chosen as the Coventry candidate. On 14 January, a solidarity rally was held at the Conway Hall, raising £1900 which helped to wipe off the overdraft. Fountaine, Tyndall and Webster were the main speakers, and they quickly co-opted Michael Stubbs on to the Directorate as the new Treasurer. Malcolm Smith, chairman of the West Herts branch, who had worked tirelessly to hold the Home Counties membership, was rewarded with a Directorate seat. Richard Verrall was left to run *Spearhead*, while Tyndall and Webster established a replacement for *Britain First*, a new broadsheet called *NF News*. Throughout January, they began to organize the first big demonstration, a by-election rally in Coventry in February, to which they bussed almost 800 supporters. On 4 March, NF women members scattered leaflets from the House of Commons gallery and called 'Traitor' during a debate on race relations.

The National Party, dispirited by its defeat in the membership struggle, held its inaugural meeting in February in Chelsea Town Hall. Only 187 people attended, although the hall holds more than 800. Kingsley Read was elected chairman with 160 votes, and a resolution to purge the party of all those with Nazi, Fascist or Communist backgrounds was defeated. £500 was collected, and a 20-strong Directorate voted into office. They included Carl Lane, Roy Painter, Richard Lawson, David McCalden, Michael Lobb, Denis Pirie, Tony Webber, Ted Arthurton and Joan Sandland. It was an impressive collection of former NF chiefs, but woefully short of Indians. Painter himself, increasingly dispirited, told his friends that he was going to retire from politics for a year, to devote himself to his successful contract cleaning business. By June, Painter was making overtures to the Conservative Party, hoping to return.

The new NP constitution was an authoritarian statement, concentrating all power in the hands of the Executive, which alone had the power to propose amendments to the statement of principles or to the constitution. Even resolutions to be chosen for debate by the membership would be at the Executive's discretion. The policy was almost indistinguishable from that of the NF, although the statement of principles boasted 'the NP takes a much harder line against immigration'. This included the compulsory repatriation of all white spouses and children of mixed marriages: 'The British people must preserve their distinct racial character by preventing all further immigration by people of non-British stock and by organizing the humane repatriation or resettlement abroad of all coloured and other racially incompatible immigrants, their dependants and descendants.' Who those 'other racial incompatibles' were, who were not coloured, was not explained. Painter's own regular complaints against the Greek, Turkish and Levantine immigration into his own Tottenham perhaps explains it.

If a clear policy line could be said to emerge from the NP, it was that of Richard Lawson in *Britain First*. His policy was a confused anti-Communist syndicalism. 'Seize the right to work', screamed one headline, to be followed by 'Smash the Red threat – there is only one force capable of stopping the Communist advance and that is the force of Racial Nationalism, a pride in our ethnic identity and a burning will to survive.' To find a source for this ideology, one has to go back to the 'soft' National Socialism of Röhm and the SD, who were wiped out by Hitler in 1934.

The NP leaders were also the subject of carefully aimed barbs from Martin Webster. In *Spearhead* (which Tyndall ensured was still widely distributed to the NP defectors), Webster recalled conversations with the Populists, quoting Kingsley Read as saying 'I'm a bigger Nazi than Tyndall ever was', and quoting a conversation with Painter in a car: 'What you don't realize is that I'm a National Socialist at heart. Only I am careful.' Both statements were quickly denied, though it was acknowledged that in the course of debates inside the NF in that year many wild things had been said that were not meant.

The weakness of the NP should not be overstated. They had taken some of the best brains, and the best organizing talents from the NF. But the NP attracted a different kind of organizer. Because of the formal political training of men like Kingsley Read and Painter inside the Conservative Party, and of Mike Lobb in the Communists, their concept of organization was a traditional one. They were concerned to build a long-lasting structure, a hierarchical chain of command, that could mobilize the vote and enforce a degree of party discipline. It was organization in depth that they sought, building up areas of strength, and proceeding from them with a long-term view of political growth firmly based upon experienced branch leaders, lists of potential canvassers and so on. It was a strategy suited to the long haul, and its successes in individual areas such as Blackburn, where the NP won two local council seats in the 1976 elections and in Deptford in June where they outpolled the NF candidate, showed its strength.

The problem was that this kind of long-term structure was wholly unsuited to the quite remarkable conditions of racial unrest and political volatility which began in the spring of 1976. The NF, on the other hand, trained in a rather flashy but effective political opportunism, through taking immediate advantage of issues as they hit the front pages of the press, were admirably poised to exploit the passions of the summer of 1976. It was the story of the Ugandan Asians all over again; organization in breadth rather than in depth. It meant organizing instant demonstrations at Gatwick and Heathrow airports as the first of the terrified Asian exiles began to land from Malawi. It meant physically wrenching Robert Relf from the British Movement when he became a kind of martyr for going on hunger strike in defiance of the Race Relations laws. It meant red paint on the door of 10 Downing Street, provocative demonstrations through the immigrant heartland in Bradford, and grabbing as much publicity and as many headlines as the NF possibly could, so that the general public came to associate the words National Front with racialism, with action and with determination. It was crude, it led to flimsy organization and a lot of fair-weather support. Although it could astonish pundits by sweeping 44,000 votes with 48 candidates in the local elections in Leicester, it could not mount the concentrated electoral force which won the NP two seats in Blackburn. Nonetheless, the NF approach was brilliantly suited to the sudden waves of racial tension which swept Britain in 1976.

It is not easy to say when it began. Some might point to the BBC's decision to screen an anti-immigrant message from the British Campaign to Stop Immigration on its public access programme, which lent an air of respectability to the stop-immigration forces. Others would suggest the 1000-strong NF march in the immigrant areas of Bradford on 24 April, which provoked young blacks into attacking and stoning the police, the overturning of two police cars, a mounted police charge and a running battle back into the near-ghetto of Lumb Lane.

The new Race Relations Bill was proceeding slowly through the House of Commons, with the Home Secretary, Roy Jenkins, a man with a reputation for liberalism and culture implicitly acknowledging at least one of the racialists' arguments with a speech in the House on 4 March: 'There is a clear limit on the amount of immigration which this country can absorb and in the

195

interests of the racial minorities this means maintaining a stric
control over immigration.' The Bill, which proposed to tighter
the laws on incitement to race hatred, forbid discrimination in
private clubs, employment, housing, education and advertising
also promised action on racial disadvantages as well as dis
crimination. It served to inflame the racialists – 'We accept th
Government's challenge,' Martin Webster wrote in *Spearhead*
while doing little to reassure the increasingly alarmed immigran
communities.

Their fears were comprehensible, given the subtle kind o
racism which suddenly appeared to rush to the head of the popu
lar press. On 24 May, in a major article entitled 'The Front-lin
families', the *Daily Mail* looked at the lives of the white neigh
bours of immigrants. The tone was unfortunate, implying as i
did that there was a social burden in having a coloured neighbour
The following day, the same newspaper splashed the announce
ment in the Commons by Enoch Powell of a confidential repor
on Asian immigration, known as the Hawley Report after it:
civil servant author, on the queues of Asians wishing to arriv
in Britain, the papers they had to obtain in order to enter Britai
(which in many cases had to be forged because they did not exis
in an underdeveloped country). Again, the tone was such as t
play into the racists' hands: 'Immigrants – how Britain is deceived'
splashed the *Daily Mail*. It spoke of 'the vast queue of peopl
all planning to surge into Britain . . . Daily the tide creeps in
Planes arrive in Britain all the year round bringing more immi
grants to this crowded island.' It is striking to note how a nationa
newspaper such as the *Daily Mail*, which editorially abhorre
the NF, was able to borrow the language, the mood and th
subconscious appeals of *Spearhead*.

This was but the beginning of a wave of articles in press, which
clearly inflamed the sensitive issue of race relations, and fo
which the British press, including the liberal *Guardian*, must bea
a heavy responsibility. The immediate cause was the exile b
Malawi of its Asian community. In an act of unnecessary folly
the West Sussex council, who took responsibility for housin
those arriving at Gatwick airport, placed the first arrivals in an ex
pensive 4-star hotel.

The press reaction began with the *Sun* on 4 May, with it
banner headline 'Scandal of £600 a week immigrants'. On
May, the *Mirror* responded, 'New flood of Asians to Britain'
and the *Daily Telegraph* headlined 'Invasion of Asians force
borough to call for help'. The borough in question, the stor
revealed, had the vast annual bill of £2100 for providing be

196

nd breakfast emergency accomodation at £4 a head. But for he *Telegraph*, 525 individual nights spent by Asians in one orough in the course of a year represents an 'invasion'. Popular leet Street newspapers began to ape *Spearhead* with headlines ke 'The passport to plenty – more Asians on the way to join -star immigrants' (*Daily Express*), "We want more money," ay the £600 a week Asians' (*Daily Mail*), 'Migrants "here ıst for the welfare handouts"' (*Daily Telegraph*). Even the *uardian* joined in, with a story on 9 May entitled 'Asians riled eighbours', the small print of which told how Asians at a eception centre to which they had been moved from a hotel ere set upon by white families.

The NF was quick to exploit the opportunity the press had ignalled, with teams of demonstrators arriving at the airports om 6 a.m. to jeer the incoming refugees. They made mistakes; t Gatwick on 23 May, a planeload of West Indians and black merican tourists were greeted with the chant 'Don't unpack – ou must go back' and 'This is England, not Pakistan'. But the V cameras and the reporters recorded the demonstrations, and ne or two were acute enough to point to the distinction between ie activist NF squad of chanting, angry people and the small NP contingent, which was simply at the airport to monitor rrivals. The NF were making the running again.

The case of Robert Relf, a former bodyguard for Colin Jordan nd Ku-Klux-Klan activist with a prison record for attacking an sian shop, then took over the headlines. He refused a judge's rder to remove a sign from outside his home, saying it was only or sale to English buyers. He was sent to prison for contempt of ourt – not for the sign itself – and went on hunger strike. After even weeks of court appearances, protests and demonstrations utside the prison, horrific bulletins from his family about his eclining health, he was released by the judge. Relf had won. Ie had been allowed to defy the Race Relations Act and the ourt, and he and his supporters were jubilant. He had originally een claimed by the British Movement of Colin Jordan and Iichael McLaughlin, but shortly after his release he announced is conversion to the NF, for whom he campaigned in the hurrock by-election. Relf had told the court: 'For the past 30 ears Germany has been embarrassed by a man called Rudolf Iess and now England is going to be embarrassed by Robert elf.' He succeeded.

Relf was but one of a series of blows to Britain's consciousness f itself as a liberal, tolerant nation in the course of that summer. igures as prominent as the Archbishop of Canterbury, Bob

Mellish the much-respected senior Labour politician and forme
chief whip, and even Bill Jarvis, the solidly socialist and dece
President of Birmingham Trades Councils, all called in publ
for a limit to immigration. But between press concern abo
race issues and racism as a political force, there is a gap. It w
perhaps fortunate that the local government elections of 197
took place in May, before the tensions of the summer were full
aroused. Even so, the NF and NP successes, following immediatel
upon the news of the arrival of the Malawi Asians, were strikin
enough.

The NF fielded 176 candidates, and 80 of them won more tha
10 per cent of the vote. In Leicester, 48 candidates won 43,73
votes, an average vote of 18·5 per cent. The highest vote wa
31 per cent. In Bradford, 21 candidates won 9,399 votes, a
average of 12·3 per cent. In Blackburn, two NP candidates, on
of them Kingsley Read, were elected. The two NF candidate
won 33 per cent of the votes in their wards. In Sandwell, in th
Midlands, eleven candidates won an average 17 per cent. Ther
were other localized successes: in Hydburn, Lancs, three cand
dates won 24 per cent; in Oadby and Wigston, two candidate
won 25 per cent. Elsewhere, the pattern was disappointing fo
the NF and NP. In Birmingham, twelve candidates won onl
4·3 per cent of the vote. In Wolverhampton, seven candidate
won only 9·1 per cent. In Coventry, five candidates scored onl
4·4 per cent.

The reasons for this were fairly clear. In Bradford and Black
burn, there had been NF and NP demonstrations shortly befor
the elections. The local press had been full of their exploit
In Leicester, a well-organized NF machine, led by Anthon
Reed-Herbert who had returned to the fold from the Populis
camp, fought a brilliant campaign, focusing on the wards wit
fewest black immigrants, and playing on their fears. Elsewher
the campaigns and NF presence had been lacklustre. The mor
for the NF was to keep hitting the headlines, keep on 'raisin
the political temperature' and wait for the votes. This conclusio
was drawn at a Directorate meeting which analysed the result
where a particular cause for concern was Coventry. The March b
election, in which Fountaine had won only 3 per cent of the vo
should have resulted in more local publicity and a better-traine
organization. The fact was that the local organization had be
badly split between NP and NF, and both were in disarray.

The other by-elections were more promising. In the sol
Conservative constituency of Carshalton, in South Lond
commuter-land, an unskilled NF organization had won 4

per cent in March. In Rotherham in June, where there had been only two NF members at the start of the campaign, they won 5 per cent of the vote, after bussing in supporters and organizers.

In June, the political temperature rose several degrees – just as Tyndall had hoped it would. In Southall, the main concentration of Asian immigrants near London, a young man, Gurdip Singh Chaggar, was stabbed to death outside a pub. First reports suggested this was part of some racial gang war, and the first police statements appeared to confirm this. Later assessments accepted that the attack had been made by a group of racially-mixed youngsters, black and white. But an ugly momentum was building. In East London, Mohamed Riaz Khan was charged with the murder of a white boy, Chris Adamson, whose three brothers sat in the same court, charged with making an affray. In Blackburn, on 16 June, local Community Relations officials presented a dossier of more than 30 attacks upon Asians and their property in the previous ten days, which they blamed upon the inflammatory activities of Kingsley Read and his supporters. In East London, among the Bengali community, vigilante patrols of young Asians were formed to patrol the streets at night and in Southall, Blackburn, Leicester and Birmingham, the militant immigrant groups, supported by the Institute for Race Relations, called for the establishment of self-defence groups within the immigrant community. It was an ugly period, with young immigrants clearly moving away from the traditional controls of their parents and elders, and confidence in the capacity of the police to maintain order being lost. The ignominious failure of the recruiting campaign among blacks by the Metropolitan Police underlined the public statement by the Police Commissioner Sir Robert Mark on 9 June that 'it is a regrettable fact that relations between the police and many black youths are bad'.

In Thurrock, on the Thames estuary, the NF were fighting yet another by-election, this time with the aid of their new star Robert Relf. It was new territory for the NF, with a small immigrant population and a safe Labour seat. The NF had little time and few supporters in the area for formal electioneering. There was no door-knocking, little canvassing, no list of prospective supporters and no car organization to drive supporters to the polls. Even so, they won 3225 votes, 6·6 per cent.

All was grist to the NF mill; the antics of General Amin of Uganda, whose decision to expel the Asians in 1972 had sparked the last surge for the NF, came to their assistance again in 1976, with his apparent collusion with the Palestinian hi-jackers who were killed in a daring Israeli rescue operation. The disappearance in Uganda, and almost certain murder, of an old British lady, Mrs Bloch, was again a gift to the racialists.

Concern within the Labour Movement mounted. The National Union of Miners called at their July conference for a ban on the NF. In Transport House, Labour officials drew up a list of 21 seats which they feared could fall to the Conservatives through NF intervention. The rather smug assumption of the early 1970s that the NF would take votes from the Conservatives had now shifted, partly through the wave of NF votes in North and East London in 1974, to an awareness that the NF was increasingly an inner-city phenomenon, not a simple sign of racism or anti-immigration, but equally a sign of the loosening loyalties of traditional working-class communities to the Labour Party. This was partly due to the bad housing, or appalling social effects of mass slum clearances and high-rise council housing which Labour councils had introduced in the 1960s. It was partly to do with rising unemployment, which was creeping slowly towards 1·5 million, and partly due to the weakening of Labour Party discipline, as party membership declined by almost 70 per cent in the 25 years after 1950. The Labour Party was no longer as involved in the working class in its homes as it had been, although its links through the trade unions remained as strong. More ominously the steady drift of keen party workers in the constituencies, which had accelerated during the Wilson era, and which contributed to the 1970 defeat, began again in 1975, and by the spring of 1976, the far left groups like the International Socialist and IMG were seeing the result in new recruits. The once-solid Labour areas of the inner cities, which had always put up with the worst housing, the worst jobs and the least employment, also had to face the increased social problems which came, quite predictably, from mass immigration.

The Labour Movement did, belatedly, respond. On 8 July, party officials agreed with respresentatives of the immigrant communities to propose a nation-wide anti-racist campaign to the Party committees. Roy Jenkins on 24 July, in a radio attack on the NF, observed that 'the NF hope by their provocative manner to provoke others into violence that will bring the publicity and advantage that can develop out of a general sense of disorder'. This was true as far as it went, but when Jenkins went on to counsel ignoring the NF, it was seen in the black community as a wholly inappropriate response to the wave of genuine fear that the events of the summer had created. Increasingly the Asians could respond to the uncompromising anti-fascism of the militant Left groups, who chose the very day of Mr Jenkins's anodyne

200

statement to steal and burn publicly in Southall Robert Relf's offending sign.

It had been clear since the 1970 election that the immigrant community was becoming an important source of Labour votes, and yet little seemed to come in return. Immigrant confidence in the Labour Government had been badly shaken by the dismissal of Alex Lyon, junior Minister at the Home Office, in April. As he left office, he said 'I have paid the price of trying to get justice for the blacks in this country.' Lyon's dismissal, the release of Relf by the courts, and the tone of the Commons debates on the Race Relations Bill during the summer, contributed to the gloomy memorandum sent to the Home Office in July by that most staid of Asian spokesmen, Tara Mukherjee, president of the Confederation of Indian Organizations, which concluded: 'We are now convinced that the overwhelming majority of MPs are prejudiced.'

The reaction of the NF to the summer of violence was a delighted 'We told you so'. Richard Verrall told *The Times* in July that 1800 new members had been signed up in June, an exaggeration but not a ludicrous one. Webster privately claimed to friends that there had been more than 1000 enquiries for membership in the month. Convinced that the time for expansion had come, Tyndall arranged to visit South Africa and Rhodesia later in the summer, to raise funds and promise support for the embattled whites.

Increasingly over-confident and unrestrained by the Populists' sense of caution about public statements, Tyndall began to give outspoken press interviews which made no secret of his idiosyncratic interpretation of the democracy he still professed.

'I would have elections and also referenda, but I'd have elections only every eight or ten years. Then as a strong Government we'd go to the people and ask if they wanted us to carry on,' he told the *Observer* in July. Asked if there would be an Opposition, he replied: 'If you mean people who have the right to criticize when things are going badly then yes, indeed. But if you mean the present automatic thwarting of effective Government then no.'

For all his new confidence, and his success in clinging on to the NF organization when the Populists threatened to wrest it from him, Tyndall and his supporters had not really exploited the political opportunities of the summer. Too much of their effort in the spring had been spent on winning control of the NF membership, and organizing the by-elections and marches and stunts by which this was ensured. The by-election results they had secured, although striking enough at Thurrock, had not begun to approach the heady impact of saving the deposit at West Bromwich, in the wake of the Ugandan Asians' arrival. The effect of the violent summer was to revive the NF from the effects of the Populist split, but there was little evidence that it had advanced far beyond that point. The structure and branch organization of the party was not as well established as it had been in late 1974. Some of the best brains and publicists had gone, to expend what seemed to be wasted energies in the National Party. The contrast between Kingsley Read's tame acquiescence to the courts and the Race Relations Board at his own hearing in May, and the hunger strike of Robert Relf, did little for NP morale. Had the organization not been split, had the opportunism of the NF leaders still been combined with the hard political skills of the NP, the summer of 1976 might have been very much uglier. The split came at a fortunate time for British race relations.

EIGHT

The End of the Golden Age – The New Politics and the British Crisis

At the end of the summer of 1976, neither the NF nor the far Left could make any convincing claim to have become a mass movement, nor to have won major support within the working class. But they both believed that the economic crisis which Britain faced, with inflation savaging living standards, a trade deficit of ten billion dollars, and steadily creeping unemployment, offered a prospect of the political breakthrough for which they had worked.

The severity of the economic crisis was matched by a fundamental and deeper-rooted shift in British voting habits. The proportion of electors who bothered to vote declined progressively throughout the 1950s and 1960s. In 1950, 83·9 per cent of the electorate voted, but by 1970, the turnout had dropped to 72 per cent. The bitterly-contested election of February 1974 brought a surge to the polls of 78·7 per cent, but by October that had fallen back to the apathetic 72 per cent of 1970. And between elections, political life had become more volatile. In the 243 by-elections between 1945 and 1966, only 21 seats changed their allegiance. But in the eight years and 81 by-elections between 1966 and 1974, no fewer than 27 seats changed hands. Traditional voting loyalties were losing their hold.

The votes were shifting away from the two major parties. In every post-war election until 1974, the Labour and Conservative Parties had collected at least 87·5 per cent, and usually well over 90 per cent of the votes cast. But in February 1974, their combined share of the vote fell to 75·4 per cent, and fell even further to 75·2 per cent in October. The Liberals and the Scottish Nationalists shared the great majority of the shifting votes, but the NF's 113,000 votes of October implied that by fighting every constituency, they might expect up to 750,000 votes, or the kind of support the Liberals received in the 1951 and 1955 elections.

This shift of votes to the minor parties had the effect of diminishing the apparent electoral authority of Governments. The minority Labour Government of March 1974, with only 37·2 per cent of the votes, and even the majority Government of October with only 39·3 per cent could hardly claim to have won an indisputable mandate from the electors. The legitimacy of a Government with such feeble support in the country could properly be questioned by its opponents.

British Governments throughout this period had elevated the nation's economic activity into a moral shibboleth, a criterion of virtue and of national virility. Bad trade results were seen as traumatic events, and recovery of solvency in the balance of payments was hailed as a triumph akin to Dunkirk. Growth was equated with virtue, and British economic stagnation became, in the rhetoric of politicians, a cause of national shame. The impact of this campaign upon national morale cannot be measured, but it must have been profound.

The official obsession with trade figures was almost as absurd as John Tyndall's own equation of the country's moral health with its performance in the Olympic Games. But it was very much more dangerous. It led to a search for scapegoats, and successive Governments picked upon the trade union movement as the cause of the nation's economic ills. No doubt the trade unions' insistence that their members share fully in the national wealth which the middle class had traditionally monopolized, and the steady advance of blue collar earnings towards the income levels which white collar workers had seen as their own prerogative alarmed those to whom the amount of disposable income was of less importance than being visibly wealthier than the neighbours. But the vaunted militancy of the trade unions was unable to prevent the British industrial wage from falling behind that of every other EEC country (except Italy) by 1971, and even the inflation pay awards so bitterly won in the past five years failed to close the gap.

Much was made of rising crime figures (although they were rising less dramatically than in the rest of the industrialized world) and of the numbers of immigrants (throughout the 1960s, Britain had a net population loss through migrant movements) and of the health problems they were alleged to bring. In fact, notifications of TB – the disease most commonly associated with immigrants – fell from 28,000 in 1960 to 14,000 in 1970.

The members of the National Front themselves show an almost pathological concern for every symptom which made up their diagnosis of the spiritual sickness of Britain. Crime, immigration, the numbers of white people who chose to emigrate, artistic creativity – and its consequent exuberant excess – all became functions of degeneracy. The reform of the divorce, the abortion and the homosexuality laws, the retreat of censorship in the arts, the new assertiveness of the young in music, in politics and in life styles – all of these forces of change were the subject of specific attack by the National Front.

The NF believed in a Britain independent, and called for resignation from NATO and from the UN; they believed in a Britain strong, and demanded more nuclear armaments; above all, they believed in a Britain that was morally earnest, utterly opposed to flippancy in the arts, unforgiving of the citizen who transgressed the law, scornful of those who did not share the dream of a new national might, uncomprehending of those who argued that the changing Britain of the 1960s was a tolerant, a civilized and an exciting country to enjoy.

The committed members of the NF could never see that, by many standards, Britain from 1950 to the 1970s had enjoyed a golden age. An Empire had disappeared, but it had been freely given away; by the standards of the French or of the Portuguese or of the Belgians, Britain had loosened the bonds of Empire with a degree of generosity, with a fund of good-will and with more than a touch of grace. If there were Hola camps in Kenya and a murder mile in Cyprus, there were the universities left in Africa and Asia, and there was a code of law which may have borne little relationship to the realities of Third World society, but which had a fair enough grounding in the common sense of common law to be almost infinitely adaptable.

The faded Britain of the 1960s had contrived to nurture a capital city that was close to being the artistic centre of the rich white world. In drama, in opera, in music, in fashion and in style, London offered the world in the 1960s rather the same magical mixture of cults and tastes and talents which Paris had created two generations earlier. It was not the American myth of Swinging London – although that kind of energy and confidence were important; it was that much of London recognized and welcomed the passions and the intensities and the moods which made the city so culturally magnetic in the sixties and found that it was enjoying its own new image.

Certainly the perspective had its shadows. There were 100,000 homeless, there were pensioners who died of cold in winter, there were retaliations by an uncomprehending legal system against much that was both exuberant and innocent. There were endless hours of mind-dulling pap on the television and endless hours of mind-dulling labour on assembly lines and packaging plants.

But to deny that the living standards of the bulk of the people were improving more rapidly than ever before would be perverse. Health care, housing, wages and salaries, full employment, ownership of the liberating motor car, or of that urban communication system the telephone, of refrigerators which transformed marketing habits, of machines which reduced the drudge of domestic labour – they comprised a material and social comfort for an unprecedented proportion of the population. The Golden Age was now.

Ironically, one of its proudest achievements developed to a degree which put that affluent and cultured (and often complacent) society on to the defensive. The spread of educational opportunity for the middle – and a lesser, but still significant, proportion of the working – classes had begun with the 1944 Education Act. Its parallel legislation in Northern Ireland had a similar effect. The expansion of opportunity in education led to an expansion of expectations among the growing numbers of graduates. A society which was creating 30,000 graduates in 1962 had to ensure that each year saw 30,000 graduate-style jobs to employ them. For if those expectations were not fulfilled, if the jobs were not available, the inevitable result would be a discontented and frustrated intelligentsia. This is precisely what happened in Northern Ireland, where the education system produced too many bright and trained Catholics for the Orange state to absorb. And the middle-class agitation of Civil Rights groups and People's Democracy provoked Orange retaliation and gave a focus to the grievances of the mass of the Catholics.

The slow explosion of Ulster was one of the widest cracks to appear in the structure. Another was Enoch Powell's speech of 1968, another was the student rebellions and the opposition to the Vietnam War. There was an irony to the state's alarmed reaction to the puny British imitations of the rioting students of Paris, New York, Warsaw and Berlin; an irony which goes some way to explain the confusion of the British body politic at its own transformation. At considerable national sacrifice, and often at considerable parental sacrifice, Britain had provided more university and college places than ever before, but was never able to decide whether it was cold-bloodedly investing in a future nation of highly-trained technocrats, or generously assuming that education was a vaguely 'good' thing which should be encouraged in the interests of a cultured community. What Britain had not expected was a generation of critics. The students, many of them coming from communities and families to whom universities were unknown, had the time and the training and the equipment to think (and they often had the academic courses to make them think) about the society and the economy which had produced them. Their thoughts may have been chaotic and insolent, and at times they may have been profound. But they were overwhelmingly critical. They were critical of the cult of economic growth (even though growth had provided the universities). They were critical of the patent examples of unfairness within the economy, even though students themselves were an almost extreme example of class privilege. They were critical of the world power structure which their nation helped to uphold, even though it had staved off major war for a generation. Having thought about their criticisms, and intermittently acted upon them, the rebellious students graduated into the society which had nurtured them so well.

In the press, in broadcasting, in social work, in junior teaching posts, in universities and polytechnics, in the lower ranks of the administrative grades of the civil service and in local government, they provided the British social mix with an unfamiliar element, a dissident intelligentsia vastly larger than that of the 1930s, and one that was very much more sure of itself. When the National Front complained about left-wing bias in the media, or complained of Marxists in the Race Relations Industry, or left-wingers in the universities, it was exaggerating the picture but it was not distorting. Social criticisms at almost every level of public life were sharper and more pungent, from the new passion of the media for investigative journalism to the pathetic sub-terrorism of the Angry Brigade.

Britain of the early 1970s was being widely compared to the Weimar Republic of Germany in the later 1920s. The imminent economic crisis, the permissiveness of cultural life spilling over into the sordid lasciviousness of Soho, the new blunt power of the trade unions, inflation, the impotence of Government – there was a sense of the brink, of instability and of fearsome, frightful collapse. As staid a newspaper as *The Times* lent its own respectability to the paranoia, an ancestral voice that prophesied doom, its headlines asking if a military coup was imminent in Britain, whether any democracy had ever survived 20 per cent inflation.

And brooding over it all was the six-year sore of Ulster, with its own 1500 victims of backstreet snipings and sneak explosions, the dreadful random hand of terrorism. Ulster alone precluded any comparison with Weimar, forcing the never-militarized British people to grow accustomed to its own aggressive soldiers patrolling familiar British streets, guarding familiar British chain stores, shooting at people like themselves.

Ulster even made redundant that other favoured analogy of those who offered comfort by saying that democracies had survived such times before: France in the 1950s, France fighting a war in the 'metropolitan homeland' of Algeria, France fighting

207

desperately against the terror bombers and assassins of the OAS, France with inflation, with strikes, with impotent and quarrelsome parliaments and an intelligentsia which campaigned against the war, against the torture it involved and the methods that it used – France, where a kind of democracy was saved by a kind of dictator.

The casting round for comparisons with other nations in other crises was an escape from the British reality, an evasion of the issue. If Weimar had no Ulster, then Britain had no Communist Party remotely comparable to that of Germany in 1930 or France in the 1950s. Britain's own crisis was wholly new. There was little, after all, that Britain could do about the most savage component of its troubles in the 1970s. The quadrupling of the cost of oil, and the accelerating surge of international inflation were beyond British control. Nor did Britain have enough economic weight to help decide whether or not there should be a world recession.

Britain pinned its hopes upon those traditions of good-will and co-operation and common sense which it had mythologized and used so often in the past. The Labour Government proposed what it called a 'social contract' with the trade union movement, under which the unions would agree to limit wage demands to keep pace with inflation, and in return, the Government should legislate to remove social injustices and anomalies and aim towards a fair society. Such a solution might appear naïve, and might have been progressively betrayed, but it can be fairly seen as a tribute to the faith which persisted at many levels of society that Britain was fundamentally a reasonable society, capable of surviving enormous disruption while preserving its democratic freedoms.

To portray the social contract as a triumph of British good sense, which its author Harold Wilson was prone to do, was to ignore the elementary fact that Government was treating the trade unions as equal partners in the business of managing the national economy. And it had been Harold Wilson who had dragged an unwilling TUC to a belated recognition of its own power of veto in a modern state. Wilson had not meant to do this, but it was almost the last – and without doubt the most important – action of his Government of 1966-70. The Labour Government's proposed mild reform of the trade union movement, which aimed at reducing the number of unofficial strikes and introducing an arbitration procedure between dispute and strike, was launched under the title 'In Place Of Strife'. The TUC, and its general secretary Victor Feather, were prepared to acknowledge that a measure of reform might not be a bad idea, but firmly maintained that it should be left to the TUC to reform tself, and no Government should have the power to draw up the rules by which workers would be permitted to withhold their labour. Unable to convince the Labour Party's left wing that he unions should be over-ruled, Wilson had to back down.

Edward Heath's Conservative Government introduced broadly similar legislation in its Industrial Relations Act. Unable to stop the Bill in Parliament, the unions resolved to oppose the Act, but had little idea of how this could be done. A General Strike was unthinkable, and by the fortunate process of doing nothing, the TUC happily hit upon its best policy; dumb insolence and non-violent refusal to acknowledge that the law had been made. When five dockers were imprisoned, quite legally, by an unfortunate judge who had to enforce the law as parliament had made it, the TUC called a strike. The Government surrendered, and the vaunted Act was quietly buried.

As if this basic lesson in the massed power of union action was not enough, the Heath Government tried to restrain wages by acting directly against the incomes of trade unionists and imposing statutory controls on wage rises. This time, there was no need for the whole TUC. The Grenadier Guards of the Labour Movement, the miners, were more than sufficient. Their strike in the winter of 1974 forced Heath to hold an election, which he lost. The result of these long and unsuccessful attempts by Governments to control the unions was to make it abundantly clear to Governments, unions and voters that the only way to dominate the unions was by coercion, and if that coercion were as half-hearted as the imprisonment of the five dockers then it was worse than useless. Short of class war, Government could not force the unions to obey the law. The social contract was an implicit recognition of this plain fact of modern British life. The astonishing thing is how long it took the unions to realize the extent of their powers.

For the implications of this, we can do worse than to examine Trotsky's explanation of the rise of Fascism. Not that Trotsky is necessarily right, but the broad outlines of his theory make it easier to understand what processes are at work. According to Trotsky, when a capitalist system is in crisis, with its stock exchange collapsed, its money supply inflating out of control, its businesses going bankrupt and its level of unemployment rising, then we have a revolutionary situation. This revolution can go in one of two directions, depending on the reaction of the petit-bourgeoisie, or lower-middle class. Once the petit-bourgeoisie begins to suffer from the crisis, once its meagre savings have disappeared and its jobs and respectability have been lost, then it can either ally with the bourgeois capitalist system which started the whole mess, or it can ally with the working class.

If the working class has evolved a revolutionary party determined and clear-headed, then the party with the support of the working class will be able to present solutions to the petit bourgeoisie which will win their support, and the socialist revolution follows, which will expel the capitalists from their control of the commanding heights of the economy, and commence the construction of a new, disciplined and socialist society.

However, Trotsky reminds us, capitalists and the bourgeoisie are neither timid nor stupid, but are determined to hang on to their economic dominance, and will pay any price to preserve their freedom to be exploiters. They will therefore examine the petit-bourgeoisie very closely to see if, in its spiralling discontent and dispossession, it has evolved any Fascist group. That is, a group which is revolutionary, and prepared to be violent, but which is not Socialist enough to be determined to overthrow the bourgeoisie, and which moreover has not begun to mobilize in the working class. Once such a movement is discerned, say Trotsky, the capitalists will encourage it with money, with publicity in the capitalist media, and with moral support from the Government the capitalists control. Every effort will be used to build the Fascist movement to the point at which it can combat the revolutionary party of the working class. Once this is done the capitalists permit the fascists to govern and to destroy the trade union movement, fitting the working class into their own structures. The capitalists will permit anything to happen, so long as their economic control is ensured.

The pre-conditions of Fascism are therefore: an economic crisis which brings unemployment, inflation and poverty to the petit-bourgeoisie; a revolutionary party within the working class which presents a real and immediate threat to the capitalist system; a Fascist revolutionary party within the petit-bourgeoisie capable of growing explosively and militant enough to take on the working-class party.

There is, however, no convincing sign of a British revolutionary movement with the trust and support of the working class. The Trotskyite parties, IS, IMG and WRP are too small and too dependent upon the intelligentsia to present any credible revolutionary threat. The British Communist Party is the British

210

Communist Party, highly trained to ignore a revolutionary situation, and too subservient to Moscow to threaten the great power détente by launching any sort of revolutionary adventure in Britain, even if its partly-geriatric membership had their wheelchairs oiled and ready.

Nonetheless, we could stretch Trotsky's version to suggest that even without a credible revolutionary party within the working class, the capitalist barons might feel frightened enough by the spectre of trade union power to unleash a Fascist paramilitary force to destroy the unions and fragment the working class.

Once it would have sufficed for a British writer to say simply that such a sense of fear, such a disentegration of national morale, could not happen here. Part of the myth by which the British defined and protected themselves was a divine right to stability and political level-headedness. That myth has appeared increasingly flimsy since the publication of recent studies on the effects of German bombing in the Second World War. The myth says that Britain battled on; Tom Harrisson's study of the Mass Observation reports suggests that towns like Southampton almost collapsed and that panic, fear and official demoralization were widespread. More recently, the economic and political crisis which began in 1974 brought a stunning combination of inflation, strikes, private armies, factory occupations, weak governments and threats to the unity of the nation which had the prime custodian of the national myth, *The Times* itself, musing on the likelihood of a military coup.

The fundamental reason for the alarm was the unusual fact that the February 1974 election brought into office a minority Labour Government. The election itself had been forced on the Conservatives by the miners' strike. Less than three months into office, the Labour Government had to watch a general strike in Ulster force the resignation of the Northern Ireland Executive, a hopeful body which was the direct result of Westminster's partisan faith in a solution for Ulster based upon Catholic and Protestant politicians sharing power. A minority Government in London, informed by the Army that it could not maintain essential services in Ulster and presiding over an inflation rate of 25 per cent, seemed too flimsy a structure to guide the nation through the crisis it faced. General Sir Walter Walker, a rabid anti-Communist from his years facing the Soviet threat as a NATO staff officer, announced that if the Government was too feeble, he would be prepared to organize a civilian force of volunteers with the skills and determination to run the country

211

in defiance of the trade unions.

Few were in doubt where the General's political sympathies lay. Shortly before he began to establish his 'Unison Movement' as the voluntary body was known, he addressed the Brent East Conservative Association, whose candidate was G. K. Young, the anti-immigration campaigner and candidate for the leadership of the Monday Club. Shortly after Unison was organized General Walker addressed the Anglo-Rhodesian Society, another haunt of the Monday Clubbers. His political views were old-fashioned even by Conservative standards, and his Blimpishness was best expressed in a signal he sent to the Royal Ulster Rifles when they were under his command. 'You are my white Ghurkas,' he told them, 'this is my highest compliment.' A racist the General was not, but one wonders how his white Ghurkas would have reacted to the advice he published in *The Times* in May 1973: 'The Army should soften up the No-Go areas in Ulster and then move in. Cut off their petrol, gas, electricity and stop food going in. Soften them up and then go in. I have engaged in campaigns against blacks, yellows and slant-eyes – why should we have one rule for whites and one for coloureds.'

The General claimed to have 100,000 volunteers by August 1974. He talked grandly of three million by October, and there were some in the Conservative Party who seemed to agree. Geoffrey Rippon, then Shadow Foreign Secretary, called in a speech in September for a Conservative Government to 'create a citizens' voluntary reserve for home defence and duties in aid of the civil power.' Rippon, a keen Monday Clubber before the Club's much-publicized row of 1972–3, hastened to clarify his speech after angry telephone calls from other Shadow Ministers. 'Nothing in my speech in any way lends support to recent suggestions for the formation of the so-called private armies,' he added, and official Conservative policy stressed that any such volunteers should work through the Territorial Army, the special constabulary and Civil Defence. Walker's Unison Movement quickly degenerated into a national joke, with some of its members calling for licensed brothels, and others for a ban on pornography, as solutions for the national ills.

Colonel David Stirling, who tried to establish a very much more professional cadre of skilled volunteers to maintain essential services, was stopped almost before he began when his planning documents were leaked to the *Guardian* and to *Peace News*. Stirling had hoped to maintain secrecy until mid-1975 but his plans were published in August 1974. Stirling's romantic background in the Second World War, where he led and organized aids behind enemy lines in North Africa, was looking tarnished by 1974. He had established a de luxe mercenary team called Watchguard to offer bodyguards, special forces and *corps d'élite* to foreign heads of state. He had been briefly involved in an abortive coup against Colonel Qadafi of Libya, but by 1974 he gave the impression of a man with a brilliant future behind him. Stirling claimed that his force of volunteers, to be called GB 75, would be politically non-aligned. This contrasted sharply with the anti-Labour tone of the GB 75 papers, which read, in part:

Wedgwood Benn's two-headed purpose, elaborately planned but naïvely camouflaged, of steady encroachment on the private enterprise system, together with the forcing of trade union members on to the executive board of public companies – and both of these tactics running in parallel with growing inflation and the exercising at will of the political strike weapon – amount between them to a realizable threat of a magnitude this country has probably never faced before.

But Stirling, like Walker, had misjudged the national mood. The predictable hostility from the trade unions and the Labour Government was matched by chill disapproval from the Conservative Party. Neither Walker nor Stirling ever got the kind of support, from national figures or from mass volunteers, for which they had hoped. The Police Federation claimed that there was 'no serious evidence' of a threat to the system which the police would be unable to handle, and attacked the private armies for political partiality. The Minister of Defence reminded all Army officers, in a classified signal issued in September, that they were forbidden to join organizations such as Unison or GB 75.

By April 1975, Colonel Stirling's GB 75 was disbanded and merged into a moderate trade union group called TRUE-MID, which had been founded by a handful of anti-communist union officials. 'There are only four of us today, but make no mistake about it, we could be four million tomorrow,' said one at the press conference. Little more was ever heard of it. Colonel Butler, the right-hand man of General Walker and brain behind Unison, quietly eased back into Hampshire retirement. The Labour Government, which had pinned its faith in the social contract and the voluntary tradition, had read the national mood correctly. The response to the confrontation between Government and trade unions was not more confrontation, but closing the gap between them by involving the trade unions directly in the process of national economic policy. By the summer of 1976, the Government and the TUC had successfully negotiated two annual deals to restrict pay demands, together with a complex package of price controls, food subsidies and taxes which reduced inflation, reduced the number of industrial disputes and made the sense of panic and talk of military coups in 1974 into a distant, almost forgotten memory.

Paradoxically, there may have been even more cause to fear for the unity of the state in 1976 than there had been two years earlier. In 1974, the Labour Movement had exerted its considerable force behind the Labour Government. Party members had worked hard in the October 1974 election to return a Government with a bare majority, but by 1976 that loyalty was in serious question. Cuts in Government spending, to guarantee international credit for the weak economy, had undermined the spirit and the letter of the social contract and had regenerated those seeds of doubt among the Party faithful which had led to demoralization in 1970. The far Left parties, particularly the Trotskyist groups, were again showing signs of growth. But most important of all, the question of devolution, or even independence, for the nations of Wales and Scotland had become urgent and immediate, with little hope of being speedily resolved.

The Labour Government had presented two successive proposals for devolution of powers to locally-elected Assemblies in Edinburgh and Cardiff. The second proposal, published in July 1976, suggested granting a large measure of Scottish and Welsh control over internal matters, particularly over the national Development Agencies, which directed and administered the key area of economic development. The Assemblies were not, however, granted the right to levy their own taxes, and above all, Scotland was not to be granted title to North Sea Oil, the promise of which had been the main agent in the growth of the Scottish National Party to 30 per cent of Scottish votes. There was little immediate prospect of the Government being able to push its proposals through Parliament, in view of opposition in its own ranks, an equally divided Conservative Party and a House of Commons where Labour no longer held a clear majority since two Scottish MPs had rejected the Labour whip to establish a separate Scottish Labour Party.

Without Scottish and Welsh votes, there would be no Labour Governments. In England alone, there is a natural Conservative majority. The Labour Government had to find some solution which would maintain its traditional working class support against the electoral appeals of Scottish and Welsh Nationalists

y devolving some measure of autonomy and responsibility
 the two nations. But it had to ensure that those Scottish and
Welsh voters maintained their full voting rights to send MPs to
Westminster, to counter the Conservative majority in England.
ooming over these fine political judgements was the question
f oil. An independent Scotland was unthinkable to any White-
all Government, because the oil in the sea off Scotland embodied
e vital hope of national economic recovery. It may have been,
s the SNP posters said 'Scotland's Oil' but a goodly proportion
f it had already been used by British Governments to guarantee
oreign loans. By December 1975, there had already been more
an a dozen amateurish bomb attempts upon Scottish oil
ipelines, and members of a pathetic 'Tartan Army' were already
 prison. But the threat was ominous.

For all its complications, the impending argument over devolu-
on is unlikely to bring the NF into further prominence. The
IF policy is to maintain the unity of Britain, but the precedent
f the anti-EEC campaigners suggests that any anti-devolution
rce which develops in British politics is unlikely to welcome
e NF into its ranks. Indeed, unless the question of race becomes
e dominant issue of British politics, it is difficult to see any
ther cause around which the NF could grow. The classic crisis,
r its purposes and in terms of Trotsky's theory of Fascism, was
at of 1974. Partly because that crisis was resolved by formal
olitical means, and partly because of its own weakness and inter-
al divisions, the NF was unable to take very much advantage
f it. Britain in 1974, contrary to the theories of General Walker
nd David Stirling, was not in a revolutionary situation. Had it
een so, neither the far Left nor the far Right were in any position
 act upon it.

he NF has known in the ten years of its existence three clear
eriods of success. The first, which sparked its fastest growth
nd came to redeem a time of party decline, was the coming of
e Ugandan Asians in 1972. The second was the period of the
vo elections in 1974, and the third, which allowed the NF to
ecover from the split and chaos caused by the departure of the
opulists, was the coming of the Malawi Asians and the racial
ension of 1976. Its attempts to win support and momentum from
ther causes have not been successful. It was unable to capitalize
reatly on the EEC Referendum, largely because mainstream
nd respectable politicians refused to work with it. The NF has
ronounced policies and staged demonstrations on the need to
upport Ulster Unionists for eight years, without making political

headway. There may be issues on the horizon from which t'
NF could profit. The impending battle for Rhodesia, and f
the future of white supremacist governments in South Afric
could provide the basis for a 'Back the Whites' campaign
Britain. But the eleven years since the Rhodesian crisis began wi
UDI hardly suggest that this is the topic to mobilize support f
British nationalism.

Today, as when it began, the NF's issue is race. The NF's ro
has been to act as a particularly effective and unprincipl
pressure group on the development of British immigratic
policies. As a political force, it has had hitherto little effect
elections. As a pressure group, keeping the issue of race alive a
a controversy which can win and lose parliamentary seats, t
NF and other anti-immigration groups have known a series
striking successes. The controls on immigration are alread
severe, and the Government's plan to redefine British nationalit
largely to exclude citizens of the remaining Colonies from citize
ship, will meet yet another old NF demand. Immigration a
such is likely to decline in importance as a political issue, althoug
the likelihood is that there will be further unexpected arrival
like those from Uganda and Malawi, upon which the NF ca
capitalize.

But the NF will still have a race issue, from the 2,000,0(
coloured people who now live in Britain, and the NF will use i
The question is how this will be done, and this depends wholly c
the way the NF develops. At its 1974 peak, before the Populi
split, the NF was moving purposefully towards the stage whe
it could claim to be a political party like any other. It stood i
elections, it was developing a regional party structure, it had
national headquarters which developed policy and so on. It ha
grown from a series of small and slightly mad groups into a
effective force of political pressure by 1973, when the We
Bromwich by-election suggested that it could find elector a
success. Under the Populists, with their background in form a
politics, this development into an election-oriented party co
tinued. It remains to be seen whether this strategy will be mai
tained under the renewed leadership of John Tyndall. It
certainly his intention, and the NF has participated in loc
and by-elections since the split. But the membership has to
built again, and the HQ organization, and the political experti
which the Populists took with them has to be recovered.

Other options are open for Tyndall. The NF could be deploye
not for elections, but simply for rallies and the kind of insta
demonstrations which greeted the arriving Ugandan and Malaw

refugees. To continue its growth and recovery from the Populist split, the NF is dependent upon taking advantage of race issues, but hitherto it has, with ingenious opportunism, taken advantage of those issues when the press or the decision of an African dictator has created them. There is now enough pride and committment to self-defence among Britain's immigrant communities for 'issues' to be made by the NF with a provocative march through a ghetto, as they did in Bradford in April 1976.

The NF tried, during 1974, to develop a wider base than simple racial appeals, by linking race and immigration to other political themes. Unemployment was explained as black workers taking British jobs; bad housing as blacks jumping the council house queue; clogged health and social services were the fault of diseased immigrants taking the place of deserving Britons; bad schools were the cause of illiterate black kids, and crime was their fault too. It was a potent and poisonous combination and it is one to which Britain is still frighteningly vulnerable, simply because the bad schools, the bad housing and the unemployment do exist. Moreover, these social evils predominate in precisely those run-down, inner-city areas with poor housing in which immigrants have tended to congregate, simply because they are cheap. The NF's electoral heartland, on the evidence of the 1974 general elections, is London's East End and its north-east inner suburbs. They are the areas of massive slum clearance where traditional communities were broken up by the new tower blocks of low quality public housing. Traditionally safe Labour areas, they are the seats where the proportion of the electorate voting has fallen most sharply in the last five elections, and where the local Party, whether as political machine or as a focus for the community, has tended most to decay. The ease with which Reg Prentice, a Cabinet Minister, lost his constituency, points to the decline, even while the success of the Left in building a majority against him points to a possible regeneration.

A council by-election in Deptford in July 1976 re-affirmed the trend. The Labour vote collapsed from its customary 75 per cent to 43·5 per cent. Between them, the NF and the NP won 44·5 per cent. Local politicians, analysing the poll, concluded that the white working class in the area, many of them Irish, had broken away from their traditional Labour affiliation simply because their Labour votes had not produced the jobs, the better housing and the social amenities that they expected. 'We have to impress on the Government that to avoid racial violence, we will have to increase public spending in this kind of deprived urban area. This has now become a national priority which must override even the spending controls of the financial recession,' Mr Andy Hawkins, Labour leader of the council, told the *Guardian*.

The same phenomenon seems to have been at work in Blackburn, where it combined with the personal vote for John Kingsley Read to give the NP two council seats in 1976. Nor were these deprived urban areas the only sources of NF strength. In the Leicester local elections, it was less the deprived working class wards with a high immigrant population which gave the biggest NF support but the respectable working class areas. Abbey Ward, with less than 5 per cent immigrants, came within 62 votes of electing a NF councillor. It could be that traditional Labour voters are unwilling to vote Tory or Liberal, and the NF wins the benefit of their protest vote when they are displeased with Labour. It could be a fundamental conversion. So far, there is too little evidence available to judge, but the degree of personal support for Enoch Powell among staunch Labour voters suggests that there is a large reservoir of Labour opinion which responds to a racial appeal. The traditional Labour defences against this kind of inroad into its electoral base are education through the trade unions and the local constituency parties, and organization among those groups to counter demonstrations and marches. The frightening thing about the 1976 council elections was that they came after a sporadic anti-NF campaign by the trade unions.

We have come a long way from the classic Trotsky thesis of the growth of Fascism. We are no longer talking of the deliberate encouragement of a violent anti-Communist party by an alarmed bourgeoisie. We are looking at a Labour Party base which is in danger of erosion after generations of complacency, and the NF seems to be an active agent in that erosion. The fact is that there is a significant proportion of the urban working class which has been failed by the Labour Party, at national and local levels. The public spending cuts of 1976 hit housing, schools and hospitals. They also hit employment, while Britain hovered just below the appalling figure of 1·5 million jobless. The National Front at least claimed to offer a solution that was clear and simple – remove the immigrants and there will be jobs and houses for all. It was a ludicrous answer, and one which any man who had been part of an even greater number of unemployed in the 1930s, when there were no immigrants, could have disputed.

But the Labour Party seemed to be offering no answers at all except the old remedy of toughening the Race Relations laws while simultaneously tightening the controls on immigration. A decade of admittedly looser Race Relations legislation had done little to affect the degree of discrimination even in a field as easy to monitor, and as susceptible to trade union pressure as employment. The authoritative Policy and Economic Planning Report of 1976 surveyed 300 factories and found that more than half practised some form of discrimination and only 8 per cent took positive anti-discriminatory steps. There were even employment ghettoes, with 74 per cent of the black workers in only 28 per cent of the plants, and they were almost twice as likely to work on regular night shifts and generally employed in unskilled, manual work. They also had to fill out, on average, twice as many job applications as white workers.

There was little faith in the powers or the ability of the official bodies to alleviate the effects, let alone the causes, of racism. There were, in 1976, 86 Community Relations Councils in the country, funded by local authorities and the Community Relations Commission. Lionel Morrison, a young black, published a report on three of them for the CRC called 'As They See It' which was bitterly critical. In particular, he attacked the tendency of the CRCs to see themselves as the only natural and authoritative representatives of the black communities: 'So obsessive a belief has this become among some CR officers that even where black organizations do exist, the CROs insist on interpreting their role in practice as being that of spokesmen for blacks in the area.' If there was any logic to national policy on race, it was to produce, largely through public employment and the developing Community Relations bureaucracies, a black middle class which would provide both a focus of ambition and a structure of community control for young blacks. This process, which I borrow from the paper 'Race, Class and the State' by Mr A. Sivanandan, director of the Institute for Race Relations, began to crack in the summer of 1976 as young Asians broke away from the traditional authority of their elders and religious leaders to respond directly to what they saw as racial attacks.

Young immigrants could with some justice react against the caution of their elders, when faced with violence, but other challenges they faced were more subtle. It was not simply a local Labour Party trying desperately to help those it saw as its own, but a clear policy of discrimination that made Newham council change its scheme for awarding council homes. As Councillor Bill Watts, chairman of the Housing Committee, put it on 23 October 1975: 'One of the reasons for the re-think is the influx of Asians. In five years we would have been doing nothing but giving homes to Asians.' The NF had won 7 and 7·8 per cent in two Newham constituencies in October 1974, and maintained an advice centre in the area which specialized in White housing problems.

The responsibility for ending racism in general, and stopping the NF in particular, now seems to rest with the Labour Movement. For its own sake, it will have to end the erosion of its once hard-core support in deprived urban areas, and the evidence suggests that it will increasingly have to challenge the NF for that support. This will mean, almost wholly, relying upon the weakest of the three elements of the Labour movement, the constituency Labour parties. The other two, the trade unions and the Parliamentary Labour Party, will have their own tasks through organizing in the workplace and passing legislation. But in fighting racism in the communities where people live, the burden is upon the CLPs and upon Labour councils. They seem, in 1976, to be ill-equipped to carry it.

Perhaps the most effective way to assess a CLP's involvement in its community is to look at what proportion of the electorate voted, how many people were knocked up to come to the polls, persuaded to vote, reminded that there was an election and so on. In October 1974, 72·8 per cent of the electorate voted. But in inner London, it was a depressingly different story: Brent South, 61·2 per cent; Brent East, 60 per cent; Woolwich East, 64·4 per cent; Hackney North, 52·8 per cent; Hackney South, 54·7 per cent; Harringey Tottenham, 56·2 per cent; Harringey Wood Green, 62·2 per cent; Islington Central, 55·4 per cent; Lambeth Central, 52·6 per cent; Lambeth Norwood, 61·9 per cent; Lewisham Deptford, 58·7 per cent; Newham NE, 58·6 per cent; Newham NW, 51·6 per cent; Newham South, 53·4 per cent; Southwark Bermondsey, 56·4 per cent; Tower Hamlets, 53 per cent; Waltham Forest Leyton, 62·7 per cent; Wandsworth Battersea South, 61·6 per cent.

This was the area in which the NF had its greatest regional success in 1974, and the correlations between high NF polls and low turn-out seems striking. But other high NF polls were then and have been since recorded during times of average or even high turnout, such as Leicester East with a 72·3 per cent turnout and a 6·4 per cent NF vote.

In the two Lambeth seats, and in Newham NW, no NF candidate stood in 1974; an omission which is unlikely to be repeated. For this would appear to be the growth area, partly because of the base they won in 1974, and partly because of the strong evidence of ineffective local Labour parties which give the NF

n opportunity. We have already seen how vital was the level
of trade union morale in preventing the NF from organizing
a dockers' march against the Ugandan Asians in 1972. In the
car factories in the Midlands in 1976, the shop stewards and the
union leadership were also to prevent a number of spontaneous
and NF-inspired marches and stoppages by workers in support
of Robert Relf. The trade unions were able to stop the NF;
the local Labour parties of inner London look considerably less
effective.

The irony of this is that the Populist split has robbed the NF
of many of the local personalities, such as Roy Painter, Mike
Lobb and Keith Squires, who seem to have been most able to
capitalize upon Labour's weakness. It was Mike Lobb who
organized the advice centre in Newham, and who led the local
NF in support of the East End strikers at the Tate and Lyle
plant in Silvertown. It was Kingsley Read who organized the
residents' associations in Blackburn. By working on these other
fronts, as well as linking bad housing and unemployment with
immigration, the Populists were able to build a coherent and
credible political presence in these communities. Whether the
NF of 1976 will be as skilful is uncertain.

Even if they can build a political base in the urban white
working class, it is likely to be a precarious one unless a momentum
of success can be maintained. This will mean widening the appeal
to other sections of society; not simply scooping up the crumbs
of Labour's inner-city failures, but attracting the Monday Club
element of the Conservative Party, the protest voters of the
Liberals and so on. Many NF votes, as C. T. Husbands suggested in a study for *New Society* (May, 1976), may be protest
votes anyway. If so, they are likely to be fickle unless their
protest appears to bear fruit, and the NF is fast gaining other
support.

There are signs that this could be done, if not by the NF
then perhaps by some other political group which could take
advantage of a two-party system in decay. The implications of
devolution in Scotland and Wales are as yet unclear, but the
growth of the nationalist parties and the Liberal revival of 1974
have already given Britain a Parliament which can no longer
easily function on the familiar old pattern of crushing Government majorities and honourable Opposition defeats. The Conservative Party itself, its electoral base being squeezed into the
affluent South of England and a middle class chastened by inflation, is not at its strongest. With a former and still energetic
Prime Minister acting as the King over the water, the new leader

Mrs Thatcher has been unwilling convincingly to exercise he authority in the Party, and is apparently unable to provid inspiration to her followers in Parliament. More ominous stil Peter Walker, a former Minister and one of Edward Heath more trusted lieutenants, launched in 1976 what promises t be one of the Conservative Party's most bitter internal debates on immigration and the social reforms which must be provide for the immigrants and their communities. Peter Walker's ca which he significantly made in the left-liberal weekly *Ne Statesman*, will have its echoes at Conservative conferences an within the Party for some years to come. The bulk of the Monda Club remains, a little more easily than under Edward Heat inside the Tory Party. Whether it would remain Tory, shoul Peter Walker's programme for massive public investment in black education, employment and housing be made party polic is unlikely.

Once again we are back to John Tyndall's analysis of th collapse of the two-party system, and back to the beginnings this chapter and the steady fall in the number of electors wh vote Tory and Labour. But as the Liberal Party has found, needs more than erosion of the two main parties to achieve a electoral breakthrough in Britain. It may need a real collapse.

The NF see the sullen continuity of economic crisis winnin them support and leading to that collapse. They are convince that rising unemployment will discredit the trade union leader ship in the eyes of the workers, and make their penetration a the easier. They are convinced that racial tensions will increas with unemployment, as unemployed whites react to the sight blacks still earning wages, or taking home more social securit money. They are convinced that unemployment among schoo leavers will create an ever-larger pool of unemployed, dissatisfie frustrated black youth in the cities, whose behaviour and mil tancy will provoke a white backlash. And the NF, less convinc ingly, still sees its other favourite issues, Law and Order, Ulste and the instabilities and higher food prices of the EEC, becomin a base for winning wider support in all the reaches of th bourgeoisie.

The future will clearly depend on the fate of the tradition parties. The great coalition that makes up the Labour Party accustomed to internal fury and divisions, and it would be naï to see the arguments between the nationalizing Left and the caut ous Labour Right leading to breakdown. Devolution, unemploy ment, deflation and unrest in the constituency parties ma sharpen the internal tensions on which the Labour Party trad ionally thrives, but it does not make it easier to stop the erosion of its inner-city voting base, nor to stop the NF's racist appeal. The Conservative Party has its own problems of maintaining unity, and they will remain as long as Edward Heath remains in Parliament but not as party leader. The Conservatives have already been the victim of some erosion by the NF, in the wake of the Ugandan Asians; there is little sign that the party leaders knew quite what was going on, and they certainly did little to stop it.

But for all their internal weaknesses, the two parties have the enormous advantage of belonging to a political system that is still enormously flexible. It adapted to the minority Government of 1974, to the Government-Union confrontations, to the bitter debates over the EEC and even to the three-day week. The country has survived three centuries without unconstitutional change, and that is important.

But partly because of those three centuries, there are signs that the system creaks and gapes open like an ancient house. It is slow to react to sudden change, just as it was slow to respond to the 1973 oil crisis. It looks even less capable of reacting to the first and most alarming British statistic, that the country produces but one half of the food it consumes. This is in itself a blunt promise of social and economic transformation in a world of declining food reserves and rising food prices.

These matters do not directly pave the way for a NF Government. But they do lead to the conditions of rapid change, of alarm and of uncertainty in which the 'great simplicities', in Enoch Powell's phrase, appear attractive. The NF's policies are based upon them, and it makes no secret of its own dedication to the collapse of the current British system. The NF sees itself as a truly revolutionary party, implacably opposed to the British Establishment. The NF's opponents see it as a loathsome graveyard echo of the old Nazism. But there is another and perhaps even more sinister way of seeing it; as an authoritarian party offering 'solutions' and demanding responsibility at a time when the great anti-authoritarian parties are faltering and failing.

It has always been a great and persistent fear of the liberal-left that the world is becoming so complex and so evil and so unfair that only an authoritarian government could redeem it – an authoritarian government which all good liberal-leftists would be bound in all conscience to oppose. All we can safely prophesy is that great social and economic upheavals are quickly reflected in new political movements. And as the old political parties are challenged by the new, they lose that assurance of

shared power which contributed so much to their survival
Perhaps the best measure of the change that has come, and
the change that may yet be, is that a bare four years ago, the
prospect of a tiny band of former Nazis, Empire Loyalists,
racists and cranks becoming the fourth party in the country was
wholly unthinkable.

Martin Walker was educated at grammar schools in Durham and London, and won the Brackenbury Open Scholarship to Balliol College, Oxford in 1965. He was President of the Stubbs Society, and took a first class honours degree in History in 1969. Before going to Oxford, he worked for a year in Africa as a journalist. Having been awarded a Harkness Commonwealth Fellowship to Harvard, he went to the US in 1969, served as resident tutor at Kirkland House, Harvard, for a year and then moved to Washington as a Congressional Fellow of the American Political Science Association. He then served on the campaign staff of Senator Ed Muskie as a researcher on the foreign policy staff and later as a speechwriter.

He has worked for the *Guardian* newspaper since 1971, as journalist, music reviewer, and columnist, covering an American Presidential campaign, interviewing Idi Amin and being the first reporter to cover the great Sahel drought in West Africa.

A regular broadcaster for the BBC, Martin Walker lives in North London. He is a qualified pilot, and his work has previously been published in an anthology of young British poets (*The Happy Unicorns*. Sidgwick & Jackson, 1971).

He has also written for the *New York Times*, the *Washington Post*, *Private Eye* and *Encyclopaedia Britannica*. In his spare time he reads Science Fiction and plays squash. He represented Great Britain at the International Frisbee Festival in Washington DC in 1971.

His next book, on British Political Cartoons and Cartoonists, will be published next year by Paladin.